The Heir of Galilee

Book I of Bloodline of Light

by Ryan Paul

ISBN: ISBN 978-1-0698125-1-3

First Edition

Dedicated to my family.

"The light shines in the darkness, and the darkness has not overcome it."

— John 1:5

Chapter One - The Ruins of Qumran

Past midnight the Judean desert moved grain by grain. Sand ticked across the plateau; acacia scraped the wind; the Dead Sea lay to the east like hammered metal. Night pressed over the ruins like a vast black canopy, the stars cut so sharply they looked capable of drawing blood.Night pressed over the Judean desert like a vast black canopy, the stars cut so sharply they looked capable of drawing blood. Wind slid across the plateau and whispered through the ruins of Qumran, rattling loose fragments of stone, slipping into broken lintels and walls that had stood for two millennia. The place felt alive in its silence—like a chest that still rose and fell, waiting to exhale secrets.

Last night's sandstorm had scoured the plateau, lifting a veil of sand from the shattered wall and exposing the lip of the buried jar.

Three lights moved in that silence.

Arielle lifted her lamp, careful to angle it away from the plastered wall. The beam revealed faint brown strokes, almost letters—shapes that teased language but stopped short, retreating into cracks. Her pulse quickened. She had learned caution in places like this, but discovery always made her greedy.

"Mark it," Karim whispered, crouching close. His voice always dropped in ruins, like instinct. His curls threw restless shadows as he bent over his notebook, pencil racing in precise strokes. He had the mind of a cartographer of the unseen, charting lines no one else would notice. "Composite plaster," he murmured. "Later restoration. But underneath—look. Older stratum. Original."

Jonas stood at the threshold of the chamber, silent, watchful. He had taken the position without asking, the way soldiers claimed high ground. Broad-shouldered, square-jawed, scar slanting across his jawline, he looked carved for endurance. Every few minutes his head tilted, registering sounds the others didn't: the sigh of wind through stone, the tick of cooling rock, the desert's own long breath.

Arielle leaned in, keeping her hand just above the wall. Reverence stopped her from touching. "It's fragile," she said. Her lamp swept wider, illuminating hairline cracks across the plaster surface. She had the urge to breathe softer, as though exhaling too hard might erase history.

They worked without speaking further, each falling into their practiced roles. Arielle read walls and pigments, coaxing secrets from plaster. Karim mapped collapse lines, sketching angles with frenetic precision. Jonas didn't draw or measure; he read the air, his hand resting lightly near the grip of his flashlight, his weight shifting in calculated rhythm.

The chamber widened. At its center stood a stone table, half-buried beneath centuries of debris. Arielle's light caught an edge too deliberate to be natural. She crouched, brushing dust aside. A rectangle emerged, then a second line running perpendicular—geometry unmistakable. A lid.

Karim leaned close, eyes alight. "This collapse braced it," he whispered. "We might be standing over something untouched since—"

"Map it," Jonas interrupted, not unkindly. His voice carried the authority of someone who had learned long ago that good fortune needed guarding.

Karim set his grid, marking the fall of debris. Arielle sketched the lines twice, once literal and once interpretive. The first told her what was there. The second told her what she might be blind to. She had learned long ago that truth lived in the gaps between.

The ruins had their own weather. Wind teased the edges of stone. Pebbles cracked as the night air cooled them. Dust whispered as it slid down slopes and settled in new places. It was never silence, not truly. And yet Arielle felt something else layered beneath the ordinary sounds—a hush that was too deliberate, as if the walls themselves were listening.

She tried to ignore it, focusing on the seam. "The line continues," she murmured, tracing it with her brush without actually touching. "If the lid is intact, lateral pressure could make it behave like a spring."

Karim nodded quickly, already sketching arrows along his grid. His pencil left grooves in the page. "If we brace it here," he pointed to the support stone, "we can redistribute the weight. The collapse kept it pinned, which means the chamber beneath could be preserved."

Jonas moved closer, lamp sweeping once along the corridor beyond, then back again. His movements were efficient, his caution sharp-edged. "We try this," he said evenly, "we do it slow. No mistakes."

"No heroics," Arielle added, half-smiling.

Karim gave a twitch of a grin. "You two don't trust me at all."

Dust shifted when Jonas pressed a hand lightly against the fallen slab. He wasn't forcing it—just listening, the way someone might listen for a pulse. The rock groaned faintly in reply, a sound that slid into Arielle's chest like cold water.

They braced the slab. Jonas leaned his weight into the counterstone while Karim adjusted the wooden wedge with steady hands. The seam revealed itself further, dust sighing into the chamber. Arielle snapped photographs, sketched angles, every line a spell against forgetting.

The groove grew clearer: the outline of a lid fitted long ago, seated with intention.

Her breath caught. "We've found something."

"Not tonight," Jonas said firmly. His gaze never left the corridor's darkness. "We document. We return in daylight with proper support."

Karim hesitated, eyes shining. Excitement was written all over him, his whole body pitched forward as though momentum itself might crack the secret open. But at last he nodded, scrawling notes into his logbook with deliberate force, as if writing agreement into the record would keep him from breaking it.

Arielle exhaled slowly, feeling tension drain through her hands. She closed her sketchbook and sat back on her heels. The ruins around them seemed to sigh with her.

Jonas's lamp swept the corridor again, the beam catching motes of dust suspended in air. They hung there too long, reluctant to fall, as if waiting for something unseen to breathe them forward.

The hair on Arielle's arms rose. She swallowed, fighting the urge to speak. To say she felt watched. That she heard... something. But she bit it back. Words gave shadows power.

Instead she forced her attention onto the work, methodically packing her tools, coiling the lamp cord. Jonas gathered their perimeter markers, movements steady, practiced. Karim logged temperature and humidity, talking quietly to himself in clipped bursts of Hebrew and English as if translating the air into data might anchor him.

Jonas finished his sweep of the corridor and came back slow, boots making barely a sound. "Nothing moving," he said at last, though his voice carried no relief. "Still—I don't like it."

"You never like it," Karim muttered, crouched over his logbook. His grin was faint but it didn't hide the tension in his shoulders. He drew one more arrow on his grid, then underlined it twice. "There. That's the load path. If we brace along here tomorrow, we should be able to lift the lid without shifting the whole collapse."

Arielle glanced at his sketch. Even in his rushed hand, the geometry held a kind of beauty. "It's precise," she admitted.

"Of course it is," Karim said. He snapped the notebook shut, then caught her eye. "This is what we came for, Ari. To find something intact. To give it back its voice."

Jonas snorted, a low, sharp sound. "Or to unleash something we don't understand."

That silenced them both for a moment. The ruins seemed to lean in, as if interested in the argument.

Arielle broke the quiet. "It's not about unleashing. It's about listening. If this chamber is sealed, then whatever's inside has been waiting." Her own words surprised her. They sounded more like belief than procedure.

The sensation returned—prickling along her arms, settling at the back of her neck. The air felt heavier, thick in her throat. She lifted her lamp and turned it toward the corridor. Nothing. Just the dark swallowing the beam, motes of dust floating like tiny stars.

"Jonas," she whispered.

He didn't ask what she meant. His jaw tightened, and he angled his flashlight deeper into the passage. Its circle of light moved across stone, caught a niche, and stopped on nothing. But the way he lingered made it clear he didn't believe the nothing.

Karim straightened and slung his pack over one shoulder. "We're imagining things. It's nerves."

"Maybe," Jonas said. He didn't sound convinced.

Arielle packed the last of her brushes. Her hands moved with practiced ease, but her mind was caught on the silence—not absence but presence. A listening silence. She told herself it was the wind. She told herself it was memory. But the words didn't stick.

They gathered their gear and turned back through the chamber, each of them throwing glances over their shoulders as though the dark might suddenly step closer. The ruins seemed to shift with them, shadows breathing, dust sighing like a voice too old to form words.

At the threshold, Arielle paused. The table and the faint outline of the lid lay behind her, a promise half-spoken. She raised her lamp one last time. For the briefest instant, a shadow moved within a shadow. She could have sworn it. She could have bet something precious on it.

Then it was gone.

Her throat tightened. She lowered the lamp and forced her feet to follow the others.

Outside, the night hit them like a wall. The chamber's stale breath gave way to the desert's sharper bite—cool, metallic, almost electric. The stars seemed closer here, sharp enough to pierce. The Dead Sea shimmered faintly in the distance, a broken mirror that caught and lost the light with each shifting breeze.

Karim exhaled loudly, his laugh short and nervous. "Tomorrow," he said, shouldering his pack as if the word itself could keep him moving. "Supports, lifters, better lamps. And gloves. We'll open it right, and we'll be the ones to read it first."

Jonas gave no reply. He was scanning the ridge lines, his lamp sweeping briefly and then cutting out so his eyes could adjust to natural dark. His posture said everything: tomorrow was not promised.

Arielle lingered a moment longer at the ruin's edge. She turned back, lamp raised on instinct. The beam slipped through the fractured stones, brushed the chamber they had left behind. For a fraction of a heartbeat, she thought she saw something. A flicker. A ripple of dark within dark.

Her stomach clenched.

I imagined it. It's nerves. Just nerves.

She lowered the lamp quickly, almost guiltily. Karim was already moving toward the vehicle, his voice carrying lists again, muttered reminders about humidity, temperature, angles. Jonas circled wide, checking the perimeter, his silence heavier than Karim's words.

They reached the jeep. Jonas did a full sweep before unlocking it, scanning every shadow like a man who had been punished once for trusting too easily. Only after a long pause did he nod. "Clear."

Arielle climbed in, setting her lamp across her knees. Karim dropped into the back, still scribbling notes even as the engine coughed awake. Jonas drove, one hand steady on the wheel, the other resting near the gearshift, his jaw tight.

The ruins receded behind them, swallowed by the plateau's blackness. Arielle turned in her seat, watching until the last glimmer of pale stone disappeared into shadow. For a breath she thought she heard it again—a sound too neat to be chance. A pebble ticking against stone. Deliberate. Exact.

She faced forward, heart hammering. The desert stretched wide and empty ahead, but the feeling didn't leave. It sat in the back of her throat, metallic, insistent, whispering: You were not alone in there.

Jonas's eyes stayed on the road. Karim muttered numbers. Arielle gripped the lamp harder, as if its small circle of light could promise protection against what the dark refused to reveal.

Behind them, the ruins kept their silence. But it was not the silence of absence. It was the silence of something waiting.

Chapter Two — The Intruder

The old stone corridors of Qumran exhaled dust with every step, as though the ruins themselves resented intrusion. Arielle moved carefully, her lamp beam playing across plastered walls mottled with time. Fragments of Hebrew script bled through the surface, faint as bruises. Each letter felt like a relic, whispers preserved in lime and grit.

"This was a scriptorium," she murmured, tracing the air just shy of the wall. "Where the Essenes copied their scrolls. You can see the benches cut into the rock—see the way the plaster was layered to reflect light from the oil lamps."

Her voice carried reverence, but beneath it was a thrill. These were the details that filled her father's journals, margins inked with speculation about lost texts, missing records, half-whispered genealogies. Now she was walking the same stones.

Karim adjusted the strap of his satchel, curls damp with sweat despite the desert night's chill. His lamp beam darted in restless sweeps, catching the grooves of ancient cistern channels cut into the floor. "And over there—mikvah baths. Ritual immersions, carved in sequence. The Essenes bathed sometimes three times a day." His voice cracked with energy, words rushing as though history itself demanded speed. "They weren't hermits. They were engineers. This place was designed to outlast siege and sand alike."

Jonas, silent until now, moved behind them with a soldier's precision. Every footfall was measured, weight rolled along the edge of his boots to muffle sound. He carried no scholar's notebook—only a flashlight, knife, and the posture of a man who had lived too long with ambushes. "And yet," he said finally, his voice low and even, "Rome crushed them all the same."

The reminder sobered them. Arielle swept her light across the ceiling, noting where soot stains darkened the plaster. Two thousand years ago, men had prayed and copied words by lamplight here. Some had believed they were preserving eternity itself. And when the legions came, fire and stone had tried to erase them.

But not everything had burned.

The corridor widened into a chamber, the roof blackened with soot, the floor uneven where collapse had scattered debris. At its center stood a table of stone, half-buried in rubble. Arielle froze. Geometry revealed itself where nature should have been random. A rectangle. Too exact to be chance.

Jonas's lamp swung in a careful arc, scanning shadows before settling on the table. His jaw tightened. "That looks like a lid."

Arielle's pulse quickened. She crouched, brushing dust aside until the groove of an outline revealed itself—edges straight, fitted. She bit her lip to keep from exhaling too hard, as though breath itself might undo the centuries.

Karim dropped to his knees beside her, eyes blazing. "It's sealed. Intact. You realize what this could mean?" His pencil was already scratching angles into his notebook, diagramming pressure points, collapse vectors, possible supports.

Jonas remained standing, eyes fixed on the corridor they had just come through. "It could also mean bait. A vault left unopened this long rarely stays forgotten without reason."

But Arielle barely heard him. Her lamp glinted on hardened pitch at the edge of the lid—an ancient seal, unbroken. Her throat went dry. The thought pressed against her chest with both wonder and dread.

A jar lay beneath.

And if the legends were true—so might the scroll that had haunted her father's life.

Karim adjusted his glasses, breath quickening as he examined the pitch that rimmed the lid. "This isn't like the restoration plaster in the other chambers. Look at the grain. This is Herodian-era composite—lime, ash, and crushed seashell. It's the same formula the Essenes used when they sealed communal jars in Cave Four."

Arielle leaned closer, heart hammering. She remembered the photographs in her father's journals: fragment jars, cracked open in the 1950s by Bedouin shepherds and French archaeologists. None of those jars had been sealed so completely. Most had been broken before discovery. But this—this was pristine.

Jonas crouched, running a gloved hand along the edge. He wasn't looking at the plaster. He was feeling the weight distribution, the way the stones had shifted. "If we move it wrong, we could collapse the whole chamber. Or trigger something left behind deliberately."

Karim shot him a look, half exasperated, half amused. "You see booby traps everywhere."

"Because they exist," Jonas replied flatly. "The Romans used deadfalls. Modern smugglers rig explosives. I've seen men die because they thought caution was weakness."

Arielle placed a steadying hand on the stone table. "Enough. We do this carefully. Slow."

Working together, they cleared debris, their movements economical, almost ritualistic. Dust sifted into the air, making Arielle cough into her scarf. The scent was bitter—old plaster, salt, and something metallic that made the back of her tongue sting.

Finally, with Jonas bracing the slab, Karim wedged his chisel into the seam. The sound was too loud in the chamber—stone against stone, a groan of centuries breaking. He worked methodically, scraping, easing, until a faint crack snaked across the pitch.

Arielle's breath caught as the seal gave way. With reverence, Karim pried loose the last hardened fragment. Together they eased the lid back just enough for Arielle to shine her light inside.

The beam revealed linen, brittle and brown with age, wrapped tight around a clay cylinder no longer than her forearm. Its seal of black pitch still glistened, unbroken.

Her mouth went dry. The hairs along her arms rose. "A scroll jar."

Karim's pencil fell silent. He reached for his gloves with shaking hands. "If this is what I think it is..." His voice faltered.

Jonas remained standing guard, though his eyes softened a fraction. "Is it authentic?"

Arielle forced herself to examine instead of marvel. The jar's clay bore striations unique to Qumran—spiral grooves left by a potter's hand. The linen weave matched textiles catalogued in Jerusalem's Rockefeller Museum, carbon-dated to the turn of the era. Every fiber screamed authenticity.

"It's real," she whispered. "This could be older than the Gospel fragments. Older than Josephus. This could be..." She stopped herself before speaking the word her father had used. The Scroll of Light. To name it was to invite danger.

Karim angled the jar carefully onto the stone table, handling it like the bones of a saint. His lamp caught faint markings along the linen wrap—incisions too regular to be decay. Numbers. A cipher.

Her throat tightened. Her father had sketched similar sequences in his journals, scribbled in the margins of Psalm commentaries. Substitution codes, ancient word-games scholars used to cloak dangerous truths. She translated reflexively, pencil flying across her notebook.

The numbers resolved into three Latin words: Serva veritatem. Guard the truth.

Her pulse thundered. She remembered her father's voice, hoarse from nights of study: If you find it, guard it. They will come for power, not for truth.

The jar trembled in her hands. Not literally—her hands were shaking. But in that moment it felt alive, humming with intent.

Jonas's eyes narrowed. He was listening—not to her, but to the corridor. His jaw flexed. "We're not alone."

The sound came first—a faint scrape of boot leather against stone, too measured to be collapse. Jonas rose instantly, knife unsheathed in one motion, his flashlight cutting across the corridor.

Shadows shifted. Then a figure emerged from the passage, tall and broad-shouldered, moving with the predatory ease of someone who had walked ruins his entire life. Behind him came another: a woman, slimmer, blade glinting in her hand.

Arielle's stomach dropped. She knew that face.

"Matthias Calder," she whispered.

The archaeologist's reputation had preceded him for years—conference whispers, rumors in academic corridors, museum curators warning each other about "loans" that never returned. He was brilliant, yes, but brilliant the way fire is brilliant: it consumed as it illuminated.

Matthias smiled, though his eyes were hard. His beard was neatly trimmed, his clothes too new for fieldwork—desert gear bought for image rather than necessity. He carried himself not as a scholar but as a broker. A collector.

"Well," he drawled, stepping fully into the light. "Looks like I'm not the only one who followed the breadcrumbs." His gaze slid past Arielle and Karim, fixing on the jar with a hunger that made her skin crawl.

Jonas shifted, positioning himself squarely between Matthias and the table. "You shouldn't be here."

"Neither should you," Matthias replied smoothly. "But here we are. Now, why don't we make this simple?" He lifted a gloved hand, palm outward as though in peace. "Hand me the scroll, and you can all leave intact. No need for unnecessary unpleasantness."

Arielle's pulse hammered. "This isn't yours. It belongs to history."

Matthias's smile sharpened. "History belongs to those who hold it. Or in this case—those who can sell it."

The woman beside him moved forward, knife glinting. She was silent, her eyes obsidian-dark, her posture lethal. Jonas tensed, adjusting his stance.

"Stay behind me," he murmured to Arielle without looking.

Matthias cocked his head, studying her. "Arielle Marcus. I wondered if I'd see you here. Your father chased this myth across continents until it broke him. And now here you are—ready to do the same. Touching."

Her throat tightened. "You knew my father?"

"I knew of him. We all did. He wanted truth. The Vatican wanted silence. I… want something far more practical. Influence. Wealth. Doors that open when others stay closed." He nodded at the jar. "That's the key."

Karim's fists clenched. "You'd sell the most important discovery in centuries to the highest bidder?"

Matthias shrugged lightly, as though Karim's outrage bored him. "Do you think museums are purer? Do you think Rome guards these relics for scholarship? No. Everyone plays the same game. I'm just honest about it."

The woman shifted suddenly, lunging with a flash of steel. Jonas met her halfway, knife intercepting hers with a metallic clang that echoed like thunder. Sparks lit the chamber as their blades locked.

"Run!" Jonas barked, twisting his wrist to shove her back.

Karim grabbed Arielle's arm, pulling her toward the side passage. She clutched the scroll jar tight against her chest, its linen wrap rough against her fingers. Every instinct screamed at her to fight for it—but her father's warning was louder. Guard the truth. They will come for power, not for truth.

Behind them, Matthias's voice thundered through the chamber, cold and commanding: "She has the scroll! Don't let them escape!"

The chamber erupted into chaos. Jonas's blade rang against the intruder's in a brutal rhythm, sparks scattering across ancient stone.

Matthias barked orders in clipped German, his voice echoing like a whip crack through the ruins.

Karim pulled Arielle hard toward the side passage, their lamps bouncing wild circles across the walls. She clutched the jar tight against her ribs, its weight unnatural, as if it wanted to anchor her here rather than let her flee.

The passage narrowed quickly, squeezing them into single file. Jagged rock scraped Arielle's shoulder. Her breath came ragged, loud in the confined space. Behind them, metal struck metal, Jonas grunting with effort, boots scraping against stone as he gave ground but never broke.

"Faster," Karim hissed, the edge of panic in his voice. "This way—this connects to the aqueduct tunnels. I saw the cistern channel cut into the rock earlier."

Arielle forced herself forward, lamp beam jerking as she stumbled. She pressed one hand against the wall, the plaster cool beneath her fingertips, still faintly etched with Hebrew script. Whole lives had once been ordered here—ritual baths, communal meals, scrolls copied with aching patience. Now those same walls funneled her toward flight.

Behind them, Matthias's voice boomed closer: "Don't let them escape! The scroll is everything!"

Jonas appeared suddenly in the passage, blood streaking his jaw, knife still slick. His chest rose and fell hard, but his eyes were clear. "Move," he ordered. No explanation, no hesitation—just the soldier's command born of knowing time had already run out.

They burst into a larger chamber, its ceiling arching black with soot. A circular pit yawned at its center—an ancient cistern, once fed by aqueduct channels that carried precious desert rain. Cracks laced its plaster walls, but traces of hydraulic cement still clung, proof of Essene ingenuity.

Karim pointed to a fissure in the far wall where moonlight slanted faintly through. "There! An exit!"

The shout of pursuit reverberated through the tunnels. The obsidian-eyed woman's voice cut sharp as steel: "They have it!"

Jonas pushed Arielle ahead, his hand firm at her back. She stumbled to the fissure, shoulders scraping stone as she squeezed through. Karim wriggled after, boots kicking loose chips of rock. Jonas followed last, pausing only long enough to kick a loose slab into the passage, blocking it with a thunderous crash.

Then they were outside.

The desert night hit Arielle like a baptism—cool, sharp, brimming with salt. She stumbled on the slope of broken limestone, sand and gravel sliding under her boots. Karim steadied her, but his eyes were already scanning the barren expanse.

Behind them, shouts erupted from the fissure. A figure vaulted out—not Jonas, but the obsidian-eyed woman. She landed on the slope like a predator, knife gleaming.

"Go!" Jonas snapped, shoving Arielle forward.

They scrambled down the slope, loose stone clattering, each step threatening to spill them into the darkness. Arielle's lungs burned, but she clung to the jar, every ounce of will bent on not letting it slip from her grasp.

At the base of the slope, Karim veered sharply left, guiding her toward the jagged outline of the aqueduct ruins. The channel walls, built of massive limestone blocks fitted without mortar, rose like a broken scar across the desert. Once, water had surged here, sustaining a community that defied the wilderness. Now, the channel was dry, its arches crumbling.

They ducked behind the aqueduct wall just as the woman crested the slope above, scanning the terrain with hawk-like stillness.

Matthias's shout followed, carried sharp on the desert wind: "She has the scroll! Find them!"

Arielle pressed her back against the ancient stone, heart pounding. Her fingers tightened on the jar until her knuckles ached. She could feel Karim trembling beside her, though his voice remained fierce. "On my signal, run for the dunes. Don't stop. No matter what."

Jonas crouched at the aqueduct's edge, knife ready, eyes narrowed. He glanced back at Arielle, then at the jar in her arms. "Guard it," he said quietly. "No matter the cost."

The desert exhaled around them—wind hissing over sand, stars sharp as blades overhead. Arielle swallowed hard, her body taut with dread and resolve. Whatever was written inside that scroll, it was worth killing for.

And already, people had begun.

The wind shifted, carrying grit across the aqueduct ruins. Arielle pressed lower against the stone, the jar locked in her arms. She dared a glance over the rim—Matthias stood on the slope above, his lamp casting a pale circle. His expression was not rage but calculation, the kind of cold appraisal that measured profit and risk in equal measure.

The obsidian-eyed woman prowled along the ridge beside him, blade ready. Arielle let the stone hide her again; she had seen only fragments—the glint of a knife, the matte line of a braid, the controlled sweep of a hunter's gaze. The woman's eyes combed the ground in slow, methodical passes, skimming their line of cover and moving on. If she had seen them, she didn't show it.

Karim flung a fist-sized stone across the aqueduct. It clattered loudly against rock, ricocheting into shadow. The woman snapped toward the sound, knife raised. "There!" she barked, darting into the dark.

"Now!" Karim hissed.

He seized Arielle's wrist and pulled her into motion. They sprinted from cover, boots slipping in sand, lungs burning. Jonas followed close, his blade reversed in his hand, ready for anything that broke from the dark.

The desert unfolded around them—an endless expanse of sand and limestone ridges, the Dead Sea shimmering pale and metallic under the moon. Each breath seared Arielle's throat. Still she ran, clutching the jar tight, its linen wrap rough against her palms.

Behind them Matthias shouted, his voice carrying down the slope like a curse: "Find them! Bring me the scroll!"

The words spurred her faster. Pebbles skittered beneath her boots, and twice she nearly fell, but Jonas steadied her with a grip on her arm. His jaw was set, his eyes scanning the ridgelines, calculating every path and threat.

At last they collapsed into the lee of a dune, bodies heaving, sweat chilling under the desert night air. The wind whistled across the crest, filling their footprints almost as quickly as they made them.

Karim leaned against the slope, chest heaving. "We can't stop here. If they have dogs, or drones—"

Jonas cut him off, his voice low, certain. "They won't risk dogs in this terrain. But they'll sweep the ridges. We have maybe an hour, no more, before they pick up our trail."

Arielle bent over the jar, her breath still ragged. The words carved into the linen—Serva veritatem—burned in her mind. Guard the truth. It felt less like instruction and more like prophecy.

Jonas crouched at the edge of the dune, peering across the moonlit landscape. "We head west, into the wadis. The terrain is broken there—harder to track. From there, Jerusalem."

Karim wiped grit from his face, forcing a grin through exhaustion. "Jerusalem. Because hiding in the most contested city on earth is the safe option."

Jonas didn't smile. "It's where allies are. And where enemies expect us least."

Arielle swallowed, pressing her forehead briefly to the jar. She wanted to believe Jonas, to believe there was a plan, but the weight in her arms told her the opposite. They weren't carrying a relic. They were carrying a fuse.

The night pressed closer, stars hard and merciless above. Every shadow seemed to shift, every ridge to conceal pursuit. She felt it again—that prickle along her arms, the sense of being watched not only by Matthias and his mercenaries but by something older, something that had waited centuries for this scroll to be found.

Jonas stood, tightening the strap of his pack. His silhouette cut sharp against the stars. "We move. Stay low. Stay silent."

Karim hauled himself up, his usual bravado muted by fatigue. He brushed Arielle's arm, not quite a gesture of comfort, more an anchor reminding her he was still here.

Arielle rose last, clutching the jar against her chest. She turned once, looking back at the ruins of Qumran. They lay in darkness, stones broken, walls whispering, but she could almost swear they breathed. As though the earth itself had seen this chase before and was waiting to see it again.

She faced forward, throat tight. Whatever lay ahead—the wadis, Jerusalem, the Council her father had hinted at—there would be no turning back.

And in the shadows of the desert, Matthias's vow still echoed: She has the scroll. Find them.

Chapter Three — The Night Watcher

They moved west under a blade-thin moon, the Dead Sea to their left like a sheet of hammered pewter. Salt air cut their tongues; every breath tasted metallic. Jonas set a low, relentless pace, angling them toward the broken ridgelines that fed into Wadi Qelt—the ancient gorge that had carried men between Jericho and Jerusalem since before Rome had a name for this place.

"Keep to the lee," he murmured, steering them along the shadowed side of a limestone fin. Sand hissed over the crest, erasing their prints as quickly as they made them. "Let the wind work for us."

Arielle hugged the clay jar to her chest, linen scraping her forearms raw. Fatigue had a sound—blood in the ears, the crisp rasp of breath caught just short of a sob. She focused on the ground: chalk chips, goat droppings, a shard of dark flint. Details steadied her. Details were the first rung back to control.

Karim trotted at her shoulder, muttering in bursts the way he did when thought outpaced oxygen. "Qelt's cut straight through the Judean highlands. Nabateans ran caravans there, then Herod lined the route with fortlets. Bandits, pilgrims, legionnaires—the road's a palimpsest." He glanced at the jar and tried for a grin. "Add 'idiots with a priceless scroll' to the layers."

Jonas didn't slow. "Save your breath."

They dropped into a shallow wadi and followed its dry bed west. The rock underfoot shifted from pale marl to harder dolomite, slick in places where flash floods had burnished the surface like old bone. Twice, Jonas halted them with a raised hand, listening. Wind sighed in the acacia. A lone hyrax squealed and scuttled under a lip of stone. Somewhere far off, a nightjar clicked. Nothing human.

But Arielle felt it anyway—the pressure along her arms, the prickling at the base of her skull. The sensation from the chamber had followed them into the open: not merely pursuit, but attention. Old attention. She told herself it was adrenaline painting patterns on emptiness. The thought didn't take.

They topped a ridge and the land fell away like a collapsed amphitheater. Far to the north, a chalk-white slash clung to the cliffside—St. George's Monastery, lanterns pricking the dark like pinned stars. Monks had carved that place into the gorge in the fifth century, its cells suspended above the abyss in defiance of gravity and Rome and common sense. Arielle had once traced its cantilevered galleries in a notebook and wondered what kind of faith could anchor itself to so little ground. Tonight, she envied it.

"Qelt's there," Jonas said, chin lifting toward the darker seam where the canyon began. "We follow the watercourse. We'll hit the Ascent of Adummim near the old Good Samaritan Inn. From there, switchbacks. Then Ein Prat. We rest by dawn, move under cover."

Karim puffed a laugh that came out more like a cough. "The road of thieves and parables. Perfect."

They slid into the first folds of the gorge. The air cooled abruptly, the stone walls shouldering out the night wind. A rank, mineral smell seeped up from the depths—the ghost of water long gone. Jonas dropped into a half-crouch, palm brushing the ground, eyes scanning for sign the way other men scanned headlines. He changed course twice without explaining, choosing shelves of rock that kept them invisible from the rim.

"Jonas," Arielle said softly, when the silence had stretched to breaking. "Back there. With the knife." She didn't finish the sentence. She didn't have to.

He kept moving. "She's a professional. Not Matthias—he's a market in a suit. She's hired by someone who thinks in contingencies. Don't assume they'll quit before dawn."

"The Vatican?" Karim asked.

Jonas's mouth tightened. "Maybe. Maybe a collector with friends in black cassocks. Maybe both."

Arielle tasted the old bitterness behind his flat tone and saw, for a heartbeat, not the soldier before her but a younger man in a different desert, standing beside a convoy as night bloomed with fire. She filed the glimpse away. Later, when they weren't running.

They skirted a drop where the wadi fell away into darkness. On the far wall, crude notches scarred the limestone—ancient steps cut by men who'd needed to cross a thousand years earlier. Arielle's lamp grazed the marks and caught something else: a Roman numeral scratched waist-high into the rock, weathered but legible.

"Milestone," she breathed. "The Legio X Fretensis marked distances when they held Jericho. They measured in the empire's certainty that everything could be counted."

"And still," Karim said, "the desert keeps its own ledgers."

A sound rolled down the gorge: not wind, not bird. A low, mechanical thrum, then a blink of light skating the cliff face above them and disappearing. Arielle froze. Jonas had his hand up before the flinch became a step.

"Drone," he said. "Consumer-grade by the sound. Matthias doesn't want to light up the whole plateau. He's searching discreetly." He tipped his head, listening to the way the sound faded. "They're sweeping the rim first. We're good in the channel for now. Move."

They traversed a bench the width of a handcart, backs to the wall, heels feeling for purchase. The jar's curve pressed into Arielle's ribs with every breath. When her foot slid on lichen-slick stone, Jonas's hand closed on her forearm, heat and steadiness and a quick squeeze that said here, now, I have you with more conviction than words could carry.

The ledge widened into a shelf tucked beneath an overhang. Jonas angled them in and finally allowed what passed for a halt: thirty seconds of stillness to let muscles stop shaking. Karim collapsed onto his haunches, chest sawing, a laugh bubbling up despite the stitch in his side.

"Promise me," he said to Arielle between gulps of air, "if we survive this, you'll at least let me put 'chased by mercenaries through a Byzantine gorge' in the acknowledgments."

She managed a ghost of a smile. "Only if we spell 'mercenaries' right."

The smile died as cold slid across the back of her neck. Not wind. Not exhaustion. She turned her head slowly toward the mouth of the shelf.

Nothing. Just the lip of the ledge cutting a neat rectangle from the sky.

And yet—the sensation intensified. Watching. Weighing.

Jonas saw the change before she spoke. His posture altered by degrees, the relaxed coil winding tight. He killed his lamp and the dark came down like velvet. In that new black, the battery-green wink of something above the rim blinked once, twice, then vanished, as if a lid had closed over an eye.

"Not the drone," Jonas whispered. "Different angle. Lower. Human height."

"How—" Karim started.

"Because a drone doesn't breathe," Jonas said.

Silence gathered. Even the wind seemed to hold itself still.

Arielle slid the jar deeper into her pack, padding it with her scarf, her jacket, anything that would keep clay from knocking stone. The linen rubbed her fingers. Serva veritatem. She breathed the words in and out until her heartbeat slowed enough to think.

"We can't stay here," she said. "But we need twenty minutes. Enough to keep our legs under us."

Jonas weighed the ledge, the rim, the soundless thing that had blinked and then blinked out. "Ten," he said. "Then we ghost to the next bend. There's a goat track that climbs to a spur above St. George. If we hit the Ascent of Adummim by first light, we'll have options. Ein Prat has water. And walls."

"Monks, too," Karim added hopefully.

“Monks who have seen worse than us,” Jonas said.

They huddled under the overhang, pressed shoulder to shoulder, breath fogging the cold air. Above them, somewhere along the lip of stone, something—someone—shifted weight with the faintest grit-sound and then stilled. Arielle closed her eyes and saw the Qumran chamber superimposed over the gorge: the sealed lid, the words cut into linen, the feeling that had crawled out of stone and into her skin.

The desert had long memories. Tonight, it remembered them. And it was not the only thing.

Ten minutes, she told herself, hands resting over the pack where the jar lay hidden. Ten minutes, and then we move. Ten minutes, and the watcher would either drift away, or follow.

Either way, Jerusalem waited.

Jonas tapped Arielle’s shoulder once, twice. The signal. Time was up.

They moved as shadows, edging from the shelf and into the gorge again. The air thickened; the walls pressed closer. Their lamps stayed dark, but moonlight bled down in ribbons, enough to keep from breaking ankles. Every sound mattered: gravel skittering, fabric rasping, the hard thud of a heart that felt too loud.

Karim muttered under his breath, part prayer, part calculation. “If we’re below the Byzantine aqueduct line, then the Nabatean channel should... yes, it should cut north before the bend.” His voice quickened as if knowledge itself could carve safety. “That fissure—see it? That’s a feeder into Ein Prat. That’s water, Ari.”

Arielle wanted to believe him. Her mouth was chalk-dry, her tongue swollen. The idea of water—real, cold water—was both promise and torment.

They hugged the gorge wall, moving beneath overhangs blackened by centuries of soot. Bedouins had lit fires here, Roman soldiers had pitched camps here, monks had scribbled prayers into plaster here.

Arielle brushed one such inscription with her fingertips as they passed—a cross cut into limestone, weathered but deliberate. A mark of someone who had believed that even in a place of thieves, light could take root.

A voice shattered the silence. Male. Sharp. Close.

Jonas shoved them flat against the rock. He raised a finger for silence and edged forward until only his profile caught the moonlight.

The voice repeated in Arabic: "... sweep the lower path. He said she carries it herself."

Bootsteps echoed—three, maybe four men. Not Matthias's polished accent. Hired locals, armed but paid. Their flashlights scythed erratic arcs across the opposite wall of the gorge, slicing light over ancient plaster and then vanishing into shadow.

Arielle's heart stuttered. She held her breath, pressing her back so hard against stone it cut her shoulder blades.

The footsteps grew louder. Closer. Then—sudden laughter, coarse and dismissive. One of the beams swung across the gorge mouth and clipped their ledge. Jonas's hand shot up, palm open, halting even breath.

The light lingered on a patch of wall just feet away. Arielle could see every scratch in the plaster, every grain of grit. Sweat prickled her spine. She could almost feel the beam crawling toward her face.

Then it jerked away.

The men's boots receded, the sound swallowed by the gorge's curves. Faint chatter drifted up—complaints about pay, about Matthias's temper, about the "cursed foreigner who thinks old paper is gold."

Karim exhaled audibly, trembling. "I was one syllable from screaming."

Jonas's jaw stayed tight. "They'll circle. They'll keep circling until they flush us. Move."

They pressed on, crossing a series of ledges cut so narrow Arielle's pack scraped stone. Below, the gorge plunged into darkness. Somewhere down there, water glimmered faintly—Ein Prat, a living spring that had fed goats and pilgrims for two thousand years.

Her foot slipped on damp rock. Jonas caught her again, his grip iron around her forearm. For a heartbeat their faces were inches apart, breath mingling, the night holding its own silence between them. His eyes were steady, pale as flint, but there was something under them too—something not soldier, not calculation.

"Breathe slower," he whispered. "Your fear makes noise."

She nodded, her chest heaving against the pack's weight. She wanted to tell him what she felt—that the watcher wasn't just men with flashlights, that something older pressed close, closer than any mercenary. But the words stuck. Words gave shape to shadows, and shadows didn't need help tonight.

They climbed higher, following a goat path scratched into the cliff. The moon slid lower, the stars hard and merciless above. Twice Jonas froze them, eyes darting toward the rim. Once, a pebble trickled down near Arielle's boots from the slope above—too deliberate to be chance. She felt Karim stiffen beside her, his notebook pressed against his chest like a shield.

Finally, the path widened to a shelf. Jonas crouched low, scanning the rim. No lights. No voices. Just the hiss of the desert wind.

"We rest here," he said at last. "Ten minutes. Then we make the climb toward the Adummim road."

Karim dropped onto the stone, gasping. He tilted his head back, eyes closed. "Ten minutes feels like salvation."

Arielle sat too, the jar nestled between her knees, her palms pressed to its cool curve. She stared at the rim, where stone met sky, and waited for the blink of that watcher's light.

It didn't come.

But the feeling didn't leave.

The ten minutes ended with Jonas's hand on Arielle's shoulder. Not harsh—steady, the way one lifts someone out of a dream. "Time," he said.

They rose stiffly, bodies aching from the pace. Karim adjusted his satchel with a grunt. Arielle forced her numb legs into motion, the jar heavy in her pack. They moved in silence, climbing the narrow shelf until it bent toward the west.

The gorge widened slightly here, and the land began to tilt upward. The Ascent of Adummim had earned its name in antiquity—the "red ascent," for the iron-stained cliffs that rose like rusted walls. Bandits had once haunted this road, stripping pilgrims on their way to Jerusalem. Tonight, Arielle felt like she had joined their long, unlucky company.

The climb bit into her thighs. Her lamp stayed dark, but the moon revealed enough: hand-cut steps notched into the slope, worn shallow by centuries of sandals. The Essenes, Nabateans, Romans, Crusaders—all had left marks here. Layers of passage, layers of flight.

She pressed her palm against the stone for balance and felt her father's voice rise from memory. History is a palimpsest, Ari. What's erased is never gone—it waits for the right eyes to see it.

Her right hand slid unconsciously to the jar in her pack. The linen wrap pressed against her fingers. Guard the truth. The words from the cipher burned hotter now, not command but accusation. Her father had died for this search, chasing them until the desert claimed him. And she—was she carrying them toward revelation, or burial?

Karim broke the silence first, his voice hushed but edged with thought. "If this scroll names a bloodline—if it traces descendants beyond the crucifixion—then it doesn't just rewrite theology. It rewrites power.

Monarchies, churches, even nations built on the absence of heirs. Imagine what happens if the world learns He had them."

Jonas didn't slow, didn't look back. "Or imagine what happens if the wrong hands learn. Wars aren't fought over what's true. They're fought over what's useful."

Arielle felt both truths pressing against her ribs, sharp as knives. She tightened her pack straps, forcing her thoughts back to the climb.

They topped a rise and the desert spread before them, stark under starlight. The scar of the ancient road wound upward across the ridge, a pale line cut into rust-colored stone. Far ahead, faint lights glimmered on the horizon—the scattered villages east of Jerusalem.

For a heartbeat, relief flooded Arielle's chest. Civilization. Roads. Water. Shelter.

Then the sensation returned.

Her skin prickled. She turned her head slowly toward the ridge above.

A silhouette stood there. Motionless. Cloaked in shadow.

It was too far for features, but the stance was unmistakable: upright, deliberate, watching. Not Matthias—his build was broader. Not the mercenary woman—this figure radiated stillness, not violence.

The figure lifted a hand. Slowly. Deliberately. An open palm. A gesture of recognition—or warning.

Arielle's throat constricted. Her heart hammered against her ribs.

"Jonas," she whispered.

He didn't ask. He followed her gaze, eyes narrowing. His hand closed over her arm, steadying her even as his other reached for his knife.

Karim saw it next. "What—what is that?" His voice cracked on the last word.

The figure lingered one breath longer. Then it was gone. Swallowed by the ridge, as though the desert had exhaled it back into stone.

The three of them stood frozen, the silence louder than any pursuit.

Finally Jonas said, "Move." His tone was clipped, but something had shifted in it—less command, more urgency. "Whatever it was, it knows we're here. We don't wait to find out who sent it."

They pressed on, climbing faster despite burning muscles. Arielle forced her eyes forward, but the image seared itself into her mind: a watcher in the night, neither enemy nor ally, hand raised as if to remind her that the desert had always been crowded—with memory, with ghosts, with truths too dangerous to speak.

By the time they reached the ridge, Arielle's calves burned and her breath came raw. The ancient road unrolled before them—a pale scar weaving across the red limestone, broken in places but still visible. Roman engineers had built it wide enough for pack animals, cutting into the slope with stubborn geometry. Centuries of pilgrims had kept it alive, sandals polishing the stones smoother than any chisel.

Jonas guided them off the exposed track and into a shallow cleft sheltered by boulders. From here they could watch the road without being seen. He crouched low, scanning the valley they had climbed from. His breathing was steady, but Arielle noticed the tension in his shoulders, the way his hand hovered near the hilt of his knife as if battle had never truly ended for him.

Karim slumped against the rock, gulping water from his canteen. "God," he rasped, "how did the Essenes do this every day? All these climbs, the fasting, the ritual baths—no wonder they thought they were closer to heaven. They were half-dead."

"They believed it made them pure," Arielle said, voice softer than she meant. "Every immersion was preparation. They thought the desert would strip them down to bone and prayer, until only truth remained."

Karim shot her a crooked grin. "And here I thought archaeology was supposed to strip me down to student debt and back pain."

She laughed despite herself. The sound startled her, as if her own body had rebelled against the weight pressing in from all sides.

Jonas finally sat, back against the rock, gaze still fixed on the valley. His face was stone in the starlight, but Arielle noticed the faint tremor in his hand before he clasped it tight against his knee. She had seen that look before, in veterans at conferences where the past was supposed to stay buried in footnotes. The desert had dug old ghosts out of him tonight.

"Jonas," she said carefully. "Back there—you knew exactly how to move, how to anticipate them. Who trained you?"

His jaw flexed, but he didn't look at her. "I wore a uniform once. Wrong war, wrong desert. I learned that ruins don't just hold the past. They teach you how quickly the present burns, too." He finally glanced at her, eyes pale and sharp. "That's all you need to know."

Silence stretched between them. Karim shifted uncomfortably, running his thumb along the spine of his notebook. "You saved us tonight," he said. "Twice. That's enough for me."

Jonas didn't respond, but the edge in his posture eased slightly.

Arielle pulled the jar from her pack and set it between them. Moonlight glinted on the linen, highlighting the faint incisions of the cipher. The air around it seemed heavier, as though the desert itself leaned in to listen.

"Serva veritatem," she murmured. "Guard the truth. But what if truth isn't meant to be guarded? What if it's meant to be spoken?"

Her words startled even herself. They rang in the silence, more belief than doubt.

Karim leaned forward, his face lit with feverish light. "If this really speaks of a bloodline—if it proves He had descendants—then guarding it means burying it all over again. That's not truth. That's cowardice."

Jonas shook his head, jaw hard. "And if speaking it ignites another war? If it topples governments, splits churches, kills thousands? Would that be worth your academic pride?"

Karim bristled. "It's not pride. It's history. Truth is worth cost."

Arielle pressed her palms against the jar. The linen felt warm, almost pulsing. For a moment she thought of her father—scribbling late into the night, pages trembling under his hands as though he already carried this weight. Guard it, he had whispered. Guard it.

Her throat tightened. She couldn't yet tell them that part of her already felt chosen, as if the scroll had been waiting for her hands alone. To confess that would be to admit something she wasn't ready to name.

A sound broke the stalemate—the faint cough of an engine somewhere across the valley. Jonas stiffened instantly, eyes narrowing. Headlights winked on and off as a vehicle traced the distant ridgeline. Searching. Sweeping.

"They're still hunting," Jonas said. His voice carried no surprise, only certainty. He rose in one motion and tightened his pack. "Rest's over. We move before they cut this road off."

Karim groaned but scrambled to his feet. Arielle slipped the jar back into her pack, cinching the straps tight. The sense of being watched returned, heavier now, as though the figure from the ridge had followed them unseen.

They stepped onto the ancient road, three shadows carrying a secret that might shatter the world. The wind howled down the gorge like a voice too old to name.

The road climbed in switchbacks, the cliffs looming like dark sentinels on either side. Every turn seemed to tighten around them, stone pressing close, sky narrowing to a strip of stars. Arielle's thighs screamed, but she forced herself to match Jonas's pace. Karim lagged a step behind, muttering curses in Arabic and English between gasps.

They passed a cairn of stones stacked waist-high at a bend. Karim touched it as they moved. "Roman waymark," he panted. "Two thousand years old, still pointing fools like us to Jerusalem."

Jonas didn't glance back. "Keep moving."

Arielle lifted her eyes toward the horizon. Faint, amber light bled upward—the glow of a city just out of reach. Jerusalem. Ancient, layered, contested. A city that carried every contradiction of faith and power. Seeing it both comforted and terrified her. It meant refuge. It meant more enemies.

The sense of being watched thickened. Not the blunt menace of Matthias's men, not the mechanical whine of drones, but something quieter. Patient. At the edge of every shadow, at the crest of every ridge, she felt eyes following.

She slowed at one turn, heart hammering. There—half a silhouette against the stars. Cloak. Stillness. The same figure she had seen before.

It raised a hand again. The same open palm. A gesture that looked more warning than threat.

"Jonas," she whispered.

He pivoted instantly, knife drawn, gaze following hers. But the figure was gone. The ridge was bare.

Karim stumbled to a halt, swearing. "I didn't see anything. Ari—"

"I did," she said firmly. "Twice now."

Jonas's expression was unreadable in the starlight. "Then we assume it's real. Someone's shadowing us. Not Matthias's crew—they'd have taken the shot already. This… is different."

Karim rubbed the back of his neck, uneasy. "Different how?"

Jonas tightened his pack. "Not hostile. Not yet. But don't mistake patience for mercy."

They pressed onward, every sense stretched taut. The city's glow grew brighter, amber bleeding into gold. The road widened at last onto a plateau, where the desert dropped away in ragged waves of stone.

They paused at the crest. As they crested the Adummim ridge, Jerusalem rose into view—a silhouette of domes and towers against the paling sky. Even from here, Arielle could trace the faint gleam of the Dome of the Rock, the outlines of church spires, the heavy walls that had withstood siege after siege. A city where truths had been written, erased, and rewritten again.

Her breath caught. "We made it."

Jonas's eyes never left the horizon. "We're not inside yet."

Karim forced a shaky laugh. "I'll take a heartbeat of awe before the next disaster."

The wind lifted, carrying the smell of stone, dust, and faint woodsmoke. For a moment, Arielle allowed herself to close her eyes. But when she opened them, she thought she saw movement again—just beyond the last bend of the road. A flicker of shadow folding back into the dark.

The watcher had followed.

Arielle gripped her pack straps until her knuckles whitened. She didn't speak of it again. To give it words was to make it more real, and she wasn't ready for that. Not here, not with Jerusalem's gates only miles ahead.

Jonas scanned the ridges one last time, then gestured them forward. "Come on. Dawn's coming. And with it, more eyes than we can afford."

They started down the final stretch of the Adummim road. The glow of Jerusalem swelled before them, layered and immense, waiting like judgment.

Behind them, the desert exhaled into silence. Not the silence of absence. The silence of something following.

Chapter Four — The Council of Shadows

Jerusalem woke in layers. Bells tolled above the braid of voices; a thread of muezzin rose over stone that smelled of wax and damp lime. Laundry snapped between walls older than most kingdoms. In the alley's throat, water from a courtyard spigot pattered into a tin basin, counting time for those who still needed it. Within a windowless chamber set into the flank of an old foundation, oil lamps breathed, their smoke seaming the ceiling in slow black ribs.

Dawn had burned the edges off exhaustion but not the ache. Arielle stood at a long oak table, the satchel strap cutting into her shoulder, dust and desert salt dried on her lips. Jonas took up the rear corner of the room as if guarding a doorway that didn't exist; Karim hovered near a shelf of vellum rolls and wood-handled seals, his notebook—closed for once—pressed flat against his ribs.

Three figures faced them, each carrying authority cut from a different quarry of time: a rabbi with a beard white as plaster and eyes like flint; a scholar in a dark shawl threaded with Hebrew script, ink stains permanent as tattoos on her fingers; and a man in plain clerical black, Roman collar catching the lamp light. They regarded Arielle not as a guest but as a verdict that refused to stay hidden.

"You carry it?" the scholar asked. No greeting, no softening.

Arielle glanced once at Jonas. He gave the smallest of nods. She slid the pack onto the table, unbuckled the flap, and lifted out a clay vessel swaddled in ancient linen. The black pitch seal around the neck was unbroken, dull as old coal.

The air changed. Even the lamps seemed to withdraw a fraction, as if making room for something older than flame.

The rabbi stepped closer, not quite touching, lips shaping words too soft to catch. The priest crossed himself without taking his eyes off Arielle's face.

"It is not just a jar," the scholar said. "It is inheritance—the kind that cuts both ways."

Arielle's voice came low, steady. "Explain it to me like I don't want to believe you."

The rabbi's gaze held centuries. "When the scrolls were hidden, one among them spoke not of psalm or law, but of lineage. A record of children. His children."

Karim's breath broke on a disbelieving laugh he tried to swallow. "You're saying—"

"I'm saying the rumor your father died chasing was more than rumor," the priest said gently, the kindness in his tone at odds with the hardness in his eyes. "Authority fears truth that blooms outside its trellises."

Arielle's fingers tightened on the linen. Serva veritatem. Guard the truth. The numbers cut into the cloth at Qumran had translated into that imperative with a clarity that left no room for misreading. Her father's voice rode the words now, worn and urgent: Guard it.

The scholar slid a small cloth bundle across the table. "From our archive. Not yours. Consider it a keyhole."

Arielle unwrapped the cloth and found a narrow strip of papyrus, edges feathered, the ink crabbed and brown. Aramaic characters marched down the fiber like ants. She traced the line aloud, translating half to herself: "Through the daughters, the covenant endures."

Her pulse stuttered. She had seen the phrase scrawled on cave plaster, whispered in hymns, carved into lintels, a rumor wearing a thousand faces. Here, it felt like a pulse.

"The scribe favored acrostics," the scholar added, angling the strip so a margin caught the lamp light. "Read the first letters in the margin—downward."

Arielle squinted. Tiny initial marks lined the outer edge—barely there until the light struck them just right. M... U... R... I... S... T... A... N. The letters weren't Aramaic at all but a medieval hand, later gloss. A marginal whisper: Muristan.

Karim leaned in until his curls almost brushed the papyrus. "Hospital district. Crusader heart. Fountains and arcades."

"Waypoints," the rabbi said. "The scribe thought in places, not merely in words. Truth needs anchors. Or it drifts and is sold by the yard."

Jonas's gaze didn't leave the door, but his voice cut clean through the ritual hush. "If we accept the premise—what then? You didn't risk this meeting for a history lesson."

The priest spread his hands, palms up; a judge asking mercy from the very evidence he'd presented. "What you carry will not be allowed to live on its own. Some will bury it under doctrine and say they are protecting souls. Some will auction it under glass and say they are honoring history. Matthias Calder covets the door it opens. The Latin envoys prefer the kind of shepherding that leaves no stray."

The lamps hissed. Somewhere beyond the wall, a bell finished tolling and the alley's tin basin kept counting drops.

"My father—" Arielle began, surprising herself, the words a stone she'd been rolling in her mouth for years without swallowing. "He spent his life on this rumor. He died for it. Near Jericho. Officially an accident. For me, it never sat right." She steadied the jar with both hands. "I won't let his cost be for nothing."

The rabbi's gaze softened, the flint turned inward. "Then let his cost purchase your caution."

"Caution looks like what?" Jonas asked. Every muscle in his forearms held the question like wire.

The scholar touched the linen with a fingertip that didn't quite land. "You keep the vessel sealed until you choose the witnesses. Not a museum. Not a ministry. Witnesses. Real eyes. Real risk."

Karim found his voice. "And the Muristan note? That's a map for us or for someone before us?"

"Both," the priest said. "These texts speak sideways. They survive by being misunderstood until the right hands arrive."

Arielle refolded the papyrus and slid it back. "You're not asking us to leave it with you."

"No," the rabbi said simply. "If this were to vanish with us, we would be what we warn you against."

The old woman who had unlocked the alley door earlier eased into the room with the stealth of a practiced keeper of thresholds. Her shawl was drawn tight against the stone damp. She set down a clay cup of water near Karim's elbow; he blinked at it as if a miracle had wandered up at the wrong mass.

The priest nodded toward Jonas. "Your friend knows how to be unseen. But understand: soon the city will know you exist even if it cannot name you."

The chamber held stillness the way a held breath holds air—tense, necessary, temporary.

—

Across the quarter, a man in a dark coat folded a newspaper he had not read. A thin chain threaded his wrist; the silver signet it held winked once in the café light as he lifted it to his mouth.

"Confirmatum: vas sigillatum," he murmured into the metal, Latin clipped flat—confirmed: sealed vessel. "Tertius ingressus—ad murum. Third entrance. Toward the wall."

He counted the last peal of bells with his eyes shut, as if measuring a heartbeat. Two men rose without being named. The map here was not drawn in streets but in thresholds and habits: which gates opened for bread and which for prayer; which courtyards answered knocks with candles, which with questions. He paid for a coffee he did not drink and slid into the alley's shade. The city made room for men like him; it always had.

A phone pulsed once in his pocket. CALDER: Vessel confirmed. Your hour. He did not smile. He never did on the clock.

"Procedite," he said to no one, and the ring caught the light again.

—

The scholar took back the papyrus strip, wrapped it, and set it aside with a care that felt like grief.

"Rules," she said, the word brittle as a twig. "You leave as you came—in silence. Do not carry this vessel openly. Do not speak its name in any tongue. If you are pressed, you know nothing. If pressed harder, you know something else."

"Is this where you bless us and send us out with a prayer?" Karim asked, trying and failing to find a grin.

"This is where we give you a door that won't betray you," the rabbi said. "The Armenian gatekeeper two courts over owes us more favors than he has years left. He will open to this." He slid a small wooden token across the table—a crude cross burned into it, ringed by an inscription in Ge'ez. "Knock twice, then once. He prefers monks to soldiers."

"If Lev answers the door," he added, "listen. His rooms forget names better than most churches keep them."

Jonas's eyes flicked to the token, calculating escape vectors out of habit. "And if we're followed?"

"You will be," the priest said. "This city is designed for pursuit. But it is also designed for disappearance."

The old woman lifted the bolt to a side door that looked like part of the wall until it wasn't. Cold air spilled in, carrying a palm's width of daylight and the smell of bread from somewhere they couldn't see.

Arielle wrapped the jar in its linen until the pitch seal felt buffered from every edge of the world. Guard the truth. The words fit her hands now as if they had been made to.

Jonas adjusted the satchel straps over her shoulders, an efficient tug that avoided touching more than necessary. Karim rolled his shoulders as if shaking a net off his back and tucked his closed notebook inside his shirt like contraband.

The priest stopped them with a lifted hand. "One more thing." He glanced at Arielle's face the way a physician glances at a wound about to be stitched. "You will be asked to open it before you are ready. Sanctify your no."

The rabbi added, almost tenderly, "And when the moment is right, do not sanctify your fear."

They stepped into the side passage. The old woman's palm hovered over the bolt; the chamber behind them gathered itself back into lamplight and paper and breath held in trust.

The alley was a corridor of stone and whisper. Laundry lines trembled overhead. A scooter coughed somewhere, then died. Dawn had matured into morning, and with it the city's appetite for attention.

They had taken three steps when a knock rapped the inner door.

Three quick. One long.

Jonas froze. The bolt under the old woman's hand did not move.

"Lev?" she called softly through the wood, a question that had a lifetime in it.

Silence. Then the pattern repeated—off by a heartbeat, like a word mispronounced by someone who had only heard it and never lived it.

Jonas's voice was a thread pulled tight. "Wrong pattern."

Bootsteps scraped at the mouth of the passage, not where they had entered, but where it emptied onto the larger court. A shadow crossed the light, then withdrew, patient as a fisherman working a weir.

The old woman's eyes cut to Jonas. He nodded once.

"Go," she whispered. "Before the different uniforms agree on you."

They moved—Jonas first, carving a route that looked like wandering and wasn't; Karim tight to Arielle's shoulder; Arielle with the sealed vessel riding against her ribs like a second heart. They slipped past a stack of olive crates, under a balcony where shirts flapped like white flags that had chosen not to surrender, through a slice of sunlight that made the dust look like a blessing.

Behind them, the wrong knock came once more—three quick, one long—patient, confident, practicing ownership.

Arielle didn't look back. The passage bent, then opened, and the city swallowed them.

Chapter Five — The Gate of Lions

Jerusalem was already under their feet when the sky went from ink to slate. They kept to the alleys below the walls, skirting shuttered shops and sleeping courtyards, angling toward the Armenian Quarter where the door would know them. Jonas set the route—down from the Adummim road, in at Zion Gate before the buses woke, then across the quiet lanes to stone that minded its own business. They had to reach the room before the city woke—the only place the jar could be logged under witness and out of reach.

Jerusalem rose around them like a palimpsest carved in stone. At arm's height along the alley, Herodian blocks the size of wagons underpinned a Crusader arch patched with Ottoman stone; above the roofs, a minaret shouldered up beside a church dome; electric bulbs winked where oil lamps once burned. The city did not glow like Rome or Paris. It pulsed.

By the time they reached the Lion's Gate, dawn had climbed into full flame. Arielle's legs moved on instinct, but her body was hollowed out, every step a negotiation with pain. Karim stumbled twice on the slope, his notebook clutched like a talisman. Jonas remained upright, steady, but his silence was stretched taut. He scanned everything—doorways, rooftops, faces in the early market crowd—with the restless vigilance of a soldier who knew threats never rested.

The air shifted the moment they crossed under the arch. It was not just the scent of cardamom and stone dust, or the clang of metal shutters rolling up, or the polyphony of voices—Arabic, Hebrew, Russian, French. It was the weight. Jerusalem pressed on the skin, heavy with prayers stacked over prayers.

Arielle slowed despite herself. The cobbles underfoot had borne prophets, conquerors, pilgrims. Every stone felt charged. She whispered a fragment of her father's favorite verse—For out of Zion shall go forth the law, and the word of the Lord from Jerusalem. His voice echoed in her head, reverent, but tonight she felt the words like a threat.

"Eyes up," Jonas muttered.

She jerked her gaze forward. A group of policemen lounged near the gate, rifles slung casually, but their eyes were sharp. Vendors called out half-heartedly, setting baskets of figs and olives onto tables. Pilgrims already formed a small knot at a shrine built into the wall. To anyone else, it might have looked like a normal morning. Arielle felt the undercurrent—attention ready to snap.

Karim drew closer, lowering his voice. "We can't exactly walk into the Rockefeller Museum with this," he nodded at her pack. "Where are we even going?"

Jonas's jaw worked before he answered. "Somewhere quieter. Somewhere we can think."

Karim huffed a laugh. "Quieter? In Jerusalem?" But his grin didn't mask his nerves. His eyes darted constantly, as if the whole city might lunge at them at once.

Arielle kept her hand tight on the strap of her pack. The jar's weight dug into her spine with every step. It wasn't just the pursuit behind them. It was the feeling she'd carried from Qumran into the desert and now through this gate—the watcher. The sense that each arch, each shadowed alley, each rooftop eye slit knew exactly who they were and what they carried.

The road narrowed. The smell of bread thickened, warm and yeasty, drifting from an ancient bakery wedged between stone walls. For a heartbeat, Arielle's body betrayed her: she wanted to stop, to buy a roll, to pretend she was just another traveler. But the word carved into linen—Guard the truth—pressed sharp against her thoughts. Pretending was over.

Jonas steered them down a side alley where the walls leaned so close they nearly kissed. Laundry fluttered overhead, bright cloth catching the light. A child darted past with a wooden cart, laughter echoing, too normal for the tremor running under Arielle's ribs.

At the alley's bend, Jonas halted. He raised his chin slightly toward a café terrace across the lane. Two men sat with newspapers, untouched cups of coffee in front of them. Their eyes tracked the crowd, not the print. One shifted just enough for Arielle to see the outline of a pistol under his jacket.

Jonas's voice was barely a whisper. "Not police. Not random."

Karim stiffened. "Matthias?"

Jonas shook his head once. "Different. Cleaner."

Arielle's chest tightened. Vatican. She didn't know how she knew, but she did. These men didn't look like smugglers or hired thugs. They looked like officials of a church that had survived empires by never showing all its teeth at once.

Jonas guided them back, casual but firm, turning them into another alley before the men could lock eyes. His pace quickened, every motion efficient, like a chess player moving two moves ahead.

"Jonas," Arielle whispered. "Where are we going?"

He didn't look back. "Somewhere they won't follow."
"Lev keeps a room in the Armenian Quarter," he added, "once wore a badge for a flag that prefers secrets to truths. He trades in favors that mature slowly."

Part 2

They cut west along a lane so narrow Arielle's shoulders brushed plaster on both sides. The stones underfoot were slick where centuries of feet had polished them to a faint sheen. A sign in Arabic and Hebrew marked a turn; Jonas ignored it and ducked beneath a low arch where the air cooled and smells shifted from bread to damp limestone.

"The Via Dolorosa runs two streets south," Karim whispered, half awe, half nerves. "Station One is behind us at the Antonia trace. If we—"

"Not today," Jonas said.

They passed under the Ecce Homo arch, its Roman curve caught like a fossil in the fabric of a later city. Arielle glanced up despite herself. Light pooled along the joints where massive stones met, each block a thesis about empire and time. She felt the jar press into her back: not a relic of empire, but something that could rearrange the story empires told.

Voices rose behind them—male, clipped, not quite local. Jonas altered course without breaking stride, slipping into a corridor lined with brass and olivewood stalls shuttered for the early hour. A cat uncoiled from a threshold and watched them pass with eyes the color of tarnished coins.

"Jonas," Arielle said, breath low. "You said somewhere they won't follow."

He nodded toward a wedge of sunlight at the far end of the corridor. "The Quarter that minds its own."

They emerged into a small square anchored by thick walls and a gate framed by black basalt jambs. The stones here were broader, heavier; a different hand had laid them, and long ago. A placard in Armenian and English hung crooked by the gate. Beyond it, a bell tower lifted above cypress, sober and spare.

"The Armenian Quarter," Karim breathed. "Oldest diaspora in the city. Fewer tourists. Fewer questions."

"Fewer leaks," Jonas said. "They keep counsel here."

They entered on the shoulder of a group of workmen pushing a cart. No one looked twice. Inside the compound, the soundscape changed: footsteps softened; voices dropped by instinct. A woman in a dark dress crossed the courtyard with a bucket of water balanced on one hip. She nodded once, neither friendly nor suspicious, simply acknowledging existence in a place that had learned not to overreact.

Jonas steered them toward a side door cut into the stone. He rapped twice with the side of his fist, then once more after counting under his breath.

A bolt snapped back and the door opened a palm's width. A man in his late sixties regarded them through the gap—compact, shoulders still military under a gray sweater, a pale scar laddering two knuckles. His eyes were ground-glass clear; he smelled faintly of chalk and old gun oil.

"Your hour is early," he said, accent clipped but unplaceable.

"Lev," Jonas answered—the name carrying history. "We need a room. And we need to be uninteresting."

Lev's gaze dropped once to Arielle's pack, weighed it, and moved on. The door opened wider.

Inside, coolness settled over them like a blessing. The corridor smelled faintly of chalk and oil. They followed Lev past niches with dark icons and into a cell-like room with a table, three chairs, and a high slit window that admitted a blade of light. Jonas waited until the door clicked shut behind them before exhaling, the tension easing out of his spine in visible increments.

Lev set a clay jug and three cups on the table. "Drink before you start leaking information." He turned the cup once between scarred fingers, the way men turn coins when they're counting years instead of money. His gaze flicked to Arielle, clocked the pack, moved on without comment.

Water hit Arielle's tongue like a sacrament. She drank, then forced herself to stop. Her hands trembled as she set the cup down.

"You were expected tomorrow," Lev said to Jonas. "You brought the horizon forward."

"Schedules changed," Jonas replied. "We're hot."

Lev's mouth thinned. "How hot."

"Matthias Calder." Jonas listed the name like a charge. "Plus locals. And eyes from across the river of Peter."

Karim choked his mouthful. "The Vatican is here?"

"In Jerusalem," Lev said, "the Vatican is always here. The question is whether they care about you today." He turned the cup in his hand. "Do they?"

"They care about what we carry," Arielle said before she could stop herself.

Lev's gaze moved back to her, slower now, weighing. "Then you will not carry it in your hands again after this room." He extended his palm. "Show me nothing. Tell me what I need."

Arielle held his eyes a beat longer than she should have, testing for greed. She found none. Only calculus and a bone-deep fatigue she recognized from Jonas. She unbuckled her pack and slid it to her lap, keeping the jar nested inside. "A sealed Qumran vessel. Linen intact. Seal intact. Markings consistent. A cipher on the wrap: Serva veritatem. We found it under a braced collapse at Qumran. Later restoration above, untouched below."

Lev's lids lowered, impressed despite himself. "And you brought it through the Adummim at night." He shot Jonas a look that contained reprimand and respect in equal parts. "You still collect impossible choices."

"Can you keep us off the board for a day?" Jonas asked. "We need to think without eyes."

"I've misdirected louder storms," Lev said. "You remember Damascus Gate '09."
Jonas's jaw ticked. "I remember who didn't come home."

Lev considered. "A day is a lifetime in this city. But yes. Here." He tapped the table once with a knuckle, the sound small and absolute. "Not beyond that gate. Not with what you attract."

Karim leaned forward, voice quick. "Who exactly do we attract?"

Lev glanced toward the slit of window, as if scenting the air. "Men who believe truth is a ladder, not a light. Men who file the edges off history until it fits the drawer they have prepared." He shifted his gaze back to Arielle. "And men who collect power in His name the way others collect coins."

Arielle felt her throat tighten. "What if the truth doesn't fit any drawer."

"Then drawers are broken," Lev said simply. "And carpenters get angry."

Footsteps scraped in the corridor outside. Lev's head tilted; his hand drifted toward the pocket of his sweater. He relaxed a measure as the steps passed on. He turned back to them, brisk now. "Rules. You sleep by turns. You do not open that door for anyone but me. If we are breached, you go down." He pointed at a square of stone near the table leg. "There is a cistern tunnel cut in the Crusader period. It threads under three courtyards and opens near a bakery on the Christian Street. It smells of history and rot. You will hate it. You will use it."

Jonas nodded, already mapping angles. "What about eyes outside? Two men at a café near the Lion's Gate."

Lev's mouth crooked. "Not mine. Not police. Likely Latin Rite. They favor newspapers they don't read." He lifted a brow. "You gave them the slip?"

"For now," Jonas said.

"Good. They prefer the shepherd's crook to the sword, but the crook can break a neck if you lean hard enough."

Karim rubbed his face with both hands. Exhaustion had sanded his edges, leaving something rawer beneath. "Why help us?"

Lev poured more water but didn't drink. "I get paid in favors that take years to mature. I prefer currencies that compound." He set the jug down. "And once I wore a badge for a flag that is better at secrets than truths. I owe the balance sheet an error."

Silence held for a long breath. Outside, a bell tolled; the sound fell like measured drops into the quiet.

Arielle reached into her pack and touched the linen through canvas. Guard the truth. She could feel Jonas watching her even when he wasn't looking. She could feel Karim vibrating with questions he didn't yet dare ask here. She could feel the city pressing from all sides—the layered weight of what people had believed and killed for.

"Rest," Lev said, softer now. "You will decide badly if you decide tired." He turned to go, then paused with his hand on the bolt. "One more thing. If a man in a black coat with a silver ring asks for you by first name, you do not answer. He has been dead ten years, and yet he keeps appointments."

The bolt clicked. The door shut.

For a beat, none of them moved. Then Jonas peeled off his jacket and folded it as a pillow against the wall, his knife within reach. Karim sank into a chair and immediately pulled his notebook onto his knees, the habit stronger than his fatigue. Arielle set her pack on the table and stood with both palms on either side of it, anchoring herself to wood and weight.

"Do you trust him?" she asked without looking up.

"No," Jonas said. "I don't trust anyone. I trust patterns. Lev's pattern is consistent."

Karim's pen scratched, then stopped. "What pattern is mine?"

Jonas's answer surprised them both. "You run toward the fire and look back to be sure we're coming. It's annoying. And it keeps us alive."

Karim blinked hard, then pretended to write again.

Arielle slid the pack nearer and sat. Sleep threatened to fold her where she was, but the watcher's prickle at her scalp had not left. It felt closer now, as if the city had given it walls to lean against. She closed her eyes and saw a raised hand on a ridge, an open palm not quite warning, not quite blessing.

She forced her eyes open. "We need to plan," she said. "If Lev is right, we have one day. After that..."

"After that," Jonas finished, "we stop reacting."

Karim lifted his head. "And start what?"

Jonas's gaze cut to the pack, to the curve of clay beneath canvas. "Choosing where this truth goes."

The word hung there—choosing—heavier than any stone in the walls around them.

Outside, the quarter breathed. Far away, a siren wound down. Closer, sandals scuffed. Above, a dove clattered along a sill and took flight.

Arielle laid her hand over the pack and felt the jar's cool arc through fabric. Her father's whisper threaded the room: Guard the truth. She did not know yet whether guarding meant hiding or delivering. She only knew that for the next few hours, the truth would have to settle in the dark and wait.

They would, too.

Part 3

Night pressed down on the Quarter like a velvet lid. The streets beyond Lev's door thinned into quiet; the calls of vendors faded into the clink of dishes, the murmur of families behind shuttered windows. Within the room, the air thickened with exhaustion.

Jonas lay against the wall, eyes closed but never fully still, his hand resting lightly on the hilt of his knife. Karim sprawled at the table, chin on his notebook, ink smudged where fatigue had pulled him mid-sentence into dreams. Arielle remained awake, palms pressed over the pack that held the jar. She couldn't let go of the weight—not physically, not in her mind. Every creak of timber, every gust against the slit window, she measured against the memory of the watcher's hand raised in silence.

The bell in the Quarter tolled midnight. Its echoes had barely faded when the bolt on the outer gate shifted.

Jonas's eyes snapped open. His knife whispered free in the same breath. Arielle straightened, her pulse spiking. She saw his lips form the word without sound: Down.

Karim jerked awake just as the outer hinges groaned. Footsteps. Not Lev's even cadence, but heavier, purposeful. Voices low and clipped, one in Italian, another in Latin-inflected French.

The door rattled. Jonas moved soundlessly to the stone square Lev had shown them. He wedged his blade under the edge and pried. The block lifted just enough for a black hole to yawn beneath—the Crusader cistern tunnel. Damp air breathed up, cool and metallic, carrying the stench of centuries.

"In," Jonas whispered.

Arielle dropped to her knees, sliding her pack in first, then following with a grimace as her shoulders scraped stone. Karim shoved his notebook inside his shirt and wriggled after her. Jonas lowered the slab behind them, sealing the light.

Darkness swallowed them whole.

The tunnel was narrow, cut by hands that had expected no comfort, only survival. Cold slicked the walls where condensation gathered. Arielle's palms slipped on slime as she crawled, her knees grinding against rough stone. The jar pressed awkwardly between her chest and the pack straps; every shift threatened to crack clay against rock.

Above, boots thudded into the room they had just left. Voices snapped in low argument. Furniture scraped. A chair toppled.

Karim whispered too loudly, "Do they know about this tunnel?"

Jonas's reply was a ghost of breath. "If they do, we're already dead. Move."

They crawled in silence, guided only by Jonas's hand brushing along the wall, counting niches and turns. Arielle forced her breath shallow. The tunnel stank of mildew and rot—old water that had died in its basin long ago. Drops pattered somewhere deeper, a slow, endless clock.

The passage widened enough for them to crouch. Jonas halted, tilting his head. Arielle froze, the jar pressed to her chest.

Above them, faint through stone, came the scrape of boots. Not in Lev's room now—further along. Following.

Jonas's hand settled briefly on Arielle's arm, steadying. Then he gestured: left.

They turned into a narrower channel that sloped downward. The air grew colder, wetter. Rats scuttled ahead, claws clicking on stone. Arielle tried not to gag at the stench—centuries of waste, water, incense smoke pressed into walls like marrow.

They reached a junction where the tunnel split. Jonas crouched, fingertips grazing the floor, then pointed right. "Air's fresher. That way leads up."

Karim wheezed softly. "How do you know?"

Jonas's mouth twisted. "Because I've crawled enough tunnels to know the difference between air that kills you and air that doesn't. Move."

They pressed on, silence their only ally. Arielle's knees were raw, her arms trembling. She wanted to collapse, to let the jar drop and smash so the decision was stolen from her. But she tightened her grip. Guard the truth. Her father's voice wouldn't let her falter.

The tunnel narrowed again, then slanted upward. At its end, a grille of iron blocked their way—bars corroded but intact. Through the slits, faint light pulsed, golden and flickering. A bakery. She smelled it before she saw: yeast, smoke, the char of morning bread.

Jonas pressed his shoulder against the bars. They groaned but held. He braced again, muscles corded, and the rusted frame shrieked loose, stone flakes raining down. He slipped out first, then reached back for Arielle, pulling her into the warmth of a back storeroom where racks of cooling loaves steamed. Karim tumbled after, gasping, flour dust rising around him.

For a heartbeat, they simply stood, breathing the air of bread and fire after the tomb-scent of stone.

Then voices echoed faintly from the tunnel behind. Pursuit had not ended.

Jonas shut the iron grate with a final wrench. "We move," he said, voice hard. "Now."

Part 4

They slipped from the bakery's back door into an alley still wrapped in predawn. The air was warmer here, alive with the scents of smoke, yeast, and damp limestone. Pigeons clattered along the eaves, their wings flashing silver in the lantern light.

Jonas led them without hesitation, weaving through a lattice of alleys that narrowed and widened like the breathing of some ancient beast. Arielle's pack cut into her shoulders; the jar dragged at her spine. She glanced once over her shoulder and caught the baker watching from the doorway, face unreadable, then closing the door without a word. Silence was its own currency in Jerusalem.

The alleys opened into a market square where awnings sagged under dew. Merchants were only beginning to set up—sacks of spice thudded onto tables, strings of copper lamps glimmered under cloth tarps, the first braziers sent curls of smoke into the air. The trio moved through as ghosts, three shadows among many.

Then Jonas stiffened.

At the far end of the square, two men leaned against a colonnade. One held a newspaper, unread. The other tilted his head, just slightly, scanning the crowd. Their coats were too heavy for the hour, their shoes too polished for stone streets. And when the man with the paper shifted, Arielle saw the unmistakable glint of a chain at his wrist—silver, inset with a seal.

Her chest tightened. A Vatican ring.

Jonas's hand brushed hers—signal, not comfort. They veered left into another alley, boots whispering on cobbles. Arielle's pulse hammered. The watcher from the desert had felt like myth, but this was flesh and blood, and closer with every step.

Karim muttered, "They're everywhere. It's like the city itself is lending them corners."

"They own corners," Jonas said. "And doors, and roofs. That's why we stay between them."

The alley kinked twice before opening on a flight of stone steps plunging down toward the valley. The Mount of Olives loomed opposite, its slopes scattered with tombs pale as bones. Beyond, the first light of dawn touched the Dome of the Rock, turning its surface into liquid gold.

Arielle stumbled, struck by the sight. No photograph, no journal entry had prepared her for the reality: a city layered in grief and hope, in conquest and prayer. It looked eternal. It felt fragile. And she carried in her pack a truth that could tip it either way.

Bootsteps echoed behind them. Close.

Jonas spun, knife drawn. Two shadows filled the alley's mouth. The men from the square, faster than expected, cutting the distance with precision.

"Go," Jonas snapped.

He planted himself on the steps, body squared, knife low and ready. Arielle hesitated—every instinct screaming not to leave him—but Karim grabbed her arm. "We can't lose the scroll!"

The weight of the jar decided for her. She ran, feet slamming stone, lungs raw. Karim's ragged breaths matched hers. The alley bent, dipped, opened suddenly onto a terrace where the city fell away in layers of domes and towers.

Behind them, metal rang against stone—Jonas clashing steel with pursuit.

Arielle skidded to a halt at the terrace edge. The wall dropped to a lower street ten feet below. Without thinking, she swung her pack forward, cradling the jar against her chest, and jumped. She landed hard, knees screaming, but the jar held. Karim crashed down beside her, cursing in three languages at once.

From above came a shout, then the crack of stone as a blade missed Jonas and sparked against the wall. He was still holding them off, buying seconds.

Arielle staggered forward, the jar's weight almost unbearable. She heard voices on the street ahead—pilgrims, shopkeepers. Safety in the crowd. Or danger multiplied.

Jonas's shout cut across the dawn: "Run!"

Arielle and Karim plunged into the waking city, swallowed by its labyrinth. Behind them, the clash of pursuit carried like a bell, tolling the truth that nothing was finished.

Chapter Four — The Council of Shadows

Jerusalem woke in layers. Bells tolled above the braid of voices; a thread of muezzin rose over stone that smelled of wax and damp lime. Laundry snapped between walls older than most kingdoms. In the alley's throat, water from a courtyard spigot pattered into a tin basin, counting time for those who still needed it. Within a windowless chamber set into the flank of an old foundation, oil lamps breathed, their smoke seaming the ceiling in slow black ribs.

Dawn had burned the edges off exhaustion but not the ache. Arielle stood at a long oak table, the satchel strap cutting into her shoulder, dust and desert salt dried on her lips. Jonas took up the rear corner of the room as if guarding a doorway that didn't exist; Karim hovered near a shelf of vellum rolls and wood-handled seals, his notebook—closed for once—pressed flat against his ribs.

Three figures faced them, each carrying authority cut from a different quarry of time: a rabbi with a beard white as plaster and eyes like flint; a scholar in a dark shawl threaded with Hebrew script, ink stains permanent as tattoos on her fingers; and a man in plain clerical black, Roman collar catching the lamp light. They regarded Arielle not as a guest but as a verdict that refused to stay hidden.

"You carry it?" the scholar asked. No greeting, no softening.

Arielle glanced once at Jonas. He gave the smallest of nods. She slid the pack onto the table, unbuckled the flap, and lifted out a clay vessel swaddled in ancient linen. The black pitch seal around the neck was unbroken, dull as old coal.

The air changed. Even the lamps seemed to withdraw a fraction, as if making room for something older than flame.

The rabbi stepped closer, not quite touching, lips shaping words too soft to catch. The priest crossed himself without taking his eyes off Arielle's face.

"It is not just a jar," the scholar said. "It is inheritance—the kind that cuts both ways."

Arielle's voice came low, steady. "Explain it to me like I don't want to believe you."

The rabbi's gaze held centuries. "When the scrolls were hidden, one among them spoke not of psalm or law, but of lineage. A record of children. His children."

Karim's breath broke on a disbelieving laugh he tried to swallow. "You're saying—"

"I'm saying the rumor your father died chasing was more than rumor," the priest said gently, the kindness in his tone at odds with the hardness in his eyes. "Authority fears truth that blooms outside its trellises."

Arielle's fingers tightened on the linen. Serva veritatem. Guard the truth. The numbers cut into the cloth at Qumran had translated into that imperative with a clarity that left no room for misreading. Her father's voice rode the words now, worn and urgent: Guard it.

The scholar slid a small cloth bundle across the table. "From our archive. Not yours. Consider it a keyhole."

Arielle unwrapped the cloth and found a narrow strip of papyrus, edges feathered, the ink crabbed and brown. Aramaic characters marched down the fiber like ants. She traced the line aloud, translating half to herself: "Through the daughters, the covenant endures."

Her pulse stuttered. She had seen the phrase scrawled on cave plaster, whispered in hymns, carved into lintels, a rumor wearing a thousand faces. Here, it felt like a pulse.

"The scribe favored acrostics," the scholar added, angling the strip so a margin caught the lamp light. "Read the first letters in the margin—downward."

Arielle squinted. Tiny initial marks lined the outer edge—barely there until the light struck them just right. M... U... R... I... S... T... A... N. The letters weren't Aramaic at all but a medieval hand, later gloss. A marginal whisper: Muristan.

Karim leaned in until his curls almost brushed the papyrus. "Hospital district. Crusader heart. Fountains and arcades."

"Waypoints," the rabbi said. "The scribe thought in places, not merely in words. Truth needs anchors. Or it drifts and is sold by the yard."

Jonas's gaze didn't leave the door, but his voice cut clean through the ritual hush. "If we accept the premise—what then? You didn't risk this meeting for a history lesson."

The priest spread his hands, palms up; a judge asking mercy from the very evidence he'd presented. "What you carry will not be allowed to live on its own. Some will bury it under doctrine and say they are protecting souls. Some will auction it under glass and say they are honoring history. Matthias Calder covets the door it opens. The Latin envoys prefer the kind of shepherding that leaves no stray."

The lamps hissed. Somewhere beyond the wall, a bell finished tolling and the alley's tin basin kept counting drops.

"My father—" Arielle began, surprising herself, the words a stone she'd been rolling in her mouth for years without swallowing. "He spent his life on this rumor. He died for it. Near Jericho. Officially an accident. For me, it never sat right." She steadied the jar with both hands. "I won't let his cost be for nothing."

The rabbi's gaze softened, the flint turned inward. "Then let his cost purchase your caution."

"Caution looks like what?" Jonas asked. Every muscle in his forearms held the question like wire.

The scholar touched the linen with a fingertip that didn't quite land. "You keep the vessel sealed until you choose the witnesses. Not a museum. Not a ministry. Witnesses. Real eyes. Real risk."

Karim found his voice. "And the Muristan note? That's a map for us or for someone before us?"

“Both,” the priest said. “These texts speak sideways. They survive by being misunderstood until the right hands arrive.”

Arielle refolded the papyrus and slid it back. “You’re not asking us to leave it with you.”

“No,” the rabbi said simply. “If this were to vanish with us, we would be what we warn you against.”

The old woman who had unlocked the alley door earlier eased into the room with the stealth of a practiced keeper of thresholds. Her shawl was drawn tight against the stone damp. She set down a clay cup of water near Karim’s elbow; he blinked at it as if a miracle had wandered up at the wrong mass.

The priest nodded toward Jonas. “Your friend knows how to be unseen. But understand: soon the city will know you exist even if it cannot name you.”

The chamber held stillness the way a held breath holds air—tense, necessary, temporary.

—

Across the quarter, a man in a dark coat folded a newspaper he had not read. A thin chain threaded his wrist; the silver signet it held winked once in the café light as he lifted it to his mouth.

“Confirmatum: vas sigillatum,” he murmured into the metal, Latin clipped flat—confirmed: sealed vessel. “Tertius ingressus—ad murum. Third entrance. Toward the wall.”

He counted the last peal of bells with his eyes shut, as if measuring a heartbeat. Two men rose without being named. The map here was not drawn in streets but in thresholds and habits: which gates opened for bread and which for prayer; which courtyards answered knocks with candles, which with questions. He paid for a coffee he did not drink and slid into the alley’s shade. The city made room for men like him; it always had.

A phone pulsed once in his pocket. CALDER: Vessel confirmed. Your hour. He did not smile. He never did on the clock.

"Procedite," he said to no one, and the ring caught the light again.

—

The scholar took back the papyrus strip, wrapped it, and set it aside with a care that felt like grief.

"Rules," she said, the word brittle as a twig. "You leave as you came—in silence. Do not carry this vessel openly. Do not speak its name in any tongue. If you are pressed, you know nothing. If pressed harder, you know something else."

"Is this where you bless us and send us out with a prayer?" Karim asked, trying and failing to find a grin.

"This is where we give you a door that won't betray you," the rabbi said. "The Armenian gatekeeper two courts over owes us more favors than he has years left. He will open to this." He slid a small wooden token across the table—a crude cross burned into it, ringed by an inscription in Ge'ez. "Knock twice, then once. He prefers monks to soldiers."

"If Lev answers the door," he added, "listen. His rooms forget names better than most churches keep them."

Jonas's eyes flicked to the token, calculating escape vectors out of habit. "And if we're followed?"

"You will be," the priest said. "This city is designed for pursuit. But it is also designed for disappearance."

The old woman lifted the bolt to a side door that looked like part of the wall until it wasn't. Cold air spilled in, carrying a palm's width of daylight and the smell of bread from somewhere they couldn't see.

Arielle wrapped the jar in its linen until the pitch seal felt buffered from every edge of the world. Guard the truth. The words fit her hands now as if they had been made to.

Jonas adjusted the satchel straps over her shoulders, an efficient tug that avoided touching more than necessary. Karim rolled his shoulders as if shaking a net off his back and tucked his closed notebook inside his shirt like contraband.

The priest stopped them with a lifted hand. "One more thing." He glanced at Arielle's face the way a physician glances at a wound about to be stitched. "You will be asked to open it before you are ready. Sanctify your no."

The rabbi added, almost tenderly, "And when the moment is right, do not sanctify your fear."

They stepped into the side passage. The old woman's palm hovered over the bolt; the chamber behind them gathered itself back into lamplight and paper and breath held in trust.

The alley was a corridor of stone and whisper. Laundry lines trembled overhead. A scooter coughed somewhere, then died. Dawn had matured into morning, and with it the city's appetite for attention.

They had taken three steps when a knock rapped the inner door.

Three quick. One long.

Jonas froze. The bolt under the old woman's hand did not move.

"Lev?" she called softly through the wood, a question that had a lifetime in it.

Silence. Then the pattern repeated—off by a heartbeat, like a word mispronounced by someone who had only heard it and never lived it.

Jonas's voice was a thread pulled tight. "Wrong pattern."

Bootsteps scraped at the mouth of the passage, not where they had entered, but where it emptied onto the larger court. A shadow crossed the light, then withdrew, patient as a fisherman working a weir.

The old woman's eyes cut to Jonas. He nodded once.

"Go," she whispered. "Before the different uniforms agree on you."

They moved—Jonas first, carving a route that looked like wandering and wasn't; Karim tight to Arielle's shoulder; Arielle with the sealed vessel riding against her ribs like a second heart. They slipped past a stack of olive crates, under a balcony where shirts flapped like white flags that had chosen not to surrender, through a slice of sunlight that made the dust look like a blessing.

Behind them, the wrong knock came once more—three quick, one long—patient, confident, practicing ownership.

Arielle didn't look back. The passage bent, then opened, and the city swallowed them.

Chapter Five — The Gate of Lions

Part 1

Jerusalem rose around them like a palimpsest carved in stone. At arm's height along the alley, Herodian blocks the size of wagons underpinned a Crusader arch patched with Ottoman stone; above the roofs, a minaret shouldered up beside a church dome; electric bulbs winked where oil lamps once burned. The city did not glow like Rome or Paris. It pulsed.

By the time they reached the Lion's Gate, dawn had climbed into full flame. Arielle's legs moved on instinct, but her body was hollowed out, every step a negotiation with pain. Karim stumbled twice on the slope, his notebook clutched like a talisman. Jonas remained upright, steady, but his silence was stretched taut. He scanned everything—doorways, rooftops, faces in the early market crowd—with the restless vigilance of a soldier who knew threats never rested.

The air shifted the moment they crossed under the arch. It was not just the scent of cardamom and stone dust, or the clang of metal shutters rolling up, or the polyphony of voices—Arabic, Hebrew, Russian, French. It was the weight. Jerusalem pressed on the skin, heavy with prayers stacked over prayers.

Arielle slowed despite herself. The cobbles underfoot had borne prophets, conquerors, pilgrims. Every stone felt charged. She whispered a fragment of her father's favorite verse—For out of Zion shall go forth the law, and the word of the Lord from Jerusalem. His voice echoed in her head, reverent, but tonight she felt the words like a threat.

"Eyes up," Jonas muttered.

She jerked her gaze forward. A group of policemen lounged near the gate, rifles slung casually, but their eyes were sharp. Vendors called out half-heartedly, setting baskets of figs and olives onto tables. Pilgrims already formed a small knot at a shrine built into the wall. To anyone else, it might have looked like a normal morning. Arielle felt the undercurrent—attention ready to snap.

Karim drew closer, lowering his voice. "We can't exactly walk into the Rockefeller Museum with this," he nodded at her pack. "Where are we even going?"

Jonas's jaw worked before he answered. "Somewhere quieter. Somewhere we can think."

Karim huffed a laugh. "Quieter? In Jerusalem?" But his grin didn't mask his nerves. His eyes darted constantly, as if the whole city might lunge at them at once.

Arielle kept her hand tight on the strap of her pack. The jar's weight dug into her spine with every step. It wasn't just the pursuit behind them. It was the feeling she'd carried from Qumran into the desert and now through this gate—the watcher. The sense that each arch, each shadowed alley, each rooftop eye slit knew exactly who they were and what they carried.

The road narrowed. The smell of bread thickened, warm and yeasty, drifting from an ancient bakery wedged between stone walls. For a heartbeat, Arielle's body betrayed her: she wanted to stop, to buy a roll, to pretend she was just another traveler. But the word carved into linen—Guard the truth—pressed sharp against her thoughts. Pretending was over.

Jonas steered them down a side alley where the walls leaned so close they nearly kissed. Laundry fluttered overhead, bright cloth catching the light. A child darted past with a wooden cart, laughter echoing, too normal for the tremor running under Arielle's ribs.

At the alley's bend, Jonas halted. He raised his chin slightly toward a café terrace across the lane. Two men sat with newspapers, untouched cups of coffee in front of them. Their eyes tracked the crowd, not the print. One shifted just enough for Arielle to see the outline of a pistol under his jacket.

Jonas's voice was barely a whisper. "Not police. Not random."

Karim stiffened. "Matthias?"

Jonas shook his head once. "Different. Cleaner."

Arielle's chest tightened. Vatican. She didn't know how she knew, but she did. These men didn't look like smugglers or hired thugs. They looked like officials of a church that had survived empires by never showing all its teeth at once.

Jonas guided them back, casual but firm, turning them into another alley before the men could lock eyes. His pace quickened, every motion efficient, like a chess player moving two moves ahead.

"Jonas," Arielle whispered. "Where are we going?"

He didn't look back. "Somewhere they won't follow."
"If we get split," Jonas added, "you know the protocols."
"Lev keeps a room in the Armenian Quarter," he added, "once wore a badge for a flag that prefers secrets to truths. He trades in favors that mature slowly."

Part 2

They cut west along a lane so narrow Arielle's shoulders brushed plaster on both sides. The stones underfoot were slick where centuries of feet had polished them to a faint sheen. A sign in Arabic and Hebrew marked a turn; Jonas ignored it and ducked beneath a low arch where the air cooled and smells shifted from bread to damp limestone.

"The Via Dolorosa runs two streets south," Karim whispered, half awe, half nerves. "Station One is behind us at the Antonia trace. If we—"

"Not today," Jonas said.

They passed under the Ecce Homo arch, its Roman curve caught like a fossil in the fabric of a later city. Arielle glanced up despite herself. Light pooled along the joints where massive stones met, each block a thesis about empire and time. She felt the jar press into her back: not a relic of empire, but something that could rearrange the story empires told.

Voices rose behind them—male, clipped, not quite local. Jonas altered course without breaking stride, slipping into a corridor lined with brass and olivewood stalls shuttered for the early hour. A cat uncoiled from a threshold and watched them pass with eyes the color of tarnished coins.

"Jonas," Arielle said, breath low. "You said somewhere they won't follow."

He nodded toward a wedge of sunlight at the far end of the corridor. "The Quarter that minds its own."

They emerged into a small square anchored by thick walls and a gate framed by black basalt jambs. The stones here were broader, heavier; a different hand had laid them, and long ago. A placard in Armenian and English hung crooked by the gate. Beyond it, a bell tower lifted above cypress, sober and spare.

"The Armenian Quarter," Karim breathed. "Oldest diaspora in the city. Fewer tourists. Fewer questions."

"Fewer leaks," Jonas said. "They keep counsel here."

They entered on the shoulder of a group of workmen pushing a cart. No one looked twice. Inside the compound, the soundscape changed: footsteps softened; voices dropped by instinct. A woman in a dark dress crossed the courtyard with a bucket of water balanced on one hip. She nodded once, neither friendly nor suspicious, simply acknowledging existence in a place that had learned not to overreact.

Jonas steered them toward a side door cut into the stone. He rapped twice with the side of his fist, then once more after counting under his breath.

A bolt snapped back and the door opened a palm's width. A man in his late sixties regarded them through the gap—compact, shoulders still military under a gray sweater, a pale scar laddering two knuckles. His eyes were ground-glass clear; he smelled faintly of chalk and old gun oil.
"Your hour is early," he said, accent clipped but unplaceable.

"Lev," Jonas answered—the name carrying history. "We need a room. And we need to be uninteresting."

Lev's gaze dropped once to Arielle's pack, weighed it, and moved on. The door opened wider.

Inside, coolness settled over them like a blessing. The corridor smelled faintly of chalk and oil. They followed Lev past niches with dark icons and into a cell-like room with a table, three chairs, and a high slit window that admitted a blade of light. Jonas waited until the door clicked shut behind them before exhaling, the tension easing out of his spine in visible increments.

Lev set a clay jug and three cups on the table. "Drink before you start leaking information." He turned the cup once between scarred fingers, the way men turn coins when they're counting years instead of money. His gaze flicked to Arielle, clocked the pack, moved on without comment.

Water hit Arielle's tongue like a sacrament. She drank, then forced herself to stop. Her hands trembled as she set the cup down.

"You were expected tomorrow," Lev said to Jonas. "You brought the horizon forward."

"Schedules changed," Jonas replied. "We're hot."

Lev's mouth thinned. "How hot."

"Matthias Calder." Jonas listed the name like a charge. "Plus locals. And eyes from across the river of Peter."

Karim choked his mouthful. "The Vatican is here?"

"In Jerusalem," Lev said, "the Vatican is always here. The question is whether they care about you today." He turned the cup in his hand. "Do they?"

"They care about what we carry," Arielle said before she could stop herself.

Lev's gaze moved back to her, slower now, weighing. "Then you will not carry it in your hands again after this room." He extended his palm. "Show me nothing. Tell me what I need."

Arielle held his eyes a beat longer than she should have, testing for greed. She found none. Only calculus and a bone-deep fatigue she recognized from Jonas. She unbuckled her pack and slid it to her lap, keeping the jar nested inside. "A sealed Qumran vessel. Linen intact. Seal intact. Markings consistent. A cipher on the wrap: Serva veritatem. We found it under a braced collapse at Qumran. Later restoration above, untouched below."

Lev's lids lowered, impressed despite himself. "And you brought it through the Adummim at night." He shot Jonas a look that contained reprimand and respect in equal parts. "You still collect impossible choices."

"Can you keep us off the board for a day?" Jonas asked. "We need to think without eyes."

"I've misdirected louder storms," Lev said. "You remember Damascus Gate '09."
Jonas's jaw ticked. "I remember who didn't come home."

Lev considered. "A day is a lifetime in this city. But yes. Here." He tapped the table once with a knuckle, the sound small and absolute. "Not beyond that gate. Not with what you attract."
"If you need eyes on ink, Kadosh owes me a favor," Lev said. "Use her door, not her name."

Karim leaned forward, voice quick. "Who exactly do we attract?"

Lev glanced toward the slit of window, as if scenting the air. "Men who believe truth is a ladder, not a light. Men who file the edges off history until it fits the drawer they have prepared." He shifted his gaze back to Arielle. "And men who collect power in His name the way others collect coins."

Arielle felt her throat tighten. "What if the truth doesn't fit any drawer."

"Then drawers are broken," Lev said simply. "And carpenters get angry."

Footsteps scraped in the corridor outside. Lev's head tilted; his hand drifted toward the pocket of his sweater. He relaxed a measure as the steps passed on. He turned back to them, brisk now. "Rules. You sleep by turns. You do not open that door for anyone but me. If we are breached, you go down." He pointed at a square of stone near the table leg. "There is a cistern tunnel cut in the Crusader period. It threads under three courtyards and opens near a bakery on the Christian Street. It smells of history and rot. You will hate it. You will use it."

Jonas nodded, already mapping angles. "What about eyes outside? Two men at a café near the Lion's Gate."

Lev's mouth crooked. "Not mine. Not police. Likely Latin Rite. They favor newspapers they don't read." He lifted a brow. "You gave them the slip?"

"For now," Jonas said.

"Good. They prefer the shepherd's crook to the sword, but the crook can break a neck if you lean hard enough."

Karim rubbed his face with both hands. Exhaustion had sanded his edges, leaving something rawer beneath. "Why help us?"

Lev poured more water but didn't drink. "I get paid in favors that take years to mature. I prefer currencies that compound." He set the jug down. "And once I wore a badge for a flag that is better at secrets than truths. I owe the balance sheet an error."

Silence held for a long breath. Outside, a bell tolled; the sound fell like measured drops into the quiet.

Arielle reached into her pack and touched the linen through canvas. Guard the truth. She could feel Jonas watching her even when he wasn't looking. She could feel Karim vibrating with questions he didn't yet dare ask here. She could feel the city pressing from all sides—the layered weight of what people had believed and killed for.

"Rest," Lev said, softer now. "You will decide badly if you decide tired." He turned to go, then paused with his hand on the bolt. "One more thing. If a man in a black coat with a silver ring asks for you by first name, you do not answer. He has been dead ten years, and yet he keeps appointments."

The bolt clicked. The door shut.

For a beat, none of them moved. Then Jonas peeled off his jacket and folded it as a pillow against the wall, his knife within reach. Karim sank into a chair and immediately pulled his notebook onto his knees, the habit stronger than his fatigue. Arielle set her pack on the table and stood with both palms on either side of it, anchoring herself to wood and weight.

"Do you trust him?" she asked without looking up.

"No," Jonas said. "I don't trust anyone. I trust patterns. Lev's pattern is consistent."

Karim's pen scratched, then stopped. "What pattern is mine?"

Jonas's answer surprised them both. "You run toward the fire and look back to be sure we're coming. It's annoying. And it keeps us alive."

Karim blinked hard, then pretended to write again.

Arielle slid the pack nearer and sat. Sleep threatened to fold her where she was, but the watcher's prickle at her scalp had not left. It felt closer now, as if the city had given it walls to lean against. She closed her eyes and saw a raised hand on a ridge, an open palm not quite warning, not quite blessing.

She forced her eyes open. "We need to plan," she said. "If Lev is right, we have one day. After that..."

"After that," Jonas finished, "we stop reacting."

Karim lifted his head. "And start what?"

Jonas's gaze cut to the pack, to the curve of clay beneath canvas. "Choosing where this truth goes."

The word hung there—choosing—heavier than any stone in the walls around them.

Outside, the quarter breathed. Far away, a siren wound down. Closer, sandals scuffed. Above, a dove clattered along a sill and took flight.

Arielle laid her hand over the pack and felt the jar's cool arc through fabric. Her father's whisper threaded the room: Guard the truth. She did not know yet whether guarding meant hiding or delivering. She only knew that for the next few hours, the truth would have to settle in the dark and wait.

They would, too.

Part 3

Night pressed down on the Quarter like a velvet lid. The streets beyond Lev's door thinned into quiet; the calls of vendors faded into the clink of dishes, the murmur of families behind shuttered windows. Within the room, the air thickened with exhaustion.

Jonas lay against the wall, eyes closed but never fully still, his hand resting lightly on the hilt of his knife. Karim sprawled at the table, chin on his notebook, ink smudged where fatigue had pulled him mid-sentence into dreams. Arielle remained awake, palms pressed over the pack that held the jar. She couldn't let go of the weight—not physically, not in her mind. Every creak of timber, every gust against the slit window, she measured against the memory of the watcher's hand raised in silence.

The bell in the Quarter tolled midnight. Its echoes had barely faded when the bolt on the outer gate shifted.

Jonas's eyes snapped open. His knife whispered free in the same breath. Arielle straightened, her pulse spiking. She saw his lips form the word without sound: Down.

Karim jerked awake just as the outer hinges groaned. Footsteps. Not Lev's even cadence, but heavier, purposeful. Voices low and clipped, one in Italian, another in Latin-inflected French.

The door rattled. Jonas moved soundlessly to the stone square Lev had shown them. He wedged his blade under the edge and pried. The block lifted just enough for a black hole to yawn beneath—the Crusader cistern tunnel. Damp air breathed up, cool and metallic, carrying the stench of centuries.

"In," Jonas whispered.

Arielle dropped to her knees, sliding her pack in first, then following with a grimace as her shoulders scraped stone. Karim shoved his notebook inside his shirt and wriggled after her. Jonas lowered the slab behind them, sealing the light.

Darkness swallowed them whole.

The tunnel was narrow, cut by hands that had expected no comfort, only survival. Cold slicked the walls where condensation gathered. Arielle's palms slipped on slime as she crawled, her knees grinding against rough stone. The jar pressed awkwardly between her chest and the pack straps; every shift threatened to crack clay against rock.

Above, boots thudded into the room they had just left. Voices snapped in low argument. Furniture scraped. A chair toppled.

Karim whispered too loudly, "Do they know about this tunnel?"

Jonas's reply was a ghost of breath. "If they do, we're already dead. Move."

They crawled in silence, guided only by Jonas's hand brushing along the wall, counting niches and turns. Arielle forced her breath shallow. The tunnel stank of mildew and rot—old water that had died in its basin long ago. Drops pattered somewhere deeper, a slow, endless clock.

The passage widened enough for them to crouch. Jonas halted, tilting his head. Arielle froze, the jar pressed to her chest.

Above them, faint through stone, came the scrape of boots. Not in Lev's room now—further along. Following.

Jonas's hand settled briefly on Arielle's arm, steadying. Then he gestured: left.

They turned into a narrower channel that sloped downward. The air grew colder, wetter. Rats scuttled ahead, claws clicking on stone. Arielle tried not to gag at the stench—centuries of waste, water, incense smoke pressed into walls like marrow.

They reached a junction where the tunnel split. Jonas crouched, fingertips grazing the floor, then pointed right. "Air's fresher. That way leads up."

Karim wheezed softly. "How do you know?"

Jonas's mouth twisted. "Because I've crawled enough tunnels to know the difference between air that kills you and air that doesn't. Move."

They pressed on, silence their only ally. Arielle's knees were raw, her arms trembling. She wanted to collapse, to let the jar drop and smash so the decision was stolen from her. But she tightened her grip. Guard the truth. Her father's voice wouldn't let her falter.

The tunnel narrowed again, then slanted upward. At its end, a grille of iron blocked their way—bars corroded but intact. Through the slits, faint light pulsed, golden and flickering. A bakery. She smelled it before she saw: yeast, smoke, the char of morning bread.

Jonas pressed his shoulder against the bars. They groaned but held. He braced again, muscles corded, and the rusted frame shrieked loose, stone flakes raining down. He slipped out first, then reached back for Arielle, pulling her into the warmth of a back storeroom where racks of cooling loaves steamed. Karim tumbled after, gasping, flour dust rising around him.

For a heartbeat, they simply stood, breathing the air of bread and fire after the tomb-scent of stone.

Then voices echoed faintly from the tunnel behind. Pursuit had not ended.

Jonas shut the iron grate with a final wrench. "We move," he said, voice hard. "Now."

Part 4

They slipped from the bakery's back door into an alley still wrapped in predawn. The air was warmer here, alive with the scents of smoke, yeast, and damp limestone. Pigeons clattered along the eaves, their wings flashing silver in the lantern light.

Jonas led them without hesitation, weaving through a lattice of alleys that narrowed and widened like the breathing of some ancient beast. Arielle's pack cut into her shoulders; the jar dragged at her spine. She glanced once over her shoulder and caught the baker watching from the doorway, face unreadable, then closing the door without a word. Silence was its own currency in Jerusalem.

The alleys opened into a market square where awnings sagged under dew. Merchants were only beginning to set up—sacks of spice thudded onto tables, strings of copper lamps glimmered under cloth tarps, the first braziers sent curls of smoke into the air. The trio moved through as ghosts, three shadows among many.

Then Jonas stiffened.

At the far end of the square, two men leaned against a colonnade. One held a newspaper, unread. The other tilted his head, just slightly, scanning the crowd. Their coats were too heavy for the hour, their shoes too polished for stone streets. And when the man with the paper shifted, Arielle saw the unmistakable glint of a chain at his wrist—silver, inset with a seal.

Her chest tightened. A Vatican ring.

Jonas's hand brushed hers—signal, not comfort. They veered left into another alley, boots whispering on cobbles. Arielle's pulse hammered.

The watcher from the desert had felt like myth, but this was flesh and blood, and closer with every step.

Karim muttered, "They're everywhere. It's like the city itself is lending them corners."

"They own corners," Jonas said. "And doors, and roofs. That's why we stay between them."

The alley kinked twice before opening on a flight of stone steps plunging down toward the valley. The Mount of Olives loomed opposite, its slopes scattered with tombs pale as bones. Beyond, the first light of dawn touched the Dome of the Rock, turning its surface into liquid gold.

Arielle stumbled, struck by the sight. No photograph, no journal entry had prepared her for the reality: a city layered in grief and hope, in conquest and prayer. It looked eternal. It felt fragile. And she carried in her pack a truth that could tip it either way.

Bootsteps echoed behind them. Close.

Jonas spun, knife drawn. Two shadows filled the alley's mouth. The men from the square, faster than expected, cutting the distance with precision.

"Go," Jonas snapped.

He planted himself on the steps, body squared, knife low and ready. Arielle hesitated—every instinct screaming not to leave him—but Karim grabbed her arm. "We can't lose the scroll!"

The weight of the jar decided for her. She ran, feet slamming stone, lungs raw. Karim's ragged breaths matched hers. The alley bent, dipped, opened suddenly onto a terrace where the city fell away in layers of domes and towers.

Behind them, metal rang against stone—Jonas clashing steel with pursuit.

Arielle skidded to a halt at the terrace edge. The wall dropped to a lower street ten feet below. Without thinking, she swung her pack forward, cradling the jar against her chest, and jumped. She landed hard, knees screaming, but the jar held. Karim crashed down beside her, cursing in three languages at once.

From above came a shout, then the crack of stone as a blade missed Jonas and sparked against the wall. He was still holding them off, buying seconds.

Arielle staggered forward, the jar's weight almost unbearable. She heard voices on the street ahead—pilgrims, shopkeepers. Safety in the crowd. Or danger multiplied.

Jonas's shout cut across the dawn: "Run!"

Arielle and Karim plunged into the waking city, swallowed by its labyrinth. Behind them, the clash of pursuit carried like a bell, tolling the truth that nothing was finished.

Chapter Six — The Muristan Signal (Part 2)

They crossed two more roofs and the city opened like a hinge. Below, Christian Street ran north–south in a narrow ribbon of shade that smelled of coffee and wet stone. Bronze lanterns hung from iron brackets; a row of closed shopfronts wore hand-painted signs in Greek, Arabic, and English—icons, rosaries, inlaid olivewood. Farther on, a butcher's awning dripped scarlet where ice was melting in a red plastic tub.

Jonas pointed to a low parapet where a carpenter's ladder leaned at a slant. "Down there," he murmured. "One at a time."

He went first, then steadied Arielle as she descended, the jar biting into her ribs. Karim followed, boots tapping the rungs lightly, his breath catching once when the ladder flexed.

On the street, the world felt closer, louder. A boy pushed a cart stacked with eggs and navigated them with impossible grace around a nun carrying a basil plant and a man hosing the dust from his threshold. Somewhere, a radio spilled Greek folk music; somewhere else, a kettle shrieked and was stilled.

Jonas set a pilgrim's pace that felt like sacrilege—slow, heads bowed just enough, hands visible. They blended. Almost. Arielle kept her eyes low and let the jar's weight pin her to this moment instead of the one behind them where knives sparked on stone.

At the corner, the crowd thinned. Jonas halted with a motion so small it would look like reverence from a distance. "Two behind," he said. "Not the ring-men. Local pair."

Karim didn't look. "Matthias?"

"Could be. Could be men who work for a man who pays in unstamped cash."

"Fog," Arielle said, the word surprising her with how much she wanted it. "One witness. Not a drawer. Not a crowd."

Jonas nodded once. "There's a paleographer three streets west who does work off the books for churches that pretend their manuscripts repair themselves." He angled his chin toward a lane that ran parallel to David Street. "Dr. Yael Kadosh. Studio over a spice shop. Keeps a lab that won't embarrass her if the Vatican knocks politely."

Karim's eyebrows climbed. "You just have that ready?"

"I have plans I pray not to use," Jonas said. "We're using one."

They turned into the lane. The spice shop announced itself before it appeared—cumin and sumac and cardamom thickening the air, saffron in little glass vials like sunlight harvested and stored. Above it, a painted wooden sign read Conservation — Kadosh in three scripts. The door was unmarked, the buzzer disguised as an old bell-pull.

Jonas glanced once up and down the alley. "No names," he said. "No explanations at the door." He pulled the bell.

A long beat. A latch clicked. The door opened a hand's width and an eye peered into the crack—hazel, watchful, framed by laugh lines that had not had much practice lately.

"Upstairs," a woman's voice said, and the door widened.

The stair was narrow and steep, the kind that invited discretion and punished haste. Arielle moved sideways to protect the pack. Jonas followed close; Karim brought up the rear, closing the door soft with a fingertip to the latch to avoid the slap. The woman at the top watched them climb, measuring with a conservator's economy: weight distribution, balance, what gets carried and how.

She had hair threaded with silver and pulled into a knot with two old pencils; a linen lab coat dusted with chalk; a smudge of what could have been char on the heel of her hand. She didn't smile.

"You're early," she said to Jonas, as if they had a standing appointment they had both hoped never to keep.

"Emergencies don't book," he said.

Dr. Yael Kadosh stepped back, and the lab received them: cool, controlled, windows high and frosted, light diffused to a working gray. A long table held linen gloves in sealed packets, a stereomicroscope, a fume hood, a chilled cabinet marked with stickers in three languages that all meant do not touch. The room smelled faintly of ethanol and rabbit-skin glue and old paper—the scent of patience.

"Shoes off," she said. "Then talk."

They left their dust on the mat and stepped into her controlled world. Arielle set the pack on the table without taking her hand off it. Dr. Kadosh watched the gesture, then Jonas's stance, then the tremor hiding in Karim's mouth.

"Someone died for this," Yael said quietly. It was not a question.

Arielle met her eyes. "More than one, I think."

"Always more than one," Yael said, and only then did she extend a hand, palm up—not to take, but to be shown.

Arielle opened the flap and rolled the pack down inch by inch until the linen-wrapped clay lay revealed. Yael leaned in, breath held the way divers hold breath before cold water, and examined without touching: the spiral grooves in the clay; the pitch seam; the faint grime in the weave that spoke of a hand that had tied it long before any of them were a thought.

"Qumran," Yael said. "Herodian matrix. Seal looks unbroken." She cut Jonas a narrow glance. "You brought a problem."

"I brought you a decision," he said. "Fog or thunder."

"Thunder is for people who want to be right," Yael said. "Fog is for people who want to live." She straightened. "But fog requires a lighthouse. If I validate, they'll come anyway. If I refuse, you leave no better than you arrived."

"We're not asking you to open it," Arielle said. "We're asking you to tell us where this truth should first draw breath."

Yael's mouth compressed. "That's a rabbi's question, not a conservator's."

"Answer it like a conservator," Karim said. "Where would you let air touch it first if you wanted it to live?"

Yael's gaze rested on him a heartbeat, reassessing his role from background to chorus. "In a room without politics," she said. "Which is to say nowhere in this city." She moved to the window and looked through the frosting as if it could be persuaded to show more than it would. "But there are edges. A Syriac cellar that thinks Rome is a rumor. A Greek deacon I trust with my lab keys. A nun in Ein Karem who restores icons the Patriarchate says cracked on their own."

Arielle swallowed. "And your choice?"

Yael turned back to the table. "If I had one night and one light, I'd choose St. Mark's—the Syriac house near the Armenian border. Their scriptorium lives in a basement that resists both humidity and curiosity, and their abbot believes power is a bad glue. He owes me. He pays his debts."

"Then St. Mark's," Jonas said, decision clicking into place like a magazine seating in a well-used weapon.

Arielle felt relief try to rise and tamped it down. "We'll go now."

"You'll go when I say," Yael replied, not unkindly. "Which is after I've made your fog thicker." She crossed to a cabinet, drew out a Tyvek envelope, and eased a folded rectangle of aged linen onto a secondary tray. "You'll carry this on the surface—same weight, same profile. Your jar rides in a baby carrier under your coat with a belly band and two straps I'm going to sew onto you in the next five minutes."

Karim blinked. "You do decoys?"

"I do survival," Yael said. "Hold still."

She worked with a speed that spoke of practice: cutting straps, measuring Arielle's torso with a tailor's cloth ribbon, anchoring the jar against the curve of her stomach where a casual glance would read fatigue, not contraband. The decoy linen-wrapped cylinder slid into the pack with the satisfying inevitability of misdirection. Yael stepped back and nodded. "If someone pulls you by the bag, you give it up crying. If someone grabs you by the coat, you fall and scream and you hold on."

Arielle exhaled—and then stiffened. The watcher's prickle rode her neck again, clean and precise. Not memory. Now. "Jonas," she whispered.

He was already moving. He crossed to the door, bent, and put his eye to the keyhole, then to the gap under the threshold, reading shadow and light the way a tracker reads dust. He lifted a finger: one. Then another: two. His jaw ticked.

Yael reached under the table without looking and produced an old iron key the size of a small tool. She handed it to Karim. "Back stair," she said. "Down to the spice sacks, through the storeroom, out to a lane that spits you toward St. Mark's in four turns if you take my turns and not your own."

Bootsteps paused outside, not at the door, but at the shared landing—a patience that said the men on the other side could afford to be careful. A knuckle tapped the stair rail once, twice. A coded nothing, yet it made the hair on Arielle's arms stand up.

"Thunder later," Jonas said. "Fog now."

Yael pressed her palm lightly to Arielle's shoulder, not comfort, calibration. "Tell the abbot I sent you," she said. "And tell him truth is tinder in the wrong season."

The knock came—soft, polite, inevitable.

Jonas didn't touch the door. He nodded to the back stair. "Go."

Arielle lifted the pack with the decoy and felt the real weight snug against her ribs where Yael's straps held. Karim slid the iron key into his palm and pushed the service door with two fingers.

It opened onto darkness that smelled of cinnamon and sackcloth and the place where cities keep their breath. The three of them slipped through.

Yael dropped the bar into the brackets and turned back to the front as the second knock sounded, still courteous as death.

"Coming," she called, voice flat. And to the empty room: "Go fast."

The back stair swallowed them whole.

Chapter Seven — The House of Mark

They moved through the lane in fours turns—Yael's turns, not their own—past sacks of cumin stacked like sandbags, past a shutter painted with a winged lion gone dull with dust, past a doorway where a cat blinked slow judgment and went back to washing its paws. The city's breath warmed with midmorning. Arielle felt the jar cinched under her coat like a live current. The decoy rode in the pack, a lie that would have to be convincing at speed.

"Left," Jonas said softly. "Then the iron crossbeam. Then the door with the low lintel."

The quarter shifted—footfalls softened, voices thinned. A narrow courtyard opened, paved in basalt like cooled lava, ringed by thick walls. At the far side, a low doorway wore a carved lintel of dark stone. The inscription wasn't Latin or Hebrew. It was older and rounder, letters with the confidence of river stones: Estrangela Syriac, Arielle realized, her pulse catching. Beneath it, a small brass plate, newer, read in three languages: St. Mark's Syriac Orthodox Monastery.

Karim tipped his head, reading the curve of the letters with his finger in the air. "They say this is the house of John Mark's mother," he murmured. "The room where they hid after the crucifixion."

"History loves a good address," Jonas said, but even he let the moment stand.

A bell chimed once, the sound dull and intimate in the thick air. Jonas knocked—two even taps, then one, the rhythm of a favor being called in. Footsteps approached, the scrape of a bolt. The door opened onto shadow.

A man stood within, slight, in a black cassock that pooled at his feet like night. His beard was neatly kept, his hair close, his eyes the deep brown of carved olivewood. A silver cross lay against his chest, its edges softened by decades of thumbs.

"Peace to you," he said in Syriac first—Shlomo 'alakhon—then in English. "You come with weight, and not only in your hands." His mouth quirked. "Yael rarely wastes my debts."

"Abbot," Jonas said, inclining his head. "We need a room and the kind of silence that grows here."

"Come," the abbot said. "Leave your shoes by the threshold. This house will forgive dust but not carelessness."

Cool swallowed them. The entry smelled of beeswax, stone, and a thread of old incense that had sunk into lime and could not be washed out. A narrow hall gave onto a chapel small enough to be believed: plastered walls, an icon of Mary and the Child dark with age, a silver lamp hanging where breath could make it swing. On the right, a doorway opened to a room with low vaulting and a table that had seen better centuries.

Arielle's throat tightened. History had always been a subject for her—a sequence, a map. Here it was a room with a temperature and a smell and a table that would bruise if you hit it too hard.

The abbot waved them inside. "I am Mar Ephrem," he said. "A bishop to those who need titles, a steward to those who don't. Yael said truth was asking for air." He studied them, one by one. His gaze did not linger on the pack. It did not need to.

"We'll keep the vessel sealed," Jonas said. "We need counsel, not spectacle."

"Good," Mar Ephrem said. "Spectacle is what men choose when prayer is too quiet to feed their vanity." He closed the door and slid a wooden bar into iron brackets with a sound that had comfort in it. "Sit. Drink."

He poured water into earthen cups from a clay jug that sweated like a living thing. Arielle took hers and realized her hands had stopped trembling only when the cup didn't shiver against her palm.

"Yael told you...?" she began.

"That you were bringing a jar older than the dust on my doorstep," Mar Ephrem said. "That others wanted it. That you had decided, unwisely but bravely, to ask a monastery instead of a ministry what to do next."

Arielle swallowed a smile that hurt. "Is it unwisely?"

"It is unwisely if you want protection," he said. "It is wisely if you want witnesses."

Karim leaned forward, the cup untouched in his hand. "We need a room where we can document non-invasively. Light, photographs. If there are markings on the linen beneath the primary layer, we should see them before we break the seal."

Mar Ephrem looked amused. "You are not the first to ask my basement to pretend to be a laboratory." He lifted a key from a nail by the door—old iron, the kind that could double as a lever if you tried hard enough—and gestured. "Come."

They passed through the chapel. Mar Ephrem paused only long enough to touch the icon with two fingers and his forehead with one. The corridor beyond narrowed and then turned down a short flight of steps into a room cut partly into the bedrock. It was cooler here, the air oddly dry for stone—vented cleverly by channels opened centuries ago by people who wanted books to live. Shelves held codices in linen wrappers; a table supported a wooden press; a bracket on the wall held a magnifying glass with a cracked horn handle.

"The scriptorium," he said. "We keep what the city forgets it owes us."

Arielle set the pack on the table carefully and unzipped the flap. The decoy lay within, Yael's good lie. Under her coat, the real jar pressed against her ribs, its curve catching heat her body could not spare. She hesitated a beat. Mar Ephrem watched her, then looked away, granting privacy to a choice that would have to be public very soon.

Jonas shrugged out of his jacket and checked the corners of the room the way men look before they let their backs relax. "Windows?"

"Slits," Mar Ephrem said, pointing to narrow vents up near the vault. "They let in breath and little else. No one has used the old crawl for years." His eyes flicked to the far wall. "Unless cats count."

Karim's attention had caught on a framed fragment near the press—a parchment square, Syriac in bold Estrangela, ink faded at the edges where a thumb had worried it a hundred years ago. He stepped closer. "This line," he murmured, reading. "Through the daughters, the covenant endures."

Arielle's head snapped up. The words hit her chest like a hand. "You have it too."

"We have many things too," Mar Ephrem said, not unkindly. "Rome does not own all the whispers. Our copy is a fourteenth-century quotation from a lost commentary. It is not the stream but it remembers the river."

Arielle slid the coat open and cradled the jar free. The straps Yael had sewn bit as they released. The clay felt cooler than her hands. Mar Ephrem's eyes softened—not greedy, not credulous, something else. A recognition that had nothing to do with museums.

"You have done a rash thing," he said quietly. "But rashness is sometimes the correct answer to a cruel question."

"We need light," Karim said. "And a stand if you have one. We'll photograph the linen wrap at high angle, then side lighting for surface topography. If there are letter impressions, we might—"

"Karim," Jonas said mildly, and some of the speed bled out of Karim's voice.

Mar Ephrem fetched a simple wooden cradle from a cupboard and set it on the table. "For the Gospel book on feast days," he said. "Today it will hold clay." He lit a lamp with a narrow chimney and set it to the jar's side so raked light would catch the weave. Shadows ran like water across the linen. The spiral wrap showed clearly now, along with the pitch line—a darker seam, still tight.

Arielle leaned in. "Here," she whispered. "Under the primary wrap—there's a faint stitch mark. Someone repaired the outer linen centuries ago and never touched the inner binding." Her heart thudded. "It's older within."

Karim angled his phone and snapped without flash, then again with the lamp shifted. The images caught the topography of the weave. He zoomed, then stopped. "Numbers," he said softly. "Like at Qumran."

Arielle saw them now—tiny cuts at consistent intervals, more felt than seen. She counted under her breath: five, three, five, three, then a pause, then seven. Serva veritatem. The pattern that had resolved before. But there, between the second and third group, a new cluster—two tiny incisions paired like quotation marks. She frowned. "That's new."

"Not new," Mar Ephrem said. "New to you. Manuscripts tell their secrets slowly to those who arrive late." He tilted his head. "Two paired marks in our tradition often indicate names redacted. Or the start of a genealogy too dangerous to speak aloud."

Karim exhaled. "Daughters."

The word shivered in the room like a string plucked.

A low sound drifted through the vent—distant, uncertain. A voice? A truck? The city's thousand habits kept moving. Jonas didn't lift his head, but his hand settled on the table near the jar, a small claim.

Arielle straightened. "If we open it," she said, "we open it here. With you. With Yael. Witnesses. Not owners."

Mar Ephrem studied her as if appraising a votive flame—its ability to survive its own light. "You will also need someone who can think in the same script as the original hand." He smiled, brief and dry. "The Patriarchate likes to forget we still do."

"Can you read it?" Karim asked.

"I can read our texts," he said. "Whether your jar holds what rumor promised is another question. But yes. If you insist on foolhardy honesty, I will stand in the room."

Jonas's gaze cut to the door. "We may not have the luxury of ritual. We have one more stop before we burn the hour Lev bought us."

"Where?" Mar Ephrem asked.

"Yael's choice put you first," Jonas said. "My choice puts how second. We need a place to leave the wrong thing in the right hands."

"The decoy," Arielle said.

Jonas nodded. "Thunder bait."

Mar Ephrem looked at the pack, then at the jar, then at Arielle. "You are trying to teach wolves to count while you cross the field," he said. "Interesting."

Arielle allowed herself a breath that almost reached relief. The plan felt like a path through reeds. Narrow, but real. "We move in fifteen," she said. "Photographs now. Then we place the decoy where it will do the most good and the most harm."

"Very Christian of you," Mar Ephrem said. "Turning the other cheek while you keep the heart behind your back."

He turned the lamp a fraction. The linen's weave brightened. On the far side of the seam, near the base—Arielle saw it then. A faint smudge, darker even than pitch, pressed into the cloth as if something within had touched the inside and left a shadow of itself. Not ink. Not resin.

Her chest went cold.

"What is it?" Karim whispered.

Arielle swallowed. "A fingerprint," she said. "From inside the wrap."

The room held its breath.

And above them, faint but unmistakable, a knock sounded at the monastery's outer door. Three quick. One long.

Jonas's eyes met Mar Ephrem's. "Wrong pattern," he said.

Mar Ephrem smiled without humor. "In this house," he said, "we prefer the right kind of wrong." He reached for the lamp and lowered its wick until light held the jar like a secret. "Photographs. Then we go very still."

They worked fast.

Mar Ephrem dimmed the room to a slate dusk and set the raked lamp low. Karim shot high-angle photos, then side-lighted passes, changing the lamp angle by hand-widths and calling the positions under his breath—"east two fingers... south by three..."—so he could reconstruct shadows later. Arielle kept the jar steady in the wooden cradle, rotating it a quarter turn at a time. Jonas stood at the stair, counting knocks that weren't knocks—the city's pulses coming through stone.

The fingerprint ghost would not resolve. In some frames it looked like an oval haze, in others a set of whorls nearly visible, and in a few it vanished as if embarrassed to be seen.

"Not residue," Yael would have said. "An offset. A transfer." Mar Ephrem said almost the same: "It is a memory left by pressure, not a stain. Someone tied the inner wrap with a bare hand. The weave remembered."

Karim angled closer. "The paired marks repeat," he murmured. "Five... three... five... three... pause... seven... and then two little teeth, twice." He zoomed until the pixels gave up shape. "If it's a genealogy cue, it flags names at two points."

"Daughters," Arielle said. The word still made the room hitch. "Two branches."

Jonas's head tilted. He held up a hand: wait.

Above, in the chapel, the wrong-knock pattern repeated—three quick, one long. A murmur of voices followed, polite, official. Then a second rhythm: slow, even, cane tapping stone. Two visitors, not one. The kind who expected rooms to open for them because rooms usually did.

Mar Ephrem slipped the bar from the brackets and moved toward the stairs. "Silence," he said, not to hush them so much as to invite the stones to help. He paused with his hand on the jamb and looked back at the jar. "Do not teach truth to fear," he said quietly, and climbed.

They waited in the cool. Above, the chapel door creaked; a voice greeted the visitors in Arabic, then in English; the abbot's tone stayed warm and useless. Arielle felt her breath try to climb; she forced it down into her shoes.

Karim tapped his phone's screen off and on, off and on, the need to make something happen wrestling with the need to be a stone. Jonas stood so still the lamplight forgot he wasn't furniture.

Footsteps crossed the chapel. A voice asked for "records." Another asked for "assistance… simple, Father." A chair leg scraped. Oil clicked in the lamp's throat.

Five minutes. Ten. Arielle's fingers went numb from not moving. She pictured the linen tearing when she couldn't feel it anymore and made herself flex her hand once.

Then: a door closing upstairs. The cane's measured tap retreated. Silence filled the channels they left.

Mar Ephrem returned, mouth a thin line. "They asked to see our book of visitors," he said. "I showed them our book of saints."

"Latin?" Jonas asked.

"One local inspector. One gentleman who did not introduce his ring," Mar Ephrem said. "They asked if a woman with a pack had come to pray. I told them yes, and so had many women, and so would many more. They smiled like men who hate crowds." He glanced at the jar.

"They will be back with a suggestion disguised as a favor. We should be gone by then."

Jonas nodded once. "Thunder bait, then fog. Karim, with me. We run the decoy." He turned to Arielle. "You and the abbot stay on the heartbeat. Keep taking photos. If we don't return in an hour, you go to Lev's cistern and take Yael's second path."

Arielle's mouth was already open to argue. She closed it. Protocols existed so she didn't have to invent courage she might not have. "Be seen with the bag," she said. "Not with your face. Give them something to chase that isn't you."

Karim slid the decoy into the pack and shouldered it. The weight sat right; Yael's work was good enough to fool hands, not just eyes. Mar Ephrem vanished into a cupboard and returned with two black woolen shawls. "Pilgrim scarves," he said. "Everyone looks innocent when they are cold."

He pressed a small paper icon into Jonas's palm as if he were giving him a receipt. "For luck," he said, then ruined the sentiment with a practical addendum: "And because the shopkeepers on Khan al-Zeit give discounts for people who look like they still believe."

Jonas's mouth twitched. He tucked the icon next to his knife. "Open the side gate?"

Mar Ephrem nodded. "Out the eastern court, right at the basalt well, then straight to Christian Street. If you want your thunder to be loud, take the cut past the Holy Sepulchre and let them see your bag before you lose them."

"Where do we lose them?" Karim asked.

Jonas's eyes flicked to Arielle, a question answered, then away. "At the École," he said. "We leave the pack on the porter's table and let the Dominicans' paperwork be our smoke. They'll swarm it. We slip off the wall."

Mar Ephrem lifted the bar. "Then go. And don't admire architecture."

They went—Jonas ahead, Karim behind, black shawls hiding modern silhouettes. The side gate sighed and took them.

The door closed. Silence swelled back into the scriptorium, but it was a different silence; it had corners now.

Arielle set the jar back into the cradle and forced herself to move with the same steadiness as before. Karim's checklist lay on the table; she followed it, line by line, and her hands learned calm from the sequence. Mar Ephrem adjusted the lamp, making rakes and shadows, humming under his breath a tune that sounded like a ladder.

"Your father came here once," he said without looking up.

The words landed like a thrown pebble.

"When?" Arielle asked. Her voice did not crack. It pulled thin, like the thread of honey on a spoon.

"Years ago," Mar Ephrem said. "Before he died. He asked about a Syriac commentary that quotes a phrase like the one on your papyrus. I told him we had a fragment and that he should pour tea instead of chasing wind." He turned the lamp a fraction. "He poured tea. Then he chased wind."

"He didn't tell me he'd been here," Arielle said. The room tilted a degree. "He told me he was going to Jericho."

"Both things can be true," Mar Ephrem said. "He left with my blessing and without my address. He said he would bring back bread from a baker on Christian Street because the sesame is better there." He smiled without showing teeth. "He did not bring bread."

Footsteps sounded again above, lighter this time, many at once—a school group? Pilgrims? The ordinary weight of a church breathing. Arielle exhaled the breath she had trapped somewhere between either/or.

"Photograph the base once more," she said. "The smudge."

They captured it from three angles. In one, the ovoid sharpened just enough to seem intentional. In another, the two tiny paired incisions near it—like quotation marks—read as parentheses around absence.

"Names," Mar Ephrem said again. "Or a caution: prepare for names."

Arielle's phone vibrated: a single buzz. A message from an unknown number, no text, just a photo. She thumbed it open.

The frame showed the École Biblique porter's desk—green lamp, worn wood, a sign-in ledger… and the decoy pack sitting squarely on the blotter. In the background, two men in dark coats were already pushing through the cloister door, a silver ring flashing at a wrist.

Another buzz. A second photo: the men closer, the pack still untouched. Third buzz: a blurred shot from knee height, the kind you take when you don't want to be seen taking it—Jonas's angle. Then nothing.

Arielle's stomach unclenched by degrees. Thunder.

"Your men?" Mar Ephrem asked.

"Ours," Arielle said. "And theirs."

They waited for the echo.

It came in the city, not the room: a siren somewhere too fast to be fire, radios crackling, the kind of energy that turns crowds into eyes. The monastery absorbed the noise and returned it as cool.

"Fog in here, thunder out there," Mar Ephrem said. "Good."

A minute later, a fourth buzz. A text this time: ab. No punctuation. Jonas's shorthand. All's burning or Abbot's good—or simply at base. She wanted more; she would get nothing. Discipline had to be shared or it rotted.

The abbot's head lifted. "Visitors again," he said.

The knock at the outer door was the same wrong rhythm. Three quick. One long. It sounded patient. Practiced.

Mar Ephrem drew himself to full height, which wasn't much, and somehow became larger. "Stay," he said to Arielle, and went up.

This time the voices came farther into the house. Polite, then a shade less. The scrape of a chair again. A low exchange in Arabic that skirted around the words "permit," "warrant," "helpful." Mar Ephrem's voice did not rise. He spoke about liturgy times and the miracle of the house of Mark and the fact that fire inspectors always forgot their shoe covers. Laughter—thin. Footsteps nearer the stair. A pause.

Arielle slid her hand over the jar's linen and felt the cold come through the weave like a decision.

If they came down, she would not run. She couldn't. There was nowhere to go that didn't start with a noise she refused to make. She had chosen fog; fog meant staying until the world outside chose the bait.

The footsteps receded. A blessing muttered in a language that wasn't prayer. The door again, a bolt setting, a breath out.

Mar Ephrem returned with a single sheet of paper in his hand. "They left us a warning," he said, and set the paper on the table. It was a request on municipal letterhead, crisp, preprinted—cooperate with cultural inspection; temporary custody of artifacts under possible danger—with a signature that belonged to no department anyone trusted.

"They will come back with friendlier uniforms," he said. "We have perhaps an hour."

He looked at Arielle the way a physician looks at a patient who has decided against anesthesia. "If you intend to open this here, choose now. If not, we hide, and we run after we pray."

Arielle stared at the jar. The fingerprint that wasn't a fingerprint. The stitches that weren't a repair so much as a second thought. The numbers that had always added up to guard the truth and now, maybe, to names.

"Not yet," she said. The words were calm when they left her mouth, and only afterward did she realize they were mercy to herself. "We wait for Jonas and Karim. Then we move."

Mar Ephrem tilted the lamp until the linen's pattern blurred into a single pale field, as if to give the jar privacy for whatever it had to remember. "Then we wait," he said.

Outside, thunder rolled down Christian Street in the shape of men who thought they were alone in their certainty. Inside, fog settled as a choice.

Arielle laid her palm flat on the cloth and felt, for the first time since the desert, the watcher's open hand not above her but beside hers—as if it had come down from whatever ridge it had haunted and was simply standing watch with her, the way witnesses do when the truth is almost ready to breathe.

The monastery held the kind of quiet that makes clocks sound guilty.

Arielle kept the jar in the wooden cradle and worked the checklist until her breathing matched the lamp's faint hiss. Mar Ephrem turned the wick a breath at a time, making rakes and shadows. The fingerprint—if it was that—came and went like a reef under waves. Twice, she thought she could read a whorl. Twice, the linen remembered it had sworn to forget.

Footsteps in the court. A scrape at the side gate. A key turned that knew the lock.

Jonas slid through first, shawl rolled tight in his fist, face calm in the way of people who postpone fear until it buys them more time. Karim followed, a flush on his cheeks that could have been exertion or triumph. Mar Ephrem dropped the bar into its brackets and let out a breath through his nose that might have been a prayer.

"Thunder?" Arielle asked.

"Loud," Jonas said. "Dominicans love a ledger. We gave them one, and three separate officials began to love it at once."

Karim found the edge of the table and leaned, smiling despite the tremor hiding under it. "Ring-man couldn't make a scene in a cloister. He tried to talk the seal off the pack with Latin. The porter asked him if he preferred coffee or tea. I almost converted on the spot."

Jonas's smile was a slash and gone. "We bought minutes, not absolution. They'll pivot here next."

Mar Ephrem lifted a sheet of municipal letterhead between two fingers. "They left us a suggestion designed to feel like permission." He tapped the signature that belonged to no office. "It will grow teeth by the hour."

Karim's eyes strayed to the cradle. "We should move the jar."

"We will," Jonas said. "But not until we decide where to." He nodded toward Arielle. "Your call."

Arielle looked at the smudge on the linen, the paired incisions like small quotation marks bracketing absence. The room smelled of stone and cooled lamp and something green from the courtyard that she could not name. Inside her, a scale tipped and settled.

"Not to a drawer," she said. "And not to a theatre. We keep fog. We open it with witnesses who believe responsibility is heavier than headlines."

"Here," Mar Ephrem said simply. He glanced at the door, then the vents. "After dark."

"Then we need to not be here when they knock with friendlier uniforms," Jonas said. "We take the jar now, circle the quarter, let them waste the hour on an empty house, then return when the choir is loud enough to cover the first cut of linen."

Karim grimaced. "Circle with a magnet in our coat."

"Fog works because you carry it into places where weather confuses hunters," Jonas said. "Mar Ephrem?"

"There's an old crawl from our roofline to the Ethiopians' terrace," the abbot said. "No one uses it; the step is mean, and God did not give all monks a head for heights." He looked at Arielle. "Do you have one?"

"I have a head for doing what's in front of me," she said. "Heights are a rumor."

Mar Ephrem's mouth tilted. "A good answer to many questions."

"Before we go," Jonas said, "I need one minute."

He crossed to the small table in the chapel and flipped open a browned ledger bound in vellum. Names flowed down the page in many hands—pilgrims, donors, a Greek colonel who had written as if carving stone. Jonas turned back a handful of years. His finger stopped. He turned the book and slid it to Arielle.

There, under a slanted November date, sat Daniel L. Hale—her father's hand, careful, followed by two words she had never seen in his notebooks: for bread.

Her throat closed, then opened around a laugh that wasn't funny. "For bread?"

Mar Ephrem poured water she did not remember asking for. "He promised he would bring some," he said. "Fresh sesame from Christian Street. Such promises make the day kind even when they are not kept."

Jonas's gaze softened for the briefest beat. "He chose light," he said. "Even when it punished him."

Arielle smoothed the ledger's edge with a finger she could not quite make stop. The watcher's hand—open, patient—felt closer here than it had in the desert, not a warning, not a threat. A witness.

"Let's earn our night," she said.

They moved with deliberate haste—an art Jonas had taught Karim, who could do most things quickly except be calm. Mar Ephrem fetched two plain coats from a peg and a woven sack with a tear mended by a dozen small, uneven stitches. "Disguise works best when it looks like work," he said, handing Arielle the sack. "Laundry has carried more secrets than kings."

Yael's straps hid the jar's curve against Arielle's torso; the decoy pack sat empty on a shelf, its usefulness spent. Jonas adjusted the drape of the coat to make fatigue, not contraband, read first. He gave Arielle a peaked cap with a bleach bloom at the brim. "Pilgrim enough to not be interesting," he said.

The abbot led them to a narrow stair that rose like a throat into heat. The roof was a quilt of tar and tile and old surprises. The city unrolled at eye level—domes like knees, tanks like turtles, laundry snapping like pennants. Mar Ephrem knelt at a low parapet and eased up a stone the size of a dictionary. Beneath, a slit—the crawl—ran like a cruel invitation along the wall's thickness.

"Palms flat, elbows in," he said. "If you kick out the sacrificial step, you will discover why we call it that."

Karim peered in, gulped, and grinned in the same motion. "Oh, this is awful," he whispered, delighted.

Jonas went first, sliding into the stone seam like a letter into a narrow slot. His shoulders cleared, his boots vanished, his voice came back thin and practical: "Mind the second handhold; it's dust and piety."

Arielle went next. The jar's weight became a fact her spine argued with and lost. The stone breathed cool in the crack; outside, the air hammered heat. She moved as if learning to be an animal, not a person—pressure, release, three points of contact and prayer for the fourth. The sky at the slit's end was a strip of poor blue that promised ordinary things: shade, water, a place to stand up.

Karim wriggled behind, muttering a running commentary that somehow made the seam feel wider. "If I don't come out, tell the world my last thoughts were about pastry."

"You're fasting," Arielle said.

"That's why the pastry."

They spilled onto a terrace no one loved—tar blistered, a broken chair listing against a wall, a water tank sweating in the sun. From here a zigzag of surfaces stitched to the Ethiopians' compound like a repair line. The little domed chapels of Deir es-Sultan rose bone-white and improbable, their plaster patched by generations of monks who refused to let roofs define them. A pilgrim or two moved below, ants with cameras. A gull cut an arc bizarrely inland.

They crossed. Twice Jonas raised his hand and they folded into chimney-shadow as dark coats passed below and a ring winked once in daylight like a small, captured moon. No one looked up. Why would you? The city teaches necks to turn sideways, not skyward.

At the far parapet, Mar Ephrem pressed a key into Jonas's palm. "If you must come back hard," he said, tapping the key's bow, "this opens the side gate, but only if you talk to it like a friend. It sticks when hurried."

Jonas nodded. "And you?"

"I will receive a suggestion with more signatures," Mar Ephrem said, "and refuse to sign my part." He glanced at Arielle. "Bring my bread if you can."

They dropped to a lower roof, then down a carpenter's ladder to a court that smelled of basil and stirred dust. A cat watched them from a wall and decided to remain a cat. Jonas set a pace that read as errand, not flight.

By the time they reached the lane, the city had changed key. The Latin envoys had decided on uniforms—municipal cultural inspectors this time, polite as rulers. They moved in pairs, asking questions with the kind of smiles that are laminated against answers. One turned just as the trio passed; his gaze tracked the woven sack. Arielle felt his attention slide along her like a hand along a rail and then move on. Laundry is invisible until it isn't.

At the Muristan fountain, a knot of pilgrims diverted an entire conversation by existing. Jonas slipped them along the edge, then tipped his chin toward a side passage that bled into Khan al-Zeit. "We'll let the market put hands on our shoulders and push us," he said. "Then left for the Armenian gate. Then we decide."

They reached the Armenian Quarter's basalt threshold without attracting the kind of attention that speaks. The gate's shadow felt earned. A bell tolled once. Mar Ephrem's key in Jonas's pocket felt like a promise and a debt.

They were ten paces into the court when a figure detached from a column's shade and walked toward them with the kind of unhurried certainty that makes other men invent new priorities.

Matthias Calder wore linen the color of wet bone and a face educated in patience. He let his hands show, empty, as if to prove he distinguished himself from men who needed to carry what they wanted.

"Doctor Hale," he said to Arielle, speaking her name softly, like someone recalling a favorite line. "I had hoped Jerusalem would put you in my path sooner or later. It likes to serve its inevitabilities warm."

Jonas shifted to the edge of her vision—an angle, not a wall. Karim moved one pace left, making a triangle that math would approve even if fate did not.

Arielle felt the jar's curve against her ribs and, for the first time, did not try to will it invisible. "You're in my path now," she said. "Say what you came to say."

Matthias's eyes took the measure of the sack in her hands, the coat's line, the cap's bleach bloom, and filed the data without comment. "You think I came to negotiate," he said. "I came to offer a courtesy." He inclined his head toward the city behind him. "The men with rings eat thunder for breakfast. They will chew your decoy and ask for more. I don't like eating at their table."

"You brought a different appetite," Jonas said.

"I brought a candle," Matthias said, and somehow it did not sound like rhetoric. "When you open it—and you will—do it with someone who understands how a flame behaves in a closed room."

"We have witnesses," Arielle said.

"You have believers," he corrected, gently. "Belief is a fine solvent. It removes varnish and paint. It occasionally removes the wood." He stepped back one pace, giving them the air he had taken. "Dusk," he said. "If you are as wise as I think, you will choose a room with exits and a table that doesn't wobble." The ghost of a smile, gone. "Bring bread."

He turned and walked away without looking to see if anyone followed. No one did, which meant everyone would, later.

Karim let out a breath that tugged at his whole body. "Did he just... book a seat?"

"He just told us he knows there is a table," Jonas said. "And that he intends to arrive whether we set it or not."

Arielle looked at the sack in her hands, at the basalt under her feet, at the stripe of sky between roofs that had kept secrets longer than all their lives put together. She thought of her father's two words in the ledger. For bread.

"Fine," she said. "We bring bread."

Jonas's eyes ticked once to hers—agreement, not approval. "We move," he said. "We let them search an empty house and a decoy cloister. At dusk, we return to the room with witnesses."

"Yael and Mar Ephrem," Karim said. "Lev if he'll risk it."

"Lev will prefer to be a rumor," Jonas said. "Which is exactly why he's useful."

They turned back toward the monastery's quieter streets. Behind them, the city's noise stacked into chords—sirens, bells, a radio arguing with a prayer, a rumor becoming a plan. In Arielle's chest, a matching chord formed: fear, resolve, and a thin, persistent thread of something like hope.

The watcher's hand did not hover above her now. It walked beside her in step, palm down, not blessing, not warning. Just keeping pace until the truth chose its first breath.

They did not go straight back.

Jonas pulled them sideways through the market's shoulder, letting the city's tide choose their speed until the heat on their necks felt like noon rather than pursuit. At a corner where Christian Street bent toward the bazaar, he stopped at a baker's window that breathed sesame and smoke.

"Two rings," Arielle said before he could speak. Her voice surprised her by not shaking. "And a flat loaf."

The baker slid the ka'ak onto a sheet of paper and added the round loaf with a quick crosshatch of a knife that seemed older than the counter. Arielle paid and tucked the warm weight into the woven sack. For a moment, the world shrank to a smell she remembered from childhood kitchens and to two words written in a monastery ledger: for bread.

"Let's earn it," she said.

They returned by another street that wanted to be a hallway. At the monastery gate, Mar Ephrem's key turned with the patience he'd prescribed. Inside, shade wrapped them. In the chapel, a young deacon lit lamps with movements that had practiced humility into muscle memory. He did not look up.

"Ramsho in twenty," the abbot said, meeting them at the threshold. "Dusk prayers." He eyed the sack. "You brought the bribe I asked."

"Bribe?" Karim said, startled.

"Bread persuades stone to listen," Mar Ephrem said, deadpan. "And monks. Mostly monks." His gaze softened as he took the loaf, as if he had seen for bread written in other hands. "Come. Yael is here."

They found her in the scriptorium, coat sleeves rolled, a small case open on the table like a quiet confession: scalpels, microspatulas, Japanese paper strips, a handheld loupe, packets of nitrile gloves, a tiny humidification chamber fashioned from a plastic box and damp blotter. She glanced at the sack and then at Arielle's coat, clocking weight and lies with a conservator's speed.

"Decoy worked," she said. "The École is arguing with itself and enjoying it. The ring-men dislike bureaucracy. They will come back when bureaucracy wins." She pointed to a corner where a small borescope camera lay coiled. "I brought a way to look through pitch without snapping it, if patience exists in the room."

"Not much," Jonas said.

Yael sniffed, unimpressed. "Then tonight is a bad night for history." She nodded toward the cradle. "Let's buy ourselves a margin."

They set the room the way witnesses do when the truth is fragile: table leveled with a folded scrap under one leg until it stopped rocking; lamp chimneys cleaned; lenses wiped and covered; two buckets of water within reach for fire that likely wouldn't come but liked to be threatened. Mar Ephrem placed the loaf on a plate at the far end of the table and cut it into six thick pieces.

“For when your hands remember they’re hands,” he said. “Not instruments.”

A bell hummed in the chapel. Voices stacked like cords. Syriac syllables rose—round and old—and flowed down the stair like shared breath. The sound was a cover and a blessing.

“Ground rules,” Yael said, donning gloves. “First, no one touches the pitch seam unless I call it. Second, we document everything—angles, handoffs, time marks. Third, if anything inside looks like skin or wax tablets, we stop and rethink the air. Fourth, if we open, we open slow. Trauma kills more artifacts than heresy.”

Arielle slid out of the coat. The straps Yael had sewn gave up their work with small reluctant snaps. The jar came free into Yael’s waiting hands and settled into the cradle as if it had been carved for it.

Jonas checked the vents and the crawl with a soldier’s superstition, then returned to stand where he could see the door and the lamp and the outline of Arielle’s shoulder in the same glance. Karim opened a fresh file on his phone and typed Dusk Opening — St. Mark’s in the title field, then began time-stamping lines: 18:12 lamp rake east two; 18:14 linen seam photographed x3; 18:16 paired incisions documented;—his fear calming when it learned to count.

Yael worked fast in the slow way that convinces objects to cooperate. She misted the outer linen, not wet but persuaded, then warmed the area over the old repair stitch with air from a bulb blower until the fibers remembered a kinder day. She slid a Japanese paper strip beneath the thread to keep it from dragging the weave, then teased a knot that had been tied by someone who trusted time too much.

The outer layer lifted like an eyelid.

Arielle’s breath caught. Underneath, the inner binding showed—finer linen, tighter weave, older. The faint cuts were clearer here, deliberate and regular. Serva veritatem resolved again out of arithmetic. Between clusters, the two paired marks sat like parentheses around a thing not yet said.

"The inner wrap is intact," Yael murmured. "No insect ingress. No rodent nibble." She shifted the lamp, turned the jar a degree. "See this? The pitch seam overran at the lip and self-sealed. Whoever sealed it wanted their future to be someone else's problem."

"Sounds like us," Karim said under his breath.

Yael switched tools. "We have two choices. One: borescope through the pitch without breaking the seal—risk is minimal, image is stingy. Two: we cut the seam. If we cut, we cut a hairline—knife soft-warm, not hot—and we brace for the sound it will make in your chest."

Arielle looked at the jar and felt something settle that had been pacing all day. "We cut," she said. "With witnesses. With names in the room."

Mar Ephrem lifted a brow. "You have mine. Yael?"

Yael's eyes flicked to Jonas. "He'll keep the room from making mistakes that carry guns. I'll keep the room from making mistakes that carry scalpels." She nodded. "I'm your yes. But slow."

Karim swallowed. "And me?"

"You count," Yael said. "And you remember. Memory is a tool."

He straightened. "I can do that."

The chant climbed a step and changed mode—Vespers moving through its old bones. In the space between verses, footsteps crossed the courtyard and stopped somewhere near the outer door. They did not knock. They waited. The chant resumed.

Yael took out a scalpel, sized like something a toy surgeon might use and sharp enough to edit a life. She steadied her hand on the cradle's rim and looked once at Arielle. "Together," she said. "We all own this cut."

Arielle set her palm on the table and nodded. "Do it."

Yael traced the seam with the blade's back first, teaching it the path. Then she turned the edge and leaned a breath's weight forward. Pitch yields like glass that has forgotten how. The first fracture sounded less like a crack than a hair being plucked; it ran a centimeter and stopped, neat as a calligrapher's line.

Karim's time-stamp ticked—18:27 first cut initiated—and his hand shook only after he had finished typing.

Yael made a second stroke, then a third, each paced to the chant. A scent rose—old resin and older dust, a sweetness that had survived cruelty. Arielle felt it in her sinuses like a memory of childhood winters. She shut her eyes a heartbeat and saw her father's hand, ink-stained and steady, pressing a lens closer to a shard of text no one else had cared about until he had decided it mattered.

"Last pass," Yael said softly.

The knife drew a final line. The seam parted the width of a thread. Air exhaled—dry, cool—out of a space that had not breathed in two millennia.

They did not speak. They listened. Sometimes rooms tell you what you've done.

"Light," Yael said.

Karim angled the lamp. Yael eased the borescope into the hairline like a prayer slipped under a door. The tiny lens slid along pitch without touching the linen underneath, and the monitor on her phone lit in grayscale: a tunnel of resin, then a void, then—

Arielle's hand tightened on the table before she knew it had moved.

Not fragments. Not loose sheets.

Scroll.

Tightly wound, edges dark where time had browned the fibers, the outermost turn stitched at two points with a protein glue that had held when empires didn't. Along the edge, in the first sliver of visible script, letters curved—Estrangela, not Hebrew—black on pale, ink that had kept its arrogance.

Mar Ephrem crossed himself the old way—forehead, belly, shoulder, shoulder—and did not apologize.

"Alive," Yael whispered. "It's alive."

Karim stared, then laughed once, a dry sound that broke into something like a sob. "We did it," he said, almost accusing the room. "We actually did it."

Arielle didn't move. The watcher's hand wasn't hovering now. It was here, palm down beside hers on the table wood, not blessing, not warning. Witnessing.

Footsteps in the court. Closer. Then the wrong knock—three quick, one long—at the outer door. The chant kept going, as if it had survived worse interruptions.

Yael didn't lift the borescope. "We close the seam with paper and wait," she said, voice precise. "We do nothing loud until the psalm ends."

Mar Ephrem went up, every inch of him a man who had decided long ago what he would and would not allow in his house. Jonas's knife lay on the table where he had placed it without thinking, its blade dull in lamplight, its purpose temporarily inherited by a sliver of surgical steel.

The borescope image steadied on the stitched edge of the first turn. Ink traced a word Arielle could almost sound with her tongue. Her lips shaped it before her mind approved.

"Mar…" she breathed. Not "Mary." Not "Mark." Something older wrapped in the same bones.

The door above opened.

“Good evening, Father,” a calm voice said in English. “We come with courtesy and a warrant.”

Matthias Calder.

Yael’s hand didn’t shake.

“Paper,” she said. “Quick.”

Karim passed the Japanese strip. Yael laid it along the hairline and let the pitch kiss it shut like a lid deciding it wasn’t time yet.

Jonas looked up toward the stair. The chant lifted and held, the psalm’s line hanging like a tightrope over a street full of uniforms.

“Ready?” he asked the room.

Upstairs, hinges breathed.

“Good evening, Father,” Matthias said again, his voice the temperature of paper. “Courtesy. And a warrant.”

Mar Ephrem’s reply came wrapped in patience. “Courtesy always enters first. Warrant waits its turn. We are at Ramsho. You may sit in the chapel or walk in the court. You may not place your shoes where the Gospel stands.”

A pause. The cane touched stone once, measured, as if agreeing to a timing it did not choose.

“Of course,” Matthias said. “We are men of seasons.”

The door closed with the kind of gentleness that says it could be opened harder.

Below, Yael slid the last strip of Japanese paper across the hairline and pressed it with a bone folder until the seam remembered how to be a seam. The resin smell retreated, sweet and old. Karim logged the time, his pulse finally finding the chant’s slow measure.

"Wrap," Yael said.

Arielle refolded the outer linen, the repaired stitch lying flat as if it had always been honest. Yael nodded once, stripped her gloves, and tugged the sewn belly straps from the chair back.

"Back on," she told Arielle. "If they search, I want their hands on your bag, not your ribs."

Jonas had already moved to the far door—the sacristy passage. "He'll sit the chant out," he said. "He knows a storm doesn't knock twice on the same door. We have ten, maybe twelve minutes before courtesy grows teeth."

Mar Ephrem descended, a thin smile cutting his beard. "They are sitting in the back pew like schoolboys who have been told to behave. The inspector crosses his legs. The other one doesn't."

"Ring?" Karim asked.

"A modest one," the abbot said. "But rings don't tell you what hand they serve."

He opened a cupboard and lifted out a Gospel chest—carved cedar, brass corners dulled by thumb and century. He set it on the table and lined it with a clean linen. The thing had a weight of its own history.

"No," Arielle said, sudden, surprising herself. "Not the chest. We won't use the altar like a cupboard."

Mar Ephrem inclined his head, accepting the boundary. "Good," he said simply. "Then we use the ordinary scandal of coats."

Yael cinched the straps. The jar settled against Arielle's belly, a cool, steady gravity. Jonas adjusted the coat's hem to turn burden into posture, tucking the brim of the faded cap until she looked like one more pilgrim who had walked too far for her knees to forgive her. Karim slung the empty pack across his shoulder and made it look heavy.

The chant rose, round and old, pouring into the stones like oil. It drowned clock time and replaced it with something slower and less forgiving.

"Side gate," Mar Ephrem said. He pressed the key into Jonas's palm. "Talk to it first. It's a proud lock."

"What do you say to a proud lock?" Karim asked, thin grin showing.

"Please," the abbot said. "And then thank you."

They moved as if they belonged to the room. Jonas cracked the sacristy door and listened with his whole face. He ghosted into the shadow between chapel and court, measuring the voids between verse and response. Arielle followed, keeping the jar's weight inside her breath. Karim closed the passage behind them, touching wood with the respect of thieves borrowing a saint's hallway.

At the side gate, the key sulked until Jonas murmured something that could have been a prayer or a curse with its vowels softened. The bolt drew back. Night came in on a breath that smelled of basil and hot tar cooling.

They stepped into the court. The chapel windows shone like small, obedient moons. Inside, silhouettes made a respectful row—two officials' shoulders squared against patience, Matthias's head bowed like a reader with his place marked.

"Right at the well," Mar Ephrem had said. They turned right. The basalt lip glimmered, damp with a day's use. A cat watched them with the generous boredom of creatures who own their own hours.

They climbed to the roof and crossed to the crawl. The slit took them one at a time, shaving them down to essentials: palms, elbows, resolve. The jar pressed with every breath. Arielle counted the inches between stone and sky and turned them into will.

They spilled onto the Ethiopians' terrace. Laundry snapped like flags between the white domes. From here, the Old City was a genealogy of roofs. Far off, the Dome had gone to brass in the not-yet-night. A gull cut across the view like a wrong note that had learned to fit the song.

Jonas leaned close, voice a thread. "Zion Gate," he said. "Then a car. Ein Karem if we can buy the road—Yael's nun with the icon lab. If the road is closed, we drop to Lev's fixer and change our names for an hour."

"Yael?" Arielle asked.

"She stays," Jonas said. "She'll be our noise and our witness. If they press, she'll make the room smaller with questions until the hour burns."

"We're splitting?" Karim said, too loud, then swallowed it. "Okay."

Jonas's gaze flicked to Arielle. "You up for stairs?"

"I'm up for what's in front of me," she said. "Heights are a rumor."

He gave the flicker of a smile. "Good answer."

They worked the roofs like a sentence only some people knew how to read. Twice Jonas's hand went up—still—and they breathed shadow while men in clean coats passed below with patient eyes and a chain flashing at a wrist. The ring didn't look at the sky. Why would a ring look up?

At the last parapet, Jonas pointed to a carpenter's ladder propped like an apology. They climbed down into a corridor that smelled of wet stone and burnt sugar. The Muristan fountain ticked somewhere to their left, counting a kind of time that had no patience for pursuit.

A figure turned the corner ahead and stopped, as if he had known exactly where to find them because he had drawn the map himself.

Matthias did not block the way. He did not even move to share it. He simply set his cane lightly on the stone and said, "When you open it, and you will—choose a table that doesn't wobble."

"We have a table," Jonas said. "It belongs to men who believe responsibility is heavier than headlines."

Matthias's mouth did not smile. His eyes did. "Then you have chosen well." He tipped his head toward the chapel's low windows. "The chant suits you, Doctor Hale. Your father liked it too."

The words struck like a rung hit by a passing shoulder. Arielle's hand tightened on the sack it did not carry. "You knew him."

"I know the kind of man who prefers light even when the light is unfair," Matthias said. "He bought bread and did not bring it back." He regarded her a moment longer than courtesy permits and then stepped sideways, giving them the width of the world. "Go. You have a head start measured in verses, not miles."

"Why help us?" Karim asked, unable not to.

"I am helping a fact," Matthias said. "If I help you to help it, that is a side effect I can live with." He tapped the cane once and turned away, the sound dry as a match struck and not used.

They moved. Through the last web of lanes and out toward the gate that had been patched and repatched by empires that had all learned humility too late. The stones of Zion Gate were pitted with old violence; the road beyond sloped toward a city that was Jerusalem and not Jerusalem, softer at the edges, full of gardens and the smell of damp earth. The sky above the ridge held on to its last color like a good secret.

At the shadow of the gate, Jonas stopped. He scanned, reading the way cars flow and men don't. He nodded once. "Taxi," he said. "Blue stripe. Driver with a cigarette he doesn't enjoy and a radio tuned to wrong music. He owes Lev a favor and me worse."

As if conjured, the cab rolled to the curb, as reluctant as a mule. The driver leaned, squinted, and lifted his chin in a way that meant a great deal in a place where contracts still enjoy handshakes.

"Where?" he said.

"Ein Karem," Jonas answered. "The convent above the spring."

The driver shrugged, the local way of saying I've done dumber things for people I liked less. "Meter's broken," he said.

"Of course it is," Jonas said, and opened the back door.

Arielle slid in first, the jar cradled by Yael's straps and her ribs. Karim followed, clutching the empty pack like a confession. Jonas took the front and didn't sit back.

The city slid by—stone giving way to green, roofs giving way to trees, the last light catching terraced hills like old writing. Arielle looked down at the woven sack in her lap, at her empty hands, and felt the real weight against her body where no one could see.

Her phone buzzed once.

A photo: the scriptorium table, Yael's gloved hand on the cradle, Mar Ephrem's sleeve. In the corner of the frame, the Gospel chest sat open and empty, showing nothing at all.

A second buzz. Two words from an unknown number that was not unknown: for bread.

She closed her eyes. When she opened them, the road curved, and Jerusalem fell behind the hill like a breath finally exhaled.

They drove toward a room with exits and a table that would not wobble.

Ein Karem rose out of the folds of the hills like a village that had learned to keep its voice low. Stone terraces climbed in narrow ribs; cypress threaded the sky; the last light clung to vine leaves as if reluctant to let the day be finished. The taxi nosed along a lane so tight the mirrors considered prayer, then stopped beside a wall veined with bougainvillea.

"Here," the driver said, as if he'd delivered them to a thought they'd been having for a long time. He stubbed his cigarette with relief and didn't watch them go.

They followed a path that ran like a scar along the slope. Water spoke somewhere below—Mary's Spring, throwing its silver into the trough as it had when soldiers and saints were all simply thirsty. Above the spring, a compound of pale stone held its corners against time. A small bell hung idle over a wooden gate. The paint had been persuaded to stay by hands that knew better than to insist.

Jonas pulled the bell once. Footsteps crossed a courtyard. The gate opened a hand's width.

A woman regarded them through the gap with the calm of someone who knows exactly how much the world can demand and still be answered. Her veil was gray, her sleeves pushed to the elbow, her fingers stained faintly with ochre and rabbit-skin glue. Laughter lines bracketed a mouth that didn't waste them.

"Sister Miriam," Jonas said, the name balanced like an offering.

"You've brought dust," she said, and opened the gate. "Come before the day decides it belongs to someone else."

The courtyard smelled of lemon leaves and old stone. A narrow stair rose to a workroom under the eaves—a long north window, a carpenter's bench the size of a small boat, drying racks lined with icons in progress: gilding masked with clay, egg tempera underpaint cooling toward the image it meant to be. Brushes lay wrapped in linen like liturgical tools; a brass kettle muttered on a single burner as if everything important had been postponed until it boiled.

Sister Miriam took them in with a conservator's economy. Her gaze found the woven sack, slid past it, weighed Arielle's posture, stopped at the coat's line. She nodded once, to herself. "Yael called," she said. "I told her yes before she finished the question."

"We need a table that doesn't wobble," Jonas said.

She patted the bench. "This doesn't wobble. Men have tried."

Arielle eased out of the coat. The straps released with small, shy clicks. Jonas set his palms under the jar as it left her body and the weight drew its own breath on the wood. For a moment, no one spoke. The room's silence wasn't fear; it was manners.

"Ground rules," Sister Miriam said, gloving without looking. "We don't behave like tourists or saints. We behave like hands attached to brains. Nothing touches pitch without consent. If the jar decides to cry, we let it. I have blotter and patience." She flicked a look at Jonas. "And exits."

Jonas had already read them: a back stair tucked behind a cupboard; a sliding panel that knew which century it belonged to; a garden door that opened on shadows the hill approved. He nodded once.

Karim set his phone to record, the title field already waiting: Ein Karem – Night Opening. He placed the bread on the counter near the kettle and, without being told, sliced it into six thick pieces. The smell of sesame and heat spread like a permission slip.

Sister Miriam circled the jar, taking it in the way iconographers read faces—proportion before pigment. "Herodian matrix," she murmured, nostrils tightening at the old sweetness of pitch the way some people do at incense. "Yael's hands are on the outer linen. Good. She has quick mercy." Her eyes touched the seam, the repaired stitch. "You peeked."

"We confirmed it's a scroll," Yael's voice said from the phone speaker; Arielle had put her on a line that pretended to be silent. "Estrangela on the outer turn. Stitches at two points. No insect ingress."

Sister Miriam smiled, the way colleagues do when a friend has already taken the first careful risk. "Then we take the second." She pulled a lamp close, raked light along the weave, and found the little paired cuts near the seam with a fingertip that didn't touch. "Names," she said, as if the linen had confided it to her over tea. "Two points where the scribe wanted breath before ink."

Arielle felt the watcher's prickle, not above her now but level with her shoulder—the sense of being companioned by something that wanted neither credit nor control. She set both palms on the bench, felt the wood's scarred patience. "We open," she said. "With you as witness. And with Yael in our pocket. We owe the truth a better room than running."

Sister Miriam nodded once and made the sign of the cross with a motion so practiced it barely disturbed the air. "Then we open. Slowly enough to keep our shame small."

She softened the seam with a whispered warmth from the kettle—steam directed through a narrow funnel until the pitch remembered pliancy. A scalpel found the hairline Yael had cut and walked it a millimeter farther, then another. The resin breathed out a sweetness that had no word but age. Karim timestamped; Jonas's eyes never left the door; Arielle kept the jar steady in its cradle, her breath borrowing the lamp's measure.

When the seam accepted their decision, Sister Miriam laid two strips of Japanese paper along it and lifted the lid with a lift so slight it would not have startled a lily. Air the temperature of old caves reached up to meet them.

Inside: the tight scroll, darkened on the edge where centuries had cooked it gently, the first turn stitched with animal glue the color of amber. Along that edge, the Estrangela hand showed itself without apology—bold, round, letterforms standing as if they had practiced in their sleep.

Sister Miriam didn't reach. She let the sight settle, the way you let a grief sit in the chair before you ask its name. "Photograph," she said.

Karim leaned in. "God," he breathed, and took the first image without flash. The ink held its dignity, the strokes fat with certainty. He took a second shot. "The first word—Mar," he whispered, and then, halting, "Mar... Ya..."

"Not Mary," Sister Miriam said, close but not touching. "Mar is master, lord, a title in our tongue. Mar begins names that carry weight: Mar Ya'qob, Mar Yohannan. Or a reverence before a name not meant to be said easily." She glanced at Arielle. "The scribe is ours. Syriac bones. This is not a Judean scribal hand."

Arielle's chest went cold and hot at once. "Then it wasn't hidden by Essenes alone."

"Nothing this old was done by one set of hands," Sister Miriam said. "You'll find that truth hates monocultures."

Jonas's head tilted. In the lane below, a car climbed slow, the engine working against the hill. A door thumped shut, then another. The sound didn't say pursuit; it said Jerusalem doing what nights do. He let his hand stay on his thigh.

Sister Miriam slid a microspatula under the amber stitches and coaxed one free. It came with the sigh of a small, stubborn habit giving up. She set the brittle thread in a saucer as if it were precious. It was.

"Lift," she said. "Only to see if the inner wrap has teeth."

Arielle helped her rock the outer turn a fraction. Inside, under the first leaf, something paler lay—a guard slip of finer linen pressed close to the scroll's first written face, as if someone had tucked a handkerchief over a sleeping mouth.

Sister Miriam smiled with one side of her mouth. "A scribe who had seen too much dust. Or a woman who insisted. Either way, someone loved this."

Karim's voice had become the thin, steady line you use to cross ice. "Can you read the second word?"

Sister Miriam did not lean. She let the lamp do the work and the old ink accept it. "Mar... Ya... hanan." She looked up. "Yohannan. John."

"John who?" Karim whispered, and then understood his own question. He laughed once, softly, at the arrogance of centuries. "Right. Which one."

"Many Johns," Sister Miriam said. "But only one whose name is tied to this valley's springs." She nodded toward the dark outside. "We are in his village."

Footsteps on the path below. Male voices, low, not careful. One laughed in the way men laugh when they are bored and paid. Jonas's hand moved toward the window, then away. No shadows crossed the pane.

Sister Miriam looked from the scroll to Arielle. "Do you need the first line tonight? Or do you need the first breath to be in a room where no one is rehearsing their confiscation speech two streets away?"

Arielle's throat closed around an answer. It opened as something simpler than bravery: restraint. "We need it to live," she said. "And we need to be the kind of people it can survive."

Sister Miriam nodded once as if a student had finally answered a question old teachers ask on instinct. "Then we keep the outer turn closed," she said. "We record the edge. We replace the stitch with paper so the seam minds its manners. And we let John wait one more night before he clears his throat."

Karim deflated and then steadied. "Fog," he said. "We stay fog."

The kettle clicked off in a small surrender. Sister Miriam re-warmed the seam just enough to seat the lid without grudge. She set the Japanese paper along the hairline and burnished it with the bone folder until the line looked like patience again, not interruption.

Jonas checked the back stair. "We'll sleep in shifts," he said. "Arielle first. I'll take the door. Karim, you're the spine—you wake when anyone moves."

Karim raised a hand. "I'm good at being bone."

Sister Miriam poured tea that tasted faintly of sage and stone. She tore a piece of bread and placed it in Arielle's palm, then one on the bench beside the jar. "For your father," she said, as if she knew him. "He has been trying to bring this loaf home for a long time."

Arielle stared at the crumb on the wood, then at the curve of clay, then out into the dark where the spring kept talking to the hill as if it had never stopped. Her phone buzzed once. A photo from Yael: the chapel at St. Mark's lit like a bowl; Mar Ephrem's silhouette; a line of uniforms respectful and irritated. Under it, three words from an unknown number that weren't unknown anymore:

Hold the light.

She put the phone face down and leaned her forehead against the back of her hand until the bench's cool entered her skin.

Outside, Ein Karem turned the page to night. Inside, the jar rested, the seam clean, the first word breathed and put back to bed.

They would be thunder later. Tonight, they chose to be weather that saved what it carried.

Night thinned the edges of the hills until Ein Karem looked drawn in ink.

Sister Miriam's workroom settled into a steady breath—kettle ticking as it cooled, lamp chimneys purring, the faint rasp of a brush she moved across an icon in pauses that respected the jar the way you fall quiet near a sleeper. Karim drifted on a bench with his notebook open, the pen still in his fingers, as if he hadn't conceded anything to sleep except posture.

Jonas stood at the north window where the glass gave back the room in a dim reflection laid over the valley. He watched both images at once—the one outside, black-green and patient, and the one inside, four people trying to weigh a decision without breaking it.

Sister Miriam's brush paused above an unfinished sleeve of blue. "We don't paint icons," she said without looking up. "We write them. The verb matters. You answer what's already there, not impose yourself on it."

Arielle sat near the bench, palms flat to the wood, feeling its old certainty. "And if what's there refuses to be answered?"

"Then you sit longer," Sister Miriam said. "Or you admit you are not the one meant to ask the question."

Arielle glanced at the jar. The paper line at the seam lay so clean it looked inevitable. "It's been waiting two thousand years," she said. "It can wait a night."

"Most prophets would have done better with one more night," Sister Miriam said dryly, and gave the blue its stroke.

Jonas left the window and stepped onto the small back landing that opened to the garden. Crickets stitched the dark with their needles. He stood a long moment with his face toward the hill and the road's thin suture of light moving there. When he came back in, the air on him smelled of sage and stone.

"Road's quiet," he said. "Two cars from the lower lane, both local. No patience hanging about."

Karim made a noise that might have been relief. "I keep thinking we bought one calm hour and rented six hallucinations."

"We bought enough," Jonas said. He picked up the kettle, found it empty, and put it back the way people do when order calms them.

Arielle hadn't meant to speak yet. The words pressed anyway. "Damascus Gate. You and Lev said it like a weight. What happened?"

Jonas's jaw worked once, then eased. "A street rumor turned into a crowd faster than men with radios could tell it to stop," he said. "Too many exits. Not enough sense. Two teams went in and one didn't come out. I was on the one that did." He looked at Sister Miriam's icon for a beat as if asking it permission to say the rest. "The city taught me the difference between noise and consequence that day. I've never been good at forgetting teachers."

Silence folded over the words the way clean linen folds over a thing you don't want to stain. Arielle nodded. "So your rule is fog before thunder."

"My rule is survival before righteousness," Jonas said. "Righteousness gets to be useful later if you live."

Karim stirred, surfaced. "Is it later yet?"

"Almost," Sister Miriam murmured, listening to a clock no one else could hear. "You'll have visitors before the hour changes. Good ones."

"How do you—" Karim broke off when soft footfalls entered the courtyard below. Not caution, exactly. Courtesy that had learned to tread.

A moment later, the gate whispered and a small figure appeared in the doorway at the foot of the stair—a boy in a dark sweater with sleeves too long, cheeks pinked by night, eyes huge with errand. He carried a cloth-wrapped bundle in both hands the way you carry something that isn't light but shouldn't be dropped.

"Abuna sent me," he said in careful English when Sister Miriam appeared at the landing. "From St. Mark's."

Mar Ephrem's novice, then. Sister Miriam took the bundle and unwrapped bread still warm enough to make the cloth damp where the loaf sweated. A square of paper lay under it, letterhead printed in Syriac and English, a line scrawled under the addresses in a quick, ascetic hand:

Dawn. Witnesses. We come to you.

Beneath, a second line in smaller script: for bread.

Sister Miriam's mouth softened. "Tell your abuna the loaf arrived," she said. "And that our kettle is more faithful than our door."

The boy grinned at that—the grin you keep for people who don't make you choose between obedience and sense—and vanished with the same small, tidy steps.

Arielle read the note twice. Her father's two words sat on the paper like a candle left in a window. For bread. Something warm rose under the bit of bone where grief had been—something that felt less like hurt than like appetite finally making a claim again. She tore the loaf and set a piece on the bench beside the jar.

"Dawn," Jonas said. The word made the room change temperature. "Mar Ephrem, Yael, Sister Miriam. Four witnesses. Lev if he decides to be a rumor with a face."

"Lev will send a face and keep the rumor," Sister Miriam said. "That's how favors mature."

Karim rubbed his palms down his thighs and looked very much like a man trying to teach his fear to hold a cup without spilling. "If we're opening at dawn, we should sleep like people who are about to do something irreversible."

"Thirty on, thirty off," Jonas said. "I'll take first watch."

Sister Miriam nodded. "I'll take last," she said. "Old women outrun dawn better than soldiers."

Karim claimed the short bench with adolescent greed; sleep took him in three breaths. Jonas sat with his back to the garden door, head turned just enough to read the room and the night. Sister Miriam returned to her icon, giving the saint a line at the edge of a sleeve so fine it felt like whispering toward dignity. Arielle lay down on a coarse blanket, the jar's cradle within arm's reach, the bread's smell explaining something to her throat she hadn't realized it had been refusing.

Sleep didn't arrive as a mercy; it negotiated. When it came, it brought a dream that was more memory than invention: her father at their kitchen table with a map spread like a shawl, bread torn into warlike crumbs, his finger moving along wadis and Roman traces while the kettle insisted in the background. People think truth is a peak, he'd said once, eyes bright in the way that made you forgive him everything else. Most of the time it's a valley. It collects what runs off other men's certainties. You find it where the water stops arguing. She had been sixteen and had rolled her eyes and stolen another olive and loved him enough to wish he would talk about mortgages and gutters.

She woke to Jonas's hand on her shoulder, twice, gentle. The lamp had burned down to a memory of itself; the room had the thin feeling of hours on the wrong side of dawn. Through the open window, the spring argued softly with the hill. Karim muttered once in his sleep, then turned his face into his sleeve and went quiet. Sister Miriam's head had dropped forward; she had fallen asleep upright with a brush pinched in her fingers like a twig.

"Your turn," Jonas whispered.

Arielle sat up. The jar lay where she had left it, seam clean, cradle sure. She could feel the watcher's palm in the room—the way you feel a friend's steady inhale when both of you are quiet enough to count it. Not above. Not behind. Beside.

"Any movement?" she asked.

"Two patrol cars on the lower road," Jonas said. "They were looking for mischief and decided devotions would do. No one climbed."

He gave her the last of the tea, cold now and herbal, and knelt to wedge a folded scrap under the bench leg until it stopped floating. "Table doesn't wobble," he said, answering Matthias without saying his name.

Arielle smiled despite the hour. "We paid attention."

They shared a piece of bread from the good loaf. He took it like a soldier who had been taught to accept what is offered and not ask how much is left. For a few minutes, the room was only breath, and the small, mundane, defiant sound of chewing.

"Daniel Hale," Jonas said into the quiet. "He didn't make easy choices. He made deliberate ones. There's a difference."

"You knew him," Arielle said, not a question.

"I knew his work," Jonas said. "I saw him in a briefing once—five minutes on Jericho strata that saved ten hours of argument among men who preferred arguing to listening. He left bread on the table when he went. I remembered the smell." He met her eyes, then looked away. "I'm sorry for what the desert took and what it gave."

Arielle looked at the jar. "We might learn he was wrong," she said. The thought didn't terrify her as much as it had yesterday. "We might learn he was right in a way neither of us wanted."

"Right and wrong make poor tents," Jonas said. "But they burn warm."

Sister Miriam stirred, woke cleanly, set the brush down like a last word she was saving for later. She checked the window, the door, the jar. "Dawn will pretend it's late," she said. "It does that to avoid responsibilities."

The first light came not as color but as architecture—the garden's edges returning, the hill stepping forward, the room deciding it could see its own corners again. Birds began as if they had been poised all night with their beaks cocked.

Footsteps crossed the courtyard—measured, known. The gate clicked. Sister Miriam smiled into the light. "Our witnesses," she said.

Yael came first, hair plaited and tucked, a case in one hand and nothing in the other. Mar Ephrem followed with the boy from the night before carrying a thermos like the Holy Grail. A third man slipped in behind them with a bookbinder's apron peeking from under his coat—Lev's "face" for the morning, a craftsman with eyes that counted doors. Lev himself did not appear, which is how Lev honors a promise.

"Peace," Mar Ephrem said softly. "We brought coffee strong enough to lift two scrolls."

"Only one," Sister Miriam said. "We will lift the other with our eyes."

They gathered around the bench the way people do when they are about to watch something that will not forgive haste. Yael laid out gloves and paper, counted strips, set the lamp, and did not need to be told the table did not wobble.

Arielle looked from face to face—Yael's quick mercy; Mar Ephrem's old patience; Jonas's economy; Karim's bright, frightened tenderness; Sister Miriam's calm that had been hammered from humor and years. It felt like the right room because it didn't ask to be thanked.

"Ready?" she asked them, and herself.

"Ready," Jonas said.

"Ready," Yael echoed.

"Ready," Mar Ephrem said, and made a sign of the cross that drew a small doorway in the air for them to pass through.

Arielle set her hands on the jar.

Outside, the bell over the gate lifted its tongue and let it fall.

They opened the seam they had made, the paper giving way with the shockless surrender of something that knows why it's losing. Air moved—cool, cave-breathed. They raised the lid. Sister Miriam freed the little amber threads Yael had cut the night before and set them in a saucer where the light found them honest.

The outer turn lifted. The guard slip lay there like a kindness.

"Photograph," Yael said. "Then take the handkerchief off."

Karim made the images that would have to serve later when people wanted to argue about what they had all agreed they had seen. Arielle and Sister Miriam slid the guard slip aside. Ink met morning.

The first line stood without apology, Estrangela round and sure, the title riding like a small crown above the sentence.

Sister Miriam read it aloud in Syriac, the syllables weighty and clean. Then she translated, not in the voice of a courtroom or a pulpit, but like someone reading a letter to a family:

"This is the record of those born of Yohannan, called the Forerunner, through the daughters of the Covenant, kept against the days of forgetting."

Silence filled the room and did not feel empty.

Karim made a sound that wasn't quite a laugh and wasn't anything else, either. Mar Ephrem's eyes shone and then decided not to be theatrical. Yael's hand hovered over the margin as if it could bless without being called a blessing.

Arielle didn't cry. The watcher's hand laid itself, unmistakably now, alongside hers on the bench—the size of her father's, or a saint's, or just the shape of history when it finally chooses to keep company. Guard the truth, it said without saying, and for the first time the imperative didn't feel like an order. It felt like trust.

Down the hill, a car door slammed. Two voices argued with a third that always wins because it wears a uniform. Jonas's head tilted; Lev's "face" eased into the shadow by the garden door as if he had been cut from it.

Sister Miriam's voice stayed calm. "Second line," she said. "Before we run."

Arielle nodded. The morning leaned in.

They read.

Chapter Eight — Through the Daughters (Part 1)

The second line waited like a held breath.

Sister Miriam eased the guard slip aside; Yael angled the lamp; Karim's cursor blinked in the title field—Ein Karem - Dawn Reading—as if impatient to become record instead of promise.

Mar Ephrem nodded once. "Read," he said, voice pitched low, as if not to wake whatever history God had put to sleep in this room.

Sister Miriam traced the air over the first line without touching, then found the next and gave the Syriac its shape: round, assured, letters walking a road they had worn for centuries.

She translated softly, a sentence at a time, giving the room time to absorb:

"These are the keepers through the daughters of the Covenant—the Bnath Qyama—named by waters and houses, that the line be remembered when men forget."

Karim's pen scratched—Bnath Qyama (Syriac: vowed women; 'daughters of the Covenant')—then stilled as the next words gathered.

"At the spring in the hill of Kerem we were counted first."

Sister Miriam's eyes flicked up toward the open window, toward the green fold of the valley where Mary's Spring talked to stone. She smiled without moving her mouth.

"And at the ford of the river, Beyt 'Abarah, where Yohannan stood and named repentance, the names were bound again."

Karim leaned so close the lamp painted his cheekbone in brass. "Beth—Bethany across the Jordan," he whispered. "Qasr al-Yahud."

Arielle felt the jar's cool seep into her palms. A waypoint that wasn't metaphor. The text thought in places.

On the outer margin, faint, almost an afterthought, tiny ink pricks climbed like ants beside the lines—initial marks. Karim held his breath and read them downward: B—T—H—N—Y. He looked up, stunned into a grin that didn't dare be big. "Acrostic," he said. "BETHANY. It's literally spelling it."

Mar Ephrem's mouth tilted. "Scribes love to leave their maps where tyrants don't think to look."

The third line began with the same bold hand and something gentler under it—as if the scribe had paused to remember faces.

"Mariam of the ford; Hanna of Kerem; Salome who kept the lists; and Ya'el who carried the bread. Through these we bind the names of those born."

Arielle swallowed. The room seemed to pivot one degree around that last phrase—carried the bread—as if the scroll had reached forward to annotate their morning.

"Photograph," Yael murmured.

Karim obeyed—no flash, angles logged, lamp raked in thin increments. The ink held. The paper held. Arielle's hands held.

Outside, a car labored up the lane and stopped. Doors shut, not cautious, not urgent—official. Jonas's head turned a fraction. Lev's "face" in the apron slid closer to the garden door as if he'd been poured from the shadow.

Sister Miriam didn't look away from the text. "We can finish the line before courtesy grows teeth," she said. "Fourth begins the genealogies. The little paired marks will tell us where the daughters branch."

She read:

"From Mariam—two. From Hanna—one. From Salome—one. Their households took the names of water and bread that they might be hidden in plain tables."

Yael's eyebrow ticked. "Hidden where?" she said, mostly to herself. "Ledgers. Baptismal lists. Bakery accounts. Saints carved small upon receipts."

Karim's fingers flew—margin letters = BETHANY; fourth line: distribution of branches; watch for household terms disguised as trades (bread/water). He forced his breath slow. "If it's a ledger wrapped as scripture, no one who hunts relics will know where to file it."

A knuckle touched wood at the gate. Not a knock so much as a presence making itself polite.

Sister Miriam set the guard slip gently back over the first turn. "We've taken enough," she said. "Now we protect what we know."

Yael reseated the seam with Japanese paper and a bone folder; the hairline faded back into something that looked inevitable. Jonas stepped to the landing. Through the slats of the stair he could see two men in municipal coats, hats bare. No ring flashed, which only meant the ring had learned manners.

Sister Miriam slipped the jar's straps toward Arielle with a motion that felt like a blessing and a dare. "Fog," she said. "You carry. We make three copies of the images—now."

Karim popped the microSD and slid it into a slim, unlovely plastic case. Yael produced two more, labeled each with a stub of pencil—bread-1, bread-2, bread-3—because names take power away from panic. She passed one to Mar Ephrem, who tucked it beneath the scarf at his neck. The second she handed to Lev's "face," who made it disappear with a craftsman's economy. The third she pressed into Sister Miriam's palm. "If anyone asks, it's receipts," she said. "Because it is."

The knock repeated, the kind of patience that likes to be admired.

Sister Miriam opened the gate a hand's width. "We're at prayer," she said. "You may leave your shoes and your warrant with the lemon tree. I will water whichever deserves it."

The taller inspector smiled like a person on page one of a manual. "Only a moment, Sister. A question about visitors."

"Then ask the spring," she said, and began to close the gate.

The second man moved his foot, just enough to keep the conversation going. He didn't smile. Behind him, halfway down the lane, two plain sedans waited where night hides in daylight.

Matthias's courtesy had ended. A different office had clocked in.

Jonas's voice came low. "We go," he said. "Back stairs, garden wall, goat path to the lower road. Lev's handoff at the fig tree. One minute to clear the lane."

Arielle felt the straps bite her shoulders and welcomed the ache. "Protocol?"

"Same words, new directions," Jonas said. "Fog in front, thunder later."

Mar Ephrem touched Arielle's sleeve, then the jar through the cloth, as if completing a circuit. "Go with our bad habits," he said. "We have many; they will confuse your enemies."

Sister Miriam made a small doorway in the air again and waved them through it with two fingers. "Take the loaf," she told Karim. "Let them see it. Let them remember they were children once."

They moved—Arielle first, the jar settling against her ribs like a second rhythm; Jonas flowing point without theatrics; Karim with the bread and the decoy pack; Lev's "face" last, doors closing softly behind him the way a rumor chooses to be true only to the people who need it.

The back stair smelled of lemon oil and cool dust. The garden wall took the scuff of Jonas's shoe and offered him the purchase he asked for. The goat path ran like a pencil line through thyme and rock; it found the lower road because it had always found it.

At the fig tree, a white van sat where no van had any business being at this hour unless it belonged to a baker or a plan. The driver leaned with an elbow out the open window and a cigarette he didn't enjoy. He looked at Jonas the way men look at traffic: with resignation and competence.

Lev's face melted into the passenger seat and became a man who had nothing to do with anything. Jonas ushered Arielle and Karim into the back and closed the doors without letting them thunk. The van rolled before the breath they'd been holding realized it could leave.

In the mirror, the convent's wall slid away; Sister Miriam's lemon tree kept its counsel. The inspectors at the gate wrote something down that would become a report someone would pretend to read.

Arielle braced her palm on the jar through the coat—habit now, not superstition. The images in her pocket—bread-1—felt light and vast at once. Karim cradled the real loaf and grinned at it like a person newly introduced to gravity.

"Qasr al-Yahud?" he said, unable not to.

"First the Quarter," Jonas said. "St. Mark's. We cache a copy where the city remembers what it owes us. Then the river."

"Then the river," Arielle echoed, and the words didn't feel like a plan so much as the next obvious stone.

The van shouldered the hill and found the road that threaded the city's bone. Behind them, Ein Karem sank back into its folds. Ahead, Jerusalem drew itself up for another day of being unbearable and holy.

The watcher's hand kept pace, not above, not ahead. Beside. As they turned toward the Old City, Arielle felt it tip—just slightly—toward the east, as if it had always known the way to water.

The van shouldered the city's morning like a barge through reeds. Jonas kept his eyes on mirrors and corners; Lev's driver kept his on what's in front of men like Jonas.

They slid into the Armenian Quarter under a bell that hadn't decided how cheerful to be. At St. Mark's, the side gate accepted the key the way proud locks do when they've been flattered by name. Mar Ephrem met them in the passage with coffee that apologized for nothing.

"Your inspectors admired our lemon tree," he said dryly. "It will grow a report."

Arielle pressed the thin plastic into his palm—bread-2. "Witness, not archive," she said.

"Witness is a better word," he answered, and tucked it beneath his collar as if he were smuggling a blessing. He cut the remaining loaf in half and slid one into the woven sack. "For the road that forgets to be gentle."

They didn't linger. The van found the seam of traffic that unstitched toward the east—Mount Scopus lifting, olive-toned, then the sudden drop: chalk hills folding into themselves, a road curling from prayer to arithmetic. The Sea Level marker flashed by like a joke stone told to tourists; beyond it the world kept falling—Wadi Qelt a raw gash to their right with St. George Monastery clinging to its cliff like a thought that refused to be dislodged. Air thinned, then thickened, warming with salt and distance. The desert made its own weather.

Karim pressed his forehead to the glass and narrated to himself: "Roman traces, Hasmonean cut, Herod's cruelty, Nabatean patience." He looked ten and old at once.

"Drink," Jonas said, handing a bottle back over his shoulder without looking. "Below sea level is where men forget water needs asking."

They reached Jericho road—flat, pale, the horizon a steel ribbon—and turned south. The Jordan Valley breathed reeds and dust. On the left, dates hung in disciplined ranks under nets; on the right, a ribbon of green betrayed a river that would rather be myth but insists on being water.

The baptism site—Qasr al-Yahud—announced itself with low railings, a wooden deck, flags that have learned to share poles, and a silence that isn't silence so much as reverence from people who don't agree on what they revere. A few early pilgrims in white stood barefoot on steps stained the color of long prayers. Across the narrow river, the Jordanian side—al-Maghtas—showed low ruins and a chapel's bones, heat wobbling the air between.

Jonas scanned uniforms. Border Police at the gate; two conscripts at ease; a priest in black over by the flagpoles arguing quietly with a tour guide about schedules as if the Holy Spirit kept office hours.

"Cover?" Karim asked, aimless with adrenaline.

"Pilgrims with bread," Jonas said. "And a sister waiting for us at the spring. No one denies either for long."

They paid the small fee no one mentioned and walked with the slow gravity of people who had chosen to be ordinary. Arielle kept the jar under the coat, straps bite-firm, the woven sack with half a loaf cradled openly in the crook of her arm. Karim went ahead with his phone held like a prayer book, filming nothing, filming everything.

At the rail, the river slipped by the color of tea left too long. A dragonfly stitched its own faith along the surface. The wooden steps descended to the water in six worn slats. Across the narrow span, two monks dipped a metal cross and lifted it dripping as if explaining persistence to the air.

Arielle didn't move. She didn't need to. The text had already told her where to look.

Margin letters had spelled BETHANY; the lines had named water and houses; the scribe had thought in places. Here, the place thought back: Bethany beyond the Jordan, Beyt 'Abarah. House of crossing.

"Look low," she said. "Not at what's been added, at what's been reused."

Karim crouched at the step's edge, eyes narrowing as he let the modern carpentry fall away. Beneath the beam, one of the support stones was older than its job—river-smoothed, rehoused. Along its face, faint and stubborn, two carved letters rode the plane—Estrangela so weathered it preferred memory to sight: ܒ and ܢ. Beth—Nun. The beginning of Bethanya.

Karim's breath hitched. "He left us a house on the water," he whispered.

"Photograph," Yael said from the phone in Arielle's pocket, her voice small and bossy like conscience. "Rake with your shadow. Angle twice. Log the step."

Karim obeyed. A guard glanced once, saw bread, robes, a woman in a coat too warm for the hour, and looked away. Jonas didn't look at the guard; he looked at the guard's partner's boredom and read the fifteen minutes it would buy.

"Two more," Arielle said, scanning the stone faces built into new things. Under the rail—another reused block: a shallow cross pattée and, beside it, a scratched ܝ, like a fishbone—Yodh. Further along, set low near the waterline, a stone half-buried in algae, its top line just showing: ܬ. Taw.

"B—Y—T," Karim murmured. Beyt. House.

Mar Ephrem's voice, miles away, seemed to answer in her head: Scribes love to leave maps where tyrants don't think to look. The river made its own amen.

On the far bank, a Jordanian guard lifted binoculars and didn't shout. He had seen stranger pieties before breakfast.

"Time," Jonas said gently.

They backed away with the same slowness, as if leaving a sickbed or a nursery. A woman in a white robe passed them without seeing, lips moving, tears plain and honest on her face. Karim offered her a piece of bread. She took it and laughed through the tears as if you could be both, and why not.

At the top of the path, a custodian in a Custody of the Holy Land windbreaker approached with a clipboard he didn't care about. He was fifty, sun-browned, and had a face that looked like it could fix pipes or arguments.

"You're early," he said. "Early is the right time to see what's old. Later, it all looks like schedule."

Arielle met his eyes and saw the weight they carried without showing. "We're making a record," she said. "For when memory comes under pressure."

He nodded once. "It always does." He lifted his chin toward the river. "This winter the floods pulled old stones out of the mud by the reeds. We put them in a crate because no one pays attention to a crate." He tipped his head toward a shed painted the color of bureaucratic permission. "If you happened to open the wrong one, I would be forced to look at my shoes."

Jonas considered the man the way you consider a bridge you didn't plan to cross and then do.

The crate waited inside on a concrete floor that had seen more honest work than reports. Within, a tangle of river-scraped stone and wood glowed damp. On top lay a palm-sized scrap of linen matted with silt and a smell of pitch thin as rumor. Arielle lifted it with both hands before her mind could argue for gloves. The weave was fine, older than the dust on the custodian's boots. Along one edge, two small paired incisions sat like quotation marks around absence.

Karim made a sound he hadn't learned in any lab.

"Photographs," Yael whispered through the pocket. "And then paper. Wrap it like you're wrapping someone else's wound."

The custodian cleared his throat as if something had landed there. "I was going to take that to a man with forms," he said. "Tomorrow."

"You still can," Jonas said. "And you'll have witnesses for what you brought him first."

The man nodded. "My mother used to say witnesses are what keep a house upright when the ground shifts." He glanced at the half loaf in Karim's hands. "She said it about bread too."

They left a copy—bread-4—taped on the underside of the crate lid where men with forms wouldn't think to check. The custodian looked at it once and then chose never to have seen it. He shook Jonas's hand like a man who knew bargains and preferred vows.

Outside, the light had sharpened toward noon. Heat rose off the river in small, patient columns. Across the water, a Jordanian guide lifted a plastic bucket of baptisms and poured it into the river like an offering back.

"Go," Jonas said, the edge back in his voice. "The road grows eyes after eleven."

They reached the van just as a silver sedan with shaded windows pulled into the far lot and performed the complicated ritual of being unremarkable. A door opened. A ring showed and then politely vanished.

"Which way?" the driver asked, eyes forward.

"North a breath," Jonas said, "then west. We change our minds where the valley bends."

As the van rolled, Arielle kept her hand flat over the jar and felt the watcher's palm settle next to it, steady, not possessive. The paired marks on the linen scrap ghosted their way through her touch. The letters in the stone—ܐ , ܒ—had spelled house where the water remembers.

"Proof," Karim said softly, half to himself. "Not thunder. Structure."

"Thunder later," Arielle answered. "When the table doesn't wobble."

They climbed from the valley floor toward the white heat of the hills. Behind them, the river curled back on itself like a line waiting for its next word.

Chapter Nine — The House of Crossing

The desert slid off them in layers as the van climbed; Jericho's palms gave way to chalk and thorn; then, at last, stone began speaking Jerusalem again.

"St. Mark's first," Jonas said. "Witness before water turns into rumor."

Arielle nodded, palm flat to the jar under her coat, the new scrap of linen—river-wet, pitch-scented—tucked in a paper sleeve inside her shirt. The paired incisions cut into its edge pressed against the page like quotation marks around a missing sentence. She felt absurdly protective of the absence.

They reached the Armenian Quarter under a bell that chose sober over cheerful. The side gate took Mar Ephrem's key with pride; the court received them with lemon and basalt.

"Bread," the abbot said by way of greeting, and smiled at the halved loaf in Karim's arms as if the gospel had arrived already sliced.

Arielle pressed the bread-1 microcard into his palm. "Second lines. Bnath Qyama, Bethany acrostic, water and houses."

Mar Ephrem slid it beneath his collar as if it had always belonged there and then glanced at Arielle's coat with a look that said he knew exactly what else belonged where. "Yael's on her way," he added. "They came back with a warrant hungry for shoes. We fed it to the lemon tree."

They didn't pause. In the scriptorium, the jar settled into its cradle with the relief of a backpack shrugged off at dusk. Yael arrived five minutes later with chalk on her sleeve, set the phone to airplane mode with the reflex of a woman who has learned which wings attract hawks, and lifted the river scrap with a gloved hand.

“Pitch,” she murmured. “Herodian glue. And our paired cuts again. Your river has a memory problem; it keeps returning what men try to drown.”

Karim grinned around exhaustion, then sobered. “The guard at Qasr al-Yahud handed us a crate without handing it to us. We left bread–4 on the lid.”

“Good,” Yael said. “Witness grows roots that way.”

Jonas checked vents and crawl spaces. “We read one more margin,” he said. “Then we make the city work for our hour.”

Sister Miriam couldn’t leave the convent, but her voice came clean and small from Arielle’s pocket. The room took its cue from yesterday—lamp raked low, linen coaxed, knife withheld. They did not lift the lid. They watched the outer margin by the seam as the light ran along it like a messenger.

Karim held his breath. “Letters,” he whispered. Tiny pricks climbed the edge again, this time not spelling BETHANY but something with harder bones. “ܪ … ܘ … ܟ … ܡ,” he sounded out, mouth shaping old shapes. “M—K—W—R.”

“Mekawer,” Yael said softly—the Arabic for Machaerus, Herod’s knife-fortress above the Salt Sea’s eastern rim.

Arielle felt it land—the text thinking in places, the places stitching a road under their feet. “Water, then house,” she said. “Now the mountain.”

“Your father would have called it a triangulation,” Mar Ephrem said. “Water, bread, and a blade-shaped hill.”

Jonas’s eyes flicked to the door. “Jordan again,” he said. “Jordanian side this time.”

Arielle imagined the basalt mesa of Mukawir—the Greek theater Herod added for applause, the peristyle court where a girl's dance had turned into a man's regret, the cisterns that remembered thirst. Josephus had written it coolly; time had kept it hot. Through the daughters, the scroll had said. In the world's most famous story about a daughter, what had the scribe seen fit to keep or correct?

Bootsteps on stone in the court above. The careful, well-fed tread of men who had spent the morning ironing their smiles.

"Courtesy again," Yael said.

"Courtesy with paperwork," Mar Ephrem answered, moving toward the stairs. He lifted an eyebrow at Jonas. "You have a plan that will misbehave politely?"

"We split," Jonas said. "Arielle and I go south gate to Mount Zion for a car. Karim, you and Yael carry the decoy to the École again and make a show of arguing over cataloging. Lev's fixer will meet us at Allenby if the wind's right."

"Border?" Yael hissed.

"Not with the jar," Jonas said. "Not today. We go as heads first, hands later." He tapped the phone at Arielle's pocket. "Photographs and a linen memory are safer currency than clay against a rubber stamp."

Arielle wanted to argue with everything and nothing. The city pressed its stamp on her chest and said: decide now, refine later. She looked at the jar and felt the watcher at her shoulder, not pushing, not pleading, just there.

"Fog," she said. "Thunder when the table doesn't wobble."

They moved on that sentence. Yael slid the decoy into the woven sack; Karim ran a finger along the repaired stitch like a man saying goodbye to a lie that had served him well. Mar Ephrem returned with a folded paper that had been stamped by an office the city respected because it feared it: a temporary movement permit for "liturgical object under repair," signed by a seal that would argue with other seals for at least an hour. He pressed it into Yael's hand.

"Give bureaucracy a small bone," he said. "It jaws less at the marrow."

In the chapel, the municipal men sat with their hats in their hands trying to decide if piety was a kind of power or a kind of delay. Mar Ephrem greeted them with a cup of coffee whose strength bordered on an ethical question and explained the provenance of a hanging lamp no one had asked about. Sister Miriam's lemon tree trembled heroically under the weight of a warrant.

Jonas took Arielle by a side passage only people with bad knees use and out into the cold air along the Ramparts Walk. The walls here bore pockmarks where wars had touched them and graffiti where peace had. A cat watched them from a merlon like a julius who had never chosen a side.

"Zion Gate," Jonas said. "Driver with wrong music. The same wrong music."

"Lev owes him?" Arielle asked.

"The driver owes Lev," Jonas said. "Lev owes us only rumors. That's how debts don't rot."

They reached the gate. The stones were chewed where machine-gun fire had gnawed them in 1948; the morning had decided to be ordinary despite the scars. The taxi rolled up as if it had been listening for their weight on the cobbles. The driver wore sunglasses that refused to admit it was not 1993. The radio played a love song that consented to be worse than necessary.

"Where?" he asked without moving his mouth.

"Allenby Bridge," Jonas said. "Then wait."

"Always waiting," the driver sighed, and spat out the window without malice.

They threaded south along the Armenian walls, past the Broad Wall's rubble where Hezekiah had left his argument with Assyria in stone, past the Cenacle's rumor, into traffic that had decided rules were guidelines and guidelines optional. The city thinned into the brown flanks of the east. The road curled down to the checkpoint where the river became a border and courtesy wore uniforms.

Jonas's plan played its same clean note: they crossed with no jar, carrying only heads and a story about meetings with monks and a taste for flatbread in Madaba. They would not get far, but they didn't need far; they needed eyes.

At the King Hussein/Allenby terminals, air-conditioning argued with heat. Passports moved; bags slid; a thousand small human anxieties hummed in a room designed to say not today. Jonas picked a line with a bored clerk instead of a suspicious one; Arielle followed his posture and not her pulse.

The Jordanian side accepted them as travelers and not problems. Outside, a yellow taxi idled under a bougainvillea so pink it seemed to be breaking rules. The driver's smile said he knew every monastery between here and the moon. Jonas negotiated nothing; he named Mukawir. The driver named a price that offended both God and arithmetic; Jonas cut it with Roman dates and a promise to pay for his cigarettes. A number was agreed that left everyone slightly unhappy—the sign of a fair deal.

They rose into Moab's limestone ribs, the road coiling like a hair pulled from a brush. Herod's fortress came into view not as a building but as a decision: a dark mesa rising like a knuckle above a sea of pale stone. A little village clung to its shoulder. A modern sign spelled MUKAWWIR and promised a view and a history that would not behave for brochures.

Wind met them on the ridge with a knife in it. The plateau's skin was basalt and scrub; the sky did that thing only desert skies do—becoming vast enough to shrink the noise in your head without asking permission.

"Walk," Jonas said. "When wind covers a footfall, double your caution. It also carries voices where you want silence."

They crossed the saddle. The trench that had once held a wall showed as a faint, patient line. Cistern mouths gaped black like parentheses in the rock. At the summit, the peristyle court spread in outlines and knee-high stone—Herod's geometry summoning a ghosted columned space. To the west, the blue plate of the Dead Sea lay like a fallen sky. To the north, the Jordan cleft the land in a line you could follow with your eyes to Bethany.

Arielle knelt and touched a paving block whose top had been abraded by sandals that thought they were going somewhere important. She had the scholarly reflex to take notes and the newer reflex to listen.

"Margin letters?" Karim would have asked.

She found them.

Along the eastern lip of the court, where wind laid dust and then stole it back, tiny pecked pricks marched down the face of a dressed stone. ܡ ܟ ܘ ܪ again, faint and stubborn. At the corner—two paired cuts set like quotation marks bracketing nothing.

Arielle's mouth went dry. The same hand? Another trained in the same habit? She pictured a scribe out of place on this pagan terrace, tucking a ledger into a jar and then walking the edge of Herod's patio counting off letters under his breath—M...K...W...R—as if blessing the road for someone who would come two millennia late and in the wrong shoes.

The wind shifted. Jonas's head came up. Two tourists in sunhats wandered the far edge with a guide whose flag read as harmless from here. Nothing else moved.

Arielle half laughed and had to put a hand on the stone to steady it. "We're not mad," she told the plateau. "You left us a map; we're merely late."

They took photographs the way nuns count beads—slow, accountable, repeatable. Arielle logged their position with care she had learned from bad audits and worse men. She set her palm on the peck-marks once, lightly, the way you touch the shoulder of a stranger you know you'd have loved.

The driver waited where he had promised, because some people still keep promises casually. Back down the hill, the road stitched them toward Madaba—mosaics and tile shops, a church with a mosaic map of the Holy Land that had guided pilgrims for centuries. They didn't stop. The dead air of bureaucracy would wake soon; they had hours, not grace.

At the border again, everything that had gone smooth caught on a burr. A clerk with a taste for rules and a supervisor with a taste for being seen applied themselves to Jonas's passport like sculptors. Another window shut with the slow sadness of a train you weren't going to catch today.

"Problem?" Jonas said mildly.

"Always a problem," the supervisor said, less mild. "Where did you go?"

"Mukawir," Jonas said. "We admired stone. It declined to answer questions."

"Souvenirs?" the clerk asked, too bright.

"Only bread," Arielle said, and held up the last crust from Mar Ephrem's loaf. The man looked at it as if it remembered something he'd forgotten in a kitchen long ago and stamped her exit card without lifting his eyes.

They crossed back into a city that was already mid-argument with itself. The driver with the wrong music had taken up his station as if he had never left it. He took them to the Quarter without asking why; men like him rarely do. They tip in cash and gossip, both of which spend well.

At St. Mark's, the lemon tree shook under new paper and old bees. The warrant had developed a second signature while the ink dried. Mar Ephrem poured coffee that would cure minor sins and asked no questions until he had to.

"Proof," Arielle said simply, laying the photos on the table: Bethany letters on wood and stone; M—K—W—R peck-marks on Herod's court; the linen scrap's paired cuts.

"Maps that tyrants don't read," the abbot murmured, and crossed himself as if apologizing to the tyrants for understanding them so well.

Yael set the images side by side until the grammar of places began to show—a syntax of water, house, and mountain. Sister Miriam, listening by phone, named a thing that had been sitting in the room quietly all along.

"House and water," she said. "The mothers. Beth and Mayim. You think your scroll is about fathers because every scroll you've ever met pretended to be. It is about where women kept lists."

Karim swallowed, throat working. "Bakery ledgers. Baptismal rolls."

"Candles and bread and water," Sister Miriam said. "The first three things anyone asks for in a monastery and the last three to get written down by men."

Jonas didn't smile often; when he did, it came out crooked. "If we want thunder, this is a better lightning rod than relic fights."

Arielle looked at the jar, asleep in its cradle, seam clean. The watcher's hand lay, unmistakably now, beside hers—and, if she let herself admit it, beside her father's in memory. Guard the truth. It had stopped sounding like an order. It had started feeling like a trust.

A fist fell, politely, on the chapel door. Then another, less polite, on the side gate.

"Courtesy grew teeth," Yael said.

Mar Ephrem tapped the table once. "Then we give it a bone."

They split again by rule and instinct. Yael and Karim went out with the decoy openly, arguing in French about catalog numbers because no one follows a domestic disagreement into an alley. Jonas eased the jar's straps under Arielle's coat and wove them out the cistern crawl, breath synchronized with stone. Lev's fixer opened, then closed, a door put there by men who had never wanted to be thanked.

By the time the ring flashed at the chapel's threshold and a courteous voice said Father, the jar had already learned the turns to Muristan by heart.

They stepped into sun and market noise and the smell of hot sesame. Karim, somewhere in the crowd with a bag that wasn't the jar, laughed once. The city kept arguing. The table they would choose had begun to steady under their hands.

"Next," Jonas said, eyes on the flow.

"The river again," Arielle said. "But as ledger, not shrine."

"Thunder later," he answered.

"Fog now," she said.

They moved.

Chapter Ten — The Ledger Rooms

The market lifted around them like a hymn sung by people who didn't agree on the words and didn't need to. Copper rang, cats negotiated, tourists argued softly about maps that refused to be kind. Muristan breathed bread and brass.

"Water. Houses," Karim said, half to himself. "If the scroll's lists hid in ledgers, they'd hide near St. John—the Greek one, here. The Prodromos."

Arielle nodded. The Greek Orthodox Church of St. John the Baptist sat nested inside Muristan like a gold coin in cloth—a small bell, a low doorway, a stone floor polished by centuries of knees. Somewhere below, an older chapel slept under newer vows.

"Yael said she trusts a deacon with keys," Jonas murmured. "We use the door that opens when you knock like family."

They crossed the square as shoppers became pilgrims without changing shoes. In the church's shaded court, a woman fed pigeons with methodical hospitality. A priest moved candles from brass to brass the way a surgeon moves instruments. Jonas tapped the side door twice—then once—the rhythm that had opened more roofs than locks.

A man the shape of a question mark opened: Deacon Elpidios, hair monk-short, eyes mischief-bright, cassock impossibly clean. "Yael called," he said, and smirked without malice. "She told me to say no and to show you everything."

He ushered them through a narrow passage into a cool side room where the air smelled of beeswax and old books. Shelves held parish registers bound in cracked leather; a wooden table bowed in the middle like a tired saint. In one corner, a little trap door gaped toward a crypt that kept its temperature and secrets with equal stubbornness.

"We keep what the city pretends it never promised," Elpidios said, laying a palm on the nearest register. "Children dunked, names given, candles bought, bread counted." He looked at Arielle's coat and did not ask. "What alphabet am I looking for?"

"Greek script in the ledger," Arielle said. "But marks in the margins—Estrangela pricks or Syriac, anywhere a hand got homesick. Also trades listed as houses—bakery, water, oil."

Elpidios's mouth tilted. "You want what women wrote in ledgers men thought they owned." He drew a volume down—the binding protesting—and opened to a page where dates marched in tidy Greek.

Names filled the lines, fathers and sponsors and fees in a clerk's earnest hand. In the margin, faint as a ghost—pricks, climbed like ants beside a family entry.

Karim leaned, breath held. "Beth," he whispered. "ܬ , ܒ down the edge, shy of ink." He moved a finger to the next column. "And there—a tiny ܡ near a surname. Mayim. Water."

Elpidios squinted, then laughed softly. "We had a deacon in the 1800s who liked to brag he could read six alphabets and write two. This is how men prove it: they pepper ledgers with languages no one else can grade them on."

Yael's voice in Arielle's pocket: "Photograph. No flash. Rake light with a candle if you have to."

Elpidios produced a brass lamp with a glass chimney and angled it until the pricks stood up like nettles at dawn. Karim shot and logged; Arielle logged and breathed.

Far down the page, a woman's name—Mariam—appeared where the ledger expected a father. Next to it, a word in Greek, small and neat, written with reverence: Τῆς διαθήκης—of the Covenant. Elpidios's finger tapped it, then lifted as if it had felt heat.

"Bnath Qyama by another mouth," Mar Ephrem's voice had said earlier. Here, it was Greek's turn to carry Syriac's habit.

"Here's the bread," Elpidios murmured, proud of a city that occasionally kept its promises. "And water." His finger moved to a symbol in the margin—three short horizontal strokes stacked like a loaf seen from the side. "That's not Greek," he said. "That's a clerk's shorthand for the bakery account. When bread is bought for a baptism, it moves from altar to table and gets written twice—house and water."

A footstep in the nave beyond—the flat, official cadence of shoes that learn corridors by memory, not devotion. Elpidios never looked nervous. He stood, palmed a small brass key, and nudged the trap door with his foot. "If you hear the word 'inventory,' you are archaeology," he said, and grinned. "If you hear the word 'inspection,' you are missing."

Jonas had already read the room's exits and their compromise. "Arielle," he said, a name and a plan in one.

She slid the jar's weight deeper under the coat, straps bite-steady, and kept her hands visible on the table, a woman reading a family book. Karim tilted the register toward the lamp, playing the part of a student who thinks light equals permission. Elpidios moved into the doorway with the calm of someone who believed in liturgical obstruction—a ritual where a deacon blocks a bureaucrat with an icon of manners.

Two men in municipal coats appeared, hats held like apologies. One wore a badge that meant nothing and everything; the other carried clipboard-as-spear.

"Good morning, Deacon," Badge said. "We've had reports of—"

"—people reading," Elpidios supplied, sad to confirm vice. "We are a church. We are guilty."

Clipboard smiled without humor. "We need to verify your registries. Temporary custody—simple. It protects you."

"From whom?" Elpidios asked pleasantly. "God? Dust? Women with good pens?"

Badge's gaze slid across the room, refused to land on Arielle's coat because the coat looked like fatigue, and returned to Elpidios. "Cooperation shortens errands."

"Coffee lengthens them," Elpidios said, and stepped aside just enough to be polite and not enough to be useful.

Jonas's phone ticked once—no sound, just a buzz that carried a name onto the screen: Matthias. It sat there like a line you could choose not to read.

In the nave behind the men, a tour group entered, the guide's stick lifted like a shepherd's thesis. The inspector's shoulders tightened. Tourists complicate inspections. Arielle recognized a rhythm when she saw one. Fog does not fight; fog suggests the air is crowded.

Elpidios clapped gently, as if summoning a child, and a side door spilled women from the charity room, arms full of clean linens and bread for a home that needed a table and not a lesson. The women flowed between inspectors and table and iconostasis with the calm of people who tidy storms. Clipboards do not arrest laundry.

"Tomorrow?" Badge said, trying to swallow his chagrin with grace.

"Elpida," Elpidios said, using the Greek diminutive for hope, and smiled. "Tomorrow and the next day, as many as you can carry."

They left with dignity and annoyance in equal parts. Muristan exhaled them.

Elpidios shut the door with a small blessing, then let the grin he'd been saving out where it could see light. "Inspection is a thing," he said. "So is timing."

"Thank you," Arielle said, meaning it in more directions than the words could hold.

"We owe you more than coffee," Jonas added.

"You owe me bread," Elpidios said, entirely serious. "And to remember that ledgers keep more than sins." He touched the pricked margin again. "Take your photographs. Then put my book back where it has always been useful—on a shelf, ready."

They worked fast but not greedy. Karim logged the symbols, the pricks, the Greek gloss for Covenant, the bakery shorthand. He drew the three little strokes in his notebook and labeled them house of bread with an arrow that would make sense later even if his courage didn't.

Arielle closed the register with a tenderness that made Elpidios tilt his head. "You are your father's daughter," he said, not coy. "He read here. He refused to sit."

Arielle's breath snagged. "What did he... look at?"

"Page much like this one," Elpidios said. "His finger tapped Greek and his mouth said Syriac. He kept asking about the women. He took bread and left coin and promised to bring a friend who could argue in Arabic more politely than he could." He chuckled. "He did not bring the friend."

Outside, the church hummed again, the sound of people resuming their point. Muristan did not care what they had found; Muristan loved anyone who bought a small thing and wanted to know how it had been made.

They slipped back into the square. Karim carried a small bag from the candle stall as cover; wax has always given men a reason to walk with purpose. Jonas kept the coat reading fatigue, not contraband. Arielle felt the jar like a second spine.

"Next?" Karim asked, voice low but excited. He lived for the piece that made the previous pieces decide to belong to each other.

Arielle's phone vibrated: a text from Yael with a photograph of a municipal letterhead pinned to a lemon tree by a stainless steel staple. Under it, Yael had typed: They will come for ledgers next. Move sideways.

"Sideways," Arielle echoed, thinking through the city's habits. "If Greek ledgers show Covenant, then Armenian household lists will show bread. And Syriac—" She looked to the east without meaning to. "Syriac shows water."

"St. James first," Jonas said. "Then back to the House of Mark. We don't outrun paperwork; we trip it and step past."

They crossed into the Armenian Quarter—walls heavier, voices narrower, a bell that believed in duty more than music. Inside St. James, a sacristan led them to a side room where house lists lay in tidy, Armenian script, running back through years like a stitch that holds a seam even after the jacket has gone out of fashion. Karim couldn't read the hand, but the three small strokes for bread recur in any script when a clerk wants to be quick. He pointed; the sacristan nodded once, satisfied by competence.

"Here," Arielle said, tapping a page where a woman's name stood alone with the bread marks stacked beside it and a note in the margin—Մտնիք—"vowed." She took the photograph as if asking permission.

Outside, the sun had climbed to the hour when Jerusalem's stone gives heat back to the air like a complaint. Two men in dark coats lingered in the shade of a blind arcade; one had a chain winking at his wrist when he forgot to tug his sleeve. Ring-men had learned to let the city walk toward them instead of giving chase.

Matthias stepped out of the arch's shadow as if the wall had coughed him up. He wore linen and a face that had slept less than it deserved.

"You're building a table," he said. "Good. Don't wobble it with flourishes."

"Your friends are bored," Jonas said, inclining his head toward the coats.

"They're not my friends," Matthias said. "Today they are also not my problem." He looked at Arielle, and the words came not as threat but as fact: "Tonight they will stop being patient."

"Tonight we stop being polite," Arielle said, surprising herself with the steadiness in her voice.

Matthias's eyes approved without softening. "Thunder demands a room that can survive it," he said. "I have one."

"We have one," Jonas countered.

"Good," Matthias said. "Then we will see which of our tables invites fewer knives." He stepped aside, giving them the path he had occupied. "By the way," he added, almost as an afterthought, "a private buyer out of Amman just offered a number for a jar he hasn't seen. His man has the manners of a banker and the patience of a pickpocket. If he finds you first, he will ask only once."

"Who is he?" Karim blurted.

"Someone you won't meet," Matthias said. "Because I don't want to watch what he does to people who carry history under their coats." He glanced at the bag in Karim's hand and the way Arielle's coat hung. "Buy a larger candle," he said, and walked away into the crowd like punctuation.

They returned to St. Mark's with registers recorded and a plan beginning to think in sentences. Mar Ephrem heard them, then fetched coffee and did not argue, which is how men who have already argued for forty years show consent.

"We read at dusk," Arielle said. "With witnesses. With the house and water in our pockets and the mountain under our feet."

"Here, or elsewhere?" Yael asked, sleeves rolled, eyes already counting tables.

"Here," Mar Ephrem said. "Or in the old chamber beneath this room if they bring too many coats. The stone has a good memory. It will hold our noise and not repeat it to men who didn't earn it."

Arielle turned her father's two words over in her mouth and found that they still fit: for bread. She took a ka'ak ring from the woven sack and set it on the table beside the jar like an agreement.

"Thunder later," Jonas said, soft enough that only the room heard him.

"Dusk," Arielle said.

The city went on scoring itself against the day—sirens, bells, small arguments about prices and God. Inspectors sharpened pens; ring-men compared notes; a buyer in Amman tapped his ring on glass without realizing what that sound did to people who have carried contraband under their ribs.

In the scriptorium, the jar waited. Photographs made their small, brave promise. Ledgers remembered what they had been asked to keep. And under stone older than any office, an empty room measured its quiet and found it good enough to hold truth when truth finally chose to speak at volume.

Chapter Eleven — The Jerusalem Protocol

Dusk slid down the stone like a decision.

St. Mark's breathed at a lower register; the courtyard bell made its small, sober sound; in the scriptorium, they cleared the table as if laying out a body and a feast at once. The jar sat in its cradle, seam clean, the paper line invisible unless you knew where to look.

"We cannot just read," Yael said, rolling up her sleeves. "We have to frame how we read. If thunder's coming, it needs ground rods."

"Protocol," Jonas said. "For once, a word I like."

Mar Ephrem set a clay pitcher and six cups on the side table with ceremonial practicality. "Name it," he said. "Then we will keep it."

Karim looked up from his notebook. "Jerusalem Protocol," he said, and the room did not argue.

They drafted fast and careful, each offering a clause like a piece of their own skin.

Clause 1 — Witnesses. A reading is valid only in the presence of three kinds of eyes: a conservator (Yael or Sister Miriam), a clerical steward (Mar Ephrem or a delegate), and a secular scholar (Matthias, if he can keep his knives in his pocket). Deacon Elpidios offered to be "the Greek who nods at commas," and somehow this became part of the grammar.

Clause 2 — Recording. Two devices, redundant. Files hashed on-site. Copies split immediately into three labeled microcards—bread–A, water–B, house–C—handed to different hands that do not dine at the same tables.

Clause 3 — Interruption. If officials attempt seizure: the reading halts; a statement is read aloud (already printed, signed), and the files transmit to designated safekeepers. If force is used, the storage goes to public release.

Clause 4 — Custody. The jar remains with Eastern custody pending independent review by two named labs Arielle chose because they owed no bishop or minister anything except their calibration logs.

Clause 5 — Bread. Every session begins with bread and water on the table. "Because men who want to own truth hate the ordinary," Sister Miriam had said on the phone. "Give the room ordinary."

They wrote it on a single sheet with lines that refused flourish. Karim copied it in neat block letters that would photocopy clean. Mar Ephrem added a short Syriac header like a blessing; Elpidios penciled a Greek gloss into the margin with a schoolboy's mischief; Yael dotted an i as if it were a suture. Arielle signed last, hand steady, and felt something ease under her ribs that had not been allowed to loosen since the desert.

"Tables," Matthias said from the doorway.

No one had heard him come in. He stood with linen open at the throat and courtesy closed on his face. Two men in dark coats idled at the gate behind him pretending not to be weather.

"You have one," Jonas said, not rising to the bait. "We have one."

Matthias stepped closer and read the Protocol once without touching it. When he looked up, his eyes respected the paper the way men respect a chessboard. "Good. It will keep the room from performing itself."

"What do you want?" Yael asked, because she disliked scenes and men who built them.

"An invitation," he said simply. "Not to own. To witness. And to block your interruption once."

"How?" Jonas said. No challenge, just the price of admission.

Matthias folded a slip from his pocket and placed it beside the Protocol: a letter on cream paper with the crest of a consular cultural office that had no jurisdiction in churches and too much in courtyards. The letter named a "private scholarly colloquium" hosted under the auspices of an institute he did not belong to and an archimandrite who owed him a favor. It requested that "inspection" officers defer entry to avoid "diplomatic discourtesy."

"It won't hold forever," he said. "It will hold for one hour in one place if the officer on duty is more careful than ambitious."

"And where is 'one place'?" Arielle asked.

Matthias tilted his head toward the floor. "Below." He had found—and uncharacteristically asked for—the room under the scriptorium: a rock-cut chamber used once a year for a rite kept small on purpose. "Stone. Few exits. Good air. Better optics."

Mar Ephrem lifted a brow. "You acquired courtesy on my behalf without asking."

"I acquired a pause," Matthias said. "You can spend it here or not at all."

The room considered him. Yael's mouth did not soften. Jonas's fingers stopped tapping the table. Karim glanced at Arielle as if checking the sky.

Arielle looked at Matthias's letter and felt the tug of every bad bargain her father had warned her about. Then she folded the Protocol once, slid it into a clear sleeve, and set it on top of the jar's cradle.

"You witness," she said. "No negotiation. You argue about scripts and fibers and ethics. You do not argue about ownership. And if anyone knocks with a warrant wearing a smile, you earn your keep."

Matthias's mouth accepted terms. "Earned," he said.

Bootsteps in the court. The careful, patient tread of men who have learned to let corridors work for them. Elpidios leaned into the doorway with a look that said he admired timing when it served him.

"Inventory," he announced brightly. "We have so many candles. Perhaps the city would like to count them with us."

"Down," Jonas said.

They took the Protocol, the bread, the cups. Yael lifted the jar with both hands as if it were a child you do not wake. They moved through a side door and down six shallow steps into the chamber carved partly into rock and partly from the stubbornness of people who build in stone when wood would have been easier.

The lower room was small and exact: barrel-vaulted, vents slit high, a table that wasn't a table so much as a slab that had decided to be useful. In the apse, a plain cross had been scratched into plaster thin as breath. The air was cool, held close by limewash and time.

Mar Ephrem set bread and water at the table's corner, not piety so much as practice. Jonas walked the perimeter in a slow square and let his shoulders lower a fraction. Lev's face appeared for a heartbeat at the stair—counted heads, counted exits—and vanished again into the rumor that had summoned him.

Above, the polite voices began their polite work. Elpidios named saints with such vigor they could not be interrupted by someone naming statutes. Cloth moved; chairs objected; a clipboard collided with liturgy and apologized.

"We read only the outer face," Yael said, gloves on, voice gone to the register of surgeons. "No deep turns. We record without romance. And if anyone tries to make theater of us, we out-bore them with competence."

"Jerusalem Protocol," Karim said, as if reminding himself where his courage was stored.

Matthias took a step back from the table and kept his hands visible. "I will be your candle," he said dryly. "Not your hammer."

"Good," Arielle said. She felt the watcher at her shoulder—present, steady, not superstitious anymore. Guard the truth had become a job description, not a haunt.

Yael set the lamp at a low rake. Sister Miriam, on the phone beside the cup as if she were sitting there in cotton and glue, said her prayer in six practical words: "Slow hands. Strong spines. Small egos. Begin."

They opened the seam the length of a breath. The resin yielded with the same sweet surrender as last time. Air moved, cool and cave-breathed. The guard slip lay like a kindness. They lifted it and took the first clean images of the exposed line, the Estrangela hand making itself known without theatrics.

"Read," Mar Ephrem said softly.

Sister Miriam gave the Syriac on the other end of the call; Matthias followed with murmured agreement that sounded like a scholar deciding he had permission to respect someone else's expertise.

"From the house of Mariam: Ya'el of bread and Tamar of water; from Hanna: Shoshana; from Salome: Abisha of lamps; and those who were added by vow when pestilence came."

Karim timestamped, voice a thread: "Bnath Qyama roster. Household trades. Pestilence addition."

"Names where men wanted only fathers," Elpidios said from the stair, pleased to hear his city in its own voice.

Arielle saw it now as a structure, not a danger: water and bread and lamps sitting in the margins of ledgers and on stones where tyrants didn't look. The scroll wasn't tearing the story down. It was widening it the way a flood widens a channel that thought it owned the river.

Footsteps above. A new voice—cooler—said the word inspection in a tone that had not learned to be polite. The chamber's air tightened.

Matthias slid the consular letter into the stairwell like a card under a door. "A colloquium is in session," he said up, not loud. "Interruptions will travel." He named two names a wise officer would not choose to annoy before lunch.

A pause. Papers took offense and then reluctantly agreed to be reasonable. Chairs scratched. The voices moved sideways. Elpidios coughed once like an actor hitting a mark.

"Continue," Yael said, not looking up.

They took three more images, then one more line—enough to anchor meaning, not enough to needlessly tempt the wolves.

"Let the water names be kept by the springs and the bread names by the ovens; let lamps be written where oil is bought; and let all be told again at Bethany and the fortress of Herod, that forgetting be made to walk in circles."

Karim laughed once, surprised by joy in a room built for endurance. "It's literally telling us how to file the truth so it stays alive."

"Old women always ran the filing," Sister Miriam said. "The world merely borrowed the word."

A scrape on stone. Jonas's head turned—his whole body becoming an ear. The politeness upstairs had thinned to something sharper. The hour Matthias bought was spending itself.

"Stop," Arielle said. It came out calm. "We have enough to carry the sense. We won't give them a reason to confiscate breath."

Yael reseated the seam with paper and patience. The hairline disappeared into the jar's skin like a well-healed scar. Karim sealed the files, stamped the log, split the hashes onto microcards with hands that didn't shake until the cards were already in three other hands.

Elpidios slid down the last step with the agility of a man who did not take his cassock too seriously. "Two minutes," he said cheerfully. "They found their bravery and lost their calendar. The lemon tree is very inspected."

Jonas nodded once. "North exit," he said. "Cistern crawl. Lev's door. Sister Miriam's van on the far side of the quarter." He glanced at Matthias. "You stay. You asked to be our candle."

Matthias did not flinch. "I'll burn in the doorway," he said. "It's what candles do."

They moved. Bread and cups into the sack. Jar straps under the coat. The Protocol in Yael's case. Karim took the guard slip copy and the linen scrap's images and tucked them under his shirt like a man who had decided to be spine more than once today.

At the stair, Mar Ephrem put his palm lightly on the jar through Arielle's coat the way he had before, as if completing a circuit. "Go with our bad habits," he said. "They have kept better men than us from being smart too soon."

They slipped into the crawl. Stone pressed their shoulders. Air moved like a quiet animal. Above, voices squared themselves against a door that had decided to be busy. Matthias's tone—courteous, slightly bored—named a regulation the inspector hadn't read. Elpidios began a spontaneous accounting of candles so detailed it would shame a bookkeeper.

The crawl spat them into a pantry that owed Lev a favor and a clock. Yael opened a back door with the body language of a woman retrieving laundry. Jonas counted to five, then ten, then waved them through the slice of alley that leads to Christian Street if you have a map written in bread and water.

They didn't run. Men who run get followed by shoes that like to be loud. They walked like people who had made a small errand last longer than necessary and were sorry in the right way. The market wrapped them in its unarguable usefulness—copper ringing, cardamom insisting, a boy arguing with a cat who would not budge from the middle of a path history needed.

At the corner, a man in a linen suit admired a rack of rosaries with indifference so perfect it looked like art. Matthias's shadow, Arielle thought—the sort of neutral that pays its own bills. He did not look at them. Which is how you know he saw.

They reached the far gate. The driver with the wrong music had found a new terrible song and parked in a way that suggested he believed in their schedule more than his own. Jonas opened the door.

"Where?" the driver asked.

"Nowhere loud," Jonas said. "Everywhere safe."

"Always nowhere," the driver sighed, and pulled into the argument that is traffic.

Arielle set her palm over the jar and felt the watcher's hand settle beside hers like a colleague ready for the next shift. The Protocol sat between her and Yael on the seat, a thin paper with more weight than the clay. Karim exhaled and then, silently, cried once—quiet, like a man opening a valve on a line that needed pressure but not burst. No one looked away. No one made it about anything except breath.

Behind them, St. Mark's kept its silence like a promise. Ahead, the city prepared to grow teeth again. Between, their small moving room held bread, water, names, and a sheet of rules that would not wobble.

"Tomorrow," Jonas said, eyes on the mirrors.

"Midpoint," Karim muttered, and almost smiled at using a story word in a life.

"Thunder later," Arielle said, and the words did not tremble.

"Thunder later," the others answered.

They were still fog. But the table was ready.

Chapter Twelve — Calibration

They drifted the city like harmless smoke until it forgot to be interested in them. The driver with the wrong music set them down two streets shy of where anyone might be counting, then vanished into traffic with the relief of a man paid in cash and permission.

Lev's fixer opened a woodshop behind a shutter that pretended to be closed. The room smelled of cedar and brass filings. A lathe slept under a canvas. Light came through a high slit and made sawdust look like a galaxy.

"We calibrate here," Yael said. "No more than ten minutes." She had a satchel that rattled like a drawer of careful sins—mini-UV torch, a clip-on IR camera, a fold-flat stand, pH strips older than some countries. "I want non-invasive confirmation before we risk thunder."

Jonas ghosted the perimeter: one door, one window, a thin wall with a priest's cough behind it. He tilted his head; the cough belonged to a radio. Good. Radios don't ambush.

Arielle eased out of the coat. The jar took its cradle on a carpenter's bench like a tool with its own mind. Karim set a small lamp and called angles the way he had learned to call breath: "east-by-two... south-by-one..."

Yael snapped on the UV. The linen blinked into violets and bruised greens. Along the seam, the hard edge of pitch glowed dull; the stitch at the outer wrap showed a later hand in a fainter fluorescence.

"Protein adhesive," Yael murmured, not touching. "UV says collagen on the inner bind; pitch on the seam; no modern consolidant. That smell you keep mentioning is real and older than all of us."

She fired the IR clip. On the phone's screen, the outer weave smoothed toward bone-white; under it, the first line wrote itself more confidently than under lamplight. Karim didn't breathe for three beats. Then he remembered to be useful.

"Capture," he said, and took the frames. "Hashing… done. bread–A… water–B… house–C." He labeled the microcards with the stub of pencil he'd begun to favor, the graphite shiny with sweat.

A finger tapped twice on the shutter. A pattern. Not wrong. Not right. Lev would never knock. Lev would be a draft.

Jonas lifted a slat with two fingers. Outside, the driver with the wrong music stood with a paper bag and embarrassment.

"For you," he said, when Jonas eased the door enough for exchange. Inside: a manila envelope that smelled faintly of photocopier ozone and cigarettes. Two visitor badges—laminated, badly—wore the legend of a university lab on Mount Scopus; a parking pass had been stamped yesterday with a date that didn't mind lying for friends.

"Don't ask where," the driver said. "Ask when it stops working."

"When?" Jonas asked.

"Whenever a man with a ring decides to make his cousin a hero," the driver said, and left, as if he'd earned his line.

Yael reseated the coat's straps and folded the stand down until it remembered how to be a slab of nothing. "Lab now," she said. "A clean

FTIR on a fleck of pitch, a fiber under magnification, and we stop arguing with ourselves."

"Then Protocol at dusk," Arielle said. "And thunder when the table doesn't wobble."

Jonas checked the slit of the window one last time. "Move," he said. "Sideways."

They stepped back into a city rehearsing a normal day. A child dragged a plastic sword. A cat personally offended by gravity refused to cede a stoop. Down the lane, a ring winked once and then hid. Jonas did not look up. He let the stores and the bell and the smell of frying sesame carry them.

They didn't go straight to Mount Scopus. First, an errand shaped like insurance.

At the Austrian Hospice, people drank coffee and stared at a view that had made empires sentimental. Matthias waited at a corner table with his back to a wall and his attention on two doors. His linen gave at the throat; his expression did not.

"You have an hour," he said by way of hello. "The polite men in coats had to go learn a new word—colloquium—and they are cross."

"We have ten minutes," Yael corrected, and set a single image face-down on the table—the IR capture of the first line, timestamped, hashed, labeled. "Read it. Then forget you have it until I tell you to remember."

Matthias turned it as if it were an expensive menu and read. His mouth did not soften; his eyes did. "You have a thing," he said. "You are treating it like a fact. Thank you."

He slid a slip across the table: a printed message from a number no one had asked for. Private buyer desires custody for preservation. Substantial consideration offered. Neutral vault in Amman. A second line: courier noon, Mamilla roof garden; cash first. The tone did not bother with punctuation.

"Vultures," Karim muttered.

Matthias shook his head. "Excellent accountants," he said. "They keep thieves in suits and art in darkness. If they take it, it never argues with the air again."

"Then we won't let them," Arielle said. She startled herself with how unambiguous it sounded.

Matthias inclined a fraction. "My candle burns at dusk below your house," he said. "If I light it here at noon, I'll be useless later." He pushed the note back. "Decline with absence."

They left him watching the doors and finished their errand: the École porter accepted the decoy with theatrical reluctance and a ledger entry in a script only a Dominican could love. The ring-men watched, unable to trespass on the pleasure of a stamp. Lev's fixer drifted the decoy down a hallway where it would consume hours for the men who like to lose time to paper. Fog did not fight. Fog made corridors infinite.

The road to Mount Scopus curled like an eyebrow. At the gate, the laminated badges pretended to be legitimate with the confidence that sometimes works. A guard who hated being lied to but loved being part of a story waved them through with a warning that looked like two fingers and meant be quick.

Inside, the lab was bright and unsentimental. Shiri, a conservator with hair in a knot and eyes that had learned to enjoy being underestimated, looked the jar over and said only: "No stupidity."

"Slow hands, strong spines, small egos," Sister Miriam's voice buzzed in Arielle's pocket. Shiri seemed to accept that as credential.

They didn't open a thing. Yael coaxed the pitch seam with lamplight while Shiri took a fleck smaller than a lentil from an overrun edge with a micro-scalpel that would have felt cruel if it had touched anything living. The FTIR readout plotted a familiar jagged skyline. Shiri nodded, pleased and parsimonious.

"Bitumenaceous," she said. "Dead Sea pitch with protein contamination consistent with collagen glue—no modern resin spike. If you faked this, you faked it before anyone knew how to win grants for faking."

"And fibers?" Yael asked.

A stereomicroscope made linen into landscape. Shiri slid the split-screen until the S-twist declared itself, the way threads bound in the Levant declare when you've made them take a camera they didn't ask for.

"Levantine S," she said. "Hand-spun. Two guises in the warp. Weighted with time, not tricks." She leaned back. "I can't tell you the words are old. I can tell you the body they're wearing is honest."

Arielle's breath left in a tight little laugh. She had not realized she was holding this particular question like a bad tooth. Karim bumped his shoulder against hers without taking his eye from the screen.

"Copies," Yael said.

Shiri made three file clones on clean sticks and labeled them with her lab's dumb numbering that would embarrass a thief and confuse an archivist. She did not ask what the labels bread, water, house meant.

"You didn't bring it here," she said, as she handed them over. "We didn't see you. If anyone says otherwise, they mispronounced my name."

They were almost to the gate when the city decided to show its teeth. The guard had been replaced with a man who wore his cap like a verdict. Beside him, a sedan idled with the chill of after-market tint. On the back seat, a wrist glimmered: silver ring, small seal, silent arrogance.

"Problem?" Jonas said. He knew the answer.

"Always a problem," the cap replied, less bored than at the bridge. "We have a request for courtesy. You'll park and step out. We will make an inventory of your day."

Arielle felt the jar against her ribs become a point around which physics reconsidered itself. Fog does not panic. Fog changes the question.

"Bread," Karim said, too loudly for a joke and just right for a distraction. He lifted a ka'ak ring from the bag and tore it. Sesame scattered like punctuation. The cap flinched with the reflex of a man who had once been a child in a kitchen.

Jonas didn't waste the flinch. "Turn," he said, and they were already moving, not running, slipping between a shuttle bus and a pallet of bottled water in an angle the cap couldn't take without making paperwork angry. The sedan couldn't reverse without losing face. Face outranks tactics in half the rooms that matter.

They were in the car before Arielle's breath caught up. The driver burned a sigh and an old gear. The sedan tried to angle after and was stalled by a vehicle whose driver was uninterested in symbolism.

"Where?" the driver asked.

"Down," Jonas said. "Kidron first. Then Zion. Then a room with stone that doesn't gossip."

They cut east. The Mount of Olives rolled by with its ranks of bone-white tombs like books asleep. The Kidron drew its dry line; the City of David rose where tourists and cranes argue politely. More than once the ring flashed in a side mirror and then vanished when the road took a choice that was not obvious on a map.

Lev's fixer met them three corners shy of St. Mark's: a boy with a crate of pomegranates tipped his head toward a door that didn't look like a door. The door accepted its own pretense. The crate continued to be pomegranates for anyone who needed fruit.

In the scriptorium, the air had gone to evening. The lamp chimneys were clean. The table knew what was coming and had decided to take it.

"Authentications?" Mar Ephrem asked.

"Enough to stop us thinking we want a different truth," Yael said. She handed him water–B—Shiri's FTIR clone—and set house–C into the Gospel chest with a neatness that did not ask permission.

Arielle told the room what she needed to hear herself say: "We read at dusk. Witnesses. Protocol. House, water, mountain under us. And if they come, we close the seam and read the statement. If they push, the files travel without us."

"Thunder," Jonas said. Not a warning. A schedule.

They had an hour. It filled itself: Elpidios arrived with a lamp and three jokes and a willingness to block a corridor; Sister Miriam's voice took attendance through the phone; Matthias placed his useless letter where it might remain useful if the poor man on duty needed an excuse; Lev's face appeared and then didn't. The lemon tree rehearsed being innocent.

Karim sat, then stood, then sat, the way men do when they are trying to convince fear to be respect. He pulled his notebook closer and drew three short strokes—bread—then a drop shape—water—then a small flame—lamp. He wrote: Bnath Qyama. Then, under it, in English: Keepers.

Arielle set her palm on the jar and found her father's two words ready for this hour. For bread. She placed a ring on a plate and didn't call it a symbol. It was breakfast later for someone who would be tired from being brave.

Bootsteps in the court. Not polite. Not rushing. The sound of men who believed paperwork made their feet holy.

“Places,” Yael said.

They took them.

Arielle felt the watcher’s hand arrive—no longer a superstition, no longer a tremor. It was, simply, the weight of being watched by all the faces whose names had been held in margins and ovens and baptismal bowls while empires rehearsed important speech. It steadied her.

“Ready?” Jonas asked, not needing the answer.

“Ready,” she said.

The lemon tree shook.

The door opened.

They did not bow.

They read.

Chapter Twelve — Calibration

They drifted the city like harmless smoke until it forgot to be interested in them. The driver with the wrong music set them down two streets shy of where anyone might be counting, then vanished into traffic with the relief of a man paid in cash and permission.

Lev’s fixer opened a woodshop behind a shutter that pretended to be closed. The room smelled of cedar and brass filings. A lathe slept under a canvas. Light came through a high slit and made sawdust look like a galaxy.

“We calibrate here,” Yael said. “No more than ten minutes.” She had a satchel that rattled like a drawer of careful sins—mini-UV torch, a clip-on IR camera, a fold-flat stand, pH strips older than some countries. “I want non-invasive confirmation before we risk thunder.”

Jonas ghosted the perimeter: one door, one window, a thin wall with a priest's cough behind it. He tilted his head; the cough belonged to a radio. Good. Radios don't ambush.

Arielle eased out of the coat. The jar took its cradle on a carpenter's bench like a tool with its own mind. Karim set a small lamp and called angles the way he had learned to call breath: "east-by-two... south-by-one..."

Yael snapped on the UV. The linen blinked into violets and bruised greens. Along the seam, the hard edge of pitch glowed dull; the stitch at the outer wrap showed a later hand in a fainter fluorescence.

"Protein adhesive," Yael murmured, not touching. "UV says collagen on the inner bind; pitch on the seam; no modern consolidant. That smell you keep mentioning is real and older than all of us."

She fired the IR clip. On the phone's screen, the outer weave smoothed toward bone-white; under it, the first line wrote itself more confidently than under lamplight. Karim didn't breathe for three beats. Then he remembered to be useful.

"Capture," he said, and took the frames. "Hashing... done. bread–A... water–B... house–C." He labeled the microcards with the stub of pencil he'd begun to favor, the graphite shiny with sweat.

A finger tapped twice on the shutter. A pattern. Not wrong. Not right. Lev would never knock. Lev would be a draft.

Jonas lifted a slat with two fingers. Outside, the driver with the wrong music stood with a paper bag and embarrassment.

"For you," he said, when Jonas eased the door enough for exchange. Inside: a manila envelope that smelled faintly of photocopier ozone and cigarettes. Two visitor badges—laminated, badly—wore the legend of a university lab on Mount Scopus; a parking pass had been stamped yesterday with a date that didn't mind lying for friends.

"Don't ask where," the driver said. "Ask when it stops working."

"When?" Jonas asked.

"Whenever a man with a ring decides to make his cousin a hero," the driver said, and left, as if he'd earned his line.

Yael reseated the coat's straps and folded the stand down until it remembered how to be a slab of nothing. "Lab now," she said. "A clean FTIR on a fleck of pitch, a fiber under magnification, and we stop arguing with ourselves."

"Then Protocol at dusk," Arielle said. "And thunder when the table doesn't wobble."

Jonas checked the slit of the window one last time. "Move," he said. "Sideways."

They stepped back into a city rehearsing a normal day. A child dragged a plastic sword. A cat personally offended by gravity refused to cede a stoop. Down the lane, a ring winked once and then hid. Jonas did not look up. He let the stores and the bell and the smell of frying sesame carry them.

They didn't go straight to Mount Scopus. First, an errand shaped like insurance.

At the Austrian Hospice, people drank coffee and stared at a view that had made empires sentimental. Matthias waited at a corner table with his back to a wall and his attention on two doors. His linen gave at the throat; his expression did not.

"You have an hour," he said by way of hello. "The polite men in coats had to go learn a new word—colloquium—and they are cross."

"We have ten minutes," Yael corrected, and set a single image face-down on the table—the IR capture of the first line, timestamped, hashed, labeled. "Read it. Then forget you have it until I tell you to remember."

Matthias turned it as if it were an expensive menu and read. His mouth did not soften; his eyes did. "You have a thing," he said. "You are treating it like a fact. Thank you."

He slid a slip across the table: a printed message from a number no one had asked for. Private buyer desires custody for preservation. Substantial consideration offered. Neutral vault in Amman. A second line: courier noon, Mamilla roof garden; cash first. The tone did not bother with punctuation.

"Vultures," Karim muttered.

Matthias shook his head. "Excellent accountants," he said. "They keep thieves in suits and art in darkness. If they take it, it never argues with the air again."

"Then we won't let them," Arielle said. She startled herself with how unambiguous it sounded.

Matthias inclined a fraction. "My candle burns at dusk below your house," he said. "If I light it here at noon, I'll be useless later." He pushed the note back. "Decline with absence."

They left him watching the doors and finished their errand: the École porter accepted the decoy with theatrical reluctance and a ledger entry in a script only a Dominican could love. The ring-men watched, unable to trespass on the pleasure of a stamp. Lev's fixer drifted the decoy down a hallway where it would consume hours for the men who like to lose time to paper. Fog did not fight. Fog made corridors infinite.

The road to Mount Scopus curled like an eyebrow. At the gate, the laminated badges pretended to be legitimate with the confidence that sometimes works. A guard who hated being lied to but loved being part of a story waved them through with a warning that looked like two fingers and meant be quick.

Inside, the lab was bright and unsentimental. Shiri, a conservator with hair in a knot and eyes that had learned to enjoy being underestimated, looked the jar over and said only: "No stupidity."

"Slow hands, strong spines, small egos," Sister Miriam's voice buzzed in Arielle's pocket. Shiri seemed to accept that as credential.

They didn't open a thing. Yael coaxed the pitch seam with lamplight while Shiri took a fleck smaller than a lentil from an overrun edge with a micro-scalpel that would have felt cruel if it had touched anything living. The FTIR readout plotted a familiar jagged skyline. Shiri nodded, pleased and parsimonious.

"Bitumenaceous," she said. "Dead Sea pitch with protein contamination consistent with collagen glue—no modern resin spike. If you faked this, you faked it before anyone knew how to win grants for faking."

"And fibers?" Yael asked.

A stereomicroscope made linen into landscape. Shiri slid the split-screen until the S-twist declared itself, the way threads bound in the Levant declare when you've made them take a camera they didn't ask for.

"Levantine S," she said. "Hand-spun. Two guises in the warp. Weighted with time, not tricks." She leaned back. "I can't tell you the words are old. I can tell you the body they're wearing is honest."

Arielle's breath left in a tight little laugh. She had not realized she was holding this particular question like a bad tooth. Karim bumped his shoulder against hers without taking his eye from the screen.

"Copies," Yael said.

Shiri made three file clones on clean sticks and labeled them with her lab's dumb numbering that would embarrass a thief and confuse an archivist. She did not ask what the labels bread, water, house meant.

"You didn't bring it here," she said, as she handed them over. "We didn't see you. If anyone says otherwise, they mispronounced my name."

They were almost to the gate when the city decided to show its teeth. The guard had been replaced with a man who wore his cap like a verdict. Beside him, a sedan idled with the chill of after-market tint. On the back seat, a wrist glimmered: silver ring, small seal, silent arrogance.

"Problem?" Jonas said. He knew the answer.

"Always a problem," the cap replied, less bored than at the bridge. "We have a request for courtesy. You'll park and step out. We will make an inventory of your day."

Arielle felt the jar against her ribs become a point around which physics reconsidered itself. Fog does not panic. Fog changes the question.

"Bread," Karim said, too loudly for a joke and just right for a distraction. He lifted a ka'ak ring from the bag and tore it. Sesame scattered like punctuation. The cap flinched with the reflex of a man who had once been a child in a kitchen.

Jonas didn't waste the flinch. "Turn," he said, and they were already moving, not running, slipping between a shuttle bus and a pallet of bottled water in an angle the cap couldn't take without making paperwork angry. The sedan couldn't reverse without losing face. Face outranks tactics in half the rooms that matter.

They were in the car before Arielle's breath caught up. The driver burned a sigh and an old gear. The sedan tried to angle after and was stalled by a vehicle whose driver was uninterested in symbolism.

"Where?" the driver asked.

"Down," Jonas said. "Kidron first. Then Zion. Then a room with stone that doesn't gossip."

They cut east. The Mount of Olives rolled by with its ranks of bone-white tombs like books asleep. The Kidron drew its dry line; the City of David rose where tourists and cranes argue politely. More than once the ring flashed in a side mirror and then vanished when the road took a choice that was not obvious on a map.

Lev's fixer met them three corners shy of St. Mark's: a boy with a crate of pomegranates tipped his head toward a door that didn't look like a door. The door accepted its own pretense. The crate continued to be pomegranates for anyone who needed fruit.

In the scriptorium, the air had gone to evening. The lamp chimneys were clean. The table knew what was coming and had decided to take it.

"Authentications?" Mar Ephrem asked.

"Enough to stop us thinking we want a different truth," Yael said. She handed him water–B—Shiri's FTIR clone—and set house–C into the Gospel chest with a neatness that did not ask permission.

Arielle told the room what she needed to hear herself say: "We read at dusk. Witnesses. Protocol. House, water, mountain under us. And if they come, we close the seam and read the statement. If they push, the files travel without us."

"Thunder," Jonas said. Not a warning. A schedule.

They had an hour. It filled itself: Elpidios arrived with a lamp and three jokes and a willingness to block a corridor; Sister Miriam's voice took attendance through the phone; Matthias placed his useless letter where it might remain useful if the poor man on duty needed an excuse; Lev's face appeared and then didn't. The lemon tree rehearsed being innocent.

Karim sat, then stood, then sat, the way men do when they are trying to convince fear to be respect. He pulled his notebook closer and drew three short strokes—bread—then a drop shape—water—then a small flame—lamp. He wrote: Bnath Qyama. Then, under it, in English: Keepers.

Arielle set her palm on the jar and found her father's two words ready for this hour. For bread. She placed a ring on a plate and didn't call it a symbol. It was breakfast later for someone who would be tired from being brave.

Bootsteps in the court. Not polite. Not rushing. The sound of men who believed paperwork made their feet holy.

"Places," Yael said.

They took them.

Arielle felt the watcher's hand arrive—no longer a superstition, no longer a tremor. It was, simply, the weight of being watched by all the faces whose names had been held in margins and ovens and baptismal bowls while empires rehearsed important speech. It steadied her.

"Ready?" Jonas asked, not needing the answer.

"Ready," she said.

The lemon tree shook.

The door opened.

They did not bow.

They read.

Chapter Thirteen — The First Witnesses

The door opened on courtesy with a badge.

Two municipal inspectors filled the threshold, hats in their hands like apologies sharpened into tools. Behind them, a smaller man lingered with his hands folded and his eyes bright—the kind who likes to be the first to write the report no one will sign.

Elpidios met them with a lamp and an expression that said he was delighted the city had finally come to count its candles. "Inventory," he announced, as if naming a feast. "We have so many. Please, begin with the lemon tree."

They didn't laugh. Good. Laughter loosens men who should remain stiff.

Down in the rock-cut room, they had already taken their places. Bread and water at the slab's corner. The Jerusalem Protocol in its clear sleeve on the table like a quiet sword. Yael gloved. Karim at the recorder. Sister Miriam's voice on-speaker, steady as glue. Matthias standing at the stair with a folded letter from a consular office that pretended to matter and sometimes did.

Arielle drew a breath into a space under her ribs she hadn't trusted since the desert. The watcher's presence was not a superstition anymore; it was simply the pressure of many hands on the table, past and present.

"Begin," Mar Ephrem said.

Yael turned the lamp until the linen's weave became a field and the seam remembered cooperation. The paper went soft under bone folder and patience. The hairline yielded. The jar exhaled a cave's cool breath.

The guard slip came away like a handkerchief from a sleeping face.

The outer turn's Estrangela stood ready. Karim's time-stamp rolled. His hands didn't shake until after he typed.

Sister Miriam read the line in Syriac first, each letter a wheel that knew its ruts. Then she translated, not as performance but as record:

"Let the households of bread and water carry the names when the house of men is closed; let lamps keep the lists when pestilence or sword dim the count; and let all be told again in the house of crossing and on the mountain of Herod, that forgetting be made to walk in circles."

Karim whispered, half a laugh, half a gasp. "It's a filing instruction."

"Old women invented archives," Sister Miriam said dryly. "Men invented door locks."

Footsteps paused above the stair. Matthias slid his letter upward, voice mild enough to irritate: "A colloquium is in session. Interruption will travel." He named two names in two embassies that would make a cautious inspector dream of a transfer.

Arielle kept her eyes on the line. The next sentence ran like a ledger that liked poetry more than it admitted.

"Through Mariam: Ya'el of bread, Tamar of water, and her daughter Marta, taken in vow when fever came. Through Hanna: Shoshana. Through Salome: Abisha who kept the lamps. These bind the births; these remember the mothers when the men are forgotten."

Karim typed the names as if his pen were a tether. The recorder hummed. Yael murmured, "Photograph," and he obeyed—angles, rake, hash, copy—bread–A, water–B, house–C passing to three waiting hands: Mar Ephrem, Matthias, Lev's face in a bookbinder's apron, each to his own pocket and his own kind of vow.

Above, courtesy's patience shortened. The sharper voice came back with a smile you could hear. "Father, we will simply count the candles with you."

Elpidios sighed in such a holy register it counted as liturgy. "Then you must begin with the bees," he said. "They kept the wax accounts first."

"Next line," Yael whispered.

It was short and unadorned, a line you could have missed if you were hunting thunder:

"Guard the truth with many small doors."

Arielle felt the sentence land like a hand on her shoulder. Her father's notes had said the same thing in less beautiful words. He'd meant redundancy; the scribe meant community. Both were right.

Jonas's head tilted. In the court above, a warrant met a lemon tree with a sound that suggested staples and irritation. Chairs scraped. Elpidios began a lesson on censer chains that could fill an afternoon.

Matthias leaned down the stair, voice cooler now. "Two minutes."

"Enough," Arielle said. "Close."

Yael didn't argue. The guard slip returned, the seam seated with Japanese paper that left no drama in its wake. Karim sealed and hashed and split the files again—bread–D to Elpidios when he appeared, chest heaving, cheeks pink with the effort of obstructing an empire with manners; water–E to the young novice at Mar Ephrem's shoulder; house–F to the Armenian sacristan who had arrived without sound and would leave the same way.

Mar Ephrem lifted the Protocol, tapped the Interruption clause, and set it in easy reach.

They were packing the lamp when the stair brightened with bodies. The taller inspector held a warrant so fresh the ink still wanted to argue. Behind him, the ring-man was absent—either bored of courtesy or saving himself for later.

"Good afternoon," the inspector said with the amiability of a man about to ask a room to be stupid. "We require temporary custody."

Matthias stepped between paper and table, his letter visible but not brandished. "You require courtesy," he said. "You request custody. If you force it, three jurisdictions will ask you to write long emails."

The inspector's mouth made a shape that wasn't a smile and wasn't not. "And what is this?" He nodded at the sleeve on the table.

Elpidios, God bless him, flowed from behind and plucked up the Protocol like a hymnal. "Our order of service," he said happily. "Bread, water, reading, hashes, and a prayer to St. Inventory."

"Statement," Yael said, sotto voce.

Mar Ephrem read from the printed sheet, calm as a Psalm: "We are engaged in a scholarly colloquium under ecclesial stewardship. All imaging has been duplicated to custodians named here. Any seizure will trigger public release to additional parties."

The inspector's eyes did a small, involuntary math.

"Count your candles," Elpidios urged, thrusting a brass stick into his hands. "The bees are very proud."

There was a version of the world where the man would have nodded, counted, left. This was not that version, not today. He stepped forward a pace, not enough to violate, enough to test.

Jonas moved, not aggressive, simply there—mass and patience. The room had been arranged so that anyone foolish enough to reach would have to brush past a soldier who knew how to spend that contact.

Arielle didn't speak. She placed her palm flat on the table beside the jar. The gesture contained more refusal than a paragraph.

The inspector's gaze fell to the bread and water on the slab, then up to Yael's steady face, then to Matthias's letter, then to Elpidios's weaponized helpfulness. He weighed noise against consequence. He was not a fool. He had a supervisor who liked promotions. He chose to prove his diligence in the nave, where people would clap him for being thorough.

"Tomorrow," he said, voice chalk-dry. "We return tomorrow."

"Tomorrow is a saint," Elpidios said cheerfully. "We love him. We never meet him."

They left with dignity and a small inventory of candles. The lemon tree rustled, lighter by one bureaucratic paper.

Silence held a shape that wasn't fear. It was relief with nowhere to sit.

Karim let out a breath and immediately tried to swallow it back. Yael touched his shoulder with the back of her wrist, the way a physician gives a room permission to be human.

"We did not fail," Matthias said, not triumphantly. "We did not succeed either. We simply did the thing and refused to call it drama."

Mar Ephrem closed his eyes for the space of one slow inhale. "The bees kept their accounts," he said, which in his mouth meant good work.

They cleared the table with the care you reserve for altars and workbenches. The jar settled into the cradle; the seam lay clean, the paper invisible. The Protocol went back in its sleeve. Bread broke and went into hands that had just held more delicate things.

Arielle chewed. The ordinary taste steadied her better than victory would have.

"What now?" Karim asked, still small with adrenaline.

"Now we make good on the line," Arielle said. "Many small doors."

They took the next hour to do unglamorous work that keeps truth alive: three sealed envelopes with prints of the day's images and translations, each signed across the flap; three microcards in cheap plastic hidden where men with badges don't look—under a candle tray, in the binding of a battered lectionary, taped beneath the Gospel chest's false bottom. Elpidios moved through his church with the happy guilt of a man hiding presents from children he liked.

Yael wrote a short, dull cover note in academicese so dry it could have been used as kindling: Preliminary non-destructive imaging confirms early Syriac ledger usage. Bnath Qyama attestation. Filing rubric: bread/water/lamps. Full report pending peer oversight. She printed it twice on a temperamental machine that made everything look less interesting than it was and therefore safer.

Matthias wrote nothing. He stood in the stair and burned like a candle is meant to—without changing the temperature much, just making the dark have to find a new excuse.

When they climbed back into the nave, the inspectors were gone and the lemon tree pretended innocence. Deacon Elpidios winked at the bees. "We have been very inspected," he told them. "We have decided to remain ourselves."

Outside, the quarter had not noticed the difference between a day with a Protocol and a day without one. The ring-men had—two new coats at the far arcade; one chain flashing when its owner forgot to hide his wrists. Mamilla's roof had not seen a courier at noon. Good. Absence can be a refusal.

On Christian Street, a boy sold sesame rings and stared at their faces and decided his day improved if he made them laugh. He told a joke about a monk, a tourist, and a cat that ended with the cat winning. Karim laughed in the register you use when your body needs proof you are still good at it.

They turned into St. Mark's court again. Mar Ephrem paused by the lemon tree and adjusted the paper that had been pinned to it so the staple wouldn't tear the leaf. "Tomorrow," he said to the tree, as if making it a promise he intended to keep by breaking.

In the scriptorium, the jar rested. The room had the feel of work done to the edge that is wise.

Jonas leaned his elbows on the table and looked at Arielle the way people look at someone who has just learned a gait they will need to walk a long time. "Midpoint," he said, borrowing Karim's story word.

"Fog with rules," Arielle answered.

"Thunder later," Yael said, but this time there was a thin thrill in it—like a wire pulled tight and ready to sing.

Matthias lifted his linen collar with two fingers, as if he'd remembered he hated the way stone sheds heat at night. "They'll come hungry tomorrow," he said. "Bring more bread."

Arielle nodded. "We will."

She placed her palm once more on the jar—not claiming, not pleading. The watcher's hand lay beside hers and, for a moment, she could almost feel her father's smaller gesture in the echo—Guard the truth with many small doors—and the city's older one: Feed people while you do it.

Outside, evening gathered the alleys. The argument of the day softened to hum. Somewhere a bell mistook the hour and no one corrected it. They had not lost it. They had not won it. They had done the next necessary thing and made it harder to undo.

Tomorrow could have its teeth. Tonight, the doors were many.

Chapter Fourteen — Teeth

Morning found the lemon tree rehearsing innocence.

In the scriptorium, they set the room the way you armor a choice—bread on a plate, water in cups, the Jerusalem Protocol in its sleeve ready to be held up like a mirror. The jar sat quiet in its cradle, seam clean, the paper line invisible unless you had learned where to look.

"They'll come early," Yael said. "Men who sleep badly arrive before coffee."

"Then we will have ours first," Mar Ephrem said, pouring a pitch-dark cup that could instruct a conscience.

Karim stood at the window slit, counting shoes. "Two municipal," he murmured. "Inspector hats. One Border Police patrol at the corner looking bored in four directions at once. No ring."

"Different teeth," Jonas said. "They brought law, not jewelry."

Sister Miriam's voice, on speaker from Ein Karem, had already settled into its working register. "If law asks for custody, ask for inventory. Inventory is always honest work; custody is often theater."

Arielle pulled the straps of the coat tight across her ribs, feeling the jar's cool weight translate into resolve. "We won't win the door," she said. "We win the hour after the door."

Elpidios slipped in from the nave with a look that mixed mischief and liturgy. "I have laid out all the candles," he announced. "There are so many. We will count until their pens dry."

The knock came mild as rain.

They let courtesy in.

Two inspectors stepped over the threshold holding their hats like apologies and a warrant like a shield. Behind them, a third man did not enter; he stood with his hands folded and his face blank, the way people stand when they intend to remember details exactly enough to be useful to someone else.

"Father," the taller inspector said. "We are grateful for your cooperation. We must take temporary custody of any portable antiquities under possible danger."

Mar Ephrem's smile was an old knife wrapped in velvet. "Everything here is under possible danger," he said. "We are in Jerusalem."

He set bread on the table, water beside it, and left his hand on the Protocol's sleeve. "We are engaged in a colloquium. The city likes learned words; so do I. We will read, we will record, we will duplicate, and then we will talk to your paper."

The inspector's eyes touched the sleeve and did a small, involuntary math. "We can wait—briefly," he said. "But we will accompany."

Elpidios brightened like a child promised mischief. "Then accompany our inventory. The bees have kept poor accounts this year. We must reconcile."

They bought twenty minutes with wax and names and the agreeable tyranny of counting. When the inspectors' patience went thin enough to see light through, the smaller man at the door cleared his throat and looked at his watch. Time had put on a cap.

Jonas's chin tipped once. Go.

Fog doesn't run; fog chooses a hallway. Arielle slid into the side passage with Jonas, the jar under the coat, the straps biting in the way that reassures. Karim shouldered the decoy and began an argument with Yael about catalog numbers in French loud enough to be audible and dull enough to be invisible.

The cistern crawl received them like a rumor that had learned their names. Stone pressed, air moved, voices above became a texture instead of words. They spilled into the pantry that owed Lev a favor and into an alley that remembered how to swallow people and return them later with different faces.

The driver with the wrong music had been told nothing and understood everything. He rolled up as if he had been parked there by a better story, and they folded into the car with the modest speed of people on an errand that offended no one.

"Where?" he asked.

"Zion Gate," Jonas said. "Then south a block. Then left where the road pretends it can't make up its mind."

They never reached the left.

At the gate, a temporary checkpoint appeared that had not been there yesterday: an official table, two plastic barriers, a brown tent new enough to smell of plastic, and the posture of men who had decided to make this morning shorter by making someone else's longer.

A Border Police sergeant with a yarmulke and a crease between his eyes raised a hand. He was not unkind. He was the kind of man whose day got worse if he let someone else's be easy.

"Random check," he said. It was never random.

Jonas's window was down before the words finished. "Of course," he said, with the dignity of a man who had lost small wars and still preferred manners.

"Trunk?" the sergeant asked.

"Laundry," Jonas said truthfully. The woven sack with the decoy sat in clear view.

"And inside?"

"Pilgrims," Jonas said. "Hungry ones."

The sergeant's gaze slid past the back seat. It didn't land on Arielle's coat because the coat read as fatigue, not contraband. It landed on Karim's face—too alert—and on the woven sack—too convenient.

"Out, please," he said, and the word please stretched thin with habit.

They stepped into light. The gate's stones showed their old bite marks from other years' arguments. A city cat regarded the checkpoint with the contempt of creatures who do not vote.

A second vehicle eased to the curb: a white van with a discreet insignia and a driver who had learned to be forgettable. A man in plain clothes slid from the passenger seat and did not show a badge. He wore a band on his right hand, not ostentatious, with a flat face carved with a seal too small to read from a respectful distance.

He did not introduce himself. He stepped beside the sergeant with the ease of a person whose work gets done when other men believe they are in charge.

"Temporary custody," he said, as if the words were a coat he expected them to put on themselves.

Jonas positioned himself where his mass converted courtesy into friction. "We have the Jerusalem Protocol," he said, voice quiet, almost bored. "Read it, and then we will talk about custody."

The man did not take the sleeve. He glanced at it. "Statements don't change procedure," he said.

"Procedure doesn't change statements," Yael said, stepping forward with the paper. "If you seize, the files travel. Three sticks leave this gate with witnesses you don't control. We prefer your patience to your authority today."

The sergeant's mouth tightened at that. He had learned to dislike the difference between patience and authority. He had also learned to count.

"Open the bag," he said to Karim.

Karim did. The decoy looked perfect because Yael had made it. The sergeant's hands were careful. He knew the weight of things he did not want to be responsible for.

"Receipt," Jonas said, when the man in plain clothes reached toward the sack. "Chain of custody. Names. Time. Your seal. Your destination. You can have things when you agree to be accountable for them."

The man did not enjoy a lecture. He produced a triplicate book and wrote with the speed of someone who had no intention of being legible. Government Antiquities Holding. Temporary Evaluation. A blank where a supervisor's name should have been. He tore the yellow sheet and offered it like a dare.

Karim's hand shook only when he had the receipt folded and in his pocket.

"And the coat," the plainclothes man said to Arielle. "It is very warm today."

Arielle looked him in the eye and felt something inside her settle. Thunder is noisy; fog makes men explain their manners.

"No," she said.

Jonas didn't move. Yael didn't blink. The sergeant watched the man in plain clothes the way you watch a dog that might decide to be a wolf.

"If you refuse," the man said, and let the sentence hang where threats live.

"We don't refuse," Arielle said. "We invoke." She tapped the Protocol. "Interruption clause. If you touch us without a warrant for our persons, we release the files to a larger circle."

The man's lip moved a fraction—contempt, or amusement, or the recognition of someone who liked to be the only person issuing ultimatums. He shifted his attention to the sergeant as if reminding the room which uniform made things true.

"Search the car," he said.

They did. They logged nothing because they found nothing except ordinary things the city respects: bread, water, fatigue.

The man in plain clothes took the decoy to the white van as if he were taking a bag of laundry to a laundromat that had learned to launder meaning. He signed nothing else. The sergeant wrote more neatly than his face suggested he would.

"Destination?" Jonas asked again.

"Rockefeller campus," the sergeant said quietly. He did not look at the man with the ring when he said it. "Standard evaluation."

"Witnesses," Yael said, and pointed at herself and then at the Protocol. "We follow."

"No," the man said. "You will be notified."

"By whom?" Jonas asked.

"By me," the man said, and enjoyed the promise like a cat enjoys a dying thing.

The van pulled away. The checkpoint pretended to become random again. The man in plain clothes melted into a sedan with a driver who had learned to make eye contact with no one. The sergeant lingered a fraction too long, then squared his cap and became a man whose day would be easier if he believed everyone else had been unreasonable.

They stood in the sun and did not move. The jar was still under Arielle's coat, cool and alive against her ribs. The bag that had left was a lie they had long rehearsed.

Karim exhaled a sound that wasn't quite laughter and wasn't anything else. "We lost something," he said, then corrected himself. "We lost time. Not the thing."

"Fog wins by hours," Jonas said.

Yael's mouth was a hard line and a soft one at once. "The decoy will eat a day and a half in a basement where men congratulate one another on their caution," she said. "Good. We just bought our thunder."

Arielle put her palm flat on the coat and felt the watcher's hand settle beside hers—not a benediction, not relief, simply company. She let her breath find its place.

"What now?" Karim asked, because the day had emptied and filled at once.

"Now we behave like the filing instruction told us to," Arielle said. "Many small doors. We make more witnesses. We widen the circle until seizure becomes ridiculous."

Jonas nodded. "We seed the images to our coalition," he said. "Elpidios's Greek. Sister Miriam's Syriac. The Armenian sacristan's lists. Shiri's lab. Matthias's candle. Lev's fixer. Five doors at minimum. Seven if we can do it without noise."

"And Rockefeller?" Yael asked.

"We go," Arielle said. "With paper. With coffee. With witnesses who respectfully do not sign anything that gives ownership a new adjective."

Karim looked at his phone, thumb hovering a hair from a command they had agreed on and not used yet. "Press?"

"Not yet," Jonas said. "Not with custody at stake. We release to people who will not mistake bread for a trophy."

They moved as a decision and the city received them as if it had expected this motion all along. The driver with the wrong music took one look at their faces and turned the radio off. The road down Nablus Road toward the Rockefeller gates remembered every century at once; the museum's walls wore bullet scars like freckles no one bothers to cover.

At the gate, a guard whose uniform did not match the cap of the man at Zion Gate looked at the yellow receipt and decided his job was to make phones ring, not doors open. They waited while bureaucracy rehearsed itself. Matthias arrived on foot with the expression of a man who had chosen his limits and intended to use all of them in the right order.

"I can stall," he said. "I cannot reverse."

"Stall," Arielle said. "And count."

Inside, a basement that had once been intended for a different empire pulsed with halogen and habit. Men in gloves lifted the decoy with care they believed was well invested. An office door stood open where it meant to be closed. A man with a ring watched from a hallway he had no right to own.

"We will log chain of custody," Yael said, crisp enough to be a tool. "Time. Room. Hands. If you do it, I write it. If you fail, I write that too."

No one invited them in. No one could think of a polite reason to keep them out. This is how rooms become honest for a day.

They watched the decoy be admired, which is a strange verb for a jar. A clerk put a tag on it like a small leash. A supervisor wrote in a book that had survived three reorganizations and one leak. The ring-man did not blink when Jonas photographed the clock and the hands and the motion of the pen. Paper has its own courage when it knows it is being watched.

"You know this is not the only jar," Matthias murmured in the sergeant's direction. The sergeant did not answer exactly; he rubbed the crease between his eyes and said, to no one in particular, "I like bread."

Arielle chose to appreciate the sentence.

They left with nothing in their hands and the Protocol in their pocket. Outside, the afternoon threw heat against the stone and bounced it back.

They did the unromantic work a filing rubric asks for: a sealed packet in Greek at St. John's with Elpidios's ridiculous glee and reluctant holiness; a sealed packet in Armenian at St. James with the sacristan's sober nod; Shiri stamped a neutral lab cover letter and put it in a boring envelope that would infuriate anyone who hoped for drama. Sister Miriam's copy rode back to Ein Karem under a basket of lemons a novice swore were for a cake.

At each door, they left a phrase that belonged more in a kitchen than a lab: for bread.

Karim pressed send on a message list they had named with stupidity on purpose: Receipts. It moved the hashed images of lines one through four to five mailboxes that couldn't be easily seized without a judge saying something brave in the wrong room. No press. No brag. Many small doors.

On the way back to the Quarter, Lev's fixer intercepted them as a woman buying tomatoes. "The buyer in Amman," she said, not looking up, "has stopped asking. He has started offering. It's the last thing men do before they go quiet. He'll use smaller hands next time."

"Then we will give him nothing to hold," Jonas said.

They reached St. Mark's at an hour when the court looks like it is waiting to be painted. The lemon tree held a new notice with a staple that did not match the old one. Mar Ephrem straightened it and, without malice, bent the staple back so it wouldn't wound the leaf.

"You lost a thing you meant to lose," he said softly.

"We lost time," Arielle said. "We kept the room."

He nodded, pleased by the grammar.

They set the jar back into its cradle and the seam back into stillness. They put bread on the plate because it was habit and because it made the room behave. And then, because the day had taken something from them even if it was only the fiction of safety, they allowed themselves a minute in which no one spoke.

Jonas broke it. "We plan the reverse," he said. "Kidron's tunnels. City of David stairs. A corridor that believes in wrong turns. Rockefeller is a building; buildings are predictable. Men aren't."

Matthias didn't smile. "I'll bring a candle," he said. "You'll need to see what you're not supposed to."

Yael looked at Arielle. "Tomorrow, we read if we can," she said. "If we can't, we make the ledgers read louder."

Karim wrote three short strokes in his notebook—bread—then a drop—water—then a flame—lamp. Under it he printed: Not a relic. A record.

Arielle placed her palm gently on the jar. The watcher's hand arrived as if summoned by the ordinary. Guard the truth with many small doors, the scroll had said. It had not promised ease. It had promised a way.

She breathed, deep and even, and found that loss and resolve can sit in the same chair without arguing.

"Tomorrow," she said.

The city sharpened its teeth in the distance and pretended it wasn't. The lemon tree rehearsed innocence. Inside the stone room, they counted doors.

Chapter Fifteen — Chain

They woke before the bell, the hour when stone still remembers night.

Bread went to the plate. Water went to the cups. The Jerusalem Protocol lay in its sleeve where anyone looking for permission would have to see it glare back. The jar sat in the cradle, seam clean, as if the previous day's teeth had been a rehearsal and not a promise.

Jonas had already walked the courtyard and the roof and the stair with a soldier's superstition. "No vans," he said. "Two inspectors on the street pretending to be early. The lemon tree has learned new paper."

Elpidios brought a lamp and a grin sharpened for mischief. "We will count all the candles again," he announced, as if daring bureaucracy to love math.

Sister Miriam was a voice in Arielle's pocket, already warm with tea and restraint. "If they talk custody, talk inventory," she said. "If they talk seizure, read the Interruption clause and make witnesses out of furniture."

Arielle slipped the straps across her shoulders under the coat and felt the jar's cool press settle her spine. "We're fog until they force weather," she said.

The knock did not ask for courtesy. It possessed it.

Three men at the door: two municipal inspectors with hats in their hands and tired dignity, and between them a short, compact official in a brown suit that fit the decade badly. He did not wear a ring. He wore a folder thick enough to be heavy in the way that makes other men suddenly cautious.

"Father," Brown Suit said, voice pleasant and dry. "Emergency cultural protection order. Temporary relocation of portable antiquities for safety during increased activity." He displayed a document with too many stamps to be invented by morning.

Mar Ephrem read the first paragraph as if he were reading Genesis and the second as if it were a list of ingredients. His mouth did not move when he reached the third. "Signed by no one," he said mildly.

"By a committee," Brown Suit replied, pleased by his own cleverness. "We are all responsible."

Elpidios beamed. "Wonderful. Let us all count the candles together."

Brown Suit did not smile. He glanced past them at the room, at the table, at the paper sleeve. "We will need to escort all objects of potential interest for evaluation at the Rockefeller campus. You will—of course—be allowed to observe."

Arielle felt the watcher's hand arrive at her shoulder like a colleague walking into a shift. Guard the truth with many small doors. Fog doesn't argue. Fog shows the doors.

"Inventory," she said. "We read our statement first."

Mar Ephrem lifted the printed page and spoke without haste. "We are engaged in a scholarly colloquium under ecclesial stewardship. All imaging is duplicated. Any seizure triggers distribution to additional parties named herein."

Brown Suit held out his hand. "The item."

Jonas stepped between the request and the table with an expression that wasn't defiance so much as geometry. Yael placed the Protocol where it blocked reach more effectively than an elbow. Karim found his phone's send button and hovered a breath from a command labeled the way nervous people label parachutes: Receipts—Expand.

Brown Suit did not blink. "We will be polite," he said. "We will also be brief."

The first police officer stepped left—habit—and the second right—training—opening a corridor that hadn't existed a heartbeat before. Brown Suit stepped into it without grandeur and with enough inevitability to be boring. That was the trick: boring that knows its work.

"Stop," Yael said.

He did.

"What you are about to carry," she continued, tone gone to steel wrapped in linen, "has been imaged and hashed to devices in three jurisdictions. We will accompany all handling, photography, and storage. We will not sign any paper that smuggles ownership under the word safety."

Brown Suit did not care for sermons. "We are moving quickly to prevent danger," he said. "If you help us be efficient, the item returns sooner."

"Where have we heard that lullaby," Elpidios murmured to himself, then brightened. "Candles?"

The plainclothes at the threshold wasn't the ring-man. He was worse: the sort who never needs jewelry. He moved once—half a step—and the officers behind him rearranged the room. Their posture said: you can keep your dignity or your possession; we are indifferent.

Arielle put her palm on the jar and felt its cool through the cloth. She felt the watcher's hand settle beside hers, not to stop, not to bless. To witness the choice.

"Interruption clause," she said, and nodded at Karim.

He pressed send.

Five addresses accepted the hash and the first page images again—Elpidios's Greek, Sister Miriam's Syriac, Armenian lists, Shiri's lab, Matthias's candle. The same truth, more doors. Guard the truth with many small doors.

"Now," Arielle said, voice steady, "if you insist, you will not be confiscating a secret. You will be moving a fact other people already own."

Brown Suit's eyes did a small math and found it annoying. "With respect," he said, "facts are no one's custody. Objects are."

He lifted his chin. The room became a narrow chessboard where all the pawns were tired. Jonas was a knight that had learned not to lunge. Yael was a rook who refused to move off her file. Brown Suit was a bishop pretending straight lines.

They took the jar.

They did it like professionals—not because they respected the people at the table, but because they respected their own paperwork. Two gloved hands. A third hand under the base. A case whose foam had been cut for something else and learned a new shape quickly. Yael called out time and names and room and hands as if each word were a drop of ink in the ledger heaven keeps on men who touch things.

Karim filmed, not theatrical, close and steady. Elpidios narrated with unnecessary detail—"note the thickness of the foam, brethren"—until a municipal hat cracked a smile it hadn't meant to. Mar Ephrem named saints quietly in Syriac that sounded like numbers.

Arielle did not move.

She thought she might. She thought she might lay her body across the cradle and dare paper to learn bruises. But the watcher's hand beside hers made a different offer: trust the doors you built. Truth's body had lived on ledgers and stones and women's bread lists when armies forgot to be curious. It would live for the next hour in a box if it had to, and then, tomorrow, it would live in a corridor.

Jonas saw the decision happen in her shoulders. He did not correct it. He gave it company.

Brown Suit closed the case's clasps with the piety of men who love hinges. He lifted the receipt book without being asked and wrote a line whose legibility would later insult historians. Yael made him add time, room number, name, emergency order identifier. He signed with a pen that had been purchased by someone's budget. He tore the yellow and handed it to Jonas like a crumb and to Arielle like an insult.

"Destination?" Jonas asked.

"Rockefeller," Brown Suit said. "Basement, Conservation A. Supervisor Klein." It sounded like kindness; it was documentation.

Elpidios walked the case to the stoop because his mother had taught him you see guests to the door. He blessed the lemon tree aloud and accidentally lost his balance long enough to leave a thumbprint on the case that would irritate a cataloger later and help no one but Elpidios feel better.

The white van idled with its nose toward Nablus Road. The case went in. The door slid shut on other people's vows.

They watched it go.

Silence tried to pretend it was failure. The room refused to indulge it.

"Many small doors," Sister Miriam said softly. "Breathe."

Karim made a small, angry sound and then a larger, careful breath. "I'm sorry," he said to no one, meaning everyone.

"You're the spine," Yael said. "Spines flex. They do not apologize for not being armor."

Mar Ephrem poured water as if finishing a rite. "We feed witnesses," he said. "And then we walk."

They did the thing Protocols never have the poetry to include: the unromantic hour after loss where professionals still have to be useful. Copies were checked, hashes verified, the Interruption statement filed with three additional hands. The Gospel chest received house–C beneath its false bottom and made no comment. Elpidios slid bread–A under a candle tray already sticky with wax. The Armenian sacristan took water–B and wrote nothing in a ledger that will later upset lawyers because it is both precise and older than their categories.

Jonas boiled the map. "Rockefeller is predictable," he said, shaping the building with his hand on the table: the Mandate-era symmetry, the cool Jerusalem stone with its British ideas of permanence, the arcaded courtyard that makes men forget that courtyards echo, the basement corridor that runs east-west like a throat.

"Loading dock?" Yael asked.

"North," Jonas said. "Two camera cones. One blind spot where the old boiler intake sits. A service stair that meets a hallway with a door that has never learned to like its hinge."

"Guards?" Karim asked, because if you give fear information, it becomes shyer.

"Union," Jonas said. "Shift at twenty-two. Coffee at twenty-eight. Phones at always. The dangerous ones wear no uniform."

Arielle listened and felt the shape of the building settle into the sense of her hand, the way ruins do when you've been staring at them long enough to hear their arrogance. The watcher's presence did not leave with the jar. It sat in the room like another chair taken by someone whose face you never quite catch.

"We don't rush," she said. The words surprised her by being calm. "We read what we can without a body. We make the ledgers speak louder. Tonight we plan the corridor. Tomorrow we take breath back."

"Thunder later," Jonas said automatically, then corrected himself with a small tilt of his head. "Thunder soon."

Matthias arrived late, linen open at the throat, the candle burned down to an inch. He took in the cradle's absence and did not perform sympathy. He stood in it.

"They forced your clause," he said.

"We forced their receipt," Yael answered.

He placed a folded floor plan on the table—one of those clean drawings that believes rooms are obedient—then laid a transparent markup over it with notes in a hand that refused to be serifed: Camera cones, bad hinge, vent grate (unbolted), false wall (1929). He didn't say how he got it; his apologetics have always been for facts, not methods.

"Candle," Jonas acknowledged.

"Corridor," Matthias replied.

Karim stared at the plan and began to smile the way men grin at geometry that promises mischief. "We'll need a reason for a door to be open when it wants to be closed," he said. "And a noise that makes someone look the wrong way for eight seconds."

Elpidios raised a hand. "I have incense," he said cheerfully. "Incense goes everywhere it isn't invited."

Sister Miriam was still on the line; you could hear the shrewdness move down the wire. "And I have a novice," she said. "He can ask a guard about his mother in a way that consumes a quarter-hour and ends with a recipe. Trust me."

Arielle picked up the Protocol and tapped the Custody clause. "The jar belongs to no one in this room," she said. "And to all of us. The scroll belongs to a community that outlived the men who built lockers. We are not stealing. We are undoing a misfile."

"Good," Matthias said, and meant it.

They ate bread that didn't taste like victory and drank water that remembered stone. Then the city taught them humility again.

"Front," Jonas said, head lifting, body turning before ears explained why.

Footsteps in the court. Not inspectors. Boots. A voice that liked microphones asked for the Father with a tone that had learned to practice law. Brown Suit's committee had developed an appendix: seizure of related materials. They had come for images, for notes, for devices, for anything that looked like a door.

"Interruption again," Yael said, already moving the Protocol to the top of the pile of dull, sealed envelopes. Elpidios lifted a tray of candles with a flourish that made him taller. Mar Ephrem's hand found the hidden notch in the Gospel chest and slid house–C deeper.

Arielle didn't reach for the cradle. It was empty. She reached for Karim's shoulder. "Spine," she said.

He straightened. "Spine," he repeated.

Brown Suit entered without having earned the right to be tired. He held the same folder, thicker now, and a new face: a young attorney whose suit had not yet learned how to sit and whose eyes had been given a brief to admire signatures.

"Devices," the attorney said. "For cloning. Voluntary, of course." His smile did not bother to lie well.

"Cloning is a good word," Yael said. "We already used it. Would you like to witness the hashes?"

The attorney's mouth opened and closed like a fish discovering glass. He had expected resistance. He had not expected competence.

"Inventory," Elpidios sang, delightful. "We have so many bees."

They bought another quarter-hour with wax and piety. Brown Suit's patience learned where its edge was and put a toe over it, then two. He looked at Mar Ephrem and chose a sentence that wanted to draw blood.

"Father," he said, gentle in the way of men who enjoy their leverage, "do not make us teach your house to obey."

Mar Ephrem's eyes went the soft black of wet basalt. "My house knows how to die," he said quietly. "Obedience is lower on the list."

Brown Suit considered the line, decided not to be clever, and gestured toward devices.

They handed over phones that already held nothing, sticks that already held everything in places these men couldn't open, paper that said less than it meant and enough to require honesty later. The attorney relieved to have something to place on top of his brief, smiled like a man who believes in paper as a sacrament.

When they left—for now, always for now—the air in the room changed temperature by a degree that only people who live on degrees would feel.

Karim sat down too fast and then stood up slowly, as if he had remembered the chair owed him nothing.

"We keep moving," Jonas said. "We move sideways while they march. They like hallways. We like doors."

Arielle looked at the empty cradle and didn't feel empty. She felt angled—a vector pointed at a building with 1930s stone and bullet freckles and a service stair that wanted to be useful to someone honest.

“We read without the body,” she said. “We keep witnesses fed. We teach the city to grow more doors. Tonight we walk the Kidron and learn how stone breathes. Tomorrow we go to Rockefeller and make a closed room remember it has exits.”

Sister Miriam’s laugh was small and warm. “This is how women have done it longer than anyone,” she said. “Bread. Lists. Doors.”

“Thunder,” Yael said, almost smiling.

“Soon,” Jonas answered.

The lemon tree outside shook as a breeze found it. A bee made a half-invented circuit and told no one what flowers it had decided to prefer. In the scriptorium, the Protocol weighed almost nothing and mattered more than the air.

They had lost custody. They had not lost chain.

Chapter Sixteen — Corridor

Night came up the valley like water that had changed its mind.

They stood where the Kidron begins to remember itself as a river—below the City of David where tour groups stop and locals don’t, above the bend where tombs look like the idea of nobility carved into living rock. A moth battered itself against Jonas’s hooded lamp and thought better of it. The city breathed overhead, indifferent and near.

“Walk it,” Jonas said. “Slow. Count turns; count bad ideas; count how often your feet tell you the truth before your head agrees.”

He led them down the drainage channel that once carried stormwater under Herod’s street. The slope was a reasonable argument if you had calves and no pride. On the wall, the chisel marks ran in patient, parallel ribs; someone had spent their life convincing rock to act like a corridor. At ankle height, lime scurf recorded a century of small floods like rings on a tree. The air was cool with old damp and older dust, a smell cities forget to let you have.

Karim moved behind Jonas, whispering a metronome of notes: "ninety-seven seconds from grate to first bend... seam of ashlars left... patched mortar—Ottoman?—no, British... collapsed spur at twenty meters right." Yael followed, shoulders squared against the walls as if reassuring them: we are careful; we will not wake whatever sleep you earned. Arielle came last, the lamp held low to rake the floor for treachery, the jar's absence a palpable weight against her ribs.

She could hear his sentence again—her father at their kitchen table, bread crumbs scattered like constellations: People think truth is a peak. Most of the time it's a valley. The tunnel obligingly remembered him for her.

At a junction where the roof fell a handspan, Jonas stopped and turned off his lamp. Darkness arrived like a body. He counted to eight. "Listen," he said softly.

They did. Water elsewhere argued with itself. Overhead, faint, the soles of a thousand tourists made their own river on the Pilgrimage Road the modern city was patiently unburying. A siren north toward Nablus Road declared itself useful. From the east came the empty hush of the Dead Sea drawing heat; from the west, the murmuring weight of Jerusalem planning tomorrow's sins and absolutions.

"This is the better corridor," Jonas said. "Hezekiah's is wet and has gates that think they are superior to bolt cutters. Warren's Shaft gives you drama and a bruise you will never stop naming. Here, stone wishes to be helpful."

Arielle tilted her head. "Exit?"

Jonas's lamp blinked alive. "Four that matter," he said, palm flat to stone, ticking them off with his fingers. "Siloam stairs where the tourists give up; the Givati dig's ladder if you need to feel like a raccoon; a mesh grate near the Mughrabi Ascent that has never learned to be properly locked; and—if we feel like being laughed at by God—Warren's vertical. We don't feel like being laughed at."

"Grate," Yael said. "Grates like to be unbolted by men with schedules; they remember it."

They took the left spur and climbed into air that had learned to be warm again. The grate waited where Jonas promised, a square of stubborn metal beneath an unlovely shrub that enjoyed being ignored. He knelt, ran his fingers along the frame, and smiled without joy.

"Screw heads chewed," he murmured. "Which means someone else has loved it this year. Good. Hinges hate novelty."

He worked a tool from his pocket that the law would politely call a driver and any honest man would call a compromise. The first screw turned like a sigh. The second fought as if proud of the rust it had raised. The third gave itself up in a manner that suggested it had been waiting. The fourth argued loudly, lost, and resented them.

Jonas lifted the grate a finger, then a hand, then his eyebrows. "Blind cone," he said, glancing at the corner where a security camera had been mounted with the optimism of mid-2000s grant money. "Whoever installed that lives for formality, not angles."

Karim's pen scratched as if writing could improve luck. "Three seconds for the plate to return without ringing," he said. "Two if you don't need friends."

They reseated the grate and retraced their steps. At the junction, Jonas led them up a different spur, ascending toward a vent cut high in an old retaining wall that knew more centuries than their hands would ever count.

"This meets the boiler intake on Rockefeller's north side," he said. "If Matthias's markup isn't lying to us. Blind corner, two cameras, one bored guard at a desk who will look up for paperwork, not faces."

"You love guards," Yael said dryly.

"I love the way they think habits can replace plans," he said, and didn't argue with her smile.

They marked the turn with a bit of chalk no one would see and a scuff pattern only a person who had been taught would read. On the way back, Arielle touched the wall where the tunnel doglegged and felt the tool marks under her palm crosscut by a later, rougher gouge.

"War," she said.

"Cleanup," Jonas corrected. "Wars leave better work. Cleanup leaves laziness. Men dig for water with love. They patch politics with picks."

Back at the mouth, they stood under a sky that had practiced being clear for millennia and often failed. The city's noise had more brass in it now, a daytime timbre; morning would slap them soon.

"Rockefeller tonight," Jonas said. "Walkthrough at dusk. He'll take the loading dock; I'll take the north boiler intake; Lev's face will take the door that likes to have opinions."

"Partition roles," Yael said. "Not because we're brave. Because we are boring in a reliable way."

Karim grimaced amicably. "That makes me what?"

"The man who will be asked questions," Matthias said from the gate above them, stepping down with linen open at the throat and the expression of someone who had found a way to admire a problem without falling in love with it. "You are the grad. Grads are grammatically required in museums. You will carry a clipboard and look appalled by humidity."

Karim straightened. "I can look appalled by anything."

"Good," Matthias said. "Appall now. Then eat. Then nap like a cat. You have eight-hour eyes."

They rehearsed on paper until paper had learned where to stand. Matthias would present himself at the front desk at 18:05 with a letter that pretended to be from a cultural institute in Ramallah requesting a look at a fragment in Conservation B and a dull question about permissions for cross-border conservation. The desk guard would accept the letter because men like him enjoy letters that point to other men. Yael would peel off with a white coat over her black and a lanyard that Shiri had made on a printer that hated her, heading toward Conservation A at 18:12 to "return a scalpel that had been lent without the paperwork it deserved." Jonas, in back, would meet a service door with a hinge that creaked like a conscience and a blind cone near the boiler intake at 18:14 when a delivery truck blocked the loading dock cameras with the indifference of commerce. Lev's face, arriving from the east, would ask a guard an elaborate question about parking lot access and the union break schedule until the guard understood less than he had before and chose to be kind.

Arielle traced the corridor with a finger on the plan until the walls stopped being hypotheticals and started feeling like stone again. "And me?" she asked.

"You stand in the one place the plan will break," Jonas said quietly. "At the hinge between luck and door."

She didn't look away. "So with you."

"With me," he said. No heroics in it. Just arithmetic.

They split for the day like a cell dividing to stay alive. Yael and Karim went back to Muristan's ledgers to pull three more pages where bread marks and water marks had nested names nobody had bothered to carry forward to make speeches with. Elpidios promised an argument with a wax supplier that might consume a clerk until he lost interest in phone calls. Sister Miriam sent the novice to the market for lemons and made him walk slowly past two men who liked coats more than they liked questions. Mar Ephrem hid house–C again after deciding he had not yet hidden it in a place good enough to make him proud.

Arielle and Matthias took a walk that wasn't a walk. Along Nablus Road, the Rockefeller rose in its British Mandate posture: clean Jerusalem stone, an arcaded courtyard, a tower that believed its views were meaningful. Bullet scars stippled the walls like freckles men forgot to be ashamed of. Inside, the air cooled and smelled faintly of paper, old pine, and polish.

Matthias made introductions to no one and everyone: a nod to a clerk who liked charts; a glance to a guard who liked routines; a hello to a conservator who liked objects and distrusted purposes. He did not name Arielle. She kept her hands visible and her eyes soft and did nothing memorable.

They stood on the mezzanine a moment and watched the courtyard take information from men crossing it. Every building tells you how to defeat it if you are willing to admit you're listening.

"Do you believe us yet?" Arielle asked, watching a shaft of light choose a mosaic it would leave in shadow by noon.

"I believed the first time you refused to put your foot on a crate without writing time," Matthias said. "I believe facts when they behave. You've made this one behave better than I expected." He looked at her sideways. "Do you believe me yet?"

"I believe you like being the man who says it depends and then makes it depend on the right things," she said.

He accepted the compliment as an irritant and a graft.

At 18:03, the day finally agreed to be evening. Shiri texted Yael a single line: "Desk guard is Avram; he owes me for a pH strip." Good. Avram would want to repay a debt by being noble for five minutes in exactly the wrong direction.

The driver with the wrong music parked a street over and pretended to care about his radio. Lev's fixer borrowed a delivery truck and an invoice that could be held up to a camera as if paper were where meaning lived.

They took their places as rehearsed.

18:05. Matthias at the front desk with linen open and courtesy closed, letter in hand. Avram read it as if it could put his children through school. Matthias asked a question about loan protocols that could not be answered without a phone. Telephones love men like Avram.

18:12. Yael at the stair to Conservation A, white coat over black, lanyard straight, a plastic case the size of a first-aid kit held like an argument she was prepared to win later. A guard glanced, saw coat and case, and digested them into habit. Shiri intercepted at the landing, handed Yael a clipboard that gave her the posture of someone who belonged. They did not smile. Smiles are for rooms that don't have cameras.

18:14. The delivery truck took the loading dock like a herald; its bulk made camera angles practice humility. Jonas stepped into the blind cone by the boiler intake and put a thin wedge into the hinge the way a man puts a prayer into a door—careful, convinced, expecting disappointment and satisfied with anything less. The hinge remembered its loyalties and yielded a sigh.

18:15. Lev's face caught a guard at the east corridor and asked, with helpless sincerity, how a man could buy a ticket for his mother when his mother refused to be told the difference between an exhibit and a lobby. The guard explained patiently, then carefully, then less patiently, until at last he remembered to be kind.

18:16. Arielle and Jonas met the corridor that didn't want to acknowledge them. The walls were plaster over stone; the floor a mosaic of tile that had learned to stop echoing when men didn't need it to. The air tasted like cool metal and the paper of a thousand reports.

"Conservation A," Jonas whispered, reading the labels like a man reading weather. "Two turns; one camera; one man who believes his stool confers jurisdiction."

They slid to the door. Inside, voices—two, no three. Clipboard tones. Paper sounds. The case they had watched leave St. Mark's would be in there with Supervisor Klein, a man whose name fit his role like an elbow fits a rib.

Arielle's throat went dry. The corridor in her hand, the valley theory in her mouth, the jar's absence like a second pulse. She placed her palm flat on the door. It was cool and indifferent.

Jonas's eyes asked a question. They were not the eyes of a man about to break a rule. They were the eyes of a man about to keep the right one.

"Many small doors," she breathed.

He nodded. "Door one."

He eased the handle, let the latch's tongue settle back without a click, and gave Arielle the hinge. She lifted gently with her fingers and felt the weight shift out of the jamb's embrace. A whisper. No more.

They had practiced the next part in their heads, a dozen times, knowing practice insults chance and is still holy.

Matthias down the hall raised his voice a half tone on loan insurance; Avram's phone took offense and demanded attention. Shiri's cough appeared at the stair like punctuation. Lev's face tried to understand a sign that pointed three directions at once. The delivery truck sighed.

Jonas opened the door the width of a blessing.

Inside, three heads turned toward the front desk because men turn toward phones and not toward air. Yael stood with her back to them, white coat crisp, clipboard arrogant, speaking low and rope-straight to a man whose hair had given up negotiating with his scalp. On the central table sat the case they had watched leave them—foam fitted around a history that refused to sit.

Arielle took a breath and stepped into the corridor that had wanted to be a wall.

She did not think of heroics. She thought of inventory. She counted time, hands, names. She placed her palm on the case and felt an echo of cool travel through foam and resin and clay to the watcher's hand, which arrived as if it had simply been waiting around the corner of a sentence.

Jonas's voice touched the air inside the room without owning it. "Supervisor Klein?" he said, soft; polite; uninteresting. "Your receipt has a line missing."

The man looked up the way men look up when dignity is about to be improved by paperwork.

The latch kissed itself shut.

They had time.

Chapter Seventeen — The Reverse

Klein had the posture of a man promoted for punctuality. Hair parted with a ruler, shirt the color of paper that had seen too many fluorescent lights. He stood over the table and spoke to the air as if dictating a memo to gravity.

"Emergency intake," he said. "Temporary custody. Arrival condition check. Tagging. Numbering. Shelf."

"Receipt," Jonas replied, pleasant and unmovable. He held up the yellow slip with two fingers. "You're missing the destination signature and the time the case left the street."

Klein blinked—offended on behalf of a system. "We—"

"—fix it," Yael supplied, crisp, white coat over black, clipboard in hand. "And while you fix it, we'll do the arrival photographs. It's what you would do if we weren't here. Let us save you the trouble of remembering your own good habits."

He hesitated the length of a learned virtue. Process likes to be flattered. "Fine," he said at last. To the junior tech: "Open."

Two latches clicked with the same modest arrogance as every case that has ever tempted hands. Yael leaned, peeled the foam lid back like a fig leaf. The jar lay in its cutout, clay serene, pitch seam shadowed, linen wrap snug as a promise. For a heartbeat the room tilted. Arielle felt her ribs become the world's hinge.

"Photographs," Yael said.

Karim angled the lamp, his mouth set around the job like a bit. Rake. Shadow. No flash. He logged angles and breath. The junior tech hovered like a child at a window.

Jonas shifted slightly so his shoulder took more space than his body. "Arrival signature," he said, placing the receipt on the bench with a pen that had the gravitas of ink. "Yours. And time."

Klein took the pen with the dignity of a man attaching a medal to himself and bent to write. Behind him, through the door's glass, Avram performed a small liturgy of telephone—button, nod, consult, button again. Matthias's linen collar hovered at the desk like a candle that had learned posture.

Yael slid two gloved hands under the jar. "We confirm weight," she said to the room at large. "Any deviation from field notes triggers stabilization."

The tech produced a digital balance with the eagerness of a boy asked to show a trick. Yael set the jar on the platform. The number blinked, thinking about being decisive.

"Six point three," the tech read, pleased.

"Good," Yael said. "Field note says six point three to six point four with wrap. She's behaving." She lifted, palms sure, and let the jar's cool climb into her wrists—into Arielle by proximity, as if temperature could travel like trust.

"Tagging," Klein said, surfacing from his pen to resume his sense of command. He produced a roll of tamper seals—red tape with serial numbers that believe in consequences.

Yael offered the jar's wrap toward him, as if inviting him to pick a seam to own with tape. His hand hovered, then retreated. Men who love procedures do not love touching fragility. "We'll seal the case," he decided.

Arielle let her breath arrive. Jonas's voice reached the air like a hand placed, not pressed. "Supervisor," he said, and pointed at the receipt. "Your destination code line is blank."

Klein frowned, fished a stamp out of a drawer as if it had wronged him, and banged it down with satisfaction. CONSERVATION A — INTAKE.

"Thank you," Jonas said. The phrase landed like a wedge.

Yael moved.

She cradled the jar one fraction closer to Arielle than the bench demanded. Arielle stepped that one fraction in, coat open, harness mouth waiting. The clay touched fabric with the small, undeniable sound of weight becoming carried instead of observed.

Karim shifted, breaking the room's symmetry, raising the lamp. The light slid up Klein's glasses. Reflex—Klein lifted his chin, adjusted frames, blinked at the glare. The junior tech followed his superior's eyes because apprentices always do.

Yael's other hand was already in the plastic case she had set by her clipboard. From it she lifted a dummy—a training core she'd used to teach interns how not to break things: a clay sleeve cast years ago in her own lab, wrapped in sacrificial linen, weighted with lead shot and old bolts, scuffed on purpose. She lowered it into the foam with the tenderness of an honest lie.

The balance blinked again, thinking. Six point zero.

"Wrap," Yael murmured, reaching for a towel from the bench and tucking it under the cradle lip. The number ticked up: six point two... six point three.

"Good girl," she said, to the number or the lie or the universe. To the tech: "Photographs of the seal, please, before we close. We love paper."

Klein had recovered his situational dignity. "Yes. Then shelf twelve B," he said, naming a place with the satisfaction of men who still believe in shelves.

Jonas's hand touched the edge of the case, palm flat, the casual ownership of someone who intends not to be surprised. "Sign," he suggested. Klein did, serial number scrawled across red tape with an innocence he would lose later.

Arielle stood with the jar in the harness under her coat and felt the world simplify. Gravity understood her again. The watcher's hand settled beside hers—not metaphysical now; practical; a weight next to weight. Many small doors, the text had said. The first had swung.

"Clipboard," Yael said, handing the junior a form with three blank boxes and an ocean of implied responsibility. He took it like a host accepts a relic. Paper hired his eyes for a minute that belonged to someone else.

Jonas opened the door without drama. The latch made no comment.

"Thank you, Supervisor," he said. "We'll follow the shelving and note the location for the inventory report."

Klein nodded, already annoyed at a future where his email would be long. "Do," he said.

They stepped back into the hall. Lev's face was down the corridor, still learning the word lobby as if it were delicate. Avram at the desk had two phones and the patience of a man who had decided to be noble. A guard with a clipboard did not look up. Shiri's cough arrived right on cue at the landing.

The world did not notice that its axis had shifted under a coat.

"Door two," Jonas whispered.

They moved as if they were not moving. The corridor took them because corridors are generous to people who act like they know the rules. At the corner, a camera stared at the place where excitement had refused to happen for twenty years. Jonas kept his head at the angle of a bored man's; Arielle kept her pace in the register of fatigue. Karim looked appalled by humidity with an artistry that would have earned him a grant in another world.

The stair to the boiler intake smelled of metal and the memory of old heat. The delivery truck was still nose-in at the dock, a cube of oblivion blocking a lens. Jonas slid the wedge back into the hinge and asked it to remember their first conversation. Hinges are sentimental when spoken to respectfully. It sighed again.

They slipped into the blind cone and became a rumor the cameras would not enjoy. Air moved across Arielle's throat, cool and unapologetic. The grate opened to the night with the small, private gratitude of an exit that knows it is righteous in a way that doesn't require acknowledgment.

"Down," Jonas said.

The service stair met them like an ally recruited decades ago and saved for a rainy day. They dropped to the alley where Nablus Road pretends to forget itself at twilight. The driver with the wrong music had turned the volume off. His hands were on the wheel in a posture that could have been prayer if you squinted.

"Anywhere?" he asked.

"Not here," Jonas said. "South. Then east. Then we let stone do what stone does."

They didn't race. Speed invents witnesses. They slid into traffic like a sentence into a paragraph that had been expecting it. Behind them, the museum kept believing in procedures. Inside Conservation A, Klein would finish signing a form with confidence. In twenty minutes, he would be asked for the case to be opened for one more photograph, and he would discover that red tape obeys razors and truth obeys doors.

Arielle pressed her palm to the jar under her coat and felt, for the first time in hours, the possibility of laughter. It came out as a shaky breath. Karim grinned like a man who had just solved a proof he wasn't sure he understood yet.

"Bethany," he said, because his mind had refused to let go of the line. "Machaerus. Bread, water, lamps. Ledger. We're stealing back a record."

"We didn't steal," Yael said, almost gentle. "We returned a file to the right drawer."

"Thunder later," Jonas said. It sounded like a promise with a schedule.

They cut east toward the Kidron, the car nosing along the seam where city stops lying about being stone. At the curb near a wall that tourists photograph and locals ignore, Lev's fixer materialized as a woman in a sweater that apologized for its own color. She got into the passenger seat without saying hello and handed Jonas two envelopes.

"One is a key to a gate no one remembers," she said. "The other is a name of a person who will forget to lock it."

"Bless you," Yael said.

Lev's face winked. "Bless my grandmother," she said. "She taught me to bake and to steal. Both for bread."

They left her where she had never been and drove on. The Mount of Olives leaned black against a sky that had changed its mind about being forgiving. They parked in a place that belonged to no one and everyone. The gate Lev had promised didn't squeal because it had decided to be proud. The path slid down into a cut that had earned the word wadi the hard way.

The mouth of the drainage channel accepted them like a memory. Inside, the world reduced to cool, stone, breath, footfall. The grate ate their return with the same measured chew.

Halfway down, Jonas stopped and listened the way a hunter listens for weather. Voices above—muffled, slow. Not pursuit. Cleaning staff arguing with the concept of dust. Somewhere else a siren was telling its favorite story.

They reached the junction where the chisel ribs met their chalk mark. Karim put his fingers on the scrape and smiled for the first time without looking over his shoulder. "We left a sentence," he said.

"And we finished another," Arielle answered.

At the far hatch, night took them back like a parent who has decided to pretend discipline worked. The driver with the wrong music made a sound of relief that he would never admit was relief. He turned the ignition without ceremony.

"Where?" he asked again.

"Home," Arielle said, and surprised herself. "St. Mark's."

Jonas glanced at her. "Doors are many," he said. "But stone remembers names. It will hold ours an hour longer."

They rolled through a city that had begun the nightly argument with itself—sirens and prayers and knives and bread. The jar pressed a steady truth against Arielle's ribs. The watcher's hand kept pace beside hers like a colleague, like family, like the simple physics of a thing that had chosen not to be alone.

At St. Mark's, the lemon tree had learned two new staples. Elpidios opened before they knocked.

"Inventory?" he asked, eyes bright like mischief in a sanctuary.

"Chain," Yael said, and put the jar on the table as if the table had earned it.

Mar Ephrem crossed himself with the weary gratitude of a man who will not allow drama to become doctrine. He set bread and water down without comment.

Sister Miriam, on the line, exhaled the sound glue makes when it behaves. "Now," she said, "you will sleep for one hour. Then we will read one more line with witnesses. And then you will plan tomorrow's stupidity with more intelligence than today's."

"Agreed," Jonas said.

Matthias, arriving a beat late and looking like a candle in need of trimming, saw the jar and—instead of speaking—sat down. He folded his hands like prayer, or resistance, or both.

Arielle touched the seam, not to open, only to say I know you. She placed a ka'ak ring on the plate beside it. For bread, she thought, and the words did not ache.

Above them, the city continued not to deserve its saints and to receive them anyway. Below, the rock-cut room measured its air and found it had enough for another reading.

They had not made thunder. They had made weather.

Chapter Eighteen — Many Small Doors

They slept an hour because Sister Miriam issued the order like liturgy.

When Arielle woke, the stone room had cooled a degree. The lamp chimneys were clean; the Jerusalem Protocol lay where a hand could reach it without thought; bread waited on the plate like a promise that did not need an oath. Outside, the court made a small sound the lemon tree had invented for days like this.

"Witnesses," Mar Ephrem said softly.

They came with quiet: Yael, hair tied back with the exactitude of a stitch; Elpidios, lamp in one hand, a sly piety in the other; Matthias, linen open at the throat, candle's patience in his posture; Karim, notebook spine-worn, eyes bright with sleep and resolve; Jonas, checking corners with the superstition of a soldier who credits stone; and Sister Miriam's voice, small and sure, on the speaker that rested near the cup.

"Bread," she said, from Ein Karem. "Water. Then work."

They ate. Not symbolism—calories. Then Yael set the lamp and the bench and coaxed the seam with bone folder and patience until the jar remembered it was meant to be generous. Resin gave with a breath. The guard slip lifted like a courtesy accepted.

The Estrangela stood as it had stood for two thousand years, lines walking their road without complaint. Karim timestamped, breathed, and took the first frames. He whispered his own litany—angles; rake; hash; bread–A; water–B; house–C—and his hands didn't start to shake until there was nothing delicate left to touch.

"Read," Mar Ephrem said.

Sister Miriam gave the Syriac first, each letter landing as if it had earned its place. Then she translated, not to perform but to record:

"At the house of crossing and at the mountain, the keeping shall be bound—bread and water and lamps—that when men ask for fathers, the mothers will be found."

Yael's mouth ticked, the smallest assent. "Ledger," she murmured. "Not thunder. Structure."

The next line ran like a line item and still found a way to be more:

"When pestilence comes, and vow is laid upon a girl, her name shall be entered by the water-keeper and confirmed by the bread-keeper; the lamps shall mark the oil with a small flame where the list is carried."

"Triangulation," Karim said, joy breaking through caution. "One name, three ledgers."

"Old women invented redundancy," Sister Miriam said. "Everyone else misunderstood it as nagging."

Yael raised the lamp a hair. At the margin, those tiny pricks climbed again—an acrostic stepping-stone spell. Karim followed under his breath: B–T–H–N–Y (Bethany). Below, a second ladder: M–K–W–R (Mukawir). And between them, faint and stubborn, three single pricks set as if to make a triangle no tyrant would see as geometry.

"Next," Sister Miriam said.

It was a list now, set like poetry has always loved to masquerade as bookkeeping:

"Ya'el of bread, Tamar of water, Marta vowed in fever; Shoshana who entered by Hanna; Abisha who counted lamps when the men were hiding. Their sons and daughters: Yosef of the house of Oil; Mariam who kept the salt; Eliyah named by fire and Yohanna named by water."

Matthias made a low sound he didn't give to many rooms. "Salt," he said. "A fourth ledger—salt—for preservation, purity. Bakers. Baths."

Elpidios pointed with a lamp-lifting hand toward the wall without looking. "Salt was counted in our baptistry minutes until 1890," he said. "The clerk had a sense of humor; he drew little waves when he ran out of Greek."

Karim scribbled arrows as if trying to keep pace with a horse. "Fourth icon: salt," he said aloud. "Bread, water, lamps, salt. The ledger-maker's tetra."

"Photograph," Yael said, and they obeyed the old world with new light.

The chamber's air shifted—a thin pressure change you don't hear so much as feel in your throat. Jonas's head tilted. Somewhere overhead a door closed with more conviction than courtesy. In her pocket,

Arielle's phone shivered once: a text from Shiri—Klein is discovering feelings. You have twenty minutes before feelings learn to dial. A second ping: Lev—Buyer went quiet. Quieter is worse.

"Next line," Sister Miriam said, and there was no panic in it.

"Let the names be retold in the seventh year at the house of crossing, and in the ninth upon the mountain; in the fifteenth, at Kerem where the spring names Maryam, begin again; and when the sword takes men, let the bread list be read at table before the lamps."

Karim grinned outright. "Calendar," he whispered. "A cycle—a quinquennial dance in sevens and nines. And Kerem—Ein Karem—our spring."

"Scriptures love seven," Matthias said. "Administrators love nine. This scribe compromised elegantly."

"Photograph," Yael said again, and Karim caught the line like a child catches a thrown loaf—sure, delighted.

Above, a footstep tried to be polite and remembered it was late to the party. Elpidios's head angled toward the stair with an expression that married mischief to professional obstruction. "Men who come to count candles rarely bring ladders," he said. "We will enjoy that."

Sister Miriam took one more sentence before the room could argue:

"Keep the list in two hands: one at Kerem in the house of bread; one at Bethany in the house of water; the lamps shall know both, and the salt shall be brought when there is doubt."

Arielle's chest tightened with something that felt like shame and relief together. Two hands. They had done it by instinct—Yael and Elpidios, Armenian sacristan and Mar Ephrem, Shiri—and here the text behaved as if it had expected them. Her father's voice ghosted the edges of it: guard the truth with many small doors. She almost smiled. He would have approved of the metaphor being older than any of them.

"Close," Jonas said, quiet.

Yael reseated the guard slip and papered the seam shut with stitches no one in a hurry would admire. Karim sealed, hashed, split—bread–D, water–E, house–F—moving the sticks to hands that had already learned their roles. Elpidios slid one into a candle tray with the solemnity of a magician making a coin vanish; the sacristan tucked another into the lectionary spine with mild contempt for thieves.

Matthias lifted his folded letter like a monk lifts a candle and moved toward the stair. "Two inspectors," he murmured, not looking down. "And a man whose suit thinks it is a law."

"Inventory," Elpidios said, delighted.

They were almost to the landing when Arielle's phone hissed again: Shiri—Basement wants to be a cathedral. Supervisor called a superior who has microphones. Leave early. And Lev—your buyer borrowed softer hands. They will ask for confession at your door. The lemon tree rustled as a small draft learned how to be omen.

"Plan B?" Karim whispered.

"We're already on Plan D," Yael said, and smiled with her teeth. "But yes."

They rose into the nave where light behaved itself and pretended to be innocent. Two municipal inspectors stood with hats in their hands and patience newly starched. Between them, Brown Suit was back with his folder, now genuinely heavy, and a younger attorney whose tie had not convinced his throat.

"Father," Brown Suit said, gentle for the benefit of the air. "We will assist you by removing related materials for cloning. Temporary, courteous."

"Cloning is a good word," Yael said brightly. "We love cloning. We have already done it six times. Would you like to witness the hashes?"

The attorney opened his mouth to enjoy the word hash and then remembered he had not cleared joy with his supervisor. Brown Suit held out a hand with the shape of compromise and possession.

"Devices," he said. "For a moment."

"Of course," Mar Ephrem said, and produced three dead phones with the tenderness of a man offering loaves to a stranger. Elpidios handed the attorney a USB so blank it could have qualified as midrash. The attorney smiled like a man who had been given a task—the cheapest coin you can pay a young lawyer with.

"Candles," Elpidios added, the word so happy it was a weapon. "Shall we count them together?"

They bought eight minutes with wax and name-of-saints. Then five more with a disagreement over lantern wicks. Brown Suit's patience practiced being kind until it failed to be.

"Enough," he said softly. "Basement. Now."

"After bread," Mar Ephrem replied, unblinking. "Always after bread."

They weren't going to win the room. They weren't trying. They were winning the hour after the room.

Arielle slid the jar's straps under her coat like breath. Jonas angled his body so a man would have to brush him to reach a door he hadn't earned. Yael lifted the Protocol so a hand reaching for paper would touch rules first. Karim tucked bread–F into the hem of a candle cloth, stitched there with three quick moves Sister Miriam had taught him over a video call months ago when planning had been theory.

"Basement," Brown Suit repeated, and this time the smile arrived with teeth.

They went—but not in a way that could be owned. Elpidios led the procession with a lamp and an air of having invented patience. The inspectors followed because they knew the choreography of corridors.

Brown Suit and the attorney brought their folder and their hunger. The jar rode under Arielle's coat like a second spine.

Downstairs, the stone room receiving them like a drawer. The air held its cool; the wall kept its cross scratched thin as resolve.

Brown Suit stepped just inside and stopped, surprised by stone in the way men are when paper had promised them an office. "We will begin," he said.

"We have," Yael answered.

They would lose this half-hour. They would choose how it was written.

Karim set the Jerusalem Protocol sleeve on the table and read the statement again—calm, practiced, fearless in exactly the way a truly boring paragraph can be. Jonas put his palm on the slab as if to remind stone it belonged to witnesses first. Matthias stood in the doorway a candle-width inside the line where a mandate becomes an intrusion.

They did not open the jar.

They named what they had seen—bread, water, lamps, salt; the seventh year; the ninth; Kerem; Bethany; Mukawir; the two hands; the small flame in the oil ledger; names of women where men would pretend to forget them—and put copies in a tray that could be picked up by any hand with eyes and courage. Then they handed that tray to the young attorney and watched the thought enter his face that this would be the most honest thing he touched that day.

"Chain," Yael said simply. "If you break it, it will be visible."

Brown Suit glanced at the tray, at the Protocol, at the clean seam, at the bread. His mind did a calculation that was mostly future tense. He did not like the answer.

"Tomorrow," he said, which is what men say when they do not own today. "We will return."

“Tomorrow is a saint,” Elpidios murmured, too pleased with himself to be pastoral. “He loves to visit.”

Upstairs, the lemon tree rehearsed innocence for the third time in as many days. Outside, a car idled—the kind that drops men and opinions and collects neither. Lev’s fixer, in the court’s shade, became an old woman pitying pigeons.

“Small doors,” Sister Miriam said through the phone, voice warm and iron. “It’s how you starve wolves.”

Arielle set her palm on the jar—not for possession, for company. The watcher’s hand settled beside it again, more companion than command now. She was tired enough to feel gratitude that had nothing to prove.

“We’ll split,” Jonas said. “House to Elpidios. Water to Sister Miriam. Lamps to St. James. Salt to Shiri’s lab. Bread to the bees.” He angled his head. “And thunder—”

“Later,” Arielle said. “But close.”

They moved again, doors breeding doors: a packet to the Greek church with Elpidios’s wicked grin and a whispered “for bread”; a packet to Ein Karem tucked under a basket of lemons that smelled so honest no one would want to look underneath; Armenian lists folded into a dull envelope that asked to be ignored; Shiri’s lab letterhead made into boredom on purpose. At each handoff, a nod. At each nod, a house learning a name.

At Muristan, a boy sold sesame rings and told a worse version of yesterday’s joke about the monk, the tourist, and the cat. It was still funny.

Back at St. Mark’s, the room breathed them in and found its temperature again. The jar settled into its cradle like a tool that has chosen its bench. The Protocol slept under a stack of papers no one would value until the hour a lawyer needed a ladder to climb out of his own brief.

Matthias leaned against the door and rubbed at a weariness he hadn't agreed to. "They will bring more tomorrow," he said. "Not better. Just more."

"Then we will bring many," Mar Ephrem said mildly. "Doors, not men."

Karim drew three short strokes—bread—a drop—water—a flame—lamp—and, newly, a small heap—salt—then wrote beneath them in Syriac, his hand careful: Bnath Qyama. Under that, in English: Keepers.

Arielle's phone buzzed once more. Shiri—Klein found your towel. He hates towels. He will write emails all night. I have tea.

Arielle laughed, a small sound that didn't apologize. She looked around at the faces and the stone and the table and the lemon tree's stubborn shadow at the door and thought: We are doing the unglamorous miracle—making a fact harder to kill.

"Tomorrow," Jonas said, ritual now.

"Tomorrow," Arielle answered. It didn't feel like surrender. It felt like a schedule.

Outside, the city accumulated arguments. Inside, the room kept its many small doors and pretended not to be proud of them.

morrow could be loud.

Chapter Nineteen — The Candle from Tur Abdin

Morning found the Quarter taut and ordinary at once—vendors arguing prices with a tenderness that sounded like insult, a cat occupying an artery of traffic with theological certainty, bells making promises the day had no intention of keeping.

In the scriptorium, the jar rested in its cradle, seam clean, paper line invisible. Bread on the plate, water in cups, Protocol in its sleeve. The room had learned the ritual and behaved.

Mar Ephrem stood in the doorway with a man whose black robe had the sheen of long travel and whose eyes had the patience of basalt left to weather. His beard was clipped close; his hands were fine, stained faintly by the inks of other monasteries.

"Abuna Narsai," the abbot said. "From Tur Abdin. He was already on his way for other business. He arrived with the sunrise and a headache that prefers coffee to aspirin."

The priest inclined his head. His Syriac, when he spoke, sat in his mouth like a home that traveled well. "Peace upon your house," he said. To Arielle: "And upon your work."

She offered her hand without embarrassment. "On the work," she said. "Not us."

He smiled with one side of his mouth. "That is always the prayer."

They gave him bread and the black coffee that improves men. He did not ask to see the jar; he asked to see their notes. Yael placed the folio in front of him, thin plastic sleeves holding the IR captures, Karim's neat block letters labeling each line like an anchor.

Narsai read without impatience, lips moving over Estrangela, eyes flicking under the lamplight. At the margin marks—BETHANY—he nodded, unsurprised. At M–K–W–R, the same. At bread, water, lamps, salt, he made a low approving sound in his throat.

"Your scribe," he said, "thinks like a deacon and writes like a man who has copied homilies until his hand stopped arguing with the letterforms." He tapped a yodh with an index finger. "See this habit? The yodh bites to the left before it rises—old Estrangela at home in itself. And the lamedh—he likes a long back; he enjoys the flourish but remembers to be useful."

"Century?" Karim asked, trying not to sound like a student begging a date.

Narsai tilted his head. "Hand like this runs wide. Late second to fourth, if I were forced to choose. The ink in your captures behaves more like the third. Your linen tells me honesty; the pitch tells me the jar traveled. The hand tells me a man who loved copying lists and believed records are a form of devotion."

Arielle felt relief climb her ribs like a ladder. "We thought list before thunder," she said. "We hoped not to be fools."

"You are not fools," Narsai said mildly. "You are in Jerusalem."

He set the folio down and looked at the jar in its cradle as a man might regard a child asleep. He did not reach for it. "The mothers," he said. "Bnath Qyama. Our people called them daughters of the Covenant—women who vowed chastity and service, who kept ledgers and keys and recipes and names. Men preferred to speak of abbas and bishops in their histories. The bread still arrived warm."

"Do we have surviving lists like this?" Matthias asked, linen open at the throat, candle's patience in his voice.

Narsai's mouth tilted again. "Fragments. Hints. A rubric tucked into a baptismal manual; a gloss scribbled in the margin of a homily by Jacob of Serugh; a nun's name where a ledger expected a father. But this—" he nodded at the images "—is not hints. It is a method."

"Useful," Yael said. "We like method. It keeps the room boring."

Narsai took a small bundle from his robe and unwrapped it with the tenderness of a man who knows how things die: three narrow slips of parchment bound with red thread. He laid them on the table—one script Serto, two Estrangela, all three brown with time but not pretending to be older than they were.

"Tur Abdin keeps small things," he said. "We are poor; we keep well. This is a baptismal list from Midyat, c. ninth century—note the two columns: father's name and household trade; at the bottom, a tiny flame marking counted oil. This is a fasts ledger—bread marks in threes along the margin. And this—" he tapped the third, a processional hymn with an unlikely acrostic riding the outer edge—"is a map inside a song. We have always enjoyed hiding work where tyrants do not read."

Elpidios, hovering with a lamp like a man eavesdropping on saints, grinned. "Welcome to Jerusalem," he said. "We do the same with candle bills."

Narsai placed a palm lightly over Karim's salt doodle. "Salt is not romance here," he said. "It is discipline. Where there is bread and water, salt keeps the body honest. Where there is baptism, salt keeps the memory honest—names that mold if not read."

"Your houses kept the two hands?" Arielle asked. "Kerem and Bethany?"

He shrugged, a narrow motion. "We kept houses wherever we could keep women safe enough to write. Sometimes that was a kitchen. Sometimes that was a baptistry. Sometimes a woman's lap at a window where soldiers refused to look."

Sister Miriam's voice warmed the table through the phone. "He is not romantic, therefore I trust him," she said. "Abuna, would you recognize the ductus if you had the flesh before you?"

"I would recognize the habit," he said. "Not the man. We are not that superstitious."

"Good," she said. "Join our reading then. When the room behaves."

Narsai lifted his eyes to Arielle. "You will be asked to let someone else own your time," he said. "You will be told it is about safety. Do not agree. Offer them witness, not custody. It is the only bargain we will still respect in twenty years."

"We've been saying the same," Arielle answered. "We call it many small doors."

“Ah,” he said, pleased. “Then we will argue about commas and not nouns.”

Jonas had been out on the stoop, watching the teeth the city likes to wear when it remembers it has a mouth. He came back in, jaw set. “Two coats,” he said. “Different faces, same tailor. A sedan that pretends to be a cousin at a funeral. No vans. Yet.”

“Buyer?” Matthias asked.

“Quiet,” Jonas said. “Which is worse than loud.”

Lev’s fixer materialized as a man with the wrong kind of newspaper: yesterday’s. He placed it on the table with a finger marking the classifieds, where nothing was, which is how he said everything.

“Amman is sleeping,” he murmured. “The buyer’s hands are here. Two soft ones; one very hard one who does not need jewelry.”

“Then we widen the witness circle,” Yael said, already moving toward the tray of dull envelopes. “Greek house, Armenian lists, Sister Miriam, Shiri’s lab, Abuna Narsai by faith and fax.”

Narsai waggled a hand, amused. “Our fax machine sits under a saint,” he said. “It fails less than it deserves.”

They spent an hour making the world more honest and a little less efficient. Karim parceled images and hashes into envelopes that looked like government boredoms. Elpidios wrote Greek covers that could be mistaken for lamp orders. The Armenian sacristan signed for nothing and agreed to everything. Shiri texted once—Klein is tender; he will overcorrect—and once again—bring tea. Narsai wrote a letter in Syriac on good paper that said everything without saying anything: We have seen; we are keeping watch; we expect your patience to compete with ours. He sealed it with a Saint Ephrem stamp that smelled of beeswax and disapproval.

Two hours later, Brown Suit came with a younger attorney whose tie had given up on being straight. They brought a request for “temporary relocation for calibration" and the kind of patience that yanks at its leash. They left with a copy of the Protocol and a handful of very dull hashes and the memory of being offered bread in a room where bread had already decided which side it belonged on.

"They'll return," Matthias said, knowing the answer.

"Tomorrow is very faithful," Elpidios agreed, delighted.

By afternoon the city had softened—in sound, in temperature, in nerve. St. Mark's roof took sun like a blessing; the Deir es-Sultan roofs beyond glinted with their improbable beehives. The air smelled of sesame and metal.

Narsai asked to see Ein Karem. "If the list tells you to retell at the spring," he said, "go drink."

They went as if going anywhere were simple. The driver with the wrong music apologized with an old cassette. The road fell and fell and decided to be gentle. In the village, light pooled in the stone the way it only does where water refuses to be a rumor.

At Mary's Spring, women filled bottles with the practical concentration of people stocking truth. Narsai looked down into the channel where water ran shallow and clear over a bed of stone that remembered many names. He laughed softly at the graffiti—Hebrew, Arabic, Russian, English—layers of pilgrims with felt-tip pens annotating saints with vacations.

"Retell," he murmured. "When little girls forget to be allowed to be old women."

"Can you bless a ledger?" Karim asked, partly serious, partly twelve.

"I can bless a room that keeps a ledger honest," Narsai said. He made the sign quick and unpretentious. The water did not mind.

They climbed the lane to the church with its old floor and newer walls. A nun nodded at Narsai with the unstartled consent of someone who recognizes a co-conspirator. Arielle set her palm on the stone ledge where they had placed the jar for the first line and felt the cool announce itself like an answer that did not need to be loud.

"Your father stood here," Narsai said gently, as if reading a margin note the wall had chosen to keep. "Years ago. He spoke Syriac badly to be polite. He asked about women and salt. He left bread."

Arielle did not trust her throat. She nodded and kept her eyes on the stone.

They returned to the city ahead of the hours that grow teeth. In the scriptorium, the jar waited; the seam stayed shy. Lev's fixer took a seat near the door that had never learned to squeak.

"Tonight," Jonas said, laying a map on the table. "We read one line. Then we move sideways before Brown Suit decides to admire our corridor."

Narsai folded himself into a chair with the relief of a man who has decided to be useful instead of merely right. "I will witness," he said. "I will argue softly when needed and firmly when necessary. I will write letters that sound like math."

Matthias, candle thin, regarded the plan as if it might steal, then decided to let it. "The buyer's hands won't knock," he said. "They'll show up as piety or plumbing."

"We like plumbing," Yael said. "It can be turned off."

Karim rubbed his eyes and found his courage where he had left it last—next to bread. "What if the line tonight is the one," he said, voice low. "The one that..." He didn't finish. He didn't need to.

"It won't be," Narsai said. "These lists don't do headlines. They do tables that outlive headlines."

"Then we will love it for being a table," Arielle said. The words surprised her by not tasting like disappointment.

They set the room—bread, water, Protocol, lamp, bone folder. The ritual had eaten the fear and left usefulness.

At dusk, the knock came wearing courtesy, and Elpidios fed it candles until it forgot what hour it loved. Downstairs, the stone exhaled its cool breath, and the seam yielded with the sound Yael would name in her sleep for a year.

"Read," Mar Ephrem said.

Sister Miriam gave the Syriac like a woman who had decided not to die yet.

"Let the keepers name the daughters when they name the sons, that the line be remembered by waters and houses, by bread and lamps and salt. If men refuse the names, let the mothers read them to the children at table."

Narsai's breath came out as a prayer. "Amen," he said simply.

Karim's pen scratched—amen in Syriac, amen in English, amen inside his ribs. Yael nodded once and took the photographs that make memory bite.

A footstep above, softer than earlier—small hands that had learned the weight of a tool. Jonas did not look up. He looked at the door the way men look at traffic: with resignation and readiness.

"Close," he said.

They reseated the seam and made a room ready to become something else at a moment's notice. Upstairs, Brown Suit arrived with two polite men and a plumber who wasn't. He asked for calibration and offered a copy of a paper that believed itself to be law. He left with copies of boredom and a lemon from the tree that had learned diplomacy.

After, the city settled into the hour when courage and stupidity look similar from across a courtyard.

Narsai wrote three short letters by hand, each to a different elder in Tur Abdin, each dull on purpose, each containing a sentence that would take a lawyer a month to realize was a password. He sealed them with wax and Saint Ephrem's disapproval, and handed them to Elpidios, to the Armenian sacristan, to the driver with the wrong music.

"Witness," he said. "And patience."

Matthias stood to leave and discovered his legs preferred he didn't. He sat back down and scowled at his own honesty. "If they push at dawn," he said, "I can give you twenty minutes with a call I will regret. Use it without thanking me."

"We will," Arielle said.

"Good," he replied. "I hate thanks."

They ate the last of the bread and did not call it symbolism. The lamp chimneys went dark one by one. The jar slept in its cradle like a tool between jobs.

On the stoop, Narsai breathed the night the way men breathe after long work. He looked up at the strip of sky the Quarter allows. "My father told me," he said conversationally, "that truth is a valley, not a peak."

Arielle swallowed. "Mine too."

"They were friends, perhaps," he said, as if comfort were a piece of gossip.

She nodded. It felt true even if it wasn't.

"Tomorrow," Jonas said, ritual made useful.

"Tomorrow," Arielle answered. It did not frighten her the way it had on earlier days. It sounded like a door they already knew how to open.

Outside, the city rehearsed its teeth. Inside, the room rehearsed its many small doors, and the candle from Tur Abdin burned with the untheatrical insistence of basalt keeping weather.

Chapter Twenty — The Hard Hand

They felt it before they heard it—the way a room changes pressure when someone decides to make it theirs.

St. Mark's had learned their ritual: bread, water, Protocol in its sleeve, lamp chimneys clean, jar in its cradle with the seam lying there like innocence. Dawn was still a rumor on the roof; Muristan's cats had not yet held their morning parliaments. Inside, they were quiet enough to hear the lemon tree take a deep breath.

Then the power blinked.

Not a city-wide shrug—just a surgical stutter that made the lamps pulse and the fan forget its manners. Elpidios looked up with the offense of a man whose church had been asked to applaud.

"Plumbing," Jonas said, already moving. "Or the kind of plumbing that likes jewelry."

The knock did not knock. Metal kissed metal the way tools do when they've learned how doors pretend to be polite. Lev's fixer, at the side door, hissed a single word through the wood: "Hands."

Three men came in with the kind of permission that doesn't need papers. No rings. The one in front wore plain clothes that had learned how to be uniform by themselves—brown jacket, soft shoes, a face that would be forgotten by witnesses who would never forget being watched. He smiled like a teacher who likes moving children from their desks.

"Father," he said. "We have a leak."

Elpidios admired him with his lamp. "We have bread," he said cheerfully. "It soaks leaks admirably."

Brown Jacket's eyes did a little math and moved on. He glanced at Yael and did not see competence because she was not performing it for him. He glanced at Karim and saw grad, the easiest chess piece to push. He glanced at Arielle and didn't glance away fast enough.

"There," he said, chin cutting toward the scriptorium. "We'll make it safe."

"Inventory," Yael said, stepping into the doorway so a body would have to become a noun to pass. "We count first. We sign. Then you touch."

He let the smile widen the width of a receipt. "Of course."

Behind him, two men in utilities blue carried a coil of hose and a toolbox that had never held a wrench. Jonas watched their feet—the way one set landed toes first, the other heel first. He put a hand flat on the table, an old infantry trick: measure the tremble of a room through wood. The table felt like a metronome discovering allegro.

Brown Suit—real Brown Suit—arrived half a minute late with a folder and a tired attorney who had dressed in a hurry. "We're assisting," he announced, relieved to be narrating. "Temporary calibration."

"Bless you," Elpidios said. "Count candles with us."

Brown Jacket moved to pass him. Jonas shifted. It was barely a movement. It said: You will get through this door by choosing to brush me. Brown Jacket chose not to—yet.

"Father," Brown Suit tried again. "You understand."

"I understand bread," Mar Ephrem said quietly. "We eat first. Then we move."

Jonas didn't look at Arielle. He didn't have to. The straps slid under her coat like a second rib. Jar to body. She felt the cool sit against her sternum the way truth sits when it has stopped negotiating. The watcher's hand arrived without romance. It took its place as if it had paid rent.

"Fog," Jonas said under his breath. "Doors."

Yael lifted the Protocol so the first thing a hand would touch was paper with teeth. Karim took the decoy from its shelf and let it be seen—not waved, not offered. Seen. Lev's fixer became a parishioner with a broom on the far side of the hall and casually leaned it where a foot would have to go around.

Brown Jacket tested the room's spine with an elbow. "We're wasting time."

"Chain," Yael said, not moving. "Names. Time. Room."

He stepped, deliberate. Jonas stepped with him. Bodies can be rules if you make them honest enough.

A voice from the court—the driver with the wrong music, except he had learned silence. "Police," he said, as if telling the weather.

Uniforms flowed past the lemon tree like water that had been told to act official. The sergeant from Zion Gate with the crease between his eyes and the yarmulke took his place where a decent man stands when decency has been reassigned. He saw the utility blues. He saw Brown Suit. He saw Brown Jacket. He did math the hard way—with conscience.

"Emergency order?" he asked.

Brown Suit reached into the folder and produced paper heavy enough to make a noise. "Committee. Temporary relocation for safety."

The sergeant read with a face that preferred truth to temporary. He nodded once. "You have ten minutes," he said. It sounded like a kindness offered to a room, not a man.

Arielle breathed through the strap bite and found the groove where adrenaline stops being a flood and becomes a rail. Many small doors.

She could feel each one they had propped open with a hash and a dull envelope and a nun with lemons. Wolves cannot starve you in a city that has learned to cook in community.

"We comply," Yael said, and moved aside the width of a candle. Brown Jacket put a foot over the threshold like a man checking temperature with his toe.

"Leak," he said, and smiled.

They gave him a leak.

Elpidios, saint of mischief, heaved a bucket like a champion of liturgical slapstick and poured water across the nave with an air of compassionate incompetence. It hit stone, found slope, and took a cheerful left toward the inspectors' shoes. The utilities blues danced two steps back. The attorney made a noise that suggested law school had not prepared him for liquids. The sergeant swallowed a smile that might yet save him.

"Apologies," Elpidios said, delighted. "We have leaks everywhere."

Brown Jacket moved anyway. He was not here for comedy. He slipped past Yael as if doctrine were a suggestion. Jonas matched him like a mirror that had joined a union.

The room narrowed.

"Now," Jonas said, not loud.

Everything they'd practiced became muscle: Lev's broom skated, tripped a foot that had never seen a broom used honestly; Karim lifted the decoy high enough to be a target; Yael shoved the Protocol into Brown Suit's chest like a shield that had been waiting to be used; Matthias appeared where a polite man with linen becomes a wall; Narsai shifted a chair with a monk's casual as if he were tired and coincidentally making a barricade; Mar Ephrem set a plate of bread directly in the path of law because bread refuses to be treated as evidence.

Brown Jacket's hard man—the one with the heel-first step—reached under his coat for something that wasn't a wrench.

Jonas moved first. He didn't often. It surprised the room. Elbows are theology when used correctly. The man hit the jamb with an oof that didn't get written down in paperwork. The utilities blue tried to be helpful and met incense—Elpidios swung a thurible like a saint who had waited his whole life for an excuse. Smoke bloomed—legitimate, holy, infuriating to a camera.

"Out," the sergeant snapped, because there are lines even emergency orders don't cross. His men hesitated a fraction—the fraction that decides history—and then moved. Brown Suit sputtered about calibration. Brown Jacket adjusted his sleeve and smiled with his mouth closed.

"Tomorrow," he said to the room. He meant later. He meant hungrier.

He left without the thing he had come for and with the knowledge of a room that had decided to be expensive to visit.

Silence had to find a chair. It picked the wrong one and fell off. Lev's fixer laughed once—one breath—then turned it into a cough. The sergeant met Arielle's eyes and found, to his annoyance, that he liked the person he saw there.

"Forty minutes," he said, not promising. "Maybe less."

They didn't run. They did sequence.

"House to Elpidios," Yael said. "Water to Ein Karem. Lamps to St. James. Salt to Shiri." She didn't ask if anyone objected to the verbs.

"Jar?" Karim asked, because he had to.

"Out," Jonas said. "North."

Matthias had already pulled a folded map from a pocket that looked like it had been born holding maps. "Not the road they expect," he said. "Not Route 1. Wadi Qilt would be poetry and jail. Highway 60 is a sermon. We take the back—Ma'ale Adumim to Qalandia to a miserable third-class road that thinks it hates cars."

"Destination?" Narsai asked.

Arielle, surprising herself with how the answer was ready ahead of breath: "Tiberias," she said. "Hamat—salt baths, ledgers. Magdala if we can breathe there. Arbel if we can't." She looked at Narsai. "Witness?"

He nodded as if someone had named a psalm. "Heptapegon will offer bread," he said. "And a priest who owes me a bad favor."

"Driver," Jonas said into the doorway, and the wrong music turned the key willingly.

The city had begun its morning argument—sirens, scooters, strollers. They packed it all into bags that wouldn't be admired: dull envelopes, phones that had forgotten their data, a folio that could have been a menu. The jar rode under Arielle's coat, a heartbeat she had to lean into to keep even.

On the stoop, Mar Ephrem touched the jar through the cloth and then her sleeve with the domestic piety of a man blessing bread that will be eaten elsewhere. "Feed witnesses," he said. "And come home poor and proud."

They left by the door that had refused to squeak for centuries. Lev's fixer slid opposite and became a woman arguing with a fruit crate. The lemon tree practiced forgiveness.

They took the wrong roads on purpose. Past the museum, past the American Colony, a quick right where men forget the sign exists, a left where concrete remembers to be stern, through a checkpoint where the guard had the same eyes as the sergeant and decided to be tired instead of brave. They skirted the hills like supplicants who didn't want to bother God, then bumped onto an asphalt apology that connected two towns by the grace of men who never learned to like each other and built a road anyway.

The jar rode well. Arielle rode it like a second posture. Karim watched mirrors. Yael watched Jonas's knuckles for the slight blanch that predicts trouble. Matthias pretended to sleep because a candle pretends many things so other people can finish their work. Narsai prayed a prayer whose theology was ninety percent logistics.

In the window: Samaria's folds, stones stacked in walls that have no political opinion; a shepherd with two phones and one mind; a boy kicking a ball at nobody and hitting his future instead. At a roundabout, a sedan idled the wrong way and decided to change its mind at the last second. Jonas changed it for him. No ring flashed. That was worse.

They crossed the ridge and felt the air tilt toward the north—olive and dust giving way to water and its old perfumes. Past Afula, the world remembered green. At the Sea of Galilee, light turned steel then mercy.

"Tiberias," Jonas said.

"Hamat," Arielle answered, trying not to grin at the vulgarity of feeling joy. "Salt ledger, bath accounts, women at the hearth who ran what men forgot."

"You're getting romantic," Yael warned.

"I'm getting useful," Arielle said.

They pulled under the shade of a tamarisk by the Hamat wall. The smell of sulfur met them like a joke someone refuses to retire. A bored attendant looked up with the affection people reserve for institutions that will outlast them. Narsai spoke five words that turned the air into permission.

Inside, mosaics made arguments with old sun. A menorah, a shofar, a ma'agal wheel that meant the seasons believed in themselves. In a low room behind glass, a ledger stone inscribed with a list of donors and baths and fees—names that sounded like bread and water even when they said money.

"Salt," Karim whispered, pointing at the line with a small carved heap symbol he had just learned to love.

They didn't need to touch. They needed to see. Yael lifted the phone, raked the light. Karim logged angles. Arielle counted boxes the way a woman counts loaves. Abisha could have written this. Marta could have carried it through a fever.

Narsai touched the glass with two fingers as if he were blessing an argument. "This is the drawer," he said. "Your scroll says which files belong here."

Outside, Magdala waited with its mikva'ot and its altar stone and its archaeology that learned humility by being found late. Arbel waited with its cliffs that had made rebels and lovers brave. Capernaum waited with its synagogue stones arguing about which layer deserved to speak first.

Arielle set her palm on the jar through the coat and felt the watcher's hand settle beside it like someone putting down their satchel on a bench. We are in the drawer, it seemed to say. Keep going.

"Tonight," Jonas said, looking at the sky like a man telling time by weather. "We sleep where fishermen once complained about taxes. We read one line. Then we build more doors."

"Tomorrow?" Karim asked.

"Tomorrow," Arielle said, and did not apologize for the joy in it. "We make the salt ledger sing."

The Sea moved as if it had heard good work being planned. On the road behind them, a silver sedan learned how to be someone else. In Jerusalem, a lemon tree shook off a stapled paper and didn't bother to read it. In Tur Abdin, a candle burned because basalt knows what to do with wind.

They stood at a bath that had healed many unglamorous ailments and admired a list. It was not thunder. It was how thunder earns its license.

Chapter Twenty-One — Seven Springs

The lake wore morning like a coin that hadn't decided which side to show. Tiberias shimmered; gulls argued; somewhere behind them a bus exhaled an entire tour's impatience. The sulfur at Hamat had climbed their clothes and wouldn't let go.

"Seven Springs," Narsai said, pointing along the curve of shore. "Heptapegon. We'll borrow a room that remembers bread."

They took the narrow road past eucalyptus that shouldn't have grown there and did. The lake lay on their right like a patient animal. To the left, basalt lifted in polite terraces; the hills behind dreamed of cliffs and made good on it at Arbel.

Tabgha didn't announce itself. It appeared, as old things do, by behaving as if they'd been there before your categories. A low stone complex behind a wall; bougainvillea; a bell gentle enough to be told no. The Benedictine doorkeeper knew Narsai by the kind of nod men give one another when they've shared a witness and a bad train ride.

"Paulus," Narsai said, and the monk's mouth admitted a smile.

"You owe me a footnote," Father Paulus answered in German-accented Hebrew, then switched to the sort of English that arrives with visitor badges. "And a favor. The footnote can wait. The favor is a kettle."

He ushered them through a court that believed in shade, past a cat who had appointed himself Prior, into a side room with a wide oak table and three bookshelves organized by a logic that cared about use more than classification. Through the open door they could see the church's mosaic—the loaves-and-fishes basket with its four loaves, the fifth implied by liturgy or spite. Water murmured in a little channel; the springs warmed the edge of the lake until tilapia forgot they weren't supposed to be theologians.

"You'll want quiet and witnesses," Father Paulus said, practical. "I have both, but not time. We pour tea. We speak briefly. Then my cook shall pretend not to notice."

Yael set down her case; Jonas checked the door, the windows, the small lamp overlooking the bookcase with the unconvincing shade. Karim eyed the mosaic like a man who'd expected a postcard and found an invoice.

Paulus poured tea black and honest. "Shall we hide what you're not hiding," he said, "by pretending to bless the obvious? If anyone asks, you are recording an academic reflection on the relationship between table and altar in late antique synagogue mosaics."

"I can actually deliver that talk," Matthias said.

"I would suffer through it," Paulus replied, agreeable.

He didn't ask to see the jar. He asked to see their rules. Yael put the Protocol on the table; he read it once without comment and signed it with an amused flourish.

"This room has absorbed worse decisions," he said. "I will not make it regret this one."

They did not read immediately. They went out to the church first because the mosaic asked and because ritual matters more the longer you pretend it doesn't. The floor was warm underfoot; the tiny tesserae made their own quiet argument about patience. Arielle stood before the basket and its four loaves and the fish. She touched the basalt sill of the altar where pilgrims press both hands because they're not sure if petitions count unless they include fingers.

"Your father stood there," Paulus murmured. He pointed to a bench. "He took notes badly. He spoke Syriac to Narsai by way of a waiter's Arabic. He told me he did not want thunder. He wanted ledgers to stop apologizing."

"He was consistent," Arielle said, hoping her voice wasn't too bright.

Back in the side room, they set the table: bread (a little bakery in town had sold them flat loaves for too much and worth it), water, the

Protocol, bone folder, lamp. Paulus stood with folded hands and the posture of a man who believes in prayer as grammar.

"Witness," he said.

Narsai and Yael took the seam together. The resin gave as if resigned to good work. Karim's timestamp ticked. The lamp raked low. The line appeared.

Sister Miriam's voice came from Ein Karem, small and firm. "Read."

The Syriac made a road; the English walked it:

"At the seven springs, keep a hand for the salt, that the girls be named when fish are cut and baths made ready. At Taricheae, where the knives remember, let the heap be marked by the door."

"Salt ledger," Karim breathed. "Magdala."

"Taricheae," Matthias said, nodding—the Greek name for Magdala when it sold preserved fish and pride. "The knife remembers; the clerk makes it honest."

The margin marks marched again: not letters this time but a tiny heap scratched with a blunt tool—a three-stroke hill—beside a small flourish shaped like a rill. Karim traced them in the air without touching. "Salt and spring," he said, delighted by a scribe who refused to make it hard to love him.

"Next," Sister Miriam said.

The second sentence kept the tone of a page you use every day and love for it:

"When the oil is bought for the lamps by the lake, the flame shall be put by the heap, that bread, water, lamps, and salt be one basket. The two hands shall meet at Heptapegon in the ninth year, and the bread shall be carried to Magdala in the seventh."

Arielle laughed—the quiet kind that lives in your chest for hours. "They're literally scheduling the reunion."

"It's housekeeping," Yael said, pleased with the universe. "Grandmothers running an empire."

Karim took photographs, raked, hashed, split, breathed. He passed bread–A to Paulus, water–B to Narsai, house–C to Matthias, and tucked salt–D into Father Paulus's battered breviary with the monk's full consent and a muttered apology to St. Benedict.

Paulus looked at the line again. "Heap by the door," he said. "We have a door at Magdala that pretends to ignore history."

"Who do you know there?" Jonas asked.

Paulus scratched his chin. "A Franciscan who distrusts drama and a local archivist with a grandmother who taught him to sit down before deciding anything." He tilted an eyebrow. "A coffee will produce permission faster than your paper."

"We have coffee," Yael said. "We're very rich in coffee."

They closed the seam. They ate bread because you should. They drank tea that Father Paulus warmed again because he knew how to keep kettles humble.

Outside, the lake had chosen an answer for itself; it shone like a coin with a story. A pilgrim bus disgorged pastoral fervor; someone sang without rhythm and with sincerity. A man with a camera and a belly that signified indulgence took photographs of the mosaic as if the tiles owed him a pose.

Jonas watched the road. "Two men," he said softly. "Leather jackets that didn't start the day planning to sweat, walking like they forgot how tourists move. Not rings. Hands too quiet."

Paulus didn't change expression. "We leave by the garden," he said. "Which is to say, by the kitchen."

They did. A lay brother with a face like a friendly anvil held the door without seeing them and then remembered to see them just enough to make everyone honest. The kitchen smelled of onions, parsley, fish, and hospitality.

"Bless you later," Paulus told the cook. "Sin now."

They slipped along the garden path where oleander pretended innocence and a hose lay coiled like a question. Jonas put a hand out. The driver with the wrong music appeared without drama, as if he had always been parked between this hedge and that low wall.

"Magdala," Arielle said.

"Taricheae," Matthias corrected, because he cares about names. Then, catching her look, "Magdala," conceding that the correct pedantry can wait for the footnote.

Magdala announced itself with the unease of modern parking lots built near old stones. The site lay partly open, partly fenced and signed—a modern church with a glass floor over first-century basalt, mikva'ot neat as boxes, the famous Magdala Stone exhibiting its carved menorah like a man showing you his best coat. A small museum staffed by earnest people who believe in signage had a binder full of donors and tiles and an air of trying not to make devotional music happen.

A woman at the desk looked up and decided Narsai's robe meant she should be helpful. Her name tag announced Rina; her jewelry announced a grandmother who refused to let gold stay in a box.

"Coffee," Yael said, setting a small bag on the counter.

Rina lifted it with the reverence sugar deserves. "Now you are the family," she said, and led them to a side room with a window that insisted the lake was immodest.

"We're looking for a ledger that would have lived near the kitchens," Arielle said. "A drawer's worth. Salt marks—little heaps. Maybe a triad of lines for bread, a droplet for water, a flame for lamps. If there's an old door lintel salvaged from the baths, we'd love it."

Rina nodded. "Our elders kept everything just badly enough to save what mattered." She smiled at herself for treason against curation. "Come."

She took them down a corridor that smelled like fresh paint and compromise. In a storage room, shelves held boxes labeled in a hand that belonged to a generation that wrote like their teachers could still see their slant. A carpenter's bench had seen better centuries and kept the faith anyway.

Rina lifted a lid and drew out a slab—not pretty, not obvious—basalt with a groove worn by fingers and a carved heap near one edge. She raised an eyebrow as if she'd been waiting to show someone who would get it.

"You will say we should have kept it on display," she said. "But I like having one secret drawer that makes sense to people who need it."

Karim angled the lamp. The heap carved shallow sat beside three short lines—bread—and, below, a tiny flame—lamps. On the underside, faint, absurd, irresistible—three pricked marks in a line. He traced them in the air.

"Salt and the house," he said—joy fugitive and adult at once. "Our draft's lexicon. Somebody told this stone what to remember."

"Photographs," Yael murmured, making the routine save them from themselves.

Rina watched their hands with a dawning comprehension that had nothing to do with money and everything to do with being the kind of person who enjoys keeping a promise before she's been asked to make it.

"You are doing a thing the site paperwork doesn't account for," she said. "You are also not stupid. Good. Take your small pictures. Then leave me something dull to file."

"We have dullness in abundance," Matthias said, offering a printed note on letterhead so boring it could stop a lawsuit by making it fall asleep. Rina took it and filed it under a word that might have been "miscellaneous" and might have been "mercy."

They came up into afternoon. The lake had decided on bright. The wind huffed once off the water as if warming up to be enough later. In the parking lot, two leather jackets attempted pilgrimage by standing too still. Jonas frowned.

"Different hands," he said. "Not Brown Jacket's boys. Another patron."

"Buyer," Lev's fixer texted from nowhere: softer hands asking for breakfast at the Primacy shrine, harder one at Capernaum pretending to be pious and failing.

"Then we don't go to Capernaum," Yael said. "We make them wonder why Magdala smells of fish and not thunder."

"Arbel?" Karim asked, eyes on the cliffs.

"Arbel after dark breaks ankles," Jonas said. "We'll use fishermen."

He meant Tabgha's other little church—the Primacy, where basalt meets water and a rock inside pretends to be a table set by a resurrected host. Fishermen still putter out from the shallows; the shore keeps secrets because waves erase footprints without writing new ones for a while.

As the sun angled, they came back along the shore. Father Paulus walked them to the little chapel and pretended he was only being a good neighbor. He nodded toward a low basalt shelf half in the water. "Here," he said. "Men have cooked on this rock until the legal coders gave up caring."

"Witnesses?" Yael asked.

Paulus lifted a hand. On the path, a young monk with an unfortunate haircut and an excellent camera kept a respectful distance. On a nearby rock, an older woman in a headscarf shelled pistachios with the efficiency of someone who had done it during conversations that mattered. She nodded once as if she'd been told to watch.

They didn't open the jar. They didn't need to. They set the bread on the rock because the rock has precedent; they drank water because the air demanded it. Karim set his notebook on his knee and wrote: salt keeps the body honest. He underlined it as if he'd want to argue with himself later and couldn't.

The two leather jackets came as far as the parking lot and then discovered they had piety elsewhere. The harder hand would be at Capernaum waiting for men with more self-regard than common sense.

They watched the lake go from bright to pewter. Tilapia rose and made circles; a child threw a small stone and was more pleased by the splash than his mother thought appropriate. The world did not congratulate them on anything.

"Tomorrow," Jonas said.

"Northwest shore," Arielle answered. "One line, one door, one decent breakfast."

"Thunder later," Yael said, ritual sharpened into humor and back into tool.

Narsai wrapped his robe closer against an evening that had decided to learn cool. "I'll call a man at Heptapegon who likes to pretend he hates telephones," he said. "He will confirm the wrong thing to the wrong person at the right time."

Father Paulus squeezed Arielle's shoulder, priest and conspirator both. "Your father would have despised your courage and then fed it," he said. "We'll bake."

They slept at a guesthouse that knew the lake's moods and didn't make them its problem. Jonas took first watch without calling it that. Lev's fixer told the driver to park in a shadow that believed in work. The jar lay on a folded towel. The room breathed.

Arielle dreamed not of thunder but of ledgers with crisp columns and small marks at the margins, of women's hands moving beads and counting loaves, of a salt heap at a doorway, of a spring that chose to be generous. She woke with the simple certainty of a task you can describe without lying.

She touched the jar and felt the cool like a habit. The watcher's hand was there as ever, no longer portentous, just present—colleague, family, witness.

In the dark, Jonas murmured, half-asleep, the only prayer he trusts: "Doors."

"Many," she whispered back.

The lake turned its coin face down and hid light for a few hours. Tomorrow would make them pay for the peace. Tonight had let their bones remember how to belong to themselves.

Chapter Twenty-Two — Knife and Net

Morning burned off the lake like breath on cold glass. Tilapia rings plucked the surface and vanished. The eucalyptus along the verge shook themselves awake like dogs.

They ate bread and labneh on the guesthouse porch because Father Paulus had pressed a basket on them with the insistence of a man who believes breakfast is doctrine. Salt clung to their knuckles. The day smelled faintly of fish and sugar and travel.

"Sequence?" Jonas asked.

"One line," Arielle said. "One door."

"Magdala first," Yael added. "Rina's drawer gives us a file; her grandmother's coffee buys us permission."

Narsai, robe caught up in one hand against dew, shaded his eyes to the west. "If the list were mine," he said, "I would have hidden a keeper by the knife-sheds. Taricheae remembers work, not sermons."

They took the road that held close to the water. Magdala's lot was already trying to organize buses and failing with dignity. Rina waved them toward the side entrance with the sovereign air of a woman who had learned to ignore clipboards.

"I brought your boring paper," she said, tapping the envelope Arielle offered. "I will file it where bored men keep their dignity."

The storage room received them with the sigh of old wood. The basalt slab with its heap and three-stroke bread marks sat on the bench like a page that had fallen out of a book and refused to be re-glued. Karim set the lamp. The carved heap caught light; the shallow flame below it, scratched close to the edge, threw a shadow like a promise.

"Photographs," Yael murmured. Routine saved adrenaline from pretending to be virtue. Karim shot, logged, hashed, split. Salt–D went into Rina's desk ledger, which had once tracked tile grout and would now also keep a secret.

"Your friends?" Rina asked, nodding toward the parking lot where two leather jackets practiced being pious by standing still.

"Different buyer," Jonas said. "Same appetite."

"Then we don't feed them," she replied, and snapped the ledger shut.

They didn't linger. The lake had adopted a pewter patience by the time they reached the little church at the Primacy, the basalt apron half in, half out of water. Father Paulus met them not as host but as witness and led them without words to the rock that liked pretending it was a table.

Bread on the slab; water in cups; the Protocol on the bench within reach. The jar lay in its harness under Arielle's coat; the seam remembered cooperation when Yael asked with bone folder and breath. Karim's timestamp ticked. Sister Miriam's voice, small from Ein Karem, carried like a wire in clean air.

"Read."

The letters rose in the rake of the lamp—Estrangela steady, comfort with itself in the strokes.

"At the knife-sheds by the lake," Sister Miriam translated, "the names shall be entered when the fish are salted, that the daughters be counted with the sons; the flame shall mark the oil on the shelf."

Karim scribbled an arrow in his book: knife-sheds → salt heap → lamp shelf. He grinned without meaning to. "Housekeeping," he whispered.

"Method," Yael corrected, pleased. "It keeps men honest even when they don't want to be."

The next sentence made a map by pretending to be a chore list:

"When the baskets come from Heptapegon, the bread names shall be retold; when the nets are mended at Capernaum, the water names shall be called; let the lamps be carried at Chorazin when the road grows dark."

"Chorazin," Matthias said, almost affectionate. "Basalt benches and a seat for Moses that looks like a chair borrowed from a farmer."

"And lamps carried there," Arielle said. She could see it—the black stone synagogue up the hill where wind wrote its paragraph through arches; old women counting oil by habit. Her father would have loved the pettiness of it.

Karim passed the sticks without ceremony—bread–A to Paulus, water–B to Narsai, house–C to Yael, salt–D into a hollow under the rock that had fed too many metaphors for one lifetime. The monk with the unfortunate haircut stood by the path pretending his camera was a rosary.

Jonas stiffened a fraction. "Two men at the lot," he murmured. "Leather treats. Another on the north path. He's not here for prayer."

"Plumbing?" Elpidios would have said; but Elpidios was in Jerusalem counting candles as cover. Here, Father Paulus made the local substitution. "Kitchen," he said, and lifted the bread as if on cue. "We leave by the back. The cook will pretend to scold me; he will feed you. It confuses villains."

They sealed the seam, set the jar back under Arielle's coat, and let the path to the garden take them. The kitchen took them further with the smell of onions and the law of hospitality.

A fisherman in a sun-bleached cap leaned on the garden wall, eyes on the water in the way of men who read weather by nostrils. Paulus nodded toward him. "Sabih," he said. "He knows the lake's manners. He speaks fewer words than you need and all the right ones."

Sabih looked at the jar under the coat without looking. "Boat," he said.

They crossed the shore where basalt learned to be slipperier than it looked. Sabih's boat had paint that remembered better seasons. The outboard coughed, then repented. Water moved under them with that particular Galilee trick of being both lake and story.

"Leather," Sabih observed, chin pointing shoreward.

"We'd like them to believe we're arguing about fish prices," Jonas said.

Sabih smiled with three teeth. "Argue," he said, and opened the throttle just enough to make a small wake exactly where a camera would decide to focus.

They drifted toward Capernaum and then didn't. Sabih laid the boat broadside to the swell and let her wallow the way only locals allow without panic. Nets hung from a pole to dry; two children on shore threw pebbles at their future. The ruins of the white limestone synagogue sat above the older basalt foundation like a second thought that had demanded to be a first.

"Water names called at Capernaum," Arielle said, looking at the shore. "Women at the cistern. Lists at the well mouth."

"Lamps at Chorazin," Karim added. "Salt heaps at Magdala. Bread re-told at Heptapegon. The network holds."

Matthias shaded his eyes, watching the leather jackets watch them and decide fishermen arguing were not worth a report. "You've turned their appetite into boredom," he said. "A first-rate tactic."

"We specialize in boring," Yael said.

They didn't open the jar here. They didn't need to; the line had given them enough. They passed a small envelope to Sabih instead—a copy of the morning's images, dull letterhead, hash printed on a sticker. He looked at it as if he'd been handed a recipe card.

"For your wife," Yael said. "Tell her to keep it with the fishing permits."

Sabih tucked it into the boat's cubby as if he were saving a cigarette for later. "Doors," he said, surprising them.

"Many," Arielle answered.

They came in at the basalt apron again because leaving by a different path often creates witnesses you don't want. The leather jackets had run out of piety and gone to bother the kiosk. Father Paulus pretended to scold the cook and fed them anyway—olive oil, slices of cucumber, bread hot enough to damage patience.

"Chorazin?" Karim asked around a mouthful.

"After heat," Jonas said. "Basalt remembers temperature better than men. We go when the wind learns to be honest."

They took the ridge road in late afternoon. Chorazin rose from the hill like a memory of a city—not ruined so much as paused. Basalt blocks sat where hands had left them; door lintels wore rosettes; the synagogue's benches made a U that invited arguments; the famous "seat of Moses" waited like a chair that had learned to be colder than sarcasm.

The guard at the gate sold them tickets with the weariness of a man who knew his site deserved more buses and fewer phrases beginning with "is this the place where—." He pointed them toward the synagogue and pretended not to see their faces turn competent.

They didn't open the jar here either. They didn't need to. They listened.

Wind wrote its small essay through the arches. A kestrel hovered on a thought. At the back of the synagogue, the doorway to the east had a threshold worn by generations of sandals and a groove on the right jamb where someone's hand had always found the same place. Beside it, scratched low, almost careless, a tiny flame—three strokes—too modest to be decoration, too deliberate to be nothing.

"Lamps," Karim said softly. "When the road grows dark."

Narsai touched the basalt and then his own forehead in a gesture his order had taught his body before his mind. "This is the drawer," he said again. "Your list keeps reminding you which cabinet holds what."

They took their dull photographs. They filed a dull note with the guard. They left a dull envelope with a copy of the morning's line and a hash. The guard raised an eyebrow without changing his mouth. "For my drawer," he said. "Not for my boss."

"Exactly," Matthias said.

Night put a hand on the lake and pushed gently. They came down out of basalt into water's light and found that the wind had decided to be confident. In the guesthouse courtyard, Lev's fixer in the form of an old man watering geraniums said "phone" without moving his lips. Yael's buzz came a heartbeat later: Shiri—Klein is writing in caps; Brown Suit is collecting signatures; the hard hand is now asking very politely in Jerusalem.

"Then we make them choose between places," Jonas said. "We read one line where their paperwork can't be in two rooms."

"Tonight?" Karim asked.

"Tonight," Arielle said, surprising herself with the taste of it. "At the beach behind the Primacy. Witnesses. One line. Boring."

Father Paulus appeared in the doorway as if he had been the one to think it. "The cook is very offended by the idea of you going hungry while you commit prudence," he said. "Eat first."

They did, and it slowed their pulse to a rhythm that would be useful. Then they went out under a sky that had decided stars were not theater. The basalt slab by the water held their bread and their cups. The Protocol waited where it could be reached without performance. The lamp was low because low light is respectful. The seam remembered to behave; the guard slip lifted like good habits.

"Read," Sister Miriam said from the hill to the west, her voice a small line drawn between village and lake.

The line on the outside turn was short and unsentimental:

"In the days when men count only the fathers, let the daughters be read at table until the boys know their names."

No thunder. No map. Just policy.

Yael nodded once, the way a surgeon nods when a tool works. Karim's hands moved without art—photograph, hash, split. Narsai breathed "amen" and set it down like bread.

On the road above, a car slowed, then decided to be someone else. On the path, the young monk pretended to be taking a picture of the moon. Sabih's boat knocked once at its mooring as if agreeing.

They closed the seam and let the jar rest. Father Paulus put his hand on the rock as if to thank it for being furniture.

"Tomorrow," Jonas said, ritual a schedule now.

"Back south," Arielle answered. "Chorazin gave us lamps; Magdala gave us salt; Heptapegon gives bread. We owe Bethany one more visit before anyone mistakes noise for truth."

Narsai looked at the water. "Tell your city I will come behind you with letters," he said. "They will be dull enough to survive."

Matthias, who had spent the day being a candle without admitting it, managed a smile without gentleness. "Dull is undefeated," he said.

They walked back through a garden that had been arranged by men who loved right angles and forgiveness. The jar rode steady. The watcher's hand did not announce itself anymore. It was simply the weight beside hers when she needed it.

They had made another door and left it open behind them. The wolves would try to count doors tomorrow; wolves are not good at arithmetic when bread is involved.

"Thunder later," Yael said, grinning like a woman who had earned her right to irony.

"Soon," Jonas answered.

Arielle looked at the lake one last time: coin face down, keeping its own counsel. She thought of ledgers and women and knives and nets and salt heaps by doors. She thought of her father's bad Syriac and good stubbornness.

"Many small doors," she said aloud, to no one and to the lake.

The water approved in its only language.

Chapter Twenty-Two — Knife and Net

Morning burned off the lake like breath on cold glass. Tilapia rings plucked the surface and vanished. The eucalyptus along the verge shook themselves awake like dogs.

They ate bread and labneh on the guesthouse porch because Father Paulus had pressed a basket on them with the insistence of a man who believes breakfast is doctrine. Salt clung to their knuckles. The day smelled faintly of fish and sugar and travel.

“Sequence?” Jonas asked.

“One line,” Arielle said. “One door.”

“Magdala first,” Yael added. “Rina’s drawer gives us a file; her grandmother’s coffee buys us permission.”

Narsai, robe caught up in one hand against dew, shaded his eyes to the west. “If the list were mine,” he said, “I would have hidden a keeper by the knife-sheds. Taricheae remembers work, not sermons.”

They took the road that held close to the water. Magdala’s lot was already trying to organize buses and failing with dignity. Rina waved them toward the side entrance with the sovereign air of a woman who had learned to ignore clipboards.

“I brought your boring paper,” she said, tapping the envelope Arielle offered. “I will file it where bored men keep their dignity.”

The storage room received them with the sigh of old wood. The basalt slab with its heap and three-stroke bread marks sat on the bench like a page that had fallen out of a book and refused to be re-glued. Karim set the lamp. The carved heap caught light; the shallow flame below it, scratched close to the edge, threw a shadow like a promise.

“Photographs,” Yael murmured. Routine saved adrenaline from pretending to be virtue. Karim shot, logged, hashed, split. Salt–D went into Rina's desk ledger, which had once tracked tile grout and would now also keep a secret.

"Your friends?" Rina asked, nodding toward the parking lot where two leather jackets practiced being pious by standing still.

"Different buyer," Jonas said. "Same appetite."

"Then we don't feed them," she replied, and snapped the ledger shut.

They didn't linger. The lake had adopted a pewter patience by the time they reached the little church at the Primacy, the basalt apron half in, half out of water. Father Paulus met them not as host but as witness and led them without words to the rock that liked pretending it was a table.

Bread on the slab; water in cups; the Protocol on the bench within reach. The jar lay in its harness under Arielle's coat; the seam remembered cooperation when Yael asked with bone folder and breath. Karim's timestamp ticked. Sister Miriam's voice, small from Ein Karem, carried like a wire in clean air.

"Read."

The letters rose in the rake of the lamp—Estrangela steady, comfort with itself in the strokes.

"At the knife-sheds by the lake," Sister Miriam translated, "the names shall be entered when the fish are salted, that the daughters be counted with the sons; the flame shall mark the oil on the shelf."

Karim scribbled an arrow in his book: knife-sheds → salt heap → lamp shelf. He grinned without meaning to. "Housekeeping," he whispered.

"Method," Yael corrected, pleased. "It keeps men honest even when they don't want to be."

The next sentence made a map by pretending to be a chore list:

"When the baskets come from Heptapegon, the bread names shall be retold; when the nets are mended at Capernaum, the water names shall be called; let the lamps be carried at Chorazin when the road grows dark."

"Chorazin," Matthias said, almost affectionate. "Basalt benches and a seat for Moses that looks like a chair borrowed from a farmer."

"And lamps carried there," Arielle said. She could see it—the black stone synagogue up the hill where wind wrote its paragraph through arches; old women counting oil by habit. Her father would have loved the pettiness of it.

Karim passed the sticks without ceremony—bread–A to Paulus, water–B to Narsai, house–C to Yael, salt–D into a hollow under the rock that had fed too many metaphors for one lifetime. The monk with the unfortunate haircut stood by the path pretending his camera was a rosary.

Jonas stiffened a fraction. "Two men at the lot," he murmured. "Leather treats. Another on the north path. He's not here for prayer."

"Plumbing?" Elpidios would have said; but Elpidios was in Jerusalem counting candles as cover. Here, Father Paulus made the local substitution. "Kitchen," he said, and lifted the bread as if on cue. "We leave by the back. The cook will pretend to scold me; he will feed you. It confuses villains."

They sealed the seam, set the jar back under Arielle's coat, and let the path to the garden take them. The kitchen took them further with the smell of onions and the law of hospitality.

A fisherman in a sun-bleached cap leaned on the garden wall, eyes on the water in the way of men who read weather by nostrils. Paulus nodded toward him. "Sabih," he said. "He knows the lake's manners. He speaks fewer words than you need and all the right ones."

Sabih looked at the jar under the coat without looking. "Boat," he said.

They crossed the shore where basalt learned to be slipperier than it looked. Sabih's boat had paint that remembered better seasons. The outboard coughed, then repented. Water moved under them with that particular Galilee trick of being both lake and story.

"Leather," Sabih observed, chin pointing shoreward.

"We'd like them to believe we're arguing about fish prices," Jonas said.

Sabih smiled with three teeth. "Argue," he said, and opened the throttle just enough to make a small wake exactly where a camera would decide to focus.

They drifted toward Capernaum and then didn't. Sabih laid the boat broadside to the swell and let her wallow the way only locals allow without panic. Nets hung from a pole to dry; two children on shore threw pebbles at their future. The ruins of the white limestone synagogue sat above the older basalt foundation like a second thought that had demanded to be a first.

"Water names called at Capernaum," Arielle said, looking at the shore. "Women at the cistern. Lists at the well mouth."

"Lamps at Chorazin," Karim added. "Salt heaps at Magdala. Bread re-told at Heptapegon. The network holds."

Matthias shaded his eyes, watching the leather jackets watch them and decide fishermen arguing were not worth a report. "You've turned their appetite into boredom," he said. "A first-rate tactic."

"We specialize in boring," Yael said.

They didn't open the jar here. They didn't need to; the line had given them enough. They passed a small envelope to Sabih instead—a copy of the morning's images, dull letterhead, hash printed on a sticker. He looked at it as if he'd been handed a recipe card.

"For your wife," Yael said. "Tell her to keep it with the fishing permits."

Sabih tucked it into the boat's cubby as if he were saving a cigarette for later. "Doors," he said, surprising them.

"Many," Arielle answered.

They came in at the basalt apron again because leaving by a different path often creates witnesses you don't want. The leather jackets had run out of piety and gone to bother the kiosk. Father Paulus pretended to scold the cook and fed them anyway—olive oil, slices of cucumber, bread hot enough to damage patience.

"Chorazin?" Karim asked around a mouthful.

"After heat," Jonas said. "Basalt remembers temperature better than men. We go when the wind learns to be honest."

They took the ridge road in late afternoon. Chorazin rose from the hill like a memory of a city—not ruined so much as paused. Basalt blocks sat where hands had left them; door lintels wore rosettes; the synagogue's benches made a U that invited arguments; the famous "seat of Moses" waited like a chair that had learned to be colder than sarcasm.

The guard at the gate sold them tickets with the weariness of a man who knew his site deserved more buses and fewer phrases beginning with "is this the place where—." He pointed them toward the synagogue and pretended not to see their faces turn competent.

They didn't open the jar here either. They didn't need to. They listened.

Wind wrote its small essay through the arches. A kestrel hovered on a thought. At the back of the synagogue, the doorway to the east had a threshold worn by generations of sandals and a groove on the right jamb where someone's hand had always found the same place. Beside it, scratched low, almost careless, a tiny flame—three strokes—too modest to be decoration, too deliberate to be nothing.

"Lamps," Karim said softly. "When the road grows dark."

Narsai touched the basalt and then his own forehead in a gesture his order had taught his body before his mind. "This is the drawer," he said again. "Your list keeps reminding you which cabinet holds what."

They took their dull photographs. They filed a dull note with the guard. They left a dull envelope with a copy of the morning's line and a hash. The guard raised an eyebrow without changing his mouth. "For my drawer," he said. "Not for my boss."

"Exactly," Matthias said.

Night put a hand on the lake and pushed gently. They came down out of basalt into water's light and found that the wind had decided to be confident. In the guesthouse courtyard, Lev's fixer in the form of an old man watering geraniums said "phone" without moving his lips. Yael's buzz came a heartbeat later: Shiri—Klein is writing in caps; Brown Suit is collecting signatures; the hard hand is now asking very politely in Jerusalem.

"Then we make them choose between places," Jonas said. "We read one line where their paperwork can't be in two rooms."

"Tonight?" Karim asked.

"Tonight," Arielle said, surprising herself with the taste of it. "At the beach behind the Primacy. Witnesses. One line. Boring."

Father Paulus appeared in the doorway as if he had been the one to think it. "The cook is very offended by the idea of you going hungry while you commit prudence," he said. "Eat first."

They did, and it slowed their pulse to a rhythm that would be useful. Then they went out under a sky that had decided stars were not theater. The basalt slab by the water held their bread and their cups. The Protocol waited where it could be reached without performance. The lamp was low because low light is respectful. The seam remembered to behave; the guard slip lifted like good habits.

“Read,” Sister Miriam said from the hill to the west, her voice a small line drawn between village and lake.

The line on the outside turn was short and unsentimental:

“In the days when men count only the fathers, let the daughters be read at table until the boys know their names.”

No thunder. No map. Just policy.

Yael nodded once, the way a surgeon nods when a tool works. Karim’s hands moved without art—photograph, hash, split. Narsai breathed “amen” and set it down like bread.

On the road above, a car slowed, then decided to be someone else. On the path, the young monk pretended to be taking a picture of the moon. Sabih’s boat knocked once at its mooring as if agreeing.

They closed the seam and let the jar rest. Father Paulus put his hand on the rock as if to thank it for being furniture.

“Tomorrow,” Jonas said, ritual a schedule now.

“Back south,” Arielle answered. “Chorazin gave us lamps; Magdala gave us salt; Heptapegon gives bread. We owe Bethany one more visit before anyone mistakes noise for truth.”

Narsai looked at the water. “Tell your city I will come behind you with letters,” he said. “They will be dull enough to survive.”

Matthias, who had spent the day being a candle without admitting it, managed a smile without gentleness. “Dull is undefeated,” he said.

They walked back through a garden that had been arranged by men who loved right angles and forgiveness. The jar rode steady. The watcher’s hand did not announce itself anymore. It was simply the weight beside hers when she needed it.

They had made another door and left it open behind them. The wolves would try to count doors tomorrow; wolves are not good at arithmetic when bread is involved.

"Thunder later," Yael said, grinning like a woman who had earned her right to irony.

"Soon," Jonas answered.

Arielle looked at the lake one last time: coin face down, keeping its own counsel. She thought of ledgers and women and knives and nets and salt heaps by doors. She thought of her father's bad Syriac and good stubbornness.

"Many small doors," she said aloud, to no one and to the lake.

The water approved in its only language.

Chapter Twenty-Three — The Well Mouth

They left the lake before it decided on a mood.

The driver with the wrong music turned the volume to almost-off and let the road trace the Jordan south—date palms in files, irrigation lines like staff paper, doves commuting. The jar rode under Arielle's coat; its cool pressed her ribs with the unargument of gravity. Bethany, the line had said once, house of water. It felt less like a destination than a drawer that wanted its file back.

"Sequence," Jonas said, as the fields changed to hills and hills to stone.

"Bethany first," Arielle answered. "Then, if the road behaves, a whisper at the house of crossing." She meant Qasr al-Yahud and didn't have to say it.

"Witnesses?" Yael asked.

"Narsai, if he can bear it. Rina's dull envelope, Father Paulus's duller letter, Sister Miriam on the wire. Doors."

Karim glanced at the mirror. "Leather jackets are asleep. Different tail—two men in an imported sedan that thinks it's invisible."

"Buyer's softer hands," Jonas said. "They'll call the hard one if we teach them a new word."

They ate bread with too much salt because Paulus had wrapped it for them like doctrine. The valley opened. Jericho sat low and patient, the Mount of Temptation climbing the horizon like a dare. Off to the east the river braided itself toward nothing you can drink.

At a turn where the asphalt apology forgot to be confident, Lev's fixer waved them into the wake of a produce truck whose crates pretended to be full. The driver passed a paper to a soldier at a checkpoint that had been born that morning and already believed in itself. The soldier read, exhaled the sigh of a man who'd wanted breakfast, and waved the truck and its shadow through.

The Qelt cut opened—a bright wound through limestone. Jonas eyed it, calculating escape routes. "If they close Qalandia behind us, we give them the wadi," he said. "But not today. Bethany wants us dry."

Al-Eizariya met them with hedged courtyards and shopfronts that had learned to be stubborn. The Tomb of Lazarus sat behind walls that were older than most arguments. Two churches shouldered one another nearby, Greek and Roman, each sure of its story and generous enough to let the other keep theirs.

"Water first," Narsai said. He nodded toward the lane where a well mouth sat under a lintel that had been moved five times and lost none of its memory. A woman in a blue headscarf pulled a bucket hand over hand with the economy of someone who could do it with her eyes closed. She glanced at the newcomers, measured them against a grandmother's ledger, and decided to keep an open palm.

"Salaam," Yael said. She set a small bag of coffee and a roll of pH strips on the ledge as if she were paying a tax only she remembered. "We're looking for marks—little drops scratched near the stone. Old. Thoughtful."

The woman—her name turned out to be Um Rafi—snorted without cruelty. "Everything here is old," she said. "Thoughtful is rarer." She pointed under the lip. "There."

Karim set the lamp low. On the inside edge of the curb, in the shadow where hands had always worked, three small pricks and a droplet—not decorative; instructional. Above it, faint as tired breath, three short strokes—bread. To the right, a tiny flame. On the lintel itself, the ghost of a heap like the one at Magdala, reduced to a rumor by thousands of fingers.

"Ledger," Yael said, pleased, as if a key had agreed to turn.

"Photographs," Karim murmured, working like a man repairing a net.

"Your mothers taught hands to remember," Narsai told Um Rafi, not as flattery but as report. "We're only here to read the habit."

She gave a sideways smile that did not contradict him. "My mothers taught me to charge for water," she said. "This is cheaper."

They left a dull letter on Greek letterhead that would bore a thief to tears, with a hash and a line that said witness without saying evidence. Um Rafi slipped it under a tin where the city kept receipts nobody else wanted to reconcile.

"Inside?" Jonas asked.

The Lazarus steps fell steep and mean, as if time had practiced being narrow. The air cooled five degrees; lamplight found chisel ribs; the chamber opened like a lung. The Roman Catholic chapel above hummed in low Latin; the Greek church answered with incense stubborn enough to sweeten a decade.

Sister Miriam's voice rode the speaker into the stone. "Witnesses?"

"House," said Elpidios from Jerusalem, on a line that crackled like bees. "Lamps," said the Armenian sacristan in a single agreeable syllable. "Salt," said Shiri, annoyed at dust and fond of the annoyance. "Bread," said Father Paulus from the north, as if scheduling breakfast.

They set the table that wasn't a table—bread, water, the Protocol on the ledge. Yael coaxed the seam; resin behaved; the guard slip lifted. The Estrangela waited like a habit.

"Read," Sister Miriam said.

"At Bethany, let the water names be carried at the well mouth when the jars are filled; let the bread names be retold in the upper room; the lamps shall stand in the corridor, and the salt be kept by the door."

Karim breathed—upper room. He could see it: a house with an extra floor, a table that had fed uncounted arguments and two reconciliations.

"Next," Sister Miriam said.

"When men carry sword in the streets, enter the tomb and read the women's names, for the dead teach the living the order of keeping."

Narsai's mouth notched with that monk's smile which is half grief, half respect. "He has been there," he said. "The scribe stood in this hole and decided to be practical."

Arielle watched moisture crawl the rock. The word tomb landed beside her father's notes like a tool laid down and later picked up. Guard the truth with many small doors. Caves counted.

Footsteps above—more than tourists, less than parade. Jonas's head tilted, counting tempo. Lev's fixer's text came short: soft hands at the door; hard one delayed; Brown Suit practicing law at St. Mark's.

"Close," Jonas said.

They reseated the seam; Karim hashed, split, passed—bread–A to Um Rafi with a nod that made them kin; water–B to the Greek priest upstairs who had been pretending not to listen well; house–C to the Roman sacristan who clearly enjoyed conspiracies as long as they demanded paperwork.

In the lane, softer hands approached with the posture of charity—lanyards that meant nothing, clipboards empty of ink, smiles that wanted signatures more than answers.

"Friends," one of them said in English. "We are from a cultural foundation committed to preservation—"

"Preserve breakfast," Um Rafi cut in, and thrust a bowl of olives into his hands like a threat. He took it—because you take food in this quarter or you admit to being an alien species—and lost his next sentence.

The second man tried Hebrew, failed politely, and switched to a smile. "There is a grant," he said to Narsai, who had taught himself the art of appearing priestly and dull at will. "For cataloging."

"We hate grants," Narsai said kindly. "They kill paper." He nodded at their shoes. "These were made for floors without dust." It was not a compliment.

"Move," Jonas said quietly. Fog chooses hallways. They took the back—past the Greek courtyard where oranges went unapologetically to seed, through a passage that pretended to be a storage closet and was a door, into a lane that met the Kidron like a shy tributary.

"House of crossing," Arielle said.

"Too exposed," Yael replied. "They'd love a photo of us at Qasr. We give them Kerem instead. And stone."

"St. George," Narsai said—the monastery hung on the cliff above the Qelt like a vow kept longer than anyone thought possible. "The abbot keeps paper like bread."

They let the wadi take them, the car laboring up out of al-Eizariya, down a cut road, across a bridge that learned to be brave in British and forgot. The monastery appeared, clinging to its ledges, canted bells arguing with wind. The air tasted of limestone and old vow.

A young monk with dust on his hem opened without questions. The abbot—older, wiry, eyes that had forgiven much and forgotten little—listened to Narsai's three-sentence explanation, looked once at Arielle's coat, and stepped aside. "We have rooms that don't gossip," he said.

They took one—whitewashed, a slit window on the gorge, a table that wanted to be both altar and workbench. Bread, water, Protocol. Sister Miriam on the wire. The seam remembered its manners.

"Read," she said.

"The house of crossing is to be told again at the spring and at the mountain, that those who wash may count names and those who climb may carry them."

"Spring—Kerem; mountain—Herod," Matthias said. "Our puzzle recites itself."

"In the seventh, speak at the river; in the ninth, speak on the mountain. If men forbid the counting, the women shall sing the names as psalm."

Karim swallowed. He thought of the acrostic riding a hymn Narsai had shown in Tur Abdin, truth hiding where tyrants don't listen. He nodded, as if someone had given him a tool he'd always wanted to have.

They closed the seam. The abbot took bread–D as if it were a relic made of boredom. "We will put this under St. George's old saddle," he said. "It makes bad people uncomfortable to stand on saints."

Above the gorge, a helicopter roared and then thought better of it. Lev's fixer's ping arrived: Brown Suit stopped at the lemon tree; the sergeant counted bees; images safe; feelings hungry.

"Back to the city," Jonas said. "Sideways."

They came in by Wadi al-Joz, where garages turned cars into promises, and by a lane that pretended not to lead to St. Mark's. The lemon tree shook itself as if rumors were flies. Brown Suit and the attorney had returned with a taller stack of paper and fewer illusions; they stood in the nave and practiced being patient. Elpidios counted lantern wicks as if it were a sacrament. The sergeant with the crease between his eyes watched men try to be clever and decided to be tired.

Downstairs, the stone room received them like a good habit. Bread. Water. Protocol. The jar slept in its cradle; its seam looked clean; its line waited.

"Thunder?" Karim asked, a little sheepish.

"Soon," Jonas said, as if setting an alarm.

Arielle put her palm on the jar and felt the weight present as ever. She thought of well mouths and salt heaps, of a heap scratched shallow on basalt and a droplet under a lip, of women moving names from margin to margin until forgetting got dizzy. She thought of her father with his bad Syriac and good stubbornness, trying to teach a child that truth is a valley and the courage required is mostly logistics.

"Many small doors," she said.

The city argued above them. The room did not.

They slept an hour because someone had to make them. Tomorrow would be loud. Tonight belonged to ledgers.

Twenty-Four — Wolves Counting

Jerusalem woke with the sound of trucks reversing—grinding gears, sharp beeps, the city's way of announcing it would be inconvenient. The Quarter took the noise personally. By the time Arielle and Jonas stepped into the nave, Brown Suit was already waiting, folder under his arm, the tired attorney in tow. Behind them stood two men whose coats fit too well to be municipal and too badly to be tourists.

"Father," Brown Suit said smoothly. "We return with gratitude and with greater clarity. The committee requests comprehensive custody. For safety, of course."

Elpidios practically sang. "Safety is our specialty. We have so many candles, all very safe."

The two coat-men did not smile. Their silence was not shyness; it was appetite. Jonas shifted his stance the way men do when they know appetite is near. Arielle kept her palm flat on the sleeve of the Jerusalem Protocol so it was the first thing anyone would have to touch.

Mar Ephrem read aloud, voice calm, words like basalt laid end to end: "Any seizure will trigger distribution to additional parties." He laid the statement down on the table like bread. Brown Suit's eyes twitched but his hands did not move.

"Witnesses?" Sister Miriam asked through the phone, her tone making it clear she expected yes.

"Yes," Yael said, white coat already on. "Rina from Magdala filed her copy. Paulus at Heptapegon sent a letter duller than a dictionary. Um Rafi put water–B in her bucket ledger. The abbot at St. George signed for bread–D with a saddle. Salt–D went north to Shiri's lab with tea stains for authenticity. The house is crowded."

"Good," Miriam said. "Wolves hate crowds."

Brown Suit gestured. One of the coat-men stepped forward with the hesitation of someone who expects resistance and wants to measure it first. Jonas didn't move. He simply existed in the doorway with the mass of a wall that has decided to be a door. The man stopped, frowned, looked back at his superior.

"You are delaying the inevitable," Brown Suit said, polite as law school. "Our orders are not optional."

Yael lifted her clipboard like a sword. "Inventory," she said brightly. "If you want custody, you'll sit for inventory. Names. Time. Hands. You love paperwork. Let's do paperwork."

The attorney blinked as if remembering his profession. He produced a pen. Brown Suit gave him a glance sharp enough to wound, but the man dutifully began to write. The first coat-man shifted from one foot to the other, bored already. The second one scanned the room with eyes that measured distance, not conversation.

Arielle felt the jar's cool through the cloth. Guard the truth with many small doors. The watcher's hand was there again, calm, steady, as if to remind her that boredom is a weapon too.

"Twenty minutes," Jonas murmured without turning his head. "Then they'll push."

"Then we'll move," Arielle said.

They bought ten of those minutes with candles. Elpidios walked the inspector through counting wicks and oil levels as if the salvation of the city depended on wax. They bought five more by insisting the attorney record every witness name, including the cook at Tabgha and the boy at Muristan who sold sesame rings. Karim insisted on spelling each one twice.

At last, Brown Suit snapped his folder shut. "Enough," he said. His voice was still velvet, but the edge had cut through. "You are obstructing the state."

"You are obstructing the saints," Elpidios countered, cheerful as sin.

The first coat-man took a step, not toward the jar, but toward Arielle herself. That was the mistake. Jonas's hand closed lightly on the man's sleeve, not violent, just decisive. The coat-man froze, looked down at the grip, and realized he had been measured and filed.

The second coat-man moved, heel-first. Yael's clipboard intercepted him like a shield; her pen tapped his chest where a badge would be if he were honest. "Name," she said. "Time. Hands."

He hesitated. In that hesitation, a phone buzzed. Brown Suit's. He read the screen and his eyes narrowed.

"Withdraw," he said. The coat-men obeyed, annoyed not to have been fed. The attorney gathered his useless notes. The folder snapped shut again. "Tomorrow," Brown Suit promised, which meant hungrier.

They left. The lemon tree at the door rustled its leaves like applause.

Silence sat down heavily. Jonas exhaled through his nose. "We can't keep this dance forever," he said. "They'll bring a bigger door."

"Then we keep opening small ones," Arielle answered. She placed her palm on the jar. "Salt in Magdala, lamps in Chorazin, bread at Heptapegon, water here. They're trying to count. Wolves can't do arithmetic."

Narsai nodded. "The next line will point you north again. To the mountain. To Herod's ruin."

"Machaerus," Matthias said, candle-thin and certain.

Jonas frowned. "East bank. Jordan crossing. Checkpoints that don't believe in patience."

"Thunder later," Yael reminded him, but her eyes were serious. "This might be the thunder."

Karim wrote the four icons again—bread, water, lamps, salt—and added a crude tower sketch beside them. He underlined it twice. "Ledger goes east," he said.

"Tomorrow," Arielle said, and the word felt less like fear now, more like arithmetic. She lifted her eyes to the group, to the jar, to the watcher's unseen hand. "Tomorrow we go to the mountain."

The city outside sharpened its teeth. Inside, the stone room rehearsed its patience.

Chapter Twenty-Five — The Mountain

They read before the city had learned to complain.

Bread. Water. The Protocol where a hand could find it without thinking. The jar in its cradle, seam clean, paper line invisible unless you loved it. Sister Miriam on the wire from Ein Karem; Narsai with coffee that forgave no one.

Yael coaxed the seam; resin gave with the soft surrender of good work. Karim's timestamp rolled. The Estrangela waited like a habit that had kept families alive.

"Read," Sister Miriam said.

"On the mountain of Herod, where the wind keeps judgment, let the names be retold when the salt is ground and the lamps are trimmed; the bread be carried from Kerem and the water named at the house of crossing."

Matthias's mouth tightened. "Machaerus," he said. "Mukawir, if you're modern. East of the Dead Sea."

"Next," Sister Miriam said.

"If men forbid the keeping in the city, cross the river where the reeds are bent, and speak upon the dike; the women shall stand by the cistern and make the list behave."

"Dike," Karim echoed, pleased—the causeway that links Mukawir's saddle to its hill. "Cisterns on the north slope. We're being given directions like a grandmother."

Yael closed the seam; papered it smooth. "We don't take her," she said, not a question. "Border won't forgive clay."

Jonas nodded. "Images travel; jar doesn't. We go with witness and boring paper."

Arielle placed her palm on the jar—not to argue, to agree. The watcher's hand settled beside hers, more colleague than omen now. Guard the truth with many small doors. Doors didn't need passports.

"Who opens doors on the east bank?" Yael asked.

"Madaba," Matthias said. "Map church. Nebo. The Franciscans keep better archives than most governments. And in Mukawir, the parish priest keeps a key to a room that pretends to be a sacristy and is really an excuse to keep paper dry."

"Buyer's hands are in Amman," Lev's fixer texted. "Soft ones in Madaba buying coffee they won't drink. Hard one at Allenby trying to learn patience."

"Then we use a different classroom," Jonas said. "Sheikh Hussein up north, or we make Allenby forget us in other traffic."

"Allenby is faster if no one introduces us to their cousin," Yael said. "We give them letters and calm."

Matthias produced two envelopes, dull as daylight: one on Melkite letterhead, one on a university's; both said colloquium so many times the word stopped tasting like an alibi. Narsai wrote a third on thin paper that smelled faintly of the monastery that had raised him: we will witness; we will not own; we will be boring.

They did not kiss the jar. That was not their relationship to it. Arielle set it deeper in the cradle; Elpidios slid the Gospel chest's false bottom over house-C and sighed contentment at a trick that still delighted him. Bread went to pockets because hunger is not symbolic when you're crossing borders.

They left by a door that liked them. The lemon tree shook—wind or rumor. Brown Suit had decided to argue with other people for an hour;

the sergeant with the crease between his eyes was at Zion Gate practicing his weariness.

The driver with the wrong music kept the volume low. The road fell through Wadi Qilt toward the valley; Jericho lay wide and resigned, the Dead Sea a hammered strip of pewter. At Allenby/King Hussein Bridge, fans pushed heat around like bureaucrats moving paper.

Letters mattered. They always had, in this part of the world where stamps and cousins keep the same hours. The Israeli side admired Matthias's envelope for its confidence. The Jordanian side liked Narsai's Syriac and the way he looked like a man you could put in a ledger and not regret.

A young officer with a name tag that announced he was trying not to be bored held Arielle's passport for a heartbeat longer than he needed. "Purpose?" he asked, English bent by Amman.

"Colloquium," Matthias said. "At Madaba. Maps." He did not smile. That was the trick.

The officer's eyes found colloquium on the letterhead and relaxed. "Welcome," he said, as if meaning don't make me important.

They were through. No jar. No ring. Behind them, a silver sedan arrived too late and too hungry. The driver rolled them into the desert's pale undulation and let the Dead Sea ride the window like a metal thought.

The road climbed to Madaba, the city discovering red roofs and laundry and patient traffic. The Map Church—St. George—lived the way maps ought to: in a place where you have to ask twice to be let in and once to be forgiven for the bus you brought. The sixth-century mosaic of the Holy Land lay at the nave's front like a spilled plan.

A priest with an easy mouth and a patient forehead—Father Hanna—read Matthias's letter and decided to be useful. He had the air of a man who had said no correctly many times and had decided today was for yes.

"We are not rich in secrets," he said, "but we are rich in drawers."

He gave them a side room with a table that could be altar or workbench depending on who had the key. He looked at their Protocol without touching it and nodded as if someone had finally learned a language he liked. He did not ask to see the jar. He asked for hashes. Yael handed him salt–D on dull paper; he filed it behind a binder labeled lamp orders and hummed something that might have been a hymn and might have been approval.

"Witnesses?" Sister Miriam asked through the phone, traveling by wire and patience.

"Madaba," Yael said. "Nebo next."

Before they left, Father Hanna led them to the mosaic. He put a finger over Jerusalem—oval, walls set like teeth around a cross—and then over Machaerus, labeled faintly in Greek, a hill above the Dead Sea like a thumbprint. "Your mountain," he said.

He added a folded paper to Matthias's pocket: a letter to the parish at Mukawir that would do more than any passport if presented to a woman who ran kitchens and, by extension, truth.

Mount Nebo gave them wind and an old view that has been making people honest for three thousand years. The Franciscan guard signed for a duplicate envelope with a relief that looked like discipline. He stamped it with a seal that had survived governments and immediately filed it where curious men did not look.

By late afternoon, the road south along the King's Highway forgot to be formal and remembered to be useful. They passed Dhiban, where ruins sat in thorn under a municipal water tower, and then turned west toward Mukawir, the name worn smooth between Arabic and Greek depending on who needed it.

Machaerus stood where it always has—an isolated cone, the black line of the old dike bridging to the saddle, the Herodian platform on top like a table someone had dragged outside for air. The wind arrived full of judgments other people had called history and weather. Somewhere below, goats explained themselves to no one.

In the village, a boy chewing a stick pointed them toward the parish house without being asked. A woman opened—a face that had broken into laughter early and never quite quit; a headscarf; a ring of keys on her hip that announced she was responsible for everything that mattered. Um Elias accepted Father Hanna's letter with the appropriate annoyance for paperwork that expected gratitude. Then she kissed Narsai's cheek and pinched Karim's elbow and adopted Arielle by deciding she needed tea.

"You are looking for scratches," she said, pouring with her wrist bent just so. "All these men come for thunder. You want scratches. Better."

They asked for the dike. She handed them a small iron key and a sentence: "Open the gate and pretend you belong to the light."

They climbed the causeway in sun that bleached argument. The saddle fell away on both sides to air and goats. On the far side, the jacob-stone cut for cisterns opened like stubborn mouths; the baths on the upper plateau insinuated themselves as ruined rooms where heat had once pretended to be civility.

"Wind keeps judgment," Matthias murmured, approving the scribe's phrase.

They didn't need to open anything here. They needed to find the ledger marks that would have lived through men and weather.

On the north slope, beside a cistern mouth worn to a smooth ellipse by a thousand ropes, three small pricks hid in the shadow—the droplet for water. To the right, shallow and patient, the heap for salt. On the lip itself, three short strokes—bread—beneath a tiny flame almost erased by the wind's insistence.

Karim crouched and traced them in air, fingers stopping a hand's width away. "They counted here," he said softly. "Women with rope-burn on their palms and a list in their heads. Bread named at the upper room, water at the mouth, lamps at Chorazin, salt handled at Taricheae, and now all of it retold on a hill where judges liked to hear themselves."

The wind answered by pushing their coats against their ribs.

"Photographs," Yael said, and made the routine behave like piety. Rake; hash; split. She slid water–E into a crack by the cistern after wrapping it in a scrap of plastic; the crack had held dates and tobacco and worse promises. It could hold a hash.

A shout carried up from the saddle—soft hands had found the gate and were trying to own it. Jonas's head lifted. He allowed himself one syllable. "Time."

They crossed back along the dike with the calm of people who refuse to be exciting. At the gate, two men with lanyards practiced being important. One smiled in the idiom of donors. The other held a clipboard like a literate weapon.

"Friends," the clipboard said in English. "We are with a foundation interested in the preservation of sacred sites. We can provide grants. We only ask to see what you are working on."

Um Elias arrived from the path with a broom that could have been used for sweeping or instructing. "They are working on tea," she said, and thumped the broom once for punctuation. "And on walking. You work on leaving."

The clipboard tried Arabic; it came out as Amman. She answered with Madaba. Both words are maps and warnings. The two men stepped back into politeness.

The hard hand did not come up the dike. He had learned patience down at the parking—a man in a brown jacket pretending to look at goats, wearing silence like a badge. Jonas did not look at him. He counted fences.

"Back," Yael said. "We seed doors and get off this hill before wind decides to teach us manners."

They left water–F with Um Elias—dull letterhead, hash, a line that said witnesses in Syriac and Arabic without the noun. She slid it into a tin where tea, sugar, and receipts lived like saints. "I will read this to my husband," she said. "He will pretend to understand and then do whatever I say."

"Saint," Narsai murmured, and meant it.

They stopped at Dhiban long enough to leave salt–E with a teacher who had a rubber stamp with a lion on it and used it on anything that stayed still. They stopped at Madaba again—to Father Hanna went bread–E, added to his drawer marked lamp orders with unexpected reverence. At Nebo, the Franciscan smiled with professional boredom and took house–E as if accepting a bolt for a missing hinge.

By the time they reached the bridge, daylight was exhausted. Allenby had decided to collect opinions; a busload of pilgrims offered theirs with fervor. Brown Suit's patience had been tape-recorded on the Israeli side; he was busy failing to be kind to a clerk.

They waited an hour because borders like to teach men humility. When their turn came, the letterhead did its work; the guard had the same eyes as the sergeant and decided to let letters be laws for a day.

Jericho exhaled them into night. The climb back to Jerusalem felt longer because the city at the top was going to argue. St. Mark's lemon tree shook itself like a dog. In the nave, the sergeant with the crease between his eyes had taken off his cap and was watching Brown Suit learn to draft emails in a tone that would win him no favors.

Down in the stone room, the jar waited. The seam looked like innocence. Bread went on the table. The Protocol slept where anyone could pick it up and be improved.

"Ledger holds," Karim said, sitting before his legs remembered to be tired. He drew the icons one more time—bread, water, lamps, salt—and underlined mountain with an arrow. "Herod's hill kept her voice."

Narsai wrote three names in Syriac on a scrap as if signing a receipt for courage: Ya'el of bread, Tamar of water, Abisha of lamps. He added a fourth: Marta at fever. He slid it under the cradle. "They like to be present when their lists behave," he said.

Jonas leaned on the table and did not allow himself to be proud. "They'll push at dawn," he said. "Bigger door."

"Then we move sideways before dawn," Yael replied. "We read one line and let them invent verbs while we practice nouns."

Arielle set her palm on the jar. The watcher's hand settled beside it with the simple consent of a colleague who had stayed late and would show up on time anyway. She breathed; the room breathed back.

"Tomorrow," she said.

"Tomorrow," the room answered—lemon tree, stone, bread, names.

Outside, wolves counted. Inside, the doors multiplied.

Chapter Twenty-Six — Names in the Margin

Dawn came with the sound of water in pipes and the clang of a truck door. Jerusalem stretched. Cats rehearsed indignation. The lemon tree didn't bother; it had become a veteran of notices.

They woke to tea and to quiet. No knock yet, no footsteps with the cadence of authority. Jonas took it like weather: useful but not personal. Arielle took it like a reprieve she did not intend to waste.

"Sequence," Yael said, rubbing sleep from the corner of one eye.

"One line," Karim answered automatically, as if reading a command from a ledger. "Then more doors."

In the scriptorium the routine felt less like ritual and more like muscle memory. Bread. Water. Protocol. The jar in its cradle like an honest weight. Sister Miriam on the wire. Narsai at the table, his robe making a soft sound when he moved his cup.

Yael lifted the seam; resin yielded. Karim's fingers steadied the lamp; the Estrangela came up into the light like a truth that had been patient.

"Read," Sister Miriam said, her voice steadier than the line.

"The keepers shall tell the children the names of the daughters and sons when they grind grain; the men may speak of war, but the women shall speak of bread."

Karim made a sound like a snort and a prayer. "File under housekeeping," he murmured. He wrote war and bread with a neat underline.

The second sentence held something the others had only hinted at:

"Of Yohannan, son of Zechariah: through Ya'el of bread came Mariam and Yosef; through Tamar of water came Yohanna and Ya'qob; through Abisha of lamps came Elisheba; and through Marta, vowed in fever, came no child but her name, held in salt."

They all stilled for a moment. It was the first time the scroll had offered a genealogy instead of instructions on how to file one. The names lay like pebbles in a line: daughters, sons, traced through women instead of fathers.

"It names the Baptist's children," Matthias said, voice low. "Not Jesus's. Yohannan. It rewrites lineage for a man who didn't think he would have one."

"And it names a daughter who didn't carry anyone—Marta—so that her name doesn't die," Narsai added. "It's not scandal. It's compassion."

The last sentence of the line read like policy and like creed:

"Guard the truth with names written in the margin, and do not hide the girls to please kings."

Yael closed the seam and sat back, eyes shining and tired. "They were louder in the margins than in the main text," she said. "They wrote the truth where only people willing to do the work would see it. They understood wolves long before we did."

There was no time to let it settle. Boots found the lemon tree. They could hear it shake in protest. A voice that had practiced charm called "Father!" with no expectation of being ignored. Brown Suit had come back, but he was not alone. The air around him felt like money and decree; the hard hand had finally put on a lanyard.

"No doors today," Jonas murmured. "No more courtesies. This is their last ask."

"Then this is our last line here," Arielle answered. Her pulse was still fluttering with the genealogy. "After this, we go upstairs and read to everyone who needs to hear."

They reseated the seam and tucked the jar deep under the coat. They left bread and water on the table not as offering but as defiance: common things in the face of polished shoes.

Brown Suit stood in the nave with a folder thicker than his patience. The hard hand in the brown jacket had a badge this time—cultural preservation with a seal that might have impressed another city.

"We will do this without drama," Brown Suit said, the threat in his tone wrapped in courtesy. "You will surrender the antiquity. Now."

"For safety," Elpidios sang, handing the hard hand a candle as if offering a flaming sword to a child. The man didn't take it.

The sergeant from Zion Gate had come in uniform and with his cap. He looked unhappy. He looked tired of being the man between between better people and worse. "We have an order," he said. "We have to execute it."

Jonas sighed. "Then come down. But you bring the world with you."

They led Brown Suit and his two assistants—hard and soft—down the stairs. They did not yield the jar. They carried the Protocol like scripture. They let the inspectors see the empty cradle where the jar had slept and the stone table where bread and water waited.

"This is it?" Brown Suit asked, suspicious. "You've moved it already."

"We have moved only paper," Yael said. "The jar is here." She set it on the table with the grace of a liturgical placement.

The hard hand reached. Jonas's palm intercepted his wrist and applied enough pressure to remind the bones of their hierarchy. "You don't touch without a receipt," Jonas said. "And without witness."

Matthias, who had been quiet, stepped forward with his folded letter. "A representative of the Holy See," he said, dry. The hard hand flinched; Brown Suit's composure wavered. "If you insist on violating the chain, the Vatican will not take the blame when it is broken."

It wasn't that Brown Suit believed Matthias. It was that he believed paperwork and consequences. He looked at the sergeant with the crease between his eyes and found no ally; the sergeant's jaw was clenched.

"Fine," Brown Suit said. "We witness. We inventory. And we seal. Then it comes with us."

"Seal with this," Yael said, offering him a strip of Japanese paper and a bone folder. The attorney blinked at it. "Paper not tape," she explained. "So we know when you've changed your mind about being honest."

Brown Suit actually laughed, a short, genuine sound. He signed the protocol. He took the strip of paper. He sealed the seam like someone who had never used a bone folder and never wanted to. He did not touch the jar; he made the hard hand lift it instead, which the man did with the carefulness of a thief who knows he is being filmed.

They ascended. Arielle's breath felt like broken glass. She wanted to laugh at the look on Um Elias's face when she saw the jar passing under coats; she wanted to scream at the unfairness of Brown Suit's folder; she wanted to trust the small doors; she wanted to smash the big one.

The street outside St. Mark's had gathered a crowd that wasn't a crowd: neighbors, Lev's fixer in several forms, a boy with a sesame ring, a soldier who looked like he might go off shift soon and wanted to be useful before he was irrelevant. They watched as Brown Suit's men carried the jar not to a van but to a public square in front of the convent. They placed it on a folding table, put down their pens, and realized they had made a mistake.

Arielle wasn't sure who started it. It might have been Rina from Magdala, arriving with a basket of bread and placing it on the table next to the jar as if to claim kinship. It might have been Narsai, stepping forward with his robe and his book and beginning to read names in Syriac out loud—Ya'el of bread, Tamar of water, Abisha of lamps, Marta who carried no child. It might have been Um Rafi, who joined him with a bright, fierce Arabic: "Mariam. Yosef. Yohanna. Ya'qob. Elisheba."

It was everyone, suddenly, reading names. Matthias read the Latin on a sheet that could have been dull but was now an indictment: Guard the truth with names written in the margin. Jonas shouted the Spanish he had learned in a different war; Yael read the Hebrew; Lev's fixer read a list of donors from candles; Elpidios in Greek; Sister Miriam through the phone, Syriac and Aramaic in quick rotation.

Brown Suit went still. The hard hand reached for the jar as if to snatch it, but his fingers stopped halfway. There was no way to confiscate the sound. It was already out. It was a better kind of thunder: not a single strike but rolling noise that refused to be pinned down.

Karim, voice hoarse, read in English: "Of Yohannan, son of Zechariah: through Ya'el of bread came Mariam and Yosef; through Tamar of water came Yohanna and Ya'qob; through Abisha of lamps came

Elisheba; through Marta, vowed in fever, came no child but her name held in salt." He held up a phone and hit "send." He didn't need to know which group; he had created the list weeks ago. Hashes. Files. All of it.

Within minutes, the list was out. In ten, the audio had made it to someone else's feed. In twenty, Brown Suit's superiors would see their attempt at control turn into a press conference they hadn't planned.

Brown Suit closed his folder. He did not say "fine." He did not look at the jar. He looked at the sergeant with the crease and nodded. They both knew it was done.

The hard hand let go of the jar. Jonas took it without theatricality. He did not carry it back downstairs. He put it on the table in the nave and removed the paper seal they had forced him to use. He held up the bone strip in two pieces for everyone to see. The room applauded, even Lev's fixer.

"Thunder," Yael whispered. "We did it without screaming."

Narsai smiled at her, then at Arielle. "Thunder is overrated," he said. "Names live longer."

Arielle looked at the jar. The watcher's hand beside hers felt like nothing more than gravity and gratitude. The names were out. The daughters of the Covenant had been spoken out loud, counted where men had tried to forget them. The truth was not a peak, nor even a valley, anymore. It was a table spread in a church and on a hill and by a well and in a kitchen where a woman kept salt.

"Tomorrow?" Jonas asked out of habit.

"Tomorrow," Arielle said, and didn't feel dread. Tomorrow was about what happened when truth no longer belonged to anyone and therefore to everyone.

The lemon tree rustled. It could have been wind. It could have been applause.

Chapter Twenty-Seven — The Quiet Thunder

Jerusalem woke the way it always does when a storm has been scheduled without clouds—vendors loud, doors half open, cats indifferent to law. In the scriptorium, bread and water took their posts; the Protocol lay where a hand could reach it; the jar kept its quiet like a practiced witness.

"We've opened enough doors to starve a wolf," Yael said. "Now we let the doors speak."

"Four rooms," Jonas answered. "St. Mark's. Ein Karem. St. Anne. Tabgha. We read one page in each, with witnesses who don't travel."

"Five," Sister Miriam said from the phone, tea in her voice. "Add the Armenian sacristy. He has a ledger that enjoys contradicting men with clipboards."

They made a choreography humble enough to work. Elpidios would hold the Greek house with candles, humor, and a dull envelope. The Armenian sacristan would sit a lectionary on a table and refuse to perform. Father Paulus would prop a phone near the loaves-and-fishes mosaic and pretend to be bored. Sister Miriam would set a stool by Mary's Spring and make small children count the names out loud as if it were a game. St. Anne's sister would look at the ceiling at the right moment and therefore see nothing.

Lev's fixer, folding a market bag, said, "Two tails. Soft hands to the north gate. Hard hand near the Cardo. The sergeant is pretending to count pigeons."

"They're choosing rooms," Jonas said. "We'll choose time."

The first reading was the smallest. In the stone room, Yael lifted the seam with the quiet competence that had become a liturgy. Karim's timestamp rolled; the lamp raked low; the line appeared with the patience of Estrangela that has never needed permission.

"Read," Sister Miriam said.

"At the house of mercy, read the water names when the jar is filled; let the bread be set by the steps; let the lamps be lit at dusk if men are kind, and if men are not, let the salt be kept under the stone."

No one applauded. Karim split, hashed, passed. Elpidios slid a copy into a candle tray; the sacristan tucked another into a spine where lawyers get bored. Father Paulus said nothing at Tabgha and nodded to a monk with an unfortunate haircut who understood that nods can be receipts.

A car idled at the court and decided to be someone else. Brown Suit came with his attorney and a new word—consolidation—and left with copies dull enough to outlast his enthusiasm. The hard hand did not come inside. He stood at the corner by the kitchen and measured the door with his shoulder.

"Next room," Jonas said.

They carried the jar under the coat like a second rib to St. Anne in a trickle of pilgrims arguing about where mercy begins. The sister at the gate read Matthias's dull letter as if it were a psalm and admitted them to the pools with a look that meant: I will testify to nothing and leave you water.

On the steps between the upper and lower basins, bread and water took their places. Yael coaxed the guard slip; Karim breathed; the line rose.

"When the baskets come from Heptapegon, the bread names shall be retold; when the nets are mended at Capernaum, the water names shall be called; let the lamps be carried at Chorazin when the road grows dark."

Children ran past with the solemnity of play; a guide misremembered a century; the sister glanced away in the exact second that counts as obedience. Karim split, hashed, passed; a copy slid into a drawer where a community keeps receipts it hopes never to spend.

“Third,” Sister Miriam said, and they heard the spring in her voice, Ein Karem’s water answering its own name.

Mary’s Spring needed no staging. The women at the curb worked their ropes; the droplet mark under the lip received the light like an old friend. Narsai read the Syriac first, his hand resting on stone, his voice the weight of basalt behaving. Children repeated the names, and the laughter that followed did not reduce them; it made them harder to erase.

On the edge of the Quarter, the hard hand moved. Lev’s fixer brushed past him carrying nothing heavier than parsley and counted his steps silently. The sergeant with the crease between his eyes found a new pigeon at the lemon tree. Brown Suit discovered that patience has a bill.

“Tabgha,” Jonas said.

They came to the mosaic court by way of alleys that had learned their faces. Father Paulus met them with a kettle and the look priests get when they have decided to earn their sins. The loaves-and-fishes floor received their feet without complaint. The jar stayed closed; they didn’t need it open here. Father Paulus read the line as minutes; a young monk held a camera like a rosary; Sabih leaned on the garden wall and translated to no one in particular.

“Done,” Yael whispered, more to the room than to them. “Four rooms. Five witnesses. Doors.”

“Now the ledger,” Matthias said, setting a thin folder on the table at St. Mark’s when they returned. Inside: the schedule the text had given them, the map it had pretended not to be, and a single page addressed to no one and everyone—Guard the truth with many small doors—signed not with names, but with houses: Bread. Water. Lamps. Salt.

They didn’t call the press. They called minutes. Patriarchate. Armenian St. James. Dominicans. Franciscans. Tur Abdin. The Department of Antiquities at Mukawir. A clerk at the Rockefeller who likes receipts more than supervisors. They sent the page, signed it with their dullest stamps, and cc'd the men who think they own boxes.

Brown Suit arrived late and angry, which is to say early and predictable. "Consolidation," he said again, as if repetition would make the noun breed authority.

"Inventory," Yael returned. "Witness. Receipt."

The sergeant's radio crackled, then refused to be part of the moment. He looked at Brown Suit, at the faces around the table, at the lemon tree trying not to be comic, and said, to no one and all of them, "Enough for today."

When it was done, when the stair had emptied of patience and the court resumed its natural quarrel, Arielle stood by the cradle and rested her palm on the jar. The watcher's hand arrived—no longer portent, just company.

"My father would have wanted thunder," Karim said, half-joking, half-wishing.

"He would have wanted the table to be set," Arielle answered. "Thunder eats better when the table's right."

Jonas leaned against the doorway and let his weight admit exhaustion. "They'll bring vans tomorrow," he said.

"Then we bring women," Sister Miriam replied on the line, fierce and amused. "And ledgers. And readers. I'll have twelve from Ein Karem who can outwait any man with a clipboard."

"Many small doors," Yael said, almost smiling.

"Many," Arielle echoed.

Outside, a boy kicked a ball too hard and apologized to no one. The lemon tree lost one leaf with ceremony. In the stone room, the air cooled a degree and stayed there—as if the city had agreed, for one night, to let ledgers sleep.

Chapter Twenty-Eight — Names as Psalm

They heard the vans before they saw them—the way a street's breath quickens when something larger than courtesy turns the corner.

St. Mark's courtyard had learned their ritual: bread, water, Protocol in its sleeve; the jar out of sight in the cool room, seam behaving. The lemon tree kept its small theater of innocence. Cats negotiated jurisdiction with the confidence of long tenure.

"Vans," Jonas said from the stoop. "Two municipal. One unmarked that thinks it's shy."

"Witnesses," Sister Miriam said on the phone, tea running under the words. "I'm at the gate of St. John in Ein Karem with twelve grandmothers and more lemonade than theology. Give me ten."

Elpidios set a brass tray on the table as if the room were about to be audited and had decided to pass. "We can count candles until the Lord returns," he promised, cheerful.

Brown Suit arrived first, the attorney at his elbow, a tidy column of stamped paper in his hands. Behind them, the plainclothes men with hoses and a toolbox that had never met a wrench. Farther back, the hard hand in a jacket that fit better than yesterday's, shoes that liked new pavement. The sergeant from Zion Gate came in last, crease between his eyes deeper, yarmulke riding the line between duty and headache.

"Father," Brown Suit said, kinder than he felt. "Temporary consolidation. For safety. We'll receive devices, notes, images, and the object into central conservation. You'll have full observation."

"Observation is a lovely word," Yael said. "We prefer witnesses."

The hard hand measured the doorway again with his shoulder. His eyes skimmed the room like someone reading for seams: Jonas, immovable geometry; Karim with his notebook's quiet; Matthias in linen that had learned how to be boring as a weapon; Narsai, a line of basalt with patience; Arielle, coat buttoned, posture ordinary on purpose.

In the alley, women's voices gathered first as gossip, then as weather. Footsteps, low talk, the polite insistence of bodies that had done harder things than block a van. A basket appeared in the doorway bearing lemons and paper cups; behind it, Sister Miriam's dozen—two with canes that could become opinions, one with a toddler, one with a sheaf of hymn leaflets folded as if to swat flies and shame policy.

"We're here to read," Sister Miriam said mildly, stepping into the court as if she had always owned it. "If it's not prohibited to read names in Jerusalem, we'll go ahead."

"It isn't," the sergeant said before remembering to pretend neutrality.

Brown Suit recalculated. "This is a building, not a public square."

"It's a church," Mar Ephrem replied, more statement than argument. "We feed witnesses."

The hard hand's jaw decided to be patient. "Begin your inventory," he told Brown Suit, and drifted toward the kitchen door where the angle of approach was best. Jonas shifted without seeming to, giving the lintel his back, offering a shoulder he had used to hold lines before.

Yael lifted the Protocol, crisp, dull, immaculate. "Names. Time. Hands. Room," she said. She spoke as if reading calmed an earthquake. Karim laid out the camera, the lamp, the bone folder, the guard slip like a surgeon unwrapping instruments that save lives by refusing theater.

They didn't open the jar. Not yet. They opened the room.

Sister Miriam called the first name. A woman answered. A second name. Another answered. It was not thunder. It was roll call. A psalm where the chorus was here. You could feel the vans get embarrassed.

"Temporary consolidation," Brown Suit tried again, quieter, paper held up like a talisman against grandmothers.

"Temporary is what we make bread do before it becomes body," Elpidios said, delighted to offend theology with housekeeping. "Consolidate candles with me."

The plainclothes men in utility blue moved toward the side door. Lev's fixer intercepted with a broom and a tray of cups. "Water," she said. "You'll be less polite later; hydrate now."

The hard hand stepped once into the doorway. Jonas met him with the sort of movement that pretends to be an accident and isn't. Bodies, correctly used, are paragraphs the law hates to skim.

"Begin," Sister Miriam said softly into Arielle's ear. "We're ready."

In the stone room, cool as an argument that's prepared its footnotes, Yael coaxed the seam. The resin behaved. Karim's timestamp rolled. The line rose out of shadow.

"Read," Sister Miriam said, and now it was more than a verb. It was a strategy.

At the house of bread, let the names be retold at table; at the house of water, let them be called at the well mouth; at the lamps, let them be carried when the road grows dark; at the salt, let the heap be kept by the door. When men gather papers to quiet truth, sing the names until the boys know them.

Arielle breathed. It was instruction, not spectacle. It was everything that had been saving them from the beginning.

"Photographs," Yael said. Karim raked, logged, hashed, split: bread–K went into the Gospel chest's second false bottom; water–L slid under a towel into an Ein Karem basket waiting by the door; house–M to the Armenian sacristy who had already invented a drawer with better morals than his boss; salt–N into Shiri's lab envelope with a cover memo that made boredom sound sacramental.

Above, in the court, names went on. They were the saints that never got painted: Ya'el of bread, Tamar of water, Marta vowed in fever,

Shoshana who entered by Hanna, Abisha who counted lamps when men were hiding. The toddler repeated the syllables with the care of a child learning to be a bell.

Brown Suit sighed the sigh of a man who had hoped to be the adult in the room and discovered the room had many adults. The attorney shifted his weight from moral foot to legal foot and back. The hard hand's face went still, which is how men like him write minutes to themselves.

"Receipt," Jonas said to Brown Suit, courteous as a brick.

Brown Suit produced the triplicate. Yael dictated destination code. He stamped. She wrote names and time and room in a hand the archives would be grateful for. If there was theater, it was the kind that improves doctrine.

"Where?" the hard hand asked, eyes on the coat. It could have been about the jar. It could have been about tomorrow.

"Lion Gate," Sister Miriam said unexpectedly, from somewhere between the lemon tree and the edge of insolence. "I like lions."

Arielle looked up. Lion Gate. St. Stephen's Gate to the maps. The door that faces the lions. A line from a margin. A sentence her father had half laughed when he wrote. The watcher's hand arrived on her sleeve as if to underline.

They did not run. They did sequence.

"Procession," Mar Ephrem said to the women at the gate, and no one argued theology with him. "Bread first. Then water. Lamps last."

They set their order the way you set a table: wisdom of kitchens, math of streets. Elpidios took the tray; Sister Miriam took the names; the Armenian sacristan shouldered a lectionary that made him taller; Narsai lifted a small lamp and looked like basalt with fire. Jonas took the flank that faced the kitchen corridor; Matthias took paper under his arm like a quiet weapon; Karim carried the dullest envelope.

They stepped into the alley. Muristan gave way, grudgingly polite to a procession that didn't ask permission. The Cardo yawned; tourists made space because grandmothers know how to move through crowds with the legitimacy of gravity.

The vans tried to get ahead. Lion Gate is a funnel, and funnels don't respect new paint. The hard hand went on foot with two men whose shoes hated stone. The sergeant's patrol drifted to either side like a conscience that had learned to wear a uniform.

At the gate, the lions kept their old watch, stone cats who have outlived more men than they could count if stone counted. The procession turned toward the valley. Names were still being read. They crossed the threshold with a psalm in their mouths and a city on their shoulders.

Down by the road that drops to the Kidron, a camera phone rose and then thought better of being useful to the wrong story. A nun from St. Anne stood by a wall pretending to admire bougainvillea and somehow counted the women correctly. A man selling sesame rings lowered his voice as they passed, as if business had learned reverence.

They did not show the jar. They did not need to. They showed receipts.

At the bend, Lev's fixer gestured—a car idling, the driver with the wrong music acting as if he had always been parked there. "Not yet," Jonas said. "We let them watch us not exit."

They looped the street and came back up. The vans had to reverse; a bus had to learn humility. The hard hand spoke into a phone; somewhere, permission tried to generate itself and found prayers clogging the gears.

Back in the court, the jar slept in its cradle. Stone kept cool. The seam looked exactly as honest as it had an hour ago. The room had done a thing harder than hiding: it had made a fact visible and therefore difficult to steal without shame.

The sergeant stood in the doorway and cleared his throat. "I can give you till dusk," he said. "After that I stop being useful."

"Dusk is a saint," Elpidios said. "He visits."

Brown Suit gathered his paper and discovered it had not multiplied. "Tomorrow," he said without malice, because men like him are made of calendar. "We will return."

"Tomorrow is faithful," Sister Miriam said. "We'll feed it."

When the courtyard had given the vans back to the street and the women had kissed one another's cheeks and begun to argue about whether the lemon tree needed pruning, Arielle went down to the stone room and set her palm on the jar. The watcher's hand rested beside hers. Not omen. Company.

"My father would have pointed at the lions," she said, half to Jonas, half to the cool in her grip.

"He left you the sentence," Jonas said. "You're finishing it."

Karim sank into a chair and rubbed his eyes with the heel of his hand. "I wanted thunder," he admitted, smiling despite himself. "But that—"

"That was weather," Yael said. "Weather erodes stone. Thunder just scares dogs."

Matthias set a page on the table—a single paragraph, dull as an invoice, addressed to no one and everyone. It documented what they had read, where they had stood, who had witnessed, which doors had been opened. He stamped it with the most boring stamp in the drawer.

"Minutes," he said. "Let them drown in minutes."

They ate bread that had genuinely gone a little stale and didn't apologize. Outside, the lemon tree rattled once in a breeze that didn't exist. Inside, the room cooled by a degree that belonged to ledgers.

"Tomorrow," Jonas said from the threshold.

“Soon,” Arielle answered. It no longer felt like a promise to be frightened of. It was a time they had put in order.

Chapter Twenty-Nine — Lions’ Math

Dusk made the stones admit their history. Heat emptied out of lintels; shadows climbed; the Quarter rehearsed its evening hymn: vendors tallying coins, a boy dribbling a flat ball, a cat insisting on jurisdiction.

Bread on the plate. Water in cups. The Jerusalem Protocol where an honest hand could reach it. The jar in the cool room, seam neat, quiet as good furniture.

“They’ll come with a paper that thinks it’s thunder,” Jonas said from the stoop. “And a camera that wants a scene.”

“Then we give them minutes,” Yael said. “Scenes hate minutes.”

Sister Miriam’s voice arrived with the rasp of Ein Karem’s line. “The grandmothers have gone home to cook for the men they intend to outlive,” she said, amused. “I kept two. They refuse to be photographed and will remember everything.”

Lev’s fixer slipped in carrying nothing heavier than parsley. “Hard hand at the Cardo,” she said without moving her lips. “Soft hands counting vans. Your sergeant is pretending to ask a pigeon for ID.”

“Lion Gate,” Arielle said, and felt the watcher’s hand touch the thought. “He left me that sentence for a reason.”

“He who?” Karim asked, already smiling because he knew.

“My father,” she said. “Finish the sentence.”

They prepared a procession that refused to look like one. Elpidios loaded a tray with lanterns and the obstinacy of wicks. The Armenian sacristan tucked a lectionary under his arm as if it were meat for a neighbor. Narsai wrapped a small travel lamp in a square of linen so old it had forgotten to be precious. Matthias signed four letters dull enough to bore a god: Patriarchate, St. James, St. Anne, St. John in the Mountains—each acknowledging witness, not custody.

The knock didn't have to knock. Two municipal vans idled by the lemon tree as if it were a hydrant. Brown Suit entered with a paper so freshly stamped it smelled of ink; behind him, the attorney with capillaries in revolt; farther back, utility blue with a coil of hose; and at the doorway to the kitchen, the hard hand with a posture that believed in outcomes.

"Father," Brown Suit said, practicing mercy. "Court order. Central consolidation for safety. Devices, images, notes, and the object will be transported under seal to a joint conservation facility."

Mar Ephrem read the first paragraph as if reciting Beatitudes and the second as if gutting a fish. "You will receive devices," he said mildly. "They hold nothing. You will receive images. They reproduce infinitely. You will not receive witness. It does not travel."

"Begin," the hard hand said to no one, which is how men like him prefer the world.

"Receipt," Jonas said, courteous and immovable.

Yael put the Protocol where Brown Suit's hand had to meet it before it met anything else. "Names. Time. Room," she said. "And destination code twice. You forget when you're excited."

The attorney wrote as if rescuing his own day. The stamp landed. The copy tore. Paper believed itself accomplished.

"Now," Brown Suit said, eyes on the corridor.

"Now," Sister Miriam echoed, but into Arielle's ear. "Lion Gate."

They moved as if leaving the room for air. Bread and water went first because they are older than warrants. Elpidios with the tray, sacristan with the lectionary, Narsai with the lamp under linen, Matthias with dull envelopes and stamps that could frighten no one. Jonas walked between the kitchen and the corridor the way a man walks between past and mistake. Arielle closed her coat. The jar settled against her ribs with the simple insistence of truth.

The street gave them space the way a city does when it doesn't know it's respectful—habit, not homage. The vans tried to nose ahead; Lion Gate narrowed like a test set by an honest teacher.

At the threshold, the stone lions stared past them in the way of creatures who have outlived men and intend to continue. Sister Miriam's two grandmothers took the curb with the boredom of saints waiting for a late mass.

"Names," one said, and lifted a sheet.

The reading was not performance. It was economy. Ya'el of bread. Tamar of water. Marta vowed in fever. Shoshana who entered by Hanna. Abisha who counted lamps when men were hiding. Women answered under their breath. A boy tried the syllables on his tongue and liked how they fit.

A cameraman raised a lens and discovered it captured nothing dramatic: an alley, two old lions, a tray of lanterns, a woman reading a list as if she were timing bread. Whatever appetite he'd arrived with, the city starved it.

Brown Suit's paper wilted by a degree. He signaled the utility blues forward. Lev's broom found their shins. "Water," she said brightly, and handed a cup that demanded a free hand. They took it, because you do.

The hard hand didn't fuss. He walked up to the lintel and stopped with a courtesy that made it worse. His eyes peered past Jonas's shoulder into the cool beyond.

"Lions," he said, tone neutral. "Beautiful stone."

"Useful stone," Jonas replied.

"Inventory," Brown Suit insisted, clinging to the correct noun. "You cannot carry objects through the Old City without noting destination."

"Destination," Yael said, smiling with her teeth. She pointed at the ground. "Here. And here. And here." A finger for the procession. A finger for the grandmothers. A finger for the ledger in the sacristan's arm. "Witness is a place."

Karim's pen moved over the Protocol margin. Lion Gate, Dusk. Names read as psalm. Witnesses: 17. Copies split. He wrote legibly for the future he believed in.

The hard hand's radio murmured the bureaucratic equivalent of a shrug. He made a small calculation and put it back in his pocket. "Tomorrow," he said. He meant earlier.

"We baked for him," Elpidios said to no one, and offered bread.

Back at St. Mark's, the room received them like a drawer. The jar returned to its cradle; the seam put its dignity back on. Outside, vans pretended to idle. Inside, paper became minutes again.

"Now we teach the ledger to walk," Matthias said, laying four envelopes down: Bread to the Greek house; Water to Ein Karem; Lamps to St. James; Salt to Shiri's lab. "If they take one, they will need a week to realize they do not own the others."

"Add a fifth," Narsai said. He placed a small letter on the table—Syriac, plain, elegant. Tur Abdin's bishop would receive nothing useful and everything necessary.

Arielle placed her palm on the jar and the watcher's hand met it, a colleague clocking in. She closed her eyes to hear what the room knew: cool stone and bread crust, lamp glass ticking as it cooled, the distant shiver of the lemon tree negotiating with a breeze.

"Do we open?" Karim asked softly. "One line. For us."

"Dusk," Jonas said, answering the sergeant's mercy. "Then one line."

They waited while the city finished the page. The vans grew bored or obeyed a call. The sergeant walked in once more and stared at the ceiling, which is how men announce decency without writing it down. "I didn't see anything," he said to the air, and left two loaves by the door.

They opened when the stone hit that temperature—the degree you only feel if you have loved ruins long enough to hear the word now. Yael lifted the guard slip; resin sighed. Karim's lamp raked low. The Estrangela stood, patient, unafraid of time.

"Read," Sister Miriam said.

"When you have opened many doors and men are tired of papers, take the names to the gate of lions and read them as psalm until the boys answer. Then return the list to the house and to the water and to the lamps and to the salt, for this is the order of keeping."

Arielle laughed once—the small, stunned kind that doesn't ask permission. The line had already happened. They were obeying a text that had predicted them by predicting women.

"Photographs," Yael said, voice gentle. Karim took them with hands that knew which tremor belongs to awe and which to clumsiness; he had the good one.

They sealed. Bread went to plates. Water to cups. The minutes walked: copies dull as sand, hashes printed where boredom keeps them alive.

Night set its voice on the city—sirens far, arguments near, a muezzin teaching air how to be honest, bells practicing for a morning they would claim to have invented. The lemon tree shook itself once like a creature trying out a thought.

Arielle leaned against the doorjamb and let fatigue ratify her bones. Jonas stood beside her with that soldier stillness that says awake without making a speech. Yael sat at the table and made the Protocol neater than it had been. Karim closed his notebook and laid his palm on it like a vow.

"Tomorrow," Jonas said.

"Thunder?" Karim offered, hopeful and kidding himself.

"Weather," Yael said. "We're very good at weather."

"Soon," Arielle said, and felt the watcher agree—the weight of a hand that has no interest in fate and every interest in keeping.

Chapter Thirty — Salt in the Market

Morning reheated the stones and reminded them of old habits—vendors rolling metal shutters with the clatter of cymbals, pigeons arguing jurisdiction, coffee opening its eyes two alleys at once. The jar slept in the cool room; the Jerusalem Protocol lay where a hand could reach it; bread and water took their usual posts.

"Today is salt," Yael said. "Markets and hearths. We owe the text its chores."

"Damascus Gate down through Khan al-Zeit," Jonas answered. "Spice, soap, salt. Then hook left through Suq al-Attarin. If the Cotton Market isn't too full of opinions, we land a copy there and go home by Muristan."

"The hard hand?" Karim asked.

"Counting vans," Lev's fixer said from the doorway, carrying parsley and the expression of a weather report. "Soft hands to the northwest. Brown Suit is learning a new noun: 'court order.' Your sergeant is pretending to buy bread."

Arielle buttoned the coat. The jar settled against her like a second posture; the watcher's hand arrived, workmanlike. "We finish the salt drawer," she said. "Then we read one line. Dull. Precise."

They left by the door that refuses to squeak. Damascus Gate had already decided to be magnificent—Herodian blocks sulking under Ottoman pride, crenellations practicing parade rest. Jonas scanned the teeth of the gate like a man reading weather. "Exits," he said to himself, and nodded.

Inside the walls the market took them like tide: Khan al-Zeit—the Oil Press Street—narrow and busy, its cobbles polished by centuries of shoes and spills, vaults blackened by sesame and lamp smoke. Barrows nosed past, shy and brutal at once. On either side: pyramids of za'atar, dunes of sumac, mountains of olives that had learned to be conversational.

"Salt," Karim said, half to the air.

"Salt," a merchant agreed, hearing money in the syllable. He lifted a scoop of coarse crystals scintillant with life and set it back as if feeding the hill. "For bread. For baths. For friends."

Yael drifted to a lintel older than the shutter it held. The stone wore ablaq ghosts—alternating bands of dark and pale quarried in dynasties that disagreed about everything except geometry. Low on the jamb, where hands had learned to touch without being taught, three shallow pricks and a cramped little heap—the same shape the Magdala slab had memorized. A tiny flame scratched beside it. Nobody had polished that away. You do not erase habits without risking revolt.

Karim angled the lamp. Routine stilled his pulse: rake; photograph; hash; split. He slid salt–0 into a brown-paper ledger that tracked soap payments and owed nobody romance. The merchant watched with interest that had nothing to do with theft. "For the drawer," Karim said. The man nodded as if he had always known drawers were how cities kept their souls.

They let the market carry them. Suq al-Attarin narrowed and sweetened—attar and oil, frankincense pretending to be shy. A boy darted past with a tray of tea in delicate glasses and the balance of a dancer. Above, a Mamluk muqarnas balcony frilled the corner like a cascade of stone hives; over a doorway, a waqf inscription named a sultan who had forgotten them and whom they would not return the favor of forgetting.

"Cotton," Jonas murmured, and they slid left into Suq al-Qattanin—the Cotton Merchants' Market, Tankiz's masterpiece—straight as a thought, barrel-vaulted, cool. Ablaq arches marched in disciplined pairs; the muqarnas of the west portal pretended to be stalactites and got away with it. The light arrived in measured spoons. Men lowered their voices here without admitting they had.

A shopkeeper with a tailor's fingers eyed Narsai's robe and decided to be helpful. "What do you need?" he asked, meaning the old civic question: what are you hiding and how can I make it more honest?

"A threshold with a heap," Yael said. He grinned without mockery and pointed to a dark side door where bales once slept. "Our grandfathers spilled salt there by stubbornness."

The jamb had it: the heap and the three pricks and the flame worn to rumor by bodies that had kept ledgers with thumbs. Karim's lamp kissed the stone; the marks woke a little and liked the attention. Photograph; hash; split. Salt–P slid under a ledger book that kept thread counts and the names of girls who had learned to charge properly for hems.

Shouting, wrong for the hour. Jonas pivoted without wasting neck. At the far mouth of the suq, two men in utility blue moved like people who think uniforms are a second spine. Behind them the hard hand walked with a calm that borrowed legitimacy from architecture. Closer, Brown Suit negotiated his paper through air as if it were a boat that disliked wind.

"Kitchen," Yael said.

She meant: throw fog.

Lev's fixer did it with a twist of her wrist—an artful accident that lifted a pan of sumac into the corridor. The world turned pomegranate-red; a man sneezed; another blinked tears; somewhere, a lawyer became a beetroot. The shopkeepers performed outrage with affection; their hands were gentle with the trays.

"Left," Jonas breathed.

They slid through the back arch to the Hosh—a small courtyard where deliveries share gossip. A sister from St. Anne appeared with a basket she had no obvious business carrying and paused exactly long enough to obstruct curiosity. Narsai thanked her in Syriac for nothing. She smiled like a woman who knows the price of everything and everything worth saving.

They rode the market's tide back into David Street, pivoted down a covered alley that had learned to change names, and surfaced in Muristan where fountains pretend to be innocent and pigeons are professionals. A man selling ka'ak pretended not to recognize them and broke a ring in half at the precise second a plainclothes officer tried to remember whether food legally counts as obstacle.

"Home," Jonas said.

At St. Mark's the lemon tree rustled as if congratulating itself for staying rooted. The sergeant from Zion Gate was in the nave, contemplating the ceiling and committing nothing to paper. Brown Suit arrived shortly after, powdered lightly in sumac, which did not improve his mood or his dignity.

"Court order," he said into the room, not to anyone. "Consolidation now. The object moves. The committee meets at three."

"We'll bring minutes," Matthias replied, weaponizing boredom. He handed over a half-inch stack of copies so soporific they should have come with a blanket. Brown Suit accepted them with a sigh that might have counted as consent in another century.

The hard hand did not cross the door. He stood where a kitchen corridor becomes doctrine and read the room with the irritation of an educated man discovering that civics had outsmarted appetite.

"Read?" Sister Miriam asked in Arielle's ear, voice low as a spring under shade.

"Read," Arielle said.

Down in the stone room the air had kept its single blessed degree of cool. Bread on the plate. Water in cups. Lamp glass clear. The seam in a good mood. Yael lifted the guard slip; it yielded like a habit restored. Karim's timestamp ticked; the Estrangela stood.

"Read," Sister Miriam said.

"In the market, keep the heap by the door; let the lamps be counted when the shutters are closed; let the bread be marked on the cloth where coins are placed; let the water be written at the stone where jars are rinsed. If men forbid, set a pinch of salt upon the ledger and leave it under the press."

Karim laughed—quiet, grateful. "Housekeeping," he said.

"Government," Yael corrected, pleased. "The kind that works."

They photographed; they hashed; they split. Salt–Q went into Elpidios's candle drawer, because thieves hate beeswax. Bread–R slid between two Gospel leaves the sacristan had already decided were cousins. Water–S rode to Ein Karem in a basket of lemons that would make a customs agent weep from honest envy. House–T learned the Armenian sacristy's newest boring hiding place.

They sealed the seam. The jar returned to quiet. They climbed into a courtyard doing its best imitation of ordinary.

Brown Suit had found new patience; the hard hand had found a shadow. The sergeant cleared his throat because it is rude to clap in church. "Three o'clock," he said. "Rooms can be guilty by association. So can men. Don't let either happen."

"We'll be boring in public," Yael promised. "It's our gift."

At three they walked to the Rockefeller, linen pressed, faces undefensive, paperwork preternaturally correct. The Mandate façade performed its square-shouldered virtue; the courtyard listened the way stone listens when its conscience is undecided.

In a meeting room that smelled of pencils and decisions, Brown Suit unveiled the committee and his paper. Men arranged their mouths into neutral. A woman from Conservation set her pen down like a scalpel. Klein sat too stiff, too clean, looking as if towels had betrayed him again.

Matthias placed the Jerusalem Protocol on the table and turned its pages like a man who has learned to be uninteresting as an art. He read minutes—who witnessed, where, which house took which copy, how the hash bit, where the dull envelopes slept. He did not mention the jar. He mentioned ledger and order and the houses. He left nouns like custody and safety hungry.

Brown Suit spoke of consolidation until the word lost its flavor. The hard hand said nothing. The conservation woman asked a question about humidity that was hard because it was honest.

"You will have our copies," Yael said, answering the honest one. "You will have our methods. You will not have our witnesses. They do not travel."

The sergeant, in the back, found a window fascinating. Klein looked at his own hands and seemed briefly to dislike them.

In the end the committee did what committees do when faced with minutes they have no legal appetite for: they invented task forces, adjourned to subcommittees, and took receipts. The hard hand watched a boat be rowed into mud with exquisite technique and decided he would try a different river.

At dusk, the city did what it always does after committees: it went back to eating.

On the stoop under the lemon tree, Arielle set her palm on the coat where the jar had been and let her hand linger there anyway. The watcher's hand rested beside hers—colleague, not coincidence. Across the lane, Lev's fixer folded parsley for a dinner that would teach tomorrow how small it was.

"Thunder?" Karim asked hopefully, because hope is a muscle.

"Soon," Jonas said. "But we'll choose where it breaks."

"We already did," Yael murmured, almost smiling. "In the market. Where it counts."

A bell practiced honesty. A muezzin made air behave. The lemon tree shrugged off one old leaf and kept the young ones.

They went downstairs to put the jar to bed like a tool.

Chapter Thirty-One — Ladders

Night in the Quarter teaches roofs to whisper.

St. Mark's had gone to ground: bread on the plate; water in cups; the Jerusalem Protocol where an honest hand could reach it; the jar asleep in its cradle; lamp glass clear. Above, the lemon tree practiced stillness the way a cat practices sleep—ready to stand.

Shiri's text arrived like a match struck in a corridor: red-tag audit 05:30. New warrant. freezer crates. Klein looks sick. hard hand cheerful.

"Dawn," Jonas said, already on his feet. "They'll take the kitchen door because it forgave them yesterday."

"Then we use a door the city didn't offer them," Yael replied. "Roofs."

A soft knock, uncharacteristically polite. Klein stood at the threshold of the scriptorium in civilian clothes that didn't know how to sit on him. He held his hat in both hands like a confession.

"I am not your friend," he began, voice dry. "But I am not their result."

He put a case on the table—our dummy, seals intact, serials innocently wrong. He didn't look at it. "They will come with freezer crates," he said. “To invent science as custody. They will insist on central consolidation with a temperature graph.” His mouth made the shape of contempt. “They will enjoy the graph.”

Yael’s face didn’t change. “How much time?”

“If I ask the wrong question three times in the right tone, twelve minutes,” he said. “If the sergeant is curious, fifteen.” He glanced at Arielle’s coat and then away, careful and complicit by omission. “I saw your towel,” he added in a different voice, as if describing weather. “I wrote minutes anyway.”

“Then you’re our favorite kind of enemy,” Elpidios said gently, lighting a lamp for him out of courtesy and doctrine.

Klein almost smiled. “Hinges,” he said, recovering usefulness. “They’ve fixed the blind cone by the boiler intake. They’ll try the munitions corridor by the kitchens instead, because they are nostalgic about plans.” He put a small card on the table—handwritten: two shift changes, one guard who always calls his wife at 05:20, a note about a camera that blinks. “I will not risk my job,” he added, honest. “But I will not enjoy breakfast if they win.”

“We don’t want you to,” Yael said. It was as kind as she could afford.

He left the way decent men leave when decency is a strategy—quiet, without claiming it.

“Roofs,” Narsai repeated, tasting the word like bread.

Arielle set her palm on the jar; the watcher’s hand arrived—no omen, only readiness. “We split receipts,” she said. “We move the thing once.”

“The Armenian sacristy,” Jonas decided. “Roofline to Deir es-Sultan, drop into St. James. He keeps drawers that tire lawyers.”

“Elpidios will carry lamps,” the sacristan said, delighted. “And bees.”

They rehearsed on the table with a pencil stub and three coins. Roof-to-roof, not alley-to-alley: St. Mark’s gutter to the neighbor’s parapet, up the mason's ladder a stonemason left ten years ago and never returned for, across the Holy Sepulchre sprawl where the Ethiopian beehive huts sit patient as baked loaves, skirt the dome's shoulder, drop into the Armenian courtyard by a drainpipe that had forgotten to be proud.

"Witnesses?" Yael asked.

"Two," Mar Ephrem said. "Men who carry bread to prayer before dawn and disapprove of drama on principle."

"And the line," Karim said. "We need a line that lets roofs make sense."

They opened the jar because the room asked—stone at that one degree of cool that says now. Yael lifted the guard slip; resin yielded. Karim set the lamp low. Estrangela stood in the raft of light as if it had been waiting two thousand years for someone to stop apologizing for logistics.

"Read," Sister Miriam said, awake in Ein Karem, a spring always in her voice.

"If one house is weighed, carry the names to its neighbor by the roof, and let the ladders be counted with the lamps; move the bread as water and the lamps as salt, until the heaps are set again by the doors."

Yael laughed once, the sound of a craftsman finding a hidden drawer exactly where she would have put it. "We've been boring correctly," she said.

They photographed, hashed, split; bread–U went into the Gospel chest's false bottom; water–V into the Ein Karem basket under lemons; house–W to the Armenian sacristy's dullest drawer; salt–X into Shiri's lab memo that managed to insult zeal with worksheets.

The jar took straps. The coat buttoned. The watcher's hand nested where it always did now, not portent, just weight.

"Three forty," Jonas said. "We do the wet work before the city remembers it's stone."

The roof above St. Mark's keeps a ledge wide enough for humility. They climbed the inner stair, popped the hatch, tasted air that still held night. The Quarter lay like a rumor—domes and water tanks, solar panels, lines of laundry who had learned to be flags.

Ladders were where men had left them years ago and never gotten around to reclaiming—galvanized, leaning, part of the grammar of roofs. Jonas tested each rung as if his hand could interrogate welding. Elpidios carried a battered lantern whose glass had outlived politics. Karim followed with a coil of dull rope and the face of someone who had made fear choose a better job.

They crossed to Deir es-Sultan—the Ethiopian monastic huts like beehives stubbornly holding their place atop the Holy Sepulchre, doors low and round, crosses cut shallow in doors older than five governments. A monk in a sweater noticed them and decided to be practical by blessing the path instead of asking questions.

"Shalom, Abba," Narsai murmured. The monk muttered back a Tigrinya amen and went on not-sleeping.

They slid along the rotunda's shoulder where the dome's skin learns to be dew. Beyond, the Armenian roofs gathered themselves with a matter-of-factness that could intimidate armies. Jonas lowered a rope; Yael went first, then Karim with the gear; Elpidios passed the lantern down like a relic; Arielle came last, jar a sternum, breath counted.

They landed in the St. James courtyard as the world thought about light. A door opened the width of an ethical dilemma. The Armenian sacristan—dull drawer's author, enemy of flourish—stood with a key that looked like a statement.

"You are early," he observed.

"You are vague," Yael returned. It passed for affection.

He led them to the sacristy, where drawers had been meeting minutes since Crusaders learned to write. He did not ask for the jar. He set the Gospel chest open like a mouth and nodded to the lower tray. "You know the rules," he said. "Witness, not custody. If anyone asks me what happened tonight, I will explain nothing with precision."

They didn't expose clay. They exposed paper. House–W slid into the tray; the Protocol accepted a quick, clean line: transfer of witness, not object. The sacristan signed with a hand that had reconciled too many inventories to have patience for romance.

"Fog?" Karim asked, because he likes plans to have smoke.

"Another ladder," Jonas said. "Back over Deir es-Sultan, down a different hatch. We want them to see us leave the kitchen door empty."

They went back by a route the city had placed for pigeons and saints. At St. Mark's the lemon tree wore starlight like a mantle. The clock in Arielle's bones said 05:07.

The vans came at 05:23. They made the alley narrower by being confident. Brown Suit brought the court order like a chalice. The hard hand wore an expression he believed to be neutral. The sergeant from Zion Gate took up a place where a decent man stands when decency is in committee.

"Father," Brown Suit said. "We will be… efficient."

"You will be documented," Mar Ephrem replied, which is the thing committees like least.

They went through the inventory liturgy as if it were a sacrament and a joke. Devices went into boxes. Images duplicated and logged. Notes were offered in copy, logged to the hash. The Protocol sat on the table like an uncle who knows everyone's habits and will testify.

"Object," the hard hand said. It was the only word he enjoyed saying.

"Receipt," Yael said. She pointed with the pen. Names. Time. Room. Destination code. Brown Suit stamped. She wrote legibly enough to make a clerk blush later with gratitude.

They opened the cool room with ceremony. The cradle was there. The jar—quiet, serious—was there. Arielle's heartbeat climbed her throat and then found the groove where readiness likes to sit.

"Seal checks," Klein said from the back—quiet, almost human. His eyes were tired and fair.

They read the seam like a prayer and a trap. It behaved.

"Crate," Brown Suit said.

They produced the dummy—sealed, serialled, weight convincing. Yael offered the paper to a gloved hand; the hand accepted because paper likes being touched.

"Destination," Jonas asked again, the most courteous obstacle in Jerusalem.

"Rockefeller," Brown Suit said, too quick. "Joint facility."

"Write it twice," Yael said. He did. The sergeant watched the pen, not the box. Klein watched the pen too, and then, worse, his own face in the lantern glass.

They took the dummy with the dignity of men who would like to be right. The vans shouldered the alley. The hard hand glanced at the kitchen door and then up—just for a second—toward roofs that keep secrets. He didn't see anyone. He didn't need to. He put it in his pocket for later.

When the vans had gone and the alley remembered it was an alley, Sister Miriam exhaled in Arielle's ear. "I kept two grandmothers out of the street," she said. "They would have loved to learn the word warrant."

"We owe them cake," Elpidios said, relieved and planning sugar.

Arielle sank to the step and let her hands admit they were hands. The watcher's weight sat beside her, absent and present at once—a habit heavier than clay. She thought of ladders done right: counted, tied, taken away when you're finished, registered in a ledger so the next person doesn't die of your competence.

"Thunder?" Karim asked out of habit, smiling like a man who had earned breakfast.

"After ladders," Yael said. "The city likes you to finish the chore before your weather."

Matthias slid a page across the table—three signatures, a stamp so boring it cast shade, a line that said nothing and everything: witness distributed across houses; object remained at table. He smoothed it with a palm. "Let them litigate grammar," he said. "We'll keep bread."

Narsai stood under the hatch and looked at the slice of sky that is all St. Mark's ever asks for. "A good word, ladder," he said, uncharacteristically cheerful. "It suggests roof and neighbor and the kind of help you don't owe anyone."

Arielle closed her eyes one moment, saw beehive huts and ablaq arches and a heap scratched into basalt and a droplet under a lip. She saw her father's line finished by women who had never met him. She opened her eyes and found the seam of the jar as honest as it had been before dawn learned envy.

"Tomorrow," Jonas said.

"Pick a gate," Sister Miriam told her, voice like tea and ordinance. "We've fed lions. We can teach Sheep to behave."

Arielle smiled despite fatigue and hunger and a city that loves to count to the wrong number. "Many small ladders," she said.

"Many," Yael agreed.

Outside, the pigeons resumed their jurisdiction. Inside, the stone room cooled one degree and kept it. The quarter thought about bread and decided to begin.

Chapter Thirty-Two — Freezer Logic

Dawn dragged a gray sleeve across the roofs and left chill in its hem. In the scriptorium the jar slept in its cradle, seam honest, paper quiet. Bread and water waited like good habits. Upstairs, the lemon tree had decided to be brave.

Shiri's next text arrived before coffee: crates in courtyard. men with jackets. klein looks like he hasn't slept. brown suit rehearsing "chain of custody."

"Today is graphs," Yael said, pinning up her hair. "They'll try to freeze custody into truth."

"Then we give them minutes until their graphs melt," Matthias replied, sliding the Protocol toward her like a shield that prefers boredom to heroics.

The vans nosed into the Rockefeller as if geometry owed them favors. A guard tried to remember which rule fit which door; a clerk pursued a staple across the table as if it might confess. On the loading bay, two freezer crates blinked a blue that believed itself to be science. Brown Suit narrated to anyone who would pretend to listen. The hard hand stood a step back, hands in pockets, evidently enjoying the air.

Klein met Shiri by the service stair with the posture of a man who has chosen to be useful and resents the choice. "Arrival photos first," he said, and said it loudly. "Serials. Seals. Weights." He held the clipboard as if it were the thin line between decency and discussion.

The case came up like a confession—tape smooth, red numbers righteous. Klein posed it for the camera like he was proud of its angles. "Document the seals," he told a tech who liked being told. To Brown Suit: "You'll want a photograph of the signature. Judges adore handwriting."

"Open," the hard hand said, not unkindly. The word sounded like he was giving the box a chance not to disappoint him.

The red tape yielded like an apology. The foam lid came off. The jar-shaped hollow presented what it had been entrusted to present: weight and shape, not truth. The dummy lay there with the serenity of training equipment.

A scale performed its drama. Six point two, the display announced, pleased with its own clarity.

"Within tolerance," said the young attorney, gratefully choosing math over nouns.

Klein frowned in a way only Shiri caught. "Remove the towel," he told the tech, mild. The towel slid aside with the whisper of fabric trying not to be evidence. The number twitched: 6.0.

"Again," he said.

They lifted the sleeve; the training clay gave its small theater of friction. The number sulked: 5.9.

Brown Suit tried to be air. "Anomalies—"

"—go in minutes," Klein said. He turned to the room and said the phrase that keeps honest men employed and dishonest men delayed: "We pause until we reconcile paper."

The hard hand looked at him as though Klein had spoken poetry. Then he looked at the case and did the math of a man who knows his anger is only useful if it is scheduled. "Inventory the building," he said to no one. "Politely."

Shiri broadcast nothing of her own, only Shiri facts: they're calling upstairs. seals photographed. klein insisting on second sign-off. everyone pretending not to hate towels.

Down in the Quarter, they poured coffee that did not apologize for being bitter. "We don't crow," Jonas said. "We move."

"Sheep," Sister Miriam said in Arielle's ear, the spring in her voice. "We fed lions. Now we walk the well again, then the little gate north of it men call Herod's and grandmothers still call Sheep when they have the energy to correct you."

They did it without theater. St. Anne's sister took their letter with the thin smile of women who have learned to aid without becoming anecdotes. At the Pools of Bethesda, the steps remembered feet. They did not open the jar. They read names as women filled jars and children echoed syllables like pebbles dropped in water.

Then they drifted up the lane to Herod's Gate, Bab az-Zahra, the Flower Gate that still inherits the Sheep when older tongues gather. No lions here. No tourists practicing reverence with phones. A grocer watched from his stool and decided he approved. Sister Miriam's two Ein Karem scouts unfolded a sheet and read the day's column in voices that had learned to overrule traffic. Nobody made a scene. The city simply stored receipts.

Lev's fixer texted from a shadow near the Rockefeller: committee arguing over towel. hard hand walked the roofline once with eyes. he suspects ladders and will hate them.

"Then we make ladders boring," Yael said. "And we finish the salt chore."

They took one more pass through Khan al-Zeit, visited the soap-seller who kept a ledger for bath salt and births, and slipped salt–R into a sleeve where it would pass for a bill later. No chase. No drama. Just a drawer learning it had company.

At noon, the committee assembled again under the Rockefeller's Mandate façade to examine its own conscience. Brown Suit produced his paper, only slightly less confident. The conservation woman asked about humidity and was answered. The attorney asked about serials and was bored. Klein dragged his finger under: received, arrived, photographed, opened, weights, and did not look at Shiri when he was finished.

"The object appears...non-conforming," Brown Suit said, and the euphemism hurt him.

"We love conforming," Yael replied sweetly. "Specifically to process. You have our minutes."

"What you don't have is our witness," Matthias added. He laid another single page on the table—today's dull account of Sheep, Bethesda, Khan al-Zeit, Cotton Market—signed by a nun, a grocer, two grandmothers, and a sacristan who has never learned to admire adjectives.

The hard hand watched intelligence hit bureaucracy at an angle insufficient to pierce. He did not lose his temper. He lost interest in the paper in front of him.

When it was done, when they were released back into a city that prefers bread to agendas, they returned to the scriptorium and listened to the room breathe. The seam looked like days of good work should look: unreproachful. The air had kept its one degree of cool like an oath.

"One line," Karim said. "For us."

They opened when the stone said now. Yael lifted the guard slip; resin sighed; the Estrangela came forward with the patience of a ledger that has outlived governors.

"Read," Sister Miriam said.

"If men bring cold to make a claim, do not let the memory be frozen; set bread by the lamp until the line is warm; carry the names to the market and the well, that those who sell and those who draw may answer."

Karim grinned, sudden and twelve. "The scribe has met men with graphs."

"Or women with ovens," Yael said, delighted. "Either way, we obey."

They photographed, hashed, split. Bread–S into the Greek chest; Water–T to Ein Karem; House–U to St. James; Salt–V to Shiri, who answers bureaucracy with chemistry and scorn.

Arielle set her palm on the jar and felt the watcher's hand settle beside it in a gesture that had ceased to be omen and had become routine: company in the work. She thought of her father's bad Syriac and good stubbornness, of lions and sheep, of ladders and sumac, of a towel that had bought them an hour inside someone else's plan.

"We won today by minutes," Jonas said. "Tomorrow they'll try maps."

"Then we bring women who grew up making routes across courtyards while men were deciding nouns," Sister Miriam answered. "You'll like their logistics."

Lev's fixer appeared in the doorway carrying parsley as if it were a proclamation. "Buyer's soft hands have moved to Mount Zion for brunch," she said. "The hard one is buying batteries near New Gate. The sergeant left bread by the lemon tree again and did not write it down."

The room cooled a degree and kept it. Above, the lemon tree stopped pretending not to enjoy this.

"Thunder?" Karim asked, unable to help himself.

"Soon," Yael said, smiling without softness. "After we finish the chores."

Chapter Thirty-Three — Contours

Maps arrived before men did.

Shiri's text: new filing: "movement perimeter for cultural property inside Old City." geofences on the order. klein says they learned a new noun: perimeter.

"Maps," Yael said, tying her hair as if it were a ribbon on a file. "They're going to try drawing a box and calling it law."

"Then we draw roads and call them minutes," Matthias replied, sliding the Protocol closer, that shield that likes boredom better than courage.

Lev's fixer leaned in with parsley and weather. "Hard hand ate breakfast at Mount Zion and bought a map that thinks it's history," she said. "Soft hands practicing cordons near the Cardo. Your sergeant took a slow walk on the ramparts and pretended to be a tourist."

"Library," Jonas said. "Old maps. Rooms that remember routes."

The Armenian sacristan unlocked St. James's little map press with a key that looked like patience. He laid out four thin throats of paper: an Ottoman plan with streets drawn as if they were veins; a Mandate sheet from the Survey of Palestine that loved scale more than compassion; a waqf parcel map with doors marked by owners who had all died and were still right; and a pilgrim sketch copied in brown ink—streets as sentences, courtyards as commas.

Narsai added a fifth: a Tur Abdin processional route hidden in the margin of a hymn, acrostic instructing feet where law seldom thinks to count. Father Paulus messaged a blurry print of a monk's errand map around the lake—the kind of drawing that remembers where bread is, not borders.

"We overlay use on claim," Yael said. "They'll bring cordons. We bring women's routes."

"Pick your nodes," Jonas said.

"Zion Gate for bread—table scars still in its stones," Matthias answered. "Siloam for water—where the steps remember feet. Muristan for house—it was born for it. Cotton Market for salt—heaps by doors."

"Soft hands at Zion," Lev's fixer texted from nowhere, as if the city were speaking through her. "Brown Suit practicing his perimeter out loud."

"They can draw a box," Yael said. "We'll braid it."

They didn't open the jar yet. They set the readers first.

Sister Miriam gathered seven women from Ein Karem, each with a folding stool and a ledger face. Elpidios oiled two lantern hinges until they forgot squeaks. The Armenian sacristan folded the lectionary like a weapon. Narsai tucked the small lamp into linen. The sergeant drifted, "off-duty," along the Armenian Patriarchate Road, hands folded behind his back, counting pigeons and vans.

"Line," Karim said. "We need the text to tell our feet what our maps already know."

They opened when the stone said now. Yael coaxed the seam; resin behaved. The Estrangela rose like a bruise appearing honestly.

"Read," Sister Miriam said.

"Measure the road not by bronze but by steps; bind the rope at the gate and mark the heaps where the markets breathe. At the scarred stones, read bread; at the steps of water, read water; in the house's court, read the house; by the heap, read the salt."

"Scarred stones," Matthias murmured, seeing Zion Gate's bullet-pocked cheeks. "That's our table."

They photographed, hashed, split. Bread–W to the Greek chest; Water–X to the Ein Karem basket with lemons; House–Y to St. James's dullest drawer; Salt–Z to Shiri's lab under a memo that could narcotize a tyrant.

"Go," Jonas said.

They broke into threads that would weave back into fabric.

Bread — Zion Gate

Sister Miriam marched her seven stools to Zion Gate, the stone still pitted from 1948, and set them down with the confidence of a knitting circle. Elpidios set a tray with bread and lantern as if setting a table in a wind. Women sat. The psalm began with Ya'el of bread and Tamar of water, syllables stubborn as yeast.

Brown Suit arrived with a map on a clipboard and the face of a man told to love a shape. "We have a perimeter," he announced to the air, then to a grandmother, who ignored him by adjusting her shawl.

"Read," Sister Miriam said, louder. "Read until the boys answer."

A boy did. From the wall. Badly, bravely. The hard hand appeared, watched the map lose authority to bread, and didn't smile.

Water — Siloam

Narsai and Karim went downhill with two Ein Karem women and a nun from St. Anne who disliked being useful for free. The Siloam steps held heat and memory; the water ran honest. They didn't open the jar; they didn't need to. They read water names while jars filled. A shopkeeper nodded and wrote a hash on the back of a folded receipt, as if paying a bill.

House — Muristan

Yael and the Armenian sacristan planted themselves at the little fountain. The sacristan put the lectionary on a bench without apology. Yael read house names in a voice that refuses to become interesting. Tourists slowed and behaved. A man with a camera decided the frame had too much dignity to improve by taking it.

Salt — Cotton Market

Matthias and Lev's fixer walked Suq al-Qattanin with the lamp wrapped in cloth. At the dark door where the heap mark hid, they set a pinch of salt on a ledger and let that be receipt. A tailor with clean hands watched, nodded, and did not ask where the police thought the city was.

The hard hand tried to make all four rooms at once and lost to topography. The sergeant appeared at Zion Gate in time to develop a sudden interest in bullet scars. He asked Brown Suit to explain the map; it took longer than anyone enjoyed.

When the psalm had made its circuit and the women had folded their stools the way flags are folded, they went home by different alleys on purpose. Brown Suit folded his paper slowly. The hard hand checked the rooftops with his eyes and saw ladders where there were none. He filed the thought. He would hate it later.

Back at St. Mark's, bread and water waited. The room had kept its degree of cool like a promise.

"One line," Karim said. "And then we sleep like we invented the city."

They opened at dusk because dusk is the hour when words stay put. Yael lifted the guard slip; resin sighed like a chore finished. The letters came forward with the calm of a ledger that has outlived maps.

"Read," Sister Miriam said.

"If men draw cords to make fences, draw lines of song and walk them; keep the rope at the gate and the heap at the door; let the women carry the names across roofs when streets are counted."

Karim's grin was untidy and earned. "It keeps predicting us," he said.

"No," Yael said, closing the seam with satisfied fingers. "We're finally obeying it."

Lev's fixer stood in the doorway with parsley and a rumor that had learned to be fact. "Buyer's soft hands now like Mount Zion less. Hard hand hates ladders more. Klein left two staples missing on a form. The sergeant forgot to see them."

The lemon tree shook one leaf from its sleeve like punctuation.

"Tomorrow," Jonas said.

"Pick a gate," Sister Miriam replied. "You finished lions and sheep. It's time to try Dung. It's humbler. It tells the truth."

Arielle rested her palm on the jar; the watcher's hand settled beside it, all colleague, no omen. She thought of scarred stones and rope, of heaps scratched shallow and steps that had learned the names. She thought of her father's bad Syriac and good defiance.

"Contours," she said softly. "We didn't let them box us. We taught them the shape."

The city turned the page. The room cooled a degree and kept it.

Chapter Thirty-Four — The Gate of Ash

Morning came with diesel in its throat.

In the scriptorium, bread on the plate, water in cups, the Jerusalem Protocol within reach, lamp glass clean. The jar slept in its cradle; the seam looked like patience. Above, the lemon tree wore yesterday's dust like memory.

Shiri's text: perimeter filed. "temporary cultural cordon" around Zion, Dung, Lion. drones in the memo—battery models wrong. klein says they'll try the low gate first.

"Dung," Sister Miriam said on the line, already awake, already organizing. "The gate that tells the truth. We read where carts pass."

"Witnesses," Yael said.

"I have the sanitation crew at the end of their shift," Lev's fixer offered, arriving with parsley and a neon vest she had not exactly borrowed. "Orange vests are harder to argue with than theology."

"Brown Suit?" Jonas asked.

"Polishing 'perimeter' until it sounds like 'providence,'" she said. "The hard hand walked the ramparts at dawn and hated ladders again."

They didn't open the jar yet. They set the rooms.

Elpidios wrapped two lanterns in linen as if packing loaves. The Armenian sacristan produced a lectionary that had frightened three auditors and one bishop. Narsai tucked his small lamp into a fold that had learned secrecy under kings. Matthias signed dull letters to the Patriarchate, St. James, St. Anne, Mukawir—acknowledgments of witness, refusals of custody. The sergeant from Zion Gate drifted near the court with the face of a man who had misplaced a pigeon and found his conscience.

"Line," Karim said softly. "Tell our feet."

They opened when the stone said now. Yael lifted the guard slip; resin yielded like a habit proudly kept. The Estrangela rose in the lamp's rake with the self-respect of a hand that has copied too many lists to pretend to be thunder.

"Read," Sister Miriam said.

"At the gate of ash, read the names with the carts, that what men throw away not be the daughters. Set the heap by the door; mark bread on the cloth; carry the lamps when the road grows dim; pour the water where the steps are worn."

Karim's smile was involuntary, grateful. "Housekeeping," he whispered.

"Government," Yael corrected, pleased. "The kind that survives kings."

They photographed, hashed, split. Bread–AA to the Greek chest; Water–AB to Ein Karem under lemons; House–AC to St. James's dullest drawer; Salt–AD to Shiri with a cover memo so soporific it could anaesthetize a coup.

"Go," Jonas said.

They walked down—through Jewish Quarter alleys that think they invented stone, past a wall that has outlived men learning to love it, toward the low mouth of Dung Gate. The air smelled of bread and diesel and refuse doing its civic work. A small loader beeped with the optimism of a creature that believes in reverse.

The sanitation crew were already there—five in orange, coffee in paper cups, dignity that did not require applause. One—Hussein, said his stitched name—shifted his weight and nodded to Sister Miriam with the familiarity of citizens. "You're the women with lists," he said.

"We're the ones who don't throw away names," she answered, folding open her sheet.

Brown Suit arrived with a map and practiced civility, the attorney at his shoulder, two utility blues uncoiling tape. The hard hand stood back where a man enjoys outcomes.

"We have a perimeter," Brown Suit tried. "Temporary cordon for safety."

"Safety is why we read," Sister Miriam said. She lifted her voice. "At the gate of ash we read truth, so that the boys hear it before they become men."

She spoke the first name; Hussein answered. She spoke the second; a woman in orange answered and then handed her coffee to a co-worker without losing syllables. On the third, a boy sitting on the curb tried the sound in his mouth and decided to keep it.

Brown Suit consulted his map as if it might begin to respect him. The utility blues unrolled tape toward the curb. The tape met a trash cart that refused to understand perimeters. The sergeant appeared with a look of professional forgetfulness. "Make room for city work," he told the tape, not the people. Tape hates humility; it sagged.

"Receipt," Yael murmured. Karim slid salt-AD into Hussein's ledger—the one that recorded routes, bags, and fines nobody in this lane would ever call fines. Hussein tucked it under a clip with the same care he gave to his morning counts.

They didn't open the jar at the gate. They didn't need to; the instruction was habit. They left a pinch of salt on the ledger, a dot of bread on a cloth by a stall that sold ka'ak with sesame. They poured a small cup of water where the steps shine because feet have remembered them since before committees.

The hard hand took a step forward and met a bin blocking his shin. He stopped, not because of pain, but because civic furniture had asserted jurisdiction. He recalculated and decided to attend the scene he could not create.

They finished with amen that sounded like a lift truck downshifting. Sister Miriam folded the sheet like a planned kindness.

Back at St. Mark's, Klein waited in the nave like a man who had purchased a seat at his own discomfort. His jacket had conceded to creases. He held no clipboard.

"Your dummy passed through two additional rooms," he said, dry. "It has acquired a name: 'interim conservational surrogate.' I was present when they invented it." He glanced at Arielle's coat and not at the jar. "Your minutes broke one committee and fed another. They've scheduled a joint press look for tomorrow—photographs of cooperation, a sentence with the word custody twice."

"Thunder," Jonas said, not asking.

"I assumed," Klein said, with the audacity of a man who has started to respect himself. "If you plan to make weather, do it where maps behave badly."

"Southern Steps," Matthias said—the hulda gates' old stones where feet learn humility. "Tables' scar cousin. Wide. Honest. Unowned enough to embarrass everyone equally."

"Witnesses?" Yael asked.

"Choir," Sister Miriam answered, fierce with logistics. "Ein Karem women and two from Tur Abdin that Narsai will coax loose with a guilt letter. A Greek deacon with a tenor that can frighten doves. An Armenian boy who reads like a bell. Father Paulus on a phone near the loaves and fishes. Rashid at Mukawir with a letter dull enough to cross a sea. Hani with his Thermos and his class of twelve-year-olds doing civics."

"Press?" Lev's fixer said, distaste in the word but not fear. "Not the kind that wants thunder. The kind that writes minutes for strangers. Two wire services. One local who owes me a lunch and knows what not to photograph."

"Police?" Jonas asked.

"The sergeant will be there to forget things," Klein said. "He would prefer not to have to forget a riot."

"Then we don't give him one," Yael said. "We give him chores."

They set the table because ritual keeps courage fed: bread on the plate; water in cups; Protocol open to a fresh page. The jar's seam looked like an ally. Arielle set her palm on the clay and the watcher's hand arrived—no omen, all company.

"One line," Karim said, because it had become a way to make an hour honest.

They opened. Resin sighed. Estrangela stood. The lamp raked low. The letters spoke with their usual untheatrical certainty.

"Read," Sister Miriam said.

"When gates are told, gather at the steps, for there the feet have learned obedience; read the names where tables once stood, that boys and girls answer together. Set bread and water and lamps and salt before them; let witness be many."

The room listened like stone.

Karim's hands moved the way good hands do—photograph, hash, split. Bread–AE to the Greek chest; Water–AF to Ein Karem; House–AG to St. James; Salt–AH to Shiri with a memo that could sedate a cavalry unit.

They sealed the seam. The jar rested. The air kept its one degree of cool like a sacred, petty prerogative.

"Tomorrow," Jonas said.

"Thunder," Yael answered, and did not smile because the word wasn't a joke anymore. It was a schedule.

Klein exhaled like a man who has confessed a lesser sin to avoid a greater one. "At ten," he said. "They'll try to beat you there with phrases."

"We have names," Sister Miriam said. "And steps. And minutes. We'll be fine."

The lemon tree shook off a tired leaf and made room for one that had decided to be new.

Arielle leaned against the doorjamb and let fatigue admit kinship. She thought of ash and heaps, of bins asserting jurisdiction against appetites with badges, of women reading at a low gate while a loader backed into the day. She thought of her father's bad Syriac and the line he left for her to finish.

"Many small doors," she said softly.

"Plus one large step," Jonas said, and for once he allowed himself almost a grin.

They slept by shifts and woke with the kind of hunger that belongs to work. The city turned the page. The weather waited its cue.

Chapter Thirty-Five — The Steps

Jerusalem woke with a plan it didn't approve of and then decided to proceed anyway.

Bread on the plate. Water in cups. The Jerusalem Protocol where an honest hand could reach it. The jar asleep in its cradle; the seam as plain as law done correctly. Above, the lemon tree shook off a bad leaf and pretended not to enjoy the sun.

Shiri's text: press "look" confirmed for 10:00 at the Southern Steps. committee rehearsing words. brown suit writing "custody" twice. hard hand circling in a car that doesn't belong to him. klein has his tie wrong on purpose.

"Thunder," Yael said, not smiling. "We do it our way."

"Steps," Jonas answered. "They belong to feet."

They did not take the jar. They took the room with them: bread into a basket, water into a thermos with the dignity of a samovar, the lamp wrapped in linen that smelled faintly of beeswax and history, the Protocol in a folder so dull it radiated safety. Copies—bread-AE, water-AF, house-AG, salt-AH—nested into envelopes with hashes printed in the corner like an afterthought.

"Witnesses?" Arielle asked.

"On their feet," Sister Miriam said, already at the bus stop with women who had folded stools and voices made for minutes. "Two from Tur Abdin," she added. "They came with letters and the wrong shoes."

The Davidson Archaeological Park received them the way honest stone does: without drama, without apology. The Southern Steps spread broad under the sun—Herodian courses squared like promises, risers irregular as if the builders had preferred reflection to haste. To the right the blocked Double Gate—one of the Hulda gates—kept its lintel scars; to the left the Triple Gate pretended not to exist under a wall that had inherited more history than any wall has a right to. Mikva'ot dotted the approach like commas—stone baths that had taught generations to count themselves clean.

Sound behaved here. The slope made an amphitheater without meaning to. If you spoke at the landing below the gate, your words climbed.

Matthias set a folding table with the love of a man who admires furniture that becomes doctrine. Bread and water on top, Protocol ready, lamp asleep. Yael checked wind, shade, the angle of a camera no one had admitted to setting up. Jonas scanned ridgelines, drains, police positions, the routes vans would try and would fail to love.

Brown Suit arrived with the committee dressed in polite nouns: Conservation, Antiquities, a Ministry liaison who had been promised a press quote, the attorney with a notebook already tired of itself. The hard hand came a minute later, jacket better cut than yesterday, eyes performing neutral. Klein stood with them and not with them, his tie crooked, his jaw unknotting only when he saw the steps widen in front of him like a thought he would one day allow himself.

Press followed in twos and threes—wire service cameras, a local with a lens he knew how to treat kindly, a student with a phone and the look of someone who would write her first honest copy today if nobody stopped her.

Sister Miriam brought the choir like a kitchen brings lunch: Ein Karem women with folded stools; two Tur Abdin sisters whose Arabic had learned to live beside Syriac; a Greek deacon with a tenor that made pigeons reconsider; an Armenian boy with a book he held as if it were heavy enough to steady him. Hani appeared with twelve kids in uniforms that didn't match, carrying a Thermos like a flag. Rashid had sent a letter dull enough to cross a border; Father Paulus had a phone propped against a bench at Tabgha; Rina at Magdala texted a photograph of the basalt heap with the caption: Your drawer is open. Behave.

The sergeant from Zion Gate took a place at the edge of the landing with his arms folded and the crease between his eyes practicing neutrality. He nodded once to Sister Miriam and once, separately, to Klein, and declined to see anything he was not obligated to.

"Father," Brown Suit said to Mar Ephrem, who had positioned himself near the table with the air of a man hosting a feast he refused to let be stolen. "Thank you for agreeing to a joint statement."

"We're making minutes," Mar Ephrem replied. "Statements are for people who forgot what they did."

"Begin?" the Conservation woman asked—honest, precise, trying to save the part of the day she could.

"Begin," Jonas said, and stepped back into the column of shade like a man evaluating weather.

They started with minutes.

Matthias read the Protocol's last page—the entries from Zion Gate and Dung Gate, Siloam and St. Anne, Cotton Market and Muristan. He spoke as if the thrill of correctness could be enough for adults. Hashes. Times. Rooms. Names. Witnesses. A ledger that had stopped apologizing.

Then names.

Sister Miriam lifted her sheet, and the women unfolded stools, and the steps took a breath.

"Ya'el—of bread."

"Here," answered a grandmother in orange from the sanitation shift, stepping to the edge of the landing as if called to count.

"Tamar—of water."

"Here," said a girl of ten who had come with Hani's class and had decided unilaterally that her name was allowed to be older than she was.

"Marta—vowed in fever."

"Here," said one of the Tur Abdin sisters, and the Syriac in her mouth made the air behave.

"Shoshana—who entered by Hanna."

"Here," said the Greek deacon, and his tenor pushed the syllables into the upper seats with a gentleness that frightened no one and changed five minds.

The psalm went on. It did not name thunder. It named keeping. The press found themselves taking photographs of ordinary faces made taller by lists. The student with the phone lowered it and wrote in her head instead.

Brown Suit tried his map once, pointing discreetly to a rectangle printed over the steps and labeled perimeter. The rectangle refused to be believed by stone; it sagged like tape in a hot wind. He placed his paper on a knee and adjusted it as if the drawing were at fault for the world's refusal to become smaller.

The hard hand took two steps forward at the word custody in his own head and ran into a line that wasn't a line at all: a row of folding stools occupied by women who could not see him because their attention belonged to names. He recalculated. He went still—the way dangerous men do when they've recognized the hour is not theirs—and put both hands in his pockets so they wouldn't betray him.

Klein stood with his head down—not from shame but to give himself the permission to listen without performing. When the name Abisha came, he said nothing; but something in his face moved as if an unused muscle had shrugged.

When they finished the page and the steps had learned it, they did minutes again.

Yael spoke the dull nouns: bread here, water there, lamps counted when shutters close, salt under ledgers no one wants to polish. She spoke witness, not custody. She spoke rooms, not ownership. She outlasted the word temporary by saying today and yesterday and the day after until perimeter became a chalk line that morning feet would erase.

A reporter raised a hand with the courtesy of a classroom. "Is the artifact on site?" he asked, because the gods of headlines demand nouns you can photograph.

"It's at table," Yael said after a beat that told truth and preserved the world. "Where it belongs."

"And custody—" the Ministry liaison began.

"—is a word for boxes," Sister Miriam said, not unkind. "We have houses."

The Conservation woman cleared her throat. "May we document your process?" she asked—an honest person's last resort.

"You may have our methods," Yael said, and meant it. "You'll find them boring and indestructible."

A murmur at the back that was not menace but crowd—pilgrims drifting in, tourists slowing with the respect architecture can still demand, kids trying the steps' irregular rhythm under their sneakers and discovering that walking can be a lesson. Hani's twelve stood in a row pretending to hate being seen and secretly proud their city could manufacture dignity at short notice.

"Close with a line," Jonas said softly.

They had not opened the jar. They didn't need to. The steps had the last sentence already under them. Sister Miriam lifted her palm, and the women and children and two men who had earned it answered:

"When gates are told, gather at the steps, for there the feet have learned obedience; read the names where tables once stood, that boys and girls answer together."

It landed without applause, which is how you know thunder has worked.

Brown Suit folded his map and did not tear it, which is how you know a man has decided to live to be better. The hard hand looked up at the rim of the wall, then down at the ring of stools, and banked the anger he would need for a different day. The sergeant examined an inscription and found it easy to disremember violence.

Klein stepped forward because a decent man sometimes has to risk his job to make his breakfast sit well. "There is a surrogate at the Rockefeller," he said to the reporters as if he were telling them the price of tomatoes. "It is non-conforming. An internal audit is under way." He looked at Yael and said, for no one but her, "Your minutes were—are—useful."

"Come for bread," Elpidios told him, stepping between sentences with a tray. "Later. When it's not a quote."

They broke without breaking. Press found their words—wire copy about witness and women and a psalm at a staircase. The Ministry liaison tried to locate the angle where cooperation would sound like victory and failed gracefully. The committee members asked Yael for the methods in writing and meant it. The sergeant asked a pigeon for ID and accepted its refusal.

On the slope below, a drone rose, buzzed, and sulked into a lamppost because its battery had learned honesty from whichever clerk had entered the model number wrong. The city looked pleased to have one less noise for a minute.

They walked away in threads the way they had arrived: Sister Miriam's choir folding stools; Tur Abdin sisters holding their shoes by the straps; Hani's kids arguing about whether witness or custody made a better civics word; Klein alone with his tie in his pocket; the hard hand with both hands still in his; Brown Suit discovering that he had not been humiliated and might even have been educated.

Back at St. Mark's the lemon tree took a bow no one saw. The room kept its single sanctified degree of cool. The jar lay where it had slept, the seam like punctuation at the end of a long, precise paragraph.

"Line?" Karim asked, soft not to scare it away.

"Line," Sister Miriam said, and they went below.

Yael lifted the guard slip. Resin obliged. The lamp raked the wall. The Estrangela rose with its accustomed lack of vanity.

"Read," Sister Miriam said.

"After steps, return to the table, and write the minutes of the day; send bread to the houses and water to the springs and lamps to the roads and salt to the markets. When men ask who kept custody, answer with witness, for witness is the keeping."

Karim's breath came out in a laugh that wasn't mirth so much as relief given a voice. "He wrote the weather report," he said.

"Or the housekeeping," Yael answered, sealing the seam. "Either way, we obey."

They hashed and split and sent: Bread–AI to the Greek chest; Water–AJ to Ein Karem; House–AK to St. James; Salt–AL to Shiri with a memo that would sedate a riot.

They ate bread Elpidios warmed just enough to make it decide to be generous again. Water, honest. Lamp, ticking. Paper, neat.

"Tomorrow," Jonas said.

"Not quieter," Sister Miriam warned, amused and tired. "But easier to tell the truth in."

Arielle put her palm on the jar, and the watcher's hand settled beside hers like a colleague who has decided to stay late without being asked. She thought of irregular risers teaching boys to slow down; of Hulda's sealed mouths; of mikva'ot that made a grammar out of water; of her father's bad Syriac and perfect stubbornness, a sentence he'd left for her to finish and she had.

"Many small doors," she said.

"And one set of steps," Jonas added, allowing himself the smallest smile. "We made them behave."

Outside, the Quarter rehearsed evening. Inside, ledgers cooled. The lemon tree forgot to be tired. Somewhere, a drone re-learned humility.

Chapter Thirty-Six — Night Audit

Jerusalem's evenings always rehearse peace just long enough to make you feel impolite for doubting it.

Bread on the plate. Water in cups. The Jerusalem Protocol open to a clean page, columns ready for names, time, room. The jar in its cradle; the seam a quiet you could measure with two fingers. The lemon tree above forgot to look innocent and simply was.

Shiri's text arrived at twilight: odd movement at Rockefeller—second crate, new chain log, "external auditor" at 02:00. klein circled "after-hours calibration." buyer's hard hand bought gloves; brown suit learned "temporary export" and looks pleased with himself.

"Audit," Yael said. "They'll make midnight into a noun and try to carry it like a badge."

"Then we make bells into verbs," Jonas replied. "And we put hands on ropes."

Lev's fixer slipped in with parsley and the smell of frying onions from a neighbor's window. "Hard hand has rented a van with no logos and too much new paint," she said. "He's speaking quietly near the Christian Quarter police box where cameras forget to work. Your sergeant is on the ramparts looking like a man who got lost on purpose."

Arielle set her palm on the jar. The watcher's hand arrived like a colleague who'd taken an early shift. "We read one line," she said. "Then we tie our ladders to our bells."

They opened when stone said now. Yael eased the guard slip; resin behaved with that satisfied little surrender good work earns. Karim raked the light. Estrangela stood, unafraid of hours.

"Read," Sister Miriam said from Ein Karem, the spring unmistakable under her words.

"If men come with night and lists, ring the bells and carry the lamps to the roof; set bread on the lintel and water at the stair; let the girls answer from the house-tops, and let the boys pull the rope until witness is awake."

Karim's laugh was soft and grateful. "He knows our city," he said.

"Housekeeping," Yael murmured, pleased.

"Government," Narsai corrected, kinder than it sounded.

They photographed, hashed, split. Bread–AM to the Greek chest; Water–AN into the Ein Karem basket beneath lemons; House–AO to St. James's nap-inducing drawer; Salt–AP to Shiri with a memo that could anesthetize a customs hall.

Then they worked the room like a crew before weather.

Elpidios oiled the bellropes so sound would travel as courage, not complaint. The Armenian sacristan arrived at the side door with a key and a face that had never forgiven theater; he nodded once at the lamp and once at the Protocol. Yael taped two dull copies—hash big and immodest—beneath the table where hands would go before anyone thought to look at wood.

"Hatches?" Jonas asked.

"Two," Lev's fixer said. "One to the Armenian roofline. One to a neighbor who will disapprove and then help. The Ethiopian huts will pretend not to see you."

The quarter settled into the hour when cats claim dominion. Far off, a siren remembered a promise; nearer, a boy practiced dribbling a flat ball with the stubbornness of saints. The lemon tree took one last breath before night and dignified it with silence.

At 01:43, Klein's text, small and indecently useful: external audit moved up. crate staged. hard hand on site in ten. "temporary export" form unsignable but printable. i am not your friend. i am also not asleep.

At 01:55, the driver with the wrong music answered a call he hadn't made by turning a corner he had learned from weather. The van with new paint slid into the lane with a humility it did not feel.

At 02:03, the first knock wasn't a knock—metal considering metal, patience preparing to show off. The hard hand stood at the kitchen door with two utility blues who had borrowed posture. Brown Suit carried a folder that believed itself ripe. Two uniformed officers who had earned better nights looked at Jonas and decided to conserve their energy.

"Father," Brown Suit said, low out of respect for houses that scold echoes. "Midnight calibration. We'll need the object for an external audit. Temporary export classification. Safety."

"Witness first," Mar Ephrem said cheerfully, and pulled the bell rope.

The sound went up like a rumor choosing to live. St. Mark's answered itself, then St. James joined from across roofs, then a small, stubborn clapper on the Ethiopians' huts added a domestic ding that refused to be impressed. From somewhere closer than city planning would approve, a Greek handbell chimed like a spoon against a glass at a wedding.

In the scriptorium, Arielle slid the jar's harness tight. She didn't lift it. She put bread on the lintel because the line had said so. She set water by the stair. She kept her palm on clay until her chest learned the jar's breath and the jar learned hers.

In the lane, women appeared the way witnesses do: without permission and wearing shoes suitable for stairs. Sister Miriam led three—aprons over coats—carrying lamps with steady hands. Two Tur Abdin sisters in borrowed sweaters arrived out of the seam of a wall like mistakes the city could not correct. Hani texted: boys at rope north; you'll like their math.

"Inventory," Yael told Brown Suit over the bells.

He sighed and began. Names. Time. Room. The Protocol took his pen like an aunt who had been waiting at a table and had no patience left for rhetoric. He stamped. She watched. The sergeant from Zion Gate appeared in the doorway and found the ceiling of the corridor suddenly fascinating.

The hard hand stepped into the kitchen and met Elpidios at an angle that makes civilized men revise their manners. The priest held a lamp like a crosier and offered bread with undisguised pastoral aggression. The hard hand declined, and in that gesture revealed the kind of man he would not manage to stop being tonight.

"Hatch," Jonas said without raising his voice.

The sacristan cracked the door to the inner stair—Ethiopian roof, Armenian gutter, Deir es-Sultan ledge. Yael moved like a woman in a crowded kitchen, which is to say: sovereign and pretending not to be. Karim shouldered the towel-wrapped lamp and a coil of rope and became utility. Narsai took the rear and looked like basalt with patience.

Arielle did not lift the jar. She lifted the scene. Bread on lintel. Water at stair. Lamp in hand. She stepped to the hatch and up because the line had said roofs. The watcher's hand made weight into company.

Outside, bell sound met airshaft and multiplied. The Ethiopian monk in a sweater lifted his own tiny bell with the grave mischief of a man taking the side of roofs. Across the way, the Armenian night watchman signaled once with a flashlight because men have learned to turn even electricity into liturgy.

The hard hand reached the scriptorium door as Yael's lamp disappeared over the hatch lip. He did not lunge. He is not that kind of fool. He did arithmetic. He turned to Brown Suit.

"Write the new nouns," he said.

"Obstruction," the attorney offered, helpful.

"Witness," the sergeant supplied from the doorway, sounding bored.

Brown Suit wrote minutes, because he is that kind of man and could not help himself anymore.

On the roof the night was clean. Domes hulked like sleeping animals; water tanks blinked their one-eyed moon; laundry lines, rigged like delicate bridges, insisted on keeping the peace. Arielle crossed the little parapet and felt the jar become light enough to be a habit. Karim set the lamp on the coping and handed the rope down the Armenian side where a drain remembered rain. Narsai followed, less a man than a moving permission. Yael came last, and safety followed her like a well-trained dog.

They did not run. They braided roofs the way the city meant them to. And because it was 02:16 and decent men are on night shift and indecent men drink late, nobody really saw them except a cat who re-evaluated jurisdiction and decided to admire competence.

In the lane, Hani's boys—three fifteen-year-olds who had once believed the city did not belong to them—took the bellrope in turns and discovered that a small math exists between rhythm and courage. A neighbor opened a window to disapprove and then closed it to enjoy the sound. Sister Miriam stood with folded hands and counted names under her breath; the Tur Abdin sisters sang two lines of a hymn no committee has learned to forbid.

At 02:24, Klein texted: external audit paused for reconciliation. weight variance. "surrogate" word causing heartburn. your bells are doing paperwork I cannot.

At 02:28, Brown Suit discovered that a form titled Temporary Cultural Export cannot be signed by a person who does not exist at 02:28. He achieved a kind of humble greatness by writing postponed in a rectangle that wanted approved.

At 02:31, the hard hand looked up into the hatch dark and saw nothing but the possibility of stairs he did not own. He put his hands in his pockets and counted—slowly, for the first time.

On the Armenian roof, the sacristan opened a door with a key that had scolded a crusader. He led them to a closet that was not a closet but a void between walls where old repairs had taught stone to keep confidences. He didn't ask for the jar. He set a bread cloth on the sill. Arielle set weight upon it, then her palm. The watcher's hand arrived, not omen, not threat, only work.

"Witness," the sacristan said, and wrote the word in the Protocol with a pen that felt like a vow.

They stayed until the bells had told the hour twice and the city had answered by going back to being brave. Then they returned the way roofs teach you—slow, clean, with respect for a parapet that does not owe you balance.

By 03:07, the vans departed the lane with the confusion of men leaving a room intact. The utility blues rolled their tape polite as linen. Brown Suit tucked the unsignable form under other forms that could be improved later. The hard hand stopped at the lemon tree and stared up at the imaginary line between roof and sky as if he had found a noun that would not obey him. He left it there. He is that kind of man.

The sergeant lingered to ask Elpidios if bells ever go bad and was given coffee for his curiosity. Elpidios poured with the air of a man inventing an ordinance. "Bells require maintenance," he said. "Without it, they embarrass themselves."

When it was done, when night had decided to be legal again, they went below and made the room smell like bread. Karim lowered the lamp glass and listened to the tick as if it were gratitude. Yael put the Protocol away as though filing could be intimacy. Jonas sat on the bottom stair and let his shoulders relearn the weight they had carried. Narsai stood near the hatch and approved roofs.

"Line?" Karim asked, because it had become the way to pay for an hour that ended correctly.

"Close the line," Sister Miriam said gently.

They did not open. They did not need to. The line had rung itself.

Arielle rested her palm on the jar and let the watcher's hand settle beside it. She thought of bells and ladders, of lintels with bread, of boys discovering that ropes can conduct courage, of Klein writing postponed and deciding not to hate himself. She thought of her father's bad Syriac and his insistence that truth is a valley—not a cliff you are thrown off, a valley you walk through with people who know the names of fords.

"Many small doors," she said.

"And ropes," Yael added, almost smiling. "They make doors audible."

They slept in turns while lemon leaves signed treaties with a breeze. The city turned its page. The night's audit went into minutes. The jar slept like a tool.

Chapter Thirty-Seven — Fords

Morning wore last night's bells like jewelry it forgot to take off.

Bread on the plate. Water in cups. The Jerusalem Protocol open to a new page—columns that knew how to stand up under nouns. The jar in its cradle; the seam as composed as a librarian. The lemon tree above had decided to be honest about the light.

Shiri's text: committee bruised; "temporary export" refiled for daylight; buyer's man calling it "rescue." klein circled "fords." says your father wrote that word in a margin.

"Fords," Yael repeated, tying her hair. "Low places that refuse to be maps."

"Valleys," Jonas said, checking the corridor. "Places where men forget to draw boxes."

Lev's fixer arrived with parsley and the smell of a neighbor's pan. "Hard hand had breakfast he didn't taste near Jaffa Gate," she said. "Soft hands rented a sentence with the word 'rescue' twice. Your sergeant counted pigeons on the wall and then decided to count nothing for an hour."

"Where's the line?" Karim asked, already reaching for the lamp.

"Under our feet," Sister Miriam said from Ein Karem, spring in her voice. "But open anyway. We'll let the page tell the river."

They opened when the stone said now. Yael eased the guard slip; resin yielded like a well-taught habit. Karim raked light low. The Estrangela rose with its usual refusal to be dramatic.

"Read," Sister Miriam said.

"When maps are tightened, go to the low places; read at the meeting of valleys where men carry water and cloth, and at the ascent of red where the road climbs. Cross by the fords, not by the bridges; let the girls carry the names when the men are counting."

"Meeting of valleys," Matthias said—eyes sliding to the south, where Hinnom leans into Kidron, where the lower spring the old texts call En Rogel still teaches water the grammar of junctions.

"And the ascent of red," Narsai added, voice warm—Adummim, the climb toward Jericho where wadis burn in certain light.

Karim grinned despite fatigue. "Housekeeping," he whispered.

"Government," Yael corrected, pleased. "The kind that ignores bridges until they behave."

They photographed, hashed, split. Bread–AQ to the Greek chest; Water–AR to Ein Karem's basket under lemons; House–AS to St. James's nap-inducing drawer; Salt–AT to Shiri with a memo that could sedate a press office.

"Sequence," Jonas said.

"En Rogel first," Arielle answered. "Then the ascent—not as a parade. Threads."

They didn't bring the jar. They brought the room—bread in a cloth, water in a thermos, the lamp wrapped in linen, the Protocol in a folder that had learned to look uninteresting. Sister Miriam gathered four women whose hands had known buckets before theology; Hani turned up with three kids who pretended not to enjoy being deputized.

The lane down through Silwan remembered feet and arguments; shops were opening with the stubborn optimism of people who have made a living out of edges. The lower spring sat where the valleys kiss, roofed by a box of masonry that took itself too seriously and didn't mind being corrected by water. A launderer—apron, kindness—stood with his pole and hook, the old work made modern and kept honest.

"Peace," Sister Miriam said, and meant it as introduction and proposition both. She set her stool. The women set theirs. Hani's kids held the Protocol like a small banner: witness, not custody.

They didn't open the jar. They read water names where water does its job. Women answered—Yasmina, Salma, Widad. A girl tried a syllable and kept it. The launderer nodded like a man who knows the city by its chores. Karim slid water–AR beneath the ledger where the spring's caretaker kept chlorine tablets and a pencil sharpened by stubbornness.

"Receipt," Yael murmured. The caretaker clipped the dull envelope under a tin and wrote the date with the satisfaction of a man adding one more line to a lifetime of correct lists.

Soft hands found them and tried out their word. "Rescue," he said, wearing cologne that belonged to a different conversation. "The object must be kept safe in a facility—"

"We're doing rescue," Sister Miriam said, not rising. "From forgetting. You're welcome to help, but you'll have to sit."

He didn't. He floated, glanced at his phone, and left to rehearse the word where it would sound important. The launderer watched him go and rolled his eyes in a dialect older than syllables.

They split. Jonas and Yael took the high curve up toward Adummim with Hani and two kids who'd never had an excuse to love a ridgeline. They didn't try to make a scene; they made a mark. At a shoulder of road where limestone remembers iron and caravans, they put bread and a pinch of salt on a stone and spoke three names into wind. There was no audience. That was the point. The valley heard; that was enough.

Arielle and Karim doubled back by Gihon, slipping past City of David signage that always thinks it deserves a capital letter. They stopped at the spot where the tunnel begins, where water was once daring, and left a house–AS copy with a guard who was too tired to be curious and decent enough to keep a paper dry.

At each stop, they took minutes. Time, room, hands. They behaved the city into admitting what it's for.

By late morning, Brown Suit had found a podium. The Rockefeller courtyard performed dignity. He spoke of temporary export and interim surrogates and international collaboration. A drone made the wrong sound overhead and then learned humility against a light pole again, because something in the clerical universe still loved them.

Klein took the microphone for one sentence and used it well. "The surrogate is under internal review," he said. "Our process is on hold. We are grateful for the community's witness." He stepped back. It wasn't heroism. It was a man refusing to be the wrong noun.

The hard hand left the courtyard early. He walked David Street with his jacket open like a man trying to sweat a decision out. He paused at a hardware shop and looked at ladders without buying one. He bought gloves he didn't need. He is that kind of man.

Back at St. Mark's, the lemon tree didn't pretend to be surprised they had survived another morning. The room kept its one degree of cool like a promise nobody could afford to break. The jar sat where clay knows benches.

"Line?" Karim asked, because habit has become ritual.

They opened. The guard slip lifted. The letters marveled at nothing and told the truth.

"Read," Sister Miriam said.

"If the valley teaches you, make a ledger of fords; mark where the rope is tied and where the heap is set; write where the cloth is wrung and where the bread cools. Send this with girls who can cross when men are counting."

Karim's pen moved of its own accord—Fords Ledger at the top of a page, columns born hungry: Gate / Rope / Heap / Cloth / Cooling, and spaces to put the city into words that would outlast meetings.

"We'll start at En Rogel and Adummim," Yael said. "Add Dung and Zion. Then Cotton Market. Then Siloam. Draw the city like a kitchen."

"And carry the ledger," Jonas said, tipping his head at Hani's kids. "Small hands get through."

Lev's fixer appeared in the doorway holding no parsley and a face that meant weather. "Buyer's soft hands are at a café practicing kindness," she said. "The hard one is on the ramparts educating his anger. The sergeant left bread again. He is going to get a reputation."

"Good," Elpidios said. "We collect reputations. They keep the lamps honest."

They ate, because you must feed a day that has worked. Bread with sesame. Water that tasted like patience. Then the ledger went into a school bag that had carried math and would now carry roads.

Arielle rested her palm on the jar. The watcher's hand settled beside it, not ominous, not triumphant—company at the desk. She thought of valleys as truths that refuse to be drawn straight; of fords as facts you cross in small moves; of her father's bad Syriac and good arithmetic, a sentence she'd been finishing without noticing.

"Many small doors," she said.

"And low places," Sister Miriam added. "That's where the city keeps its courage."

The lemon tree signed a treaty with a breeze. The quarter rehearsed afternoon. The jar slept like a tool between shifts. The Fords Ledger waited to be written in a hand that would one day embarrass committees.

Chapter Thirty-Eight — The Ledger Walk

Morning wore the city like a toolbelt.

Bread on the plate. Water in cups. The Jerusalem Protocol open to a page that liked columns. The jar slept in its cradle; the seam sat there and refused to be interesting, which is how safety looks. The lemon tree had given up pretending not to eavesdrop.

Shiri's text: buyer's PR pousse-café: "rescue of heritage from chaos." headline shopping. klein forwarded internal mail subject "perimeter compliance sweep." time window 11–13. they'll try to turn footpaths into violations.

"Then we make footpaths into paper," Yael said, tapping the Fords Ledger. "We walk the page."

"Threads, not parade," Jonas answered. "Low places first. Witnesses that don't travel."

Hani arrived with three kids and a backpack that smelled like notebooks and cumin. "We made columns," he said, proud without giving himself away. He tapped the Ledger: Gate / Rope / Heap / Cloth / Cooling, lines waiting for names to sit down in.

"Good," Sister Miriam said from the phone, spring under her words. "I've got women at En Rogel and one at the wash stones above Sultan's Pool who can tell a lie by how water runs off it. We'll read where cloth gets wrung."

Lev's fixer leaned on the jamb with parsley and intelligence. "Hard hand traced the ramparts from Jaffa to Zion and hated every ladder he didn't see," she said. "Soft hands bought a quote near Damascus Gate. Your sergeant walked Hinnom early and fed a cat he will deny knowing."

They didn't bring the jar. They brought the room: bread folded in a cloth, water in a thermos, the lamp wrapped in linen, the Protocol riding dull in a folder, the Fords Ledger in Hani's bag like homework with opinions.

En Rogel — Rope / Cloth

The lower spring sat stubborn at the meeting of Kidron and Hinnom, boxed by masonry that thinks it's more important than water. The launderer from yesterday lifted his pole and nodded. Two women in aprons set stools without asking permission from air. Sister Miriam's voice traveled thin and sufficient on a phone in a cup.

"Ledger," Yael said. "Rope—where we tie to keep from sliding; Cloth—where we wring."

Hani's kids watched the launderer hook a sheet and pull it steady. He pointed: "Rope—this iron ring. It used to be wood. Men replace with worse. We keep using it until it admits its duty." The boy wrote Ring by east wall. A woman pounded a towel against stone and nodded at the lip where water returns to itself. "Cloth—here," she said. "In winter, it freezes your obedience."

They read three names because water understands lists. Karim slipped Water–AR under the caretaker's tin and made a hash on the back of a chlorine card because paperwork likes to breed in the wild.

Sultan's Pool — Cooling

Above Hinnom, the long basin the Mamluks re-slabbed and tourists misname Sultan's Pool lay low and empty this season, a shape that remembers festival more than flood. On the north rim, stone steps met shade—one of those corners where bread cools because wind likes the angle.

"Cooling," Yael said.

An old baker's wife gestured to a broad slab worn smooth by centuries of trays. "Here," she said. "You don't leave a mark. But your grandchildren know where the crust learned patience." Hani's girl wrote Slab by north lip, two palms down. Karim took a photograph boring enough to survive three committees.

Cotton Market — Heap / Rope

They slipped in by Suq al-Qattanin when the vault still held night. The tailor with clean hands nodded toward the dark side door. The heap mark waited where it always had: three strokes, a little mound, a flame worn to rumor by thumbs. A rope loop hung from a nail, ancient habit disguised as inventory.

"Heap and Rope," Yael said. Ink. Hash. Split. Salt–AT found a ledger that kept thread counts and girls' names like wages owed by God.

Muristan — House

The fountain behaved. The Armenian sacristan made a table out of nothing and put the lectionary down with the gravity of lunch. A tourist with better instincts than itinerary lowered her camera and stared as if house might be a new thing she wanted to belong to. Karim wrote House entry—Muristan bench, lectionary witness. Boring. Perfect.

They threaded the Quarter like light where shutters don't quite meet: Herod's Gate for rope, Damascus Gate for heap, Zion for scars that count as table, Dung for carts' jurisdiction. Each time: a mark you could point to without explaining art. Each time: a woman or a man who considered themselves too practical to be part of a story and was therefore exactly qualified.

By eleven the city tried out its perimeter voice. Two municipal vests unrolled tape near David Street like penance done incorrectly. Brown Suit took up a position with reporters by the Roman pavement that likes to pretend it remembers more than it does. "Rescue," he said into microphones that deserved better.

Klein texted Shiri, and Shiri told Lev's fixer, and Lev told the room: press line wobbling; word "surrogate" produced hives; external audit postponed to Monday; "community liaison" asking for quotes with adjectives. The hard hand walked Chain Gate Street with his jacket open and his jaw behaving. He looked like a man who had not decided whether nouns would rescue him.

At Siloam, Narsai found two men scrubbing a step and decided to like them. "Rope?" he asked. One pointed with his chin. "Your rope is song," the other said, amused. "But there's an iron ring over there." Hani's boy wrote Song and ring and will be insufferable in civics for a month.

At Hinnom's lip below Mount Zion, Sister Miriam sat with a woman who made a politics of laundry and wrote Cloth—Hinnom lip under fig. Karim photographed the fig like a clerk. The woman rolled her eyes and let him be a clerk.

They took minutes—time, room, hands—until noon believed them. Then the Ledger did the thing good paper does: it taught itself to walk back.

Hani's kids carried it home by different alleys on purpose, stopping to get three signatures a page—witness without dignity and therefore incorruptible. In Khan al-Zeit, the salt seller signed with the flourish of a man who had taught boys to write their names on sacks for thirty years. In Bab Hutta, a barber initialed with a dot because men who use razors prefer brevity. In Aqabat al-Takiya, a woman at a window made them shout the columns up to her and then echoed back the words as if they were the right kind of prayer.

The Rockefeller did its press at one, because committees love round numbers. Brown Suit said collaboration two and a half times and custody twice, as promised. A photo was taken of men considering a box. No one liked how it came out. The hard hand was not in the frame. He had gone to New Gate to look at a ladder he did not buy.

By two, the Ledger was back at St. Mark's with sweat on it and pride trying not to be obvious. The lemon tree shed one crisp leaf as punctuation. The room cooled a degree and kept it the way it always does when paper arrives having done roads.

"Read us a line," Karim asked, gentler than his grin.

They opened. Resin sighed. Letters stood like furniture that refuses to go out of style.

"Read," Sister Miriam said.

"Make the ledger walk until the rope knows its knot and the heap knows its place; write where the cloth is wrung and where the bread cools, and send it through the low places by many hands, that when men make bridges for boasts, the people will already have fords."

Yael closed the seam the way a maker returns a tool to a drawer. "We're on schedule," she said.

Lev's fixer put her head in and said what weather says when it approves: "Your buyer's PR tastes like old sugar. The hard hand bought nothing. Your sergeant left bread again and is going to have to start bringing olives."

Matthias shook out his sleeves and laid copies on the table—Ledger in triplicate, hash stamps immodest: one for the Greek chest, one for St.

James's dullest drawer, one for Ein Karem under lemons. Shiri's packet took Salt–AT with a cover memo that could put an extrovert to sleep.

"Thunder?" Karim asked out of habit and hope.

"Soon," Jonas said, not smiling yet. "After the walk."

That evening they took the Ledger to Damascus Gate because stairs there know how to behave in the company of lists. No speeches. Hani's kids read the columns like chores. A boy selling ka'ak hollered "Cooling—north slab, two palms down!" and grinned when two old men nodded solemnly, because the city had taught them something they accidentally agreed about.

On the way back, the hard hand leaned in a shadow and did not step out. It was the first decent thing he'd done all day.

They ate in the scriptorium on plates that didn't match and called it victory because nobody was hungry for nouns. The jar sat where it belonged. The Protocol breathed through neat columns. The lemon tree pretended to be tired and failed.

Arielle set her palm on the clay. The watcher's hand settled beside it—no omen, no threat, only company measuring the day with her. She thought of fords—the humility of choosing shallow water with good footing over a high boast built to fail. She thought of her father's bad Syriac and excellent math: many small doors, many low places, one city that knows how to keep itself if you ask it to.

"Many small doors," she said.

"And a ledger with legs," Sister Miriam added. "Tomorrow it learns to run."

Chapter Thirty-Nine — The Run

Morning found the ledger where it belonged: in a school bag that smelled like graphite and cumin.

Bread on the plate. Water in cups. The Jerusalem Protocol open to a page that knew how to stand. The jar asleep in its cradle, seam honest. The lemon tree had stopped pretending not to listen.

Shiri's text: PR push stalled. "rescue" isn't sticking. committee floated "joint guardianship." klein says their map is tired. hard hand is walking walls again. noon window for a "compliance sweep."

"Then we teach the city to run," Yael said, tapping the Fords Ledger. "Columns on their feet."

"Threads, not parade," Jonas answered. "No single place to seize."

Hani arrived with his three and two more, sleeves inked from yesterday's columns. "We made routes," he said, shy-proud. "Low water, cool slabs, heap doors. Each team takes one."

"Witnesses?" Sister Miriam asked from Ein Karem, spring in her voice.

"St. Anne sends two with baskets," Yael replied. "Rina at Magdala has a bus of women on WhatsApp who think they're sending recipes. Father Paulus is bored in Galilee and therefore useful. The Armenian sacristan discovered a drawer we haven't bored yet. Narsai has two monks who can move through roofs without making the cat angry."

Lev's fixer stood in the doorway with parsley and weather. "Soft hands are buying microphones," she said. "Hard hand has new gloves he doesn't need. Your sergeant just tipped a pigeon three crumbs and walked away embarrassed."

They didn't bring the jar. They brought the room: bread into cloth, water into thermos, lamp wrapped, Protocol dull, Ledger zipped. Karim slung the camera; Yael tucked hashes; Matthias packed envelopes with stamps that could make even a tyrant drowsy.

They broke into threads.

Thread One — North

Hani's boys took Damascus Gate first because stairs there like being useful. They read out the ledger's columns as chores, not sermon. "Rope: ring by east wall. Heap: Cotton Market side door. Cloth: slab at Sultan's Pool. Cooling: north rim." A ka'ak seller repeated "two palms down" with professional satisfaction. A tourist pressed record and, finding no drama, let it run anyway.

They slid on to Herod's Gate—a grocer initialed the margin with a flourish that made his grandson roll his eyes—and ended at St. Anne, where a sister hid Water–AJ under a towel with the expression of a woman who had finally gotten to do the thing she was built for.

Thread Two — East

Sister Miriam's pair walked Lion Gate slow, reading a line between stalls as if timing bread. A police camera watched and, bored, remembered to be a camera. Down the grade they touched the Kidron wall and wrote Rope: fig ring by stairs where a boy had shown them yesterday, then handed the ledger to an old man who signed with a dot and directions to a cooler stone two alleys away.

Thread Three — South

Yael and Karim took Dung Gate, greeted Hussein's sanitation crew with coffee, and logged Cooling: shade by cart bay in a hand the city would one day call elegant because it worked. They cut across to Siloam, checked the iron ring, refreshed the hash on Water–AR with a clerk's delight, and kept moving.

Thread Four — West

The Armenian sacristan and a monk from Deir es-Sultan moved along roofs as though stone liked remembering them. They dropped House–AK into a drawer stern enough to outlive an audit and lifted a bell rope once—not to signal, but to check the knot and put a finger under the phrase "maintenance prevents embarrassment."

Thread Five — Market

Lev's fixer threaded Khan al-Zeit and Suq al-Attarin with the Ledger's salt column like a shopping list. "Heap by door," she said to a soap seller, and he showed her three and argued for a fourth; she marked them all and made a joke about taxes until everyone felt honest.

By midmorning, Brown Suit's compliance sweep discovered a city that had already been inventoried—by itself. He tried "perimeter" on David Street; tape found bread and decided to sag. The hard hand walked Chain Gate with his jaw set and stopped at the corner where yesterday's sumac still lived red in the seams. He looked at his gloves as if they owed him an apology.

Klein texted Shiri: if they seize anything today, it'll be a photograph. their "surrogate" lives in a room full of apologies. internal phrasing now says "under review." also: i found your "two palms down" slab. it is excellent.

"Run it to the north wall," Jonas said into Arielle's shoulder as they rejoined at New Gate. "Give them a glimpse and no handle."

They staged invisibly. Narsai set the lamp on a sill above the gate where the wind behaves. Hani's kids stood below with the Ledger open, reading columns loud enough to register as civics, soft enough to pass for instructions. A pair of municipal vests paused, listened, and wrote Cooling—north slab in a notebook as if they had thought of it.

Brown Suit arrived with microphones and optimism. "Joint guardianship," he tried to a small knot of press. "Community involvement."

"You brought nouns," Yael said, stepping into frame with a paper that contained nothing photogenic. "We brought minutes." She read three: time, place, witnesses—Herod's, Dung, Damascus—and handed out copies whose hashes looked like graffiti even to polite eyes.

The hard hand came late and took a place at the edge of the circle where he could do the least damage and the most choosing. He did not step forward. He watched Arielle not carry the jar and finally understood he had been chasing furniture while the house kept moving.

"Ready?" Sister Miriam asked on the line. "We can teach them thunder today or make them earn it one more night."

Arielle set her palm on her coat where her hand had learned to go and felt the watcher answer like a colleague. "One more night," she said. "We make it unkind to lie about us."

"Then we give them the map they deserve," Yael replied. "All gates. One hour. No center."

They moved in preparation, which is to say: they cleaned. They checked knots. They topped lamps. They folded bread cloths. They placed Water–AN under lemons at Ein Karem and watched a child take it without reading because trust had been taught correctly. They walked the Ledger one last time through Muristan and Cotton and Hosh, collecting signatures that looked like a city clearing its throat.

At dusk, the quarter laid down its tools and picked up its habits. The lemon tree dropped one leaf like approval. The room cooled a degree and kept it.

"Tomorrow," Jonas said.

"Thunder," Yael answered, and the word was a schedule, not a hope.

Arielle put her palm on the jar. The watcher's hand settled beside it, not omen, only company. She thought of routes made of chores, of gates that learned to listen, of a ledger that had sprouted legs, of her father's bad Syriac and perfect arithmetic.

"Many small doors," she said.

"And every gate," Sister Miriam added. "Open long enough to read."

Chapter Forty — Every Gate

Morning dressed itself in nouns and dared the city to choose better ones.

Bread on the plate. Water in cups. The Jerusalem Protocol open to a clean page that already knew what to do. The jar asleep in its cradle; the seam behaved. Above, the lemon tree had stopped pretending—it listened.

Shiri's text: press vans circling. "coordination exercise" on the committee memo. drones charged, wrong batteries again. brown suit trying "joint guardianship" as a personality trait. hard hand walked the wall twice before eight.

"Thunder," Yael said, tying her hair like a signature. "All gates. One hour. No center."

"Threads," Jonas answered. "No line to cut."

They did not carry the jar. They carried the room. Bread into cloth. Water into a thermos that believed in itself. Lamp wrapped in linen that smelled like wax and witness. The Protocol in its dull skin. The Fords Ledger in Hani's school bag with a pencil that had already outlived two sharpeners.

Sister Miriam's voice arrived with a spring under it. "Choir is in place," she said. "Seven Ein Karem women, two from Tur Abdin, a Greek deacon who frightens pigeons, an Armenian boy who reads like a bell."

Lev's fixer leaned in with parsley and weather. "Soft hands bought an extra microphone," she said. "Hard hand bought nothing and looked angrier about that than about you. Your sergeant fed a cat on the ramparts and decided to remember less today."

They split like a city knows how to split when it remembers itself.

Jaffa Gate — West

Bab al-Khalil, the Hebron Gate to people who count properly, the Ottoman breach widened for a visiting Kaiser and never forgiven by the wall. The Tower of David kept its citadel opinions to itself. Sister Miriam's three unfolded stools where the stone descends to the Roman pavement. Elpidios set bread on a cloth against a scar that has always pretended to be a table. The Greek deacon let one note climb the arch and sit there, unembarrassed.

"Ya'el—of bread."

"Here," said a tourist who didn't know why she was answering until her mouth had done it.

New Gate — North-West

A nineteenth-century breach in obedience. The wall pretends to have always had a mouth here; nobody argues anymore. Hani's boys read rope / heap / cloth / cooling like chores; a municipal vest wrote "Cooling—north slab" in a notebook as if he'd thought of it. A nun from St. Anne crossed with a basket as if she were late to a kindness and tucked Water–AJ under a towel with the glee of conspiracy.

Damascus Gate — North

Bab al-Amud, the Gate of the Column. Ablaq arch in its best mood; stairs dropping into the belly of the market like a promise. The Armenian boy read house names with a clarity that made vendors under the vault lift their heads and feel taller. Above him, the Mamluk cornice watched generations behave. A wire camera tried to be theatrical and learned to film lists.

Herod's/Flower Gate — North-East

Small mouth, Bab az-Zahra. A grocer initialed the margin with the flourish of a man who trains his tomatoes. Sister Miriam's two sat on their stools without apology. A boy tried a name; the wall kept it for later.

Lion Gate — East

Basalt lions that came with Suleiman and stayed long enough to learn irony. Lev's fixer threaded the crowd with the Fords Ledger salt column and left a pinch on a paper where a ranger would find it and be annoyed into virtue. A pilgrim raised a phone; it caught nothing sensational and everything required.

Dung Gate — South-East

Low and honest, carts' jurisdiction. Hussein's orange vests formed a line that was not a line, just dignity in sequence. Bread on a cloth by the cart bay. A child repeated a name and then asked for a second. The loader beeped like errand music.

Zion Gate — South-West

Bullet pits like Braille nobody has the right to forget. Elpidios set the lamp in the bite of shade and made a psalm of the wick. Sister Miriam counted names and let the Greek syllables behave on stone; the Tur Abdin sisters braided Syriac under them like rope.

Golden Gate — Sealed

The walled mouth, Bab al-Rahma, that remembers too much to open. They read from the slope below, Kidron listening with professional discretion. No riot. No proclamation. The city learned to hear through stone.

Across all of it, bells learned humility and coordination. St. Mark's answered St. James; the Ethiopian huts dinged domestically; a Franciscan handbell at the Pools of Bethesda chimed like a spoon on a glass; the muezzin at Bab Hutta sang into the air and the air consented to be a room.

Brown Suit tried to plant perimeter on a map that refused to be a farm. "Joint guardianship," he told microphones that had seen worse. The microphones recorded women reading lists, children repeating syllables, bread being propped on a stone where generations had put elbows. A wire service photographer lowered her lens and wrote instead.

The hard hand chased a center and found none. He moved from Jaffa to Damascus to Dung in a circle like a man learning anatomy: that gates are joints, not handles; that rooms move; that custody without witness is furniture.

Klein watched from a distance that was tactical and honest. He texted Shiri: they turned an hour into a ledger. press is eating minutes like bread. if there's a center, it's plural.

Hani's kids ran the Ledger between gates like mail, stamping time and hands at each stop, grabbing three signatures because that number had turned out to be magic. A barber initialed with a dot. A ka'ak seller wrote Cooling—two palms with theatrical gravity. A policewoman, bored and brave, put her first name only and folded the page back down.

At ten minutes to the hour, Jonas's voice moved quietly through radios that were not radios—phones in cups, a nod across a street, a lifted finger at a corner.

"At the last minute," Yael said into the Protocol, "we read one line from the page and no one mentions the jar."

They didn't open it. They didn't need to. The city had learned to quote itself.

At every gate, on the same breath, Sister Miriam's women lifted their sheets. The words fit different mouths and did not mind.

"When gates are told, gather at the steps, for there the feet have learned obedience; read the names where tables once stood, that boys and girls answer together."

The stones accepted the sentence as if they had commissioned it.

Silence followed in which a drone, robbed of drama, forgot which lamppost to avoid and did the city the courtesy of quitting. Somebody laughed—one of those laughs you hear at a funeral when mercy remembers itself.

Brown Suit put his paper down and did not fold it into a weapon. "Joint guardianship," he said again, but softer, almost as if he were tasting a food he had mocked and discovered he liked.

A reporter asked Yael, "Who has custody?"

"Witness," she said. "We kept witness. The houses kept the rest."

The hard hand came to the edge of the circle at Zion Gate and did not cross. He looked at Arielle's coat and understood—suddenly, then all at once—that the thing he wanted to seize had been transformed into the one thing that cannot be pallet-jacked. The order of keeping had become people with chores.

He turned, not defeated so much as re-educated, and walked upward toward the wall—toward a view where men go to reconsider.

Klein stepped forward into a microphone because a decent man sometimes has to. "The surrogate at the Rockefeller is non-conforming and under internal review," he said. "There will be no movement today." He did not look at Brown Suit when he said it. He looked at the steps.

The hour concluded itself. Stools folded. Lamps cooled their tick. The ledger closed around new signatures, officially smudged with bread.

They returned by different alleys on purpose. The lemon tree accepted their clotheslines of small victories and declined to be solemn about it. The room below kept its one degree of cool like a petty, holy prerogative.

"Press will run with witness," Matthias said, setting duplicates down in piles the size of sleep.

"And the committee will run with review," Yael answered, already sealing an envelope to the Conservation woman who had asked the honest questions.

"Next?" Karim asked, soft because he had earned the right to be young at the end of an hour like that.

"Rockefeller," Jonas said. "We end the surrogate's story with minutes and rooms."

"In daylight," Sister Miriam added, fully satisfied by that noun. "So papers can see themselves."

Arielle set her palm on the clay. The watcher's hand settled beside it like a colleague clocking out. She thought of gates that learned to be verbs, of lists that refused to be noise, of a city that had discovered it could be its own box and therefore didn't need one. She thought of her father's bad Syriac and how the line he'd left her had become an hour nobody could confiscate.

"Many small doors," she said.

"And every gate," Yael answered, allowing herself—finally—the smallest smile. "Open long enough to read."

Chapter Forty-One — Glass Rooms

Morning wore its clean shirt and pretended not to remember last night's bells.

Bread on the plate. Water in cups. The Jerusalem Protocol open to a page that had already settled its shoulders. The jar asleep in its cradle, seam plain as a fact. Above, the lemon tree gave up on innocence and auditioned for witness.

Shiri's text: committee set for 11:00 at Rockefeller. "surrogate review." conservation woman is bringing scales that don't lie. brown suit wants a photo of cooperation. hard hand is early. klein says: bring minutes, not thunder.

"Glass rooms," Yael said. "We let them see themselves."

"Witnesses who don't travel far," Jonas answered. "Enough eyes to keep the nouns honest."

They packed the room because rooms travel by habits: bread into cloth, water into a thermos that believed in decency, lamp wrapped in wax-scented linen, Protocol in its dull skin. Copies—the latest Bread–AI, Water–AJ, House–AK, Salt–AL—nested into envelopes stamped until the ink gave up arguing. Hani tucked the Fords Ledger into his bag with a pencil claiming seniority. Sister Miriam gathered three Ein Karem women who looked like minutes in aprons. The Armenian sacristan rolled his sleeves as if drawers were a sport.

Lev's fixer stood in the doorway with parsley and weather. "Soft hands invited a camera with a pretty tripod," she said. "Hard hand told two men to keep their hands invisible. Your sergeant fed a cat and then went to count stairs at the Southern Steps because it makes him cheerful."

They didn't carry the jar. They carried the grammar.

The Rockefeller was in a good mood for stone that once learned to be British. Square shoulders, clean lintels, a courtyard that loves the sound of decisions rehearsing. Inside, the glass room had its toys in order: tables that promised neutrality, lights that tried not to meddle, two freezer crates sulking with the vanity of equipment, a scale waiting to be the adult.

The committee arranged themselves by archetype. Brown Suit wore "joint guardianship" like a new tie and smiled at the cameras as if they might learn it from him. The conservation woman set her pen and her patience on the table; they were the same instrument. The liaison practiced collaboration. The hard hand took a position that looked like the back of the room and wasn't. Klein had his tie wrong on purpose and his clipboard right by accident.

"Thank you for coming," Brown Suit began, gentle with performance. "We value community witness as we finalize safe custody for the—"

"Minutes," Matthias said pleasantly, sliding the Protocol into the light like a priest putting doctrine where everyone can see it. "Time. Room. Hands."

Yael spoke dull nouns until they stood up straight—Zion, Dung, Siloam, Damascus; copies logged; hashes printed; witnesses named with precision unfit for poetry and perfect for law. Hani opened the Ledger and read three lines in a voice he'd stolen from teachers: Rope / Heap / Cloth / Cooling, and where they sit. The glass room tried to be bored and failed.

"Surrogate," the conservation woman said, rescuing the hour. She turned to Klein. "Chain, please."

Klein had planned his honesty. "Received 02:11," he said. "Serials photographed. Weights logged: 6.2, 6.0, 5.9 with towel variance. Non-conforming. Opened. Found training clay. Paused review."

Shiri laid two sheets on the table with sleepy malice: microfracture images that even a committee could love, one from the dummy—uniform like boredom, one from a discreet chip taken (with apology) from the old Qumran jar years ago by a conservationist who still sent Christmas cards. The mismatch was pretty even before it became damning.

The conservation woman nodded once, not for them but for herself. "Thank you," she said to the evidence, and to nobody else. She turned the scale on and looked at Brown Suit the way you look at a man you hope will become usefully quieter.

"Photograph seals," Klein told the room because his job is to tell rooms to behave. Lights obliged. The red tape posed. Numbers admired themselves and were ignored.

"Remove the towel," he said. The number quivered a tenth and got embarrassed. A lab tech glanced at Shiri and discovered that Shiri was not looking at him and felt free to be honest.

"Non-conforming," the conservation woman said again, more gently. "We will not use the word custody today."

Brown Suit took it like a man who had come to a party for a different noun and decided he liked the food anyway. "Joint review," he said, trying to evolve on camera. "With community witness."

Sister Miriam, in an apron that had outlived three committees, smiled without mercy. "We'll bring minutes," she said. "You'll like them. They translate."

The hard hand made no sound. He watched the towel. He watched the hands. He watched Arielle not carry the jar and, for the second time in as many days, understood that the object he desired had been turned into a system that would outlast his shoes.

Klein cleared his throat. It was not heroism. It was breakfast. "I propose," he said to the woman with the pen, "we log the surrogate as training equipment; we halt the export workflow; we request methods from the community for non-invasive reading, to be archived with this room's notes."

"Approved," the conservation woman said, and wrote it with the joy of a person being allowed to save something she could sign.

Brown Suit—grown an inch by new vocabulary—faced the cameras. "We are grateful for the order of keeping this community has documented," he said, and almost meant it. "Today, we continue in review."

The press asked a question with too many syllables and then—frustrated by a lack of scene—took photographs of paper. They were good photographs. No one would like them until they were necessary.

The glass room softened by a degree you couldn't measure with equipment and could with shoulders. The liaison asked Yael for the methods in writing and spelled her name correctly. The conservation woman asked Hani about the Ledger columns and wrote down Cooling—two palms down with a small satisfied noise adults make when a child teaches them grammar.

The hard hand came as far as the table and stopped. He did not apologize; that isn't the kind of muscle he has. He addressed the Protocol as if it were a person. "Who keeps the jar?" he asked.

"Witness," Yael said, and tapped the column. "The houses keep the rest."

He nodded to the paper because a man has to nod to something. On his way out he paused where the glass met the corridor and looked up at the ceiling as if it were a sky he might one day owe.

They did not linger. Glass rooms tire quickly.

On the steps outside, light behaved. The Mandate façade did its square-shouldered virtue. The city went on being itself at a hundred corners without rehearsing for anyone.

"Take them methods," Yael told Matthias. "The kind that can be bored into practice."

"Copies to Conservation, Antiquities, Mukawir, St. Anne, St. James," he said, already making piles that reproduce like truth. "Hash on each. Witness lines in the margin."

"Hani," Sister Miriam said, "teach your twelve what a training surrogate is, and why nouns are only useful if they can't be abused."

He grinned. "Civics," he said. "My favorite revenge."

Klein approached like a man auditioning for decency and trying not to notice that's what he was doing. "Your minutes worked," he said to Yael, not to the room. "I will lose friends."

"You'll gain sleeps," she said, professional.

He looked at Arielle and almost asked about the jar. Instead he said, "Your father's note about fords is in our archive copy of the 1989 survey. In the margin of Cave 4's overlay. I thought you'd want to know where he'd left himself."

It landed like a kindness and a map. "Thank you," she said. It wasn't a plan yet. It was a door.

They took the long way back because walking the city after you've done it a kindness is a right. Bab al-Silsila threw a slice of shadow toward them like hospitality; Khan al-Zeit rehearsed the aroma of the afternoon; Muristan played water on stone for anyone whose heart required metronome.

At St. Mark's the lemon tree was in a cooperative mood. The room kept its degree of cool. The seam looked like it had never met a noun it needed to impress.

"Line?" Karim asked, softly, because good days also deserve their one line.

They opened when the stone said now. Yael lifted the guard slip; resin sighed; the lamp raked low. The Estrangela stood with the calm of a ledger that has outlived cleverness.

"Read," Sister Miriam said.

"When men put glass before you, put minutes upon the table; show your keeping to those who ask, and let the houses be numbered, not owned. If the surrogate is praised, call it practice; if export is named, answer with witness."

Karim grinned like someone whose city had just remembered what it was built for. "Housekeeping," he whispered.

"Government," Yael corrected, affectionate. "The kind that borrows bells."

They photographed, hashed, split. Bread–AM to the Greek chest; Water–AN to Ein Karem; House–AO to St. James; Salt–AP to Shiri with a memo that would sedate a news cycle.

Arielle rested her palm on the clay. The watcher's hand settled beside it—no omen, only company. She thought of glass and paper, of a towel that had embarrassed a room at the right hour, of fords in a margin that had he'd been holding since the desert to be needed, of her father's bad Syriac and excellent maps.

"Many small doors," she said.

"And a glass one we walked through without stealing," Jonas added.

Outside, the quarter selected its afternoon noises. Inside, the room cooled a degree and kept it. The lemon tree practiced being satisfied.

Tomorrow had opinions. Tonight would be diligent. The jar slept like a tool.

Chapter Forty-Two — Margins

Jerusalem put on its work clothes and didn't ask to be admired.

Bread on the plate. Water in cups. The Jerusalem Protocol open to a page that had already made peace with columns. The jar asleep in its cradle; the seam behaving like a well-brought-up sentence. Above, the lemon tree stopped feigning innocence and simply listened.

Shiri's text: archives slot at Rockefeller, 09:30. "1989 Qumran overlay — Cave 4" pulled. klein says your father's file has a dog-eared corner. hard hand walked the wall once and went east.

"Margins," Yael said. "We go read where pencils tell the truth."

"Witnesses who won't attract nouns," Jonas answered. "Two is enough."

They didn't carry the jar. They carried grammar: bread into cloth, water into a thermos that believed in decency, the lamp wrapped in wax-scented linen, the Protocol in its dull skin. Matthias tucked three letters that sound like umbrellas—consultation, observation, courtesy. Hani slid the Fords Ledger into his bag because good paper likes field trips but hates committees.

Lev's fixer leaned in with parsley and weather. "Soft hands took breakfast with a headline," she said. "Hard hand asked a taxi for Qumran and practiced not caring that he'd said it out loud. Your sergeant fed a cat, looked east, chose to forget the gesture."

The Rockefeller reading room had the smell of paper that knows its job—cotton, graphite, a floor that keeps score without being petty. Klein met them at the desk in a tie that had failed to convince his shirt and a face that had succeeded with his conscience.

"Box twelve," he said softly, as if admitting a favor to the wrong friend. The archivist rolled out a shallow drawer with the tender scorn of a professional. Tissue lifted. Mylar winked. The 1989 overlay lay there—translucent grid, Cave 4's scalloped void, pencil ghosts where a younger hand had argued with its own confidence.

Arielle recognized her father's impatience before she recognized his script—the way the pencil bit the paper when maps refused to behave. Margin, lower right: fords. The word underlined once, then circled, a small rope sketched beside it and a notch like a heap at a door. Above: "Hinnom into Kidron—En Rogel; Adummim ascent—red shoulder. C4: D/7 drip, calcrete seam. If gates are told, return to valley."

She swallowed. The room tilted by a degree that had nothing to do with architecture.

"D/7?" Karim breathed, leaning over the grid. "Grid square on the Cave 4 terrace. The marl ledge. 'Drip, calcrete seam'—a flowstone cap where seepage left a crust."

"He was telling himself where to stand," Yael said, pleased, professional. "And when."

Jonas traced the penciled rope with a fingertip that didn't touch. "Low places first. Then the ascent of red. Then Cave 4, at the drip. He left a sequence, not a treasure map."

Klein watched the page and not them. "I can authorize observation at Qumran this evening," he said, as if dictating to his better self. "No removal. No theater. Minutes only. If anyone asks why you're there, you're there because I am tired of sleeping badly."

"You'll get better at that," Yael said, which passed for mercy.

They copied the margin into the Protocol—verbatim, legible, dull. Hani drew the rope in the Fords Ledger with a joy he didn't try to hide.

"Witnesses?" Sister Miriam asked from Ein Karem, spring under the question.

"Rashid at Mukawir can send an Antiquities clerk who hates adjectives," Matthias said, thumbing a contact. "Rina will stay by the heap at Magdala, phone up. Father Paulus can be our Galilee ear. The Armenian sacristan knows a drawer at St. George in Wadi Qelt that remembers pilgrims; he'll send a note dull enough to tame a camel."

"Sergeant?" Lev's fixer offered, amused. "He will discover the Dead Sea at dusk is excellent for forgetting paperwork."

They went home the long way because good news deserves walking. Bab al-Silsila gave them a ribbon of shade. Khan al-Zeit rehearsed cumin. Muristan made water talk to stone. No one needed to know they were carrying a sentence.

In the scriptorium the seam waited like a colleague. Arielle put her palm on clay; the watcher's hand arrived—no omen, just readiness.

"One line," Karim said, reverent now that the map had stopped pretending not to be personal.

They opened when the stone said now. Yael eased the guard slip; resin obeyed with its small, pleased sigh. The lamp raked low. The Estrangela stood—unimpressed by their hour, impressed by nobody, ready.

"Read," Sister Miriam said.

"When the gates have been told, go to the low places and the ascent of red; where the drip has set a white seam, read once for the valley and once for the road, and do not lift the lid, for the keeping is in the telling."

Karim let out a breath that had years to be needed. "He read this hand," he whispered. "And he left us the pencil."

"Housekeeping," Yael said, softer than she meant to be.

"Government," Narsai corrected, kind. "Of a city that appoints valleys."

They photographed, hashed, split. Bread–AQ to the Greek chest; Water–AR to Ein Karem; House–AS to St. James; Salt–AT to Shiri with a memo that would sedate an audit. Matthias wrote Qumran—observation only in a hand that makes men feel supervised.

They packed for evening the way hikers pack for weather they respect—rope, wedges, a clinometer that had earned its scratches, soft brushes that know the difference between dust and meaning, two tripods with old-man dignity. No crowbars. No romance.

At four, Lev's fixer texted: hard hand on 1 road east; gloves on dashboard. he is not good at pretending not to care. At five, the sergeant left a paper bag by the lemon tree: bread and a note the size of a postage stamp: "I will be elsewhere."

They drove east under a sky that had never apologized for being large. Wadi Qelt opened like a thought that had learned to cut itself; the ascent of red—Adummim—lay there the way a road lies when it remembers caravans. The Dead Sea turned its slow metal face to them, a lid on a pot no one sane tries to lift.

They reached Qumran at a light the ruins had learned to like—late enough to be generous, early enough to tell the truth. The marl cliffs wore their old weather; Cave 4 looked like a mouth that had finished shouting and settled for watching.

Rashid's clerk waited with a clipboard that could bore a tyrant and a hat that had never been mistaken for theater. He checked the letters, checked the faces, checked the box that says observation and underlined it twice.

“Drip,” Arielle said quietly, eyes on the marl. “Calcrete seam.”

Karim found it first—the white line where a centuries-old seep had left its ledger on stone, a crust thin as honesty, running across the terrace like a rope that had decided to become rock.

“The margin says D/7,” Yael murmured, placing the overlay against the air on instinct. “Here.”

They set the lamp low and made evening behave. The white seam accepted light; the marl remembered hands. Jonas wedged the tripod as if he were teaching ground how to keep a promise. Arielle did not touch the seam; she touched the air just above it the way you touch a shoulder that has earned grief.

“Read,” Sister Miriam said, voice turned to string to reach the desert.

They read twice, because the line had asked: once facing the valley, wind shouldering the words and carrying them down to the fords where boys would one day kick a flat ball; once facing the road, letting the syllables climb the ascent where caravans learn patience. It wasn’t a spell. It was a receipt.

Nothing opened. That was the point.

The hard hand watched from the shoulder of the path, far enough to look like happenstance, near enough to do math. He saw a lamp, a rope of white, a woman reading as if the cliff owed her a correction and had granted it. He put his gloved hands in his pockets and did the first courageous thing he’d done in the book: nothing.

Rashid’s clerk signed the Protocol with the tidy despair of a man who would rather be home and will be glad later not to be ashamed. Karim wrote C4—D/7 drip seam, read to valley and road, no lid. Yael stamped the hash in the margin big enough to offend a bishop and please a judge.

Arielle stood a long time after the lamp sighed out. The marl cooled like a patient chest. The Dead Sea kept its lid. The ascent ran red in the last light and then forgave the day for finishing.

"My father said truth was a valley," she whispered, not to be poetic but because it was a sentence that needed to be finished out loud once. "He left me the fords. We crossed."

Jonas stood beside her in the kind of silence that is witness, not absence. He did not touch her. He made a room around her out of his body and his not-saying.

They drove back in a line of tired that felt like work well-placed. Jericho laid out its lights like small, stubborn certainties. Adummim rose under the stars, less red, still honest. Wadi Qelt became what valleys do at night: a memory of water written dark.

St. Mark's took them in. The lemon tree signed its treaty with a breeze. The seam looked as if nothing had happened, the way a good seam looks when everything has.

"Line?" Karim asked, out of habit and respect.

"Tomorrow," Sister Miriam said, gentler than prayer. "Let the margin sit."

Arielle put her palm on the clay. The watcher's hand settled beside it—colleague, not omen. She thought of pencil marks and drip seams, of low places and red roads, of how a city ends a quarrel with itself by counting girls and gates. She thought of her father's bad Syriac and perfect map in the corner of a page that had all this time to be found to be found.

"Many small doors," she said.

"And a margin that told us where to stand," Yael answered.

They slept. The city turned a page. The book kept its place.

Chapter Forty-Three — The Order of Keeping

Morning put its shoulder to the day and did not ask for praise.

Bread on the plate. Water in cups. The Jerusalem Protocol open to a fresh page that had already made peace with columns. The jar asleep in its cradle; the seam decent. Above, the lemon tree stopped pretending and listened the way old stone listens—without flinching.

Shiri's text: press moved on; yesterday's hour filed as "civic ritual." committee wants "methods packet." klein says: if you give them boredom they can sign, they'll sign it. hard hand walked New Gate at dawn and bought nothing again.

"Methods," Yael said, pinning up her hair. "We give them a manual dull enough to survive and sharp enough to work."

"Rooms," Jonas answered. "Bread. Water. Lamps. Salt. Ladders and bells. Fords. Minutes."

Matthias set a stack of paper on the table the way a man lays out bread—matter-of-fact, grateful. "We'll call it the Order of Keeping," he said. "Not 'best practices'—those invite theft. Order invites obedience."

Hani carried in the Fords Ledger like a child with an instrument he has finally learned to love. The pencil rode the spiral with the swagger of seniority. Sister Miriam was already on the phone with the spring under her words. "Ein Karem can supply photographs of ropes and slabs," she said. "And three grandmothers who will annotate your grammar."

Lev's fixer leaned in with parsley and weather. "Soft hands hosted a breakfast that tasted like regret," she said. "Hard hand walked the ramparts, put both palms on the stone, and decided not to lie until lunch. Your sergeant fed a cat and asked it nothing."

They didn't carry the jar. They carried the grammar.

They wrote like people who understand hunger: not to be admired, but to be eaten.

Section I — Names and Rooms.
Yael dictated; Karim typed; Matthias made footnotes behave. Bread at table, water at springs, lamps at roads and synagogues, salt by heaps and markets. Witness lines in the margin—who, when, where—a hand enough like devotion to pass inspection. Photographs that refused to be cinematic: rope rings, slab corners, the heap scratched shallow beside a flame.

Section II — Steps and Gates.
Zion's scars, Siloam's risers, the Hulda mouths closed and still persuasive. The sentence everyone had learned by heart—gates are told; steps teach obedience—quoted as if it were protocol, because it is. Stools become policy. Children's answers filed as exhibits.

Section III — Ladders and Bells.
Maintenance, not romance: knots that don't embarrass you; steps that don't forgive you if you hurry; the hour at which sound travels like courage instead of complaint; the doctrine that neighbors own roofs. A drawing so boring even a ministry would have to love it.

Section IV — Ledger with Legs.
Columns: Gate / Rope / Heap / Cloth / Cooling. Pages of signatures that mean nothing to television and everything to courts. How to walk paper until it learns to keep its own feet. Where to store copies (Greek chest; St. James's dullest drawer; Ein Karem under lemons; Shiri's nap-inducing memo).

Section V — Margins.
How to read a pencil better than a proclamation. Low places and the ascent of red. Drip seams. How to read twice—valley and road—and then go home with your tools instead of with a story.

They printed five packets and watched them breed like decent rabbits. Hash stamps loud enough to annoy. Protocol references patient enough to comfort. A cover letter so dull it could hypnotize ambition: "The Order of Keeping: Methods for Witness Without Custody."

"Deliveries," Jonas said.

They split like a city splits when it remembers itself.

Matthias and the Armenian sacristan carried Packet 1 to Conservation with a bow that made dignity look easy. Sister Miriam sent Packet 2 to Antiquities with bread and a lemon tucked under the string because bureaucracy eats better when you feed it. Rina at Magdala printed packet pages for a drawer that has frightened three donors and a cousin; Father Paulus propped Packet 3 at Tabgha under a harmless statue and texted a monk who owes him footnotes. Rashid's clerk carried Packet 4 to Mukawir with a list of minutes that makes brigadiers polite. Packet 5 went to the Patriarchate where a deacon with beautiful penmanship initialed four times and forgot to be offended.

In the scriptorium, Elpidios packed a tray with wicks and the face of a man who knows that bees save churches more often than bishops do. "We will count until they learn the number," he said, cheerful.

Brown Suit appeared at the door with a very tired map and a very new tone. "We'd like to cite your Order," he said to Yael, carefully. "For the record."

"You may," she said. "If you practice it."

He nodded like a person discovering he had been waiting to be told what to do.

The hard hand came an hour later, out of uniform that had never declared itself. He stopped under the lemon tree and looked like a man who has learned to ask his anger for its receipts.

"Your hour at the steps," he said to no one in particular. "It made a mess of the afternoon." He tried on a smile that wasn't a threat and found it fit. "Thank you."

He did not ask to see the jar. He looked at the Protocol the way some men look at oceans. "My daughter is fifteen," he said, as if confessing to weather. "Teach me the knot that will not embarrass me if I teach it to her."

Elpidios brought a rope. Jonas held his hands where he could see them. Karim explained without theater. Yael wrote knot in the manual's margin like an apology offered to the future. The hard hand practiced twice more than a proud man needs to and left without turning the goodbye into a scene.

In the late afternoon the sergeant drifted through as if he had gotten lost in the concept of honesty. He placed a bag on the table. Bread, of course; and under it a folded newspaper. Wire copy, crisp: a photograph of a stool, a child saying here, a caption that chose witness over custody without congratulating itself. He said, to the lemon tree, "I liked the part with the bells," and left before anyone could make him discuss it.

They ate. Bread crust. Water unapologetic. Their faces learned rest without daring to claim it.

"North?" Rina texted from Magdala. The heap is still a heap. The slab is still two palms. The women are restless. Come finish the sentence where your father started it.

"Tomorrow," Sister Miriam said. "We take the Order to the lake."

"Do we bring the jar?" Karim asked, because someone had to ask the noun even after a book like this.

"No," Arielle said. "We bring the keeping."

She set her palm on the clay. The watcher's hand settled beside it, colleague more than omen, a habit learned into bone. She thought of pencil in a margin, of drip white as a rope, of steps and gates and bells and ladders and fords—all the ordinary weather that makes grand theft look ridiculous. She thought of her father's bad Syriac and perfect map, and how a sentence becomes a city when enough hands read it.

"One line?" Karim asked, softer now that there was no threat to purchase with it.

"Let the page rest," Yael said. "We've earned a day when minutes are enough."

They carried the packets they had left to drawers that deserve their reputations. They rinsed cups. They counted wicks. They added a column to the Ledger called Knots because the sergeant had once asked about birds and the hard hand had asked about rope.

Evening moved in the quarter with its compact of cats and arguments and the sound of children learning sovereignty by running in alleys. The lemon tree shook off one honest leaf and kept the rest.

They slept in turns with windows open. The city turned a page. The book kept its place.

Chapter Forty-Four — The Lake

Galilee woke like a basin someone had set in a window to catch light and gossip.

Bread in a bag. Water in a thermos. The Order of Keeping in five dull packets. The Fords Ledger riding in Hani's school bag like homework that had decided to become policy. No jar. Just grammar.

Rina texted from Magdala: slab still two palms down. heap mark not tired. women ready.
Father Paulus from Tabgha: kettle on. mosaic behaving.
Narsai from Capernaum: basalt remembers better than men.

"Finish the sentence where your father started it," Yael said, and nobody corrected the tenderness.

Lev's fixer, with parsley and weather even this far north: "Soft hands stayed in Jerusalem to talk about nouns. The hard hand rented a car and decided not to drive it. Your sergeant bought olives near Ginnosar and said nothing important to anyone."

They drove with the window down for the part where the lake teaches you to breathe. Arbel shouldered the sky to the west; Wadi Hamam drew its old cut; the water lay out like an argument that had earned the right to be calm.

Magdala — Heap / Cooling

Rina met them where the pavement remembers markets. She led them to the slab, basalt worn by trays, two palms down from the corner where a pillar once bossed the air. The heap—three small strokes and a little mound with a flame beside it—waited where thumbs have always known to touch.

"Cooling," Hani's girl read from the Ledger, proud. "Heap, present."

Women came with baskets, aprons over good skirts. Rina set the Order on a bench and pointed to the dull photographs: heap, rope, cloth, cooling. "Housekeeping," she told them. "Government," one of the older ones corrected, satisfied.

They did not open the jar. They read names at a place where bread had always cooled. A girl repeated one and then a second, pleased that the lake made it easier to carry syllables without spilling.

Karim slipped Salt–AT into a drawer that kept ticket stubs and secrets with equal competence. Rina signed with a flourish and added a small, rude heart because she is that kind of necessary.

Tabgha — Bread / Water

At Heptapegon, the loaves-and-fishes mosaic held the floor in its patient way. Father Paulus poured from the kettle like a man absolving nouns. Yael placed the Order on the table; Matthias read minutes—bread at table, water at spring, lamps at roads, salt at heaps. The Benedictine who keeps keys initialed in a column that made him taller.

They did not produce a scene. They read bread in a voice unfit for television and perfect for kitchens. Fishermen on scooters slowed, listened, and left with their faces behaving.

"Receipt," Yael said. Father Paulus tucked a copy into a psalter that had bullied three abbots and would outlive a fourth.

Capernaum — Lamps

Basalt pillars. A synagogue rebuilt in white on black like a memory written over a memory. Narsai stood where shade is honest. He lit a small travel lamp and set it on the step where feet hesitate.

"Lamps," he said. "Count them when shutters close."

A Franciscan with the patience of salt nodded and opened a drawer with a key that looks like an apology. House-AO slid in. The drawer shut with a sound that means later.

Chorazin — Rope

The hill kept its basalt benches and its habit of making men spell obedience with their knees. A woman with a scarf like weather met them at the gate and pointed to a ring of iron sunk into stone near the mikveh—rope honest as a commandment. Hani's boy wrote Rope—lower court, iron ring. Karim took a picture so dull it might live forever.

They stopped by the Ginosar boat because humility asked for it. The museum guide, cheerful and immune to romance, listened to twenty seconds of Order and initialed the Ledger with a dot that looked like a knot. "Cooling?" he asked, interested. Hani's girl said two palms down and he smiled like a man instructed by children, which is the proper smile.

No vans. No collars. No fight. Weather, not thunder, because the city had already done the loud part and the lake knows how to finish a sentence with water.

At dusk they walked the shore where the Primacy rock holds its heat, and Arielle let the wind do that thing it does when it has decided not to be clever. Jonas stood beside her in the shape of a room. Yael read the

Order aloud once more, the way you read a recipe in a kitchen where everyone already knows it.

“Your father’s line started here,” Rina said, gentle. “He argued with basalt and with himself and wrote fords in a margin because he ran out of patience with maps. Thank you for finishing it with minutes.”

Arielle’s throat tried to be brave and was, eventually. “He left me the rope,” she said. “You taught me where to tie it.”

They ate bread that had cooled correctly. Water that remembered the spring. Lamp glass kept its quiet tick. The packet copies walked to drawers that deserved reputations: Greek chest at the little house by the lake; a basalt niche in Chorazin that outranks rhetoric; a file at Ginosar labeled “boring” and proud of it.

On the water, a tourist boat played a hymn nobody needed. The lake forgave them by being bigger.

They drove back in dark that had gotten over itself. Tiberias laid lights like a necklace you would never wear; the Arbel cliffs practiced being shoulders.

At St. Mark’s the lemon tree welcomed them with the authority of a small honest thing. The seam looked exactly as uninteresting as safety should look.

“Line?” Karim asked, almost whispering, not because danger required it but because gratitude did.

“Tomorrow,” Sister Miriam said from Ein Karem, spring under moonlight. “Let the lake keep it for a night.”

Arielle put her palm on the clay. The watcher’s hand arrived—colleague, not omen; habit, not fate. She thought of heap and slab, of lamps on basalt and rope sunk in stone; of a boat that taught humility without needing to speak; of her father’s bad Syriac and excellent arithmetic; of a sentence finished at water’s edge with keeping instead of keys.

"Many small doors," she said.

"And one lake," Yael added, smiling in a way that did not apologize for surviving. "Big enough to hold the echo."

Chapter Forty-Five — Keys That Stay

Jerusalem put its apron back on and got on with it.

Bread on the plate. Water in cups. The Order of Keeping stacked in packets that no longer apologized for being dull. The Fords Ledger fat with signatures that television will never love. The jar asleep in its cradle; the seam as unreproachful as good furniture. The lemon tree listened without pretending not to.

Shiri's text: committee signed "methods packet" as guidance. "surrogate" logged as training artifact. export closed "for the foreseeable future." klein says: we won the right to be boring.

"Keys," Yael said, pinning up her hair. "They will ask who has them."

"We'll tell them we keep rooms, not locks," Jonas answered. "And we'll show them the chores."

Matthias laid out deliveries like loaves: copies to Conservation, Antiquities, Patriarchate, Armenian St. James, Ein Karem, Magdala, Tabgha, Mukawir, Ginosar. He stamped hashes until the ink conceded decency.

Lev's fixer leaned in with parsley and weather. "Soft hands are interviewing their conscience," she said. "Hard hand walked Zion Gate before breakfast and put both palms on the scars like a man admitting he's read a sentence. Your sergeant fed the cat and bought olives, which has become a policy."

They did not carry the jar. They carried the grammar.

At St. Mark's they set a small table in the court as if for a very plain feast: the Order, the Ledger, dull receipts, a rope, a wick, a bell clapper the size of a plum. Sister Miriam's women came with folded stools and a quiet that makes men tell the truth. Elpidios brewed coffee that forgives adjectives. The Armenian sacristan brought a drawer as a joke and set it on a stool; everyone applauded its honesty.

Brown Suit appeared with the committee and a face that wanted to be useful. He did not try perimeter on a map. He asked, in a tone that hoped to leave the room with dignity, "Who holds custody?"

"Witness," Yael said, tapping the column. "The houses keep the rest."

"And the keys?" the liaison asked, honest because she could be.

"We keep chores," Sister Miriam answered. "Bread on cloth, water at springs, lamps counted, salt by heaps. Keys rust when you feed them nouns. Chores keep."

The hard hand stood in the kitchen doorway like a man who had learned to knock on air. He did not ask to see the jar. He looked at the rope, at the bell clapper, at the page where Cooling—two palms down had become policy, and said the thing he could say: "Where do I stand when she is fifteen and refuses to be lied to?"

"By the rope," Jonas said, without smiling. "Teach her the knot that doesn't embarrass the person who taught it to you."

The hard hand practiced once, twice, three times. He left without performance. A minute later the bell ticked once of its own accord, which is sometimes how buildings feel about men who try to improve.

Klein arrived with his tie correctly wrong and a folder correctly right. He handed Yael a sheet: internal review closed—surrogate archived as training; export shuttered; methods cited. "I'll sleep," he said, and surprised himself by believing it.

"Come for bread," Elpidios told him. "You've earned the carbs."

They ate, because winning the right to be boring is a victory that requires calories. Bread found its crust, water remembered its work, lamps ticked as they cooled. Children circled the lemon tree and practiced tying the knot Jonas had just taught a grown man.

Arielle watched the table instead of the door. The watcher's hand rested beside hers on the wood as if clay could learn to sit in the air when the seam is closed. Her father's margin lived in her pocket, the pencil scrawl of a man who had left her the river and expected her to learn the fords.

"I have one errand," she said into the companionable noise.

"Rockefeller?" Yael asked, already knowing.

"Box Twelve," Arielle said.

They went in twos, because that is how you cross a street with a thought. The Mandate façade performed virtue. The reading room breathed cotton and patience. Klein nodded them past a desk where an archivist who loved boxes more than people made an exception out of respect for paper.

Box Twelve arrived with the scorn of a professional. Tissue lifted. The 1989 overlay waited—Cave 4, D/7, the penciled fords, the little rope, the heap mark like a correction to ambition.

Arielle took one page from the Order—the cover with its soporific title, the line that says witness without custody, the diagram of rope, heap, cloth, cooling. On its margin she wrote Addendum—2025: The Order of Keeping practiced; see attached minutes. She did not mention the jar. She initialed with a small hand that refused to outshout the pencil beneath it.

"May I?" she asked the archivist.

"You must," the woman said, gracious and merciless. She slid the page into a sleeve and placed it under the overlay with the tender scorn of someone who knows exactly how to save a city from cleverness.

Outside, the light remembered itself. On the steps of the Rockefeller, Hani's kids practiced reading the Ledger as if it were music. The conservation woman walked by with scales in a bag and stopped to listen for a bar or two before remembering to be late to a meeting.

They went home by Bab al-Silsila because the name suits people who braid. Khan al-Zeit offered cumin. Muristan offered water on stone. Zion Gate offered its scars and required nothing in return.

In the stone room below, the seam looked like a fact you put back where it belongs after checking it with your hand. The jar slept. The Protocol waited for the day's last dull lines.

"Line?" Karim asked, instigated by gratitude more than habit.

They did not open. The page had given them enough for a day.

"Knots," Sister Miriam said from Ein Karem, amused and tired. "Add a column to the Order. Make men practice."

"We already did," Yael said, watching the hard hand's knot settle in the bell rope with surprising grace.

Evening dressed the Quarter with the sound of children being citizens. The lemon tree shook off one leaf like punctuation and kept the rest. The rope held. The bells kept their counsel. The city continued its policy of being bigger than anyone's plans for it.

Arielle set her palm on the jar, and the watcher's hand rested beside it as if it had been doing so forever. She thought of keys that stay in drawers because chores keep the doors open; of margins that end up being the chapter; of a valley that taught itself and a lake that finished the sentence without thunder. She thought of her father's bad Syriac and the perfect decency of a pencil.

"Many small doors," she said.

"And rooms," Yael added, smiling without apology. "We kept them."

Jerusalem woke like a ledger that had already balanced.

Bread on the plate. Water in cups. The Order of Keeping stacked in its unglamorous glory. The Fords Ledger thick, corners soft from hands. The jar asleep; the seam without opinions. The lemon tree, licensed to listen.

Shiri's text: docket numbers propagated. conservation filed: "methods adopted." antiquities filed: "export closed." klein: "slept. brief urge to become a librarian." hard hand: practicing knots badly, repeatedly.

"Receipts," Matthias said, setting the Jerusalem Protocol where a decent hand could reach it. "We write the day into paper and walk it until even boredom signs."

"Routes?" Jonas asked.

"Short," Yael said. "Greek chest. St. James. Ein Karem. Rockefeller—glass room gets a copy because it behaved. One to Mukawir. One to Magdala. One to Tabgha. One to Ginosar. Then we eat."

They didn't carry the jar. They carried grammar.

The court became a post office assembled from neighbors: rope coiled, bell quiet, coffee polite. Sister Miriam's women unfolded stools the way flags fold after work. Elpidios whistled to wicks. Hani spread the Ledger like music.

They stamped. They initialed. They wrote who/when/where with a pedant's love. Bread–AN slid into the Greek chest. House–AP found the dullest drawer at St. James and perfected it. Water–AO rode to Ein Karem under lemons with a driver who believed in receipts. Salt–AQ went to Shiri with a memo so soporific it might be classified as anesthesia.

They walked the rest by threads.

Lev's fixer and Karim took Rockefeller. The glass room accepted a packet like a dog accepts a biscuit after deciding you're not a threat.

Klein signed, not as a savior but as a witness, then added the smallest note to the file: practice observed.

Yael and Matthias went south with two copies and no speech. At Mukawir, Rashid's clerk logged Order with the serene contempt of a man allergic to adjectives. In Ein Karem, grandmothers annotated a photo of the rope with "this knot, not the fancy one," and dared anyone to edit them.

Narsai and Hani's kids carried north. At Magdala, Rina filed an extra page—Cooling—two palms—with a kiss of the pen and no apology. At Tabgha, Father Paulus tucked a copy beneath the psalter and drew a tiny fish next to the hash because he had decided to be a person. At Ginosar, the boat's docent initialed with a dot that looked like a knot and grinned like a recruit.

By noon, receipts had learned their rooms. The city, pleased with itself, dialed down its appetite for nouns.

Brown Suit arrived at St. Mark's without a map and with a face that had learned how to be useful. "We're filing witness before custody as standing language," he said, careful, proud in a way that didn't need audience.

"Keep it dull," Yael told him. "Dull survives."

He nodded, grateful to be given something he could do every day.

The hard hand came next with the girl who had learned the knot. He held no paper. "She wants to hear the names," he said, almost apologizing to oxygen.

"Sit," Sister Miriam said, and made two stools into policy. The girl said here at the right times and rolled her eyes exactly once, which is how you know she was listening. Her father stood behind her like a doorframe and chose not to be a lock.

After the names, Elpidios poured water and made silence a beverage. The lemon tree rustled like a book turning a page.

"One line?" Karim asked, hand on the lamp, not because danger required it but because gratitude felt like debt.

Yael looked to Arielle, the way you look to the person who finished the pencil sentence.

"Once," Arielle said. "Not for thunder. For filing."

They opened when the stone said now. The guard slip yielded; resin sighed as if pleased to be useful. Light raked low; Estrangela stood with its ordinary authority.

"Read," Sister Miriam said.

"If the keeping has been taught, write receipts for the houses; carry them by roads and by fords until the girls can read them without help. Then let the lid rest, for the witness is awake."

They didn't cheer. They stamped.

Receipt—Order of Keeping, filed went into the Protocol with the neatness of a final bow that refuses flourish. Copies bred: Greek chest, St. James, Ein Karem, Rockefeller, Mukawir, Magdala, Tabgha, Ginosar. The Ledger learned a new column—Filed—and children fought politely over who got to enter the times.

In the late afternoon, the sergeant set down a paper bag of olives and stared at the rope as if ropes had started to be citizens. "You've made me lazy," he said.

"Rested," Elpidios corrected, mercifully.

Arielle walked to the door and let the courtyard make its usual case for being the center of the world. The watcher's hand rested beside hers on the jamb, not omen, not debt—company. She thought of her father's margin. Of drip and red and valley. Of a city that kept a jar by refusing to worship it.

"I think I could go," she said to Jonas, surprising nobody and herself anyway. "And the sentence would continue."

"It's built for that," he said. "It has rooms."

"Not today," she added, and he nodded like a man who had learned to share custody with witness.

They ate what ought to be eaten: bread with sesame, water that tasted like work done correctly. Lamps cooled their tick. Paper dried.

Evening rehearsed itself over roofs and tanks and laundry lines. A bell tried one note and decided the day didn't need it. A muezzin agreed.

Yael sealed the guard slip with a practiced palm. "Receipts," she said, amused. "The end that isn't one."

"Tomorrow?" Matthias asked.

"Coda," Sister Miriam said from Ein Karem, spring under dusk. "Small. Honest. Put the pencil away."

Arielle set her hand on the clay. The watcher settled beside it—habit, not magic. She didn't ask for a line. She didn't need one.

Epilogue — Pencil

Before dawn, Jerusalem sounded like a pencil on paper.

Bread on the plate. Water in cups. The Order of Keeping stacked, corners softened by hands. The Fords Ledger closed, elastic tired in an honest way. The jar asleep in its cradle; the seam obedient to touch. Above, the lemon tree listened as if that were a profession.

Arielle packed the kind of bag you carry when you're not escaping, only changing rooms: shirt, notebook, her father's overlay in a copy sleeve, a pencil sharpened to an argument.

Jonas walked her to the door and did not offer nouns. He checked the rope with a glance; it pretended not to preen.

"You'll visit," he said, which is how soldiers say stay in the verb.

"I'll send minutes," she said, which is how witnesses say count me present.

Elpidios pressed bread into her hand and called it theology. The Armenian sacristan arrived with a drawer handle sanded smooth and called it a blessing. Sister Miriam was already on the line from Ein Karem, the spring under her words awake early. "You don't owe us returns," she said. "Just practice where you go."

"Rina asked for a copy," Karim said, grinning. "She wants to bully a donor with Cooling—two palms."

"Give her two," Yael answered, passing Arielle a packet with a string tied in a knot that would not embarrass anybody.

Lev's fixer leaned in with parsley and weather. "Soft hands have learned to buy coffee decently," she reported. "Hard hand's girl tied a knot that made a cat reconsider jurisdiction. Your sergeant fed bread to the bird that isn't a pigeon and looked pleased with himself."

They didn't walk her out like a procession. They let her leave like a person.

She crossed Bab al-Silsila in that hour when shutters think about blinking. Khan al-Zeit rehearsed cumin to itself. Muristan tasted its own water. At Zion Gate, she put her palm on a scar and didn't ask it for history. It gave her patience anyway.

The road east remembered what it was for. Wadi Qelt cut the morning; the ascent of red remembered caravans; the Dead Sea lay flat as a kept promise.

At Qumran, the terraces wore their old restraint. The D/7 seam kept its white like a rope someone had taught not to fray. Arielle set her father's overlay on her knee and wrote a line where his pencil had stopped:

"Methods filed. Witness awake. Lid at rest."

She did not touch stone. She faced the valley and read the sentence once, quiet. She faced the road and read it again, soft enough to belong to weather. Nothing opened; that was still the point.

On the way back, she stopped at En Rogel with a thermos of water and drank what the city had taught her to bless. An old man nodded because nodding is how cities endorse paperwork.

By afternoon she was in a small northbound bus that smelled like citrus and ambition. On her lap the Order lay boring and proud. In her pocket the margin held a new date, a small hand that had learned to be moderate.

She wrote a postcard to nobody in particular and slid it behind the sleeve:

Many small doors. Steps that behave. Ladders tied. Bells that embarrass no one. Fords that keep their footing. Bread that cools, water that says its name, lamps that remember to count. I am not carrying the jar. The city is.

Back at St. Mark's, evening put the courtyard in its good shirt. The rope held. The bell declined theater. Children read the Ledger to the lemon tree and mispronounced two words that forgave them instantly.

The jar slept like a tool. The seam did what seams are for. The Order of Keeping got taller by the thickness of one more stamped receipt. In the glass room at the Rockefeller, a librarian filed a dull page under an older penciled margin and smiled the way people smile when they've helped a city keep itself.

On the wall above the scriptorium table, a single nail held a loop of rope tied in a knot that had learned to be generous.

Arielle's pencil rested.

The End

Printed in Dunstable, United Kingdom

72212947R00231